Geo. Wm. Parker

THE ETERNAL CITY

"WHAT YOU SAID SHALL BE SACRED."

The ETERNAL CITY

By

HALL CAINE

Author of "The Christian," etc.

*"He looked for a city which hath foundations
whose builder and maker is God."*

GROSSET & DUNLAP
PUBLISHERS : : NEW YORK

PREFACE TO THIS EDITION

Has a novelist a right to alter his novel after its publication, to condense it, to add to it, to modify or to heighten its situations, and otherwise so to change it that to all outward appearance it is practically a new book? I leave this point in literary ethics to the consideration of those whose business it is to discuss such questions, and content myself with telling the reader the history of the present story.

About ten years ago I went to Russia with some idea (afterwards abandoned) of writing a book that should deal with the racial struggle which culminated in the eviction of the Jews from the holy cities of that country, and the scenes of tyrannical administration which I witnessed there made a painful and lasting impression on my mind. The sights of the day often followed me through the night, and after a more than usually terrible revelation of official cruelty, I had a dream of a Jewish woman who was induced to denounce her husband to the Russian police under a promise that they would spare his life, which they said he had forfeited as the leader of a revolutionary movement. The husband came to know who his betrayer had been, and he cursed his wife as his worst enemy. She pleaded on her knees that fear for his safety had been the only motive for her conduct, and he cursed her again. His cause was lost, his hopes were dead, his people were in despair, because the one being whom heaven had given him for his support had delivered him up to his enemies out of the weakness of her womanly love. I awoke in the morning with a vivid memory of this new version of the old story of Samson and Delilah, and on my return to England I wrote the draft of a play with the incident of husband and wife as the central situation.

How from this germ came the novel which was published last year under the title of " The Eternal City " would be a long story to tell, a story of many personal experiences, of reading, of travel, of meetings in various countries with

v

statesmen, priests, diplomats, police authorities, labour leaders, nihilists and anarchists, and of the consequent growth of my own political and religious convictions; but it will not be difficult to see where and in what way time and thought had little by little overlaid the humanities of the early sketch with many extra interests. That these interests were of the essence, clothing, and not crushing the human motive, I trust I may continue to believe, and certainly I have no reason to be dissatisfied with the reception of my book at the hands of that wide circle of general readers who care less for a contribution to a great social propaganda than for a simple tale of love.

But when the time came to return to my first draft of a play, the tale of love was the only thing to consider, and being now on the point of producing the drama in England, America, and elsewhere, and requested to prepare an edition of my story for the use of the audiences at the theatre, I have thought myself justified in eliminating the politics and religion from my book, leaving nothing but the human interests with which alone the drama is allowed to deal. This has not been an easy thing to do, and now that it is done I am by no means sure that I may not have alienated the friends whom the abstract problems won for me without conciliating the readers who called for the story only. But not to turn my back on the work of three laborious years, or to discredit that part of it which expressed, however imperfectly, my sympathy with the struggles of the poor, and my participation in the social problems with which the world is now astir, I have obtained the promise of my publisher that the original version of " The Eternal City" shall be kept in print as long as the public calls for it.

In this form of my book, the aim has been to rely solely on the humanities and to go back to the simple story of the woman who denounced her husband in order to save his life. That was the theme of the draft which was the original basis of my novel, it is the central incident of the drama which is about to be produced in New York, and the present abbreviated version of the story is intended to follow the lines of the play in all essential particulars down to the end of the last chapter but one. H. C.

Isle of Man, *Sept.* 1902.

THE ETERNAL CITY

PROLOGUE

I

HE was hardly fit to figure in the great review of life. A boy of ten or twelve, in tattered clothes, with an accordion in a case swung over one shoulder like a sack, and under the other arm a wooden cage containing a grey squirrel. It was a December night in London, and the Southern lad had nothing to shelter his little body from the Northern cold but his short velveteen jacket, red waistcoat, and knickerbockers. He was going home after a long day in Chelsea, and, conscious of something fantastic in his appearance, and of doubtful legality in his calling, he was dipping into side streets in order to escape the laughter of the London boys and the attentions of policemen.

Coming to the Italian quarter in Soho, he stopped at the door of a shop to see the time. It was eight o'clock. There was an hour to wait before he would be allowed to go indoors. The shop was a baker's, and the window was full of cakes and confectionery. From an iron grid on the pavement there came the warm breath of the oven underground, the red glow of the fire, and the scythe-like swish of the long shovels. The boy blocked the squirrel under his armpit, dived into his pocket, and brought out some copper coins and counted them. There was ninepence. Ninepence was the sum he had to take home every night, and there was not a halfpenny to spare. He knew that perfectly before he began to count, but his appetite had tempted him to try again if his arithmetic was not at fault.

The air grew warmer, and it began to snow. At first it was a fine sprinkle that made a snow-mist, and adhered wherever it fell. The traffic speedily became less, and things looked big in the thick air. The boy was wandering aimlessly

1

through the streets, waiting for nine o'clock. When he thought the hour was near, he realised that he had lost his way. He screwed up his eyes to see if he knew the houses and shops and signs, but everything seemed strange.

The snow snowed on, and now it fell in large, corkscrew flakes. The boy brushed them from his face, but at the next moment they blinded him again. The few persons still in the streets loomed up on him out of the darkness, and passed in a moment like gigantic shadows. He tried to ask his way, but nobody would stand long enough to listen. One man who was putting up his shutters shouted some answer that was lost in the drumlike rumble of all voices in the falling snow.

The boy came up to a big porch with four pillars, and stepped in to rest and reflect. The long tunnels of smoking lights which had receded down the streets were not to be seen from there, and so he knew that he was in a square. It would be Soho Square, but whether he was on the south or east of it he could not tell, and consequently he was at a loss to know which way to turn. A great silence had fallen over everything, and only the sobbing nostrils of the cab-horses seemed to be audible in the hollow air.

He was very cold. The snow had got into his shoes, and through the rents in his cross-gartered stockings. His red waistcoat wanted buttons, and he could feel that his shirt was wet. He tried to shake the snow off by stamping, but it clung to his velveteens. His numbed fingers could scarcely hold the cage, which was also full of snow. By the light coming from a fanlight over the door in the porch he looked at his squirrel. The little thing was trembling pitifully in its icy bed, and he took it out and breathed on it to warm it, and then put it in his bosom. The sound of a child's voice laughing and singing came to him from within the house, muffled by the walls and the door. Across the white vapour cast outward from the fanlight he could see nothing but the crystal snowflakes falling wearily.

He grew dizzy, and sat down by one of the pillars. After a while a shiver passed along his spine, and then he became warm and felt sleepy. A church clock struck nine, and he started up with a guilty feeling, but his limbs were stiff and he sank back again, blew two or three breaths on to the squirrel inside his waistcoat, and fell into a doze. As he dropped off into unconsciousness he seemed to see the big, cheerless house, almost destitute of furniture, where he lived with

PROLOGUE

thirty or forty other boys. They trooped in with their organs and accordions, counted out their coppers to a man with a clipped moustache, who was blowing whiffs of smoke from a long, black cigar, with a straw through it, and then sat down on forms to eat their plates of macaroni and cheese. The man was not in good temper to-night, and he was shouting at some who were coming in late and at others who were sharing their supper with the squirrels that nestled in their bosoms, or the monkeys, in red jacket and fez, that perched upon their shoulders. The boy was perfectly unconscious by this time, and the child within the house was singing away as if her little breast was a cage of song-birds.

As the church clock struck nine a class of Italian lads in an upper room in Old Compton Street was breaking up for the night, and the teacher, looking out of the window, said:

"While we have been telling the story of the great road to our country a snowstorm has come, and we shall have enough to do to find our road home."

The lads laughed by way of answer, and cried: "Good-night, doctor."

"Good-night, boys, and God bless you," said the teacher.

He was an elderly man, with a noble forehead and a long beard. His face, a sad one, was lighted up by a feeble smile; his voice was soft, and his manner gentle. When the boys were gone he swung over his shoulders a black cloak with a red lining, and followed them into the street.

He had not gone far into the snowy haze before he began to realise that his playful warning had not been amiss.

"Well, well," he thought, "only a few steps, and yet so difficult to find."

He found the right turnings at last, and coming to the porch of his house in Soho Square, he almost trod on a little black and white object lying huddled at the base of one of the pillars.

"A boy," he thought, "sleeping out on a night like this! Come, come," he said severely, "this is wrong," and he shook the little fellow to waken him.

The boy did not answer, but he began to mutter in a sleepy monotone, "Don't hit me, sir. It was snow. I'll not come home late again. Ninepence, sir, and Jinny is so cold."

The man paused a moment, then turned to the door and rang the bell sharply.

II

HALF-AN-HOUR later the little musician was lying on a couch in the doctor's surgery, a cheerful room with a fire and a soft lamp under a shade. He was still unconscious, but his damp clothes had been taken off and he was wrapped in blankets. The doctor sat at the boy's head and moistened his lips with brandy, while a good woman, with the face of a saint, knelt at the end of the couch and rubbed his little feet and legs. After a little while there was a perceptible quivering of the eyelids and twitching of the mouth.

"He is coming to, mother," said the doctor.

"At last," said his wife.

The boy moaned and opened his eyes, the big helpless eyes of childhood, black as a sloe, and with long black lashes. He looked at the fire, the lamp, the carpet, the blankets, the figures at either end of the couch, and with a smothered cry he raised himself as though thinking to escape.

"Carino!" said the doctor, smoothing the boy's curly hair. "Lie still a little longer."

The voice was like a caress, and the boy sank back. But presently he raised himself again, and gazed around the room as if looking for something. The good mother understood him perfectly, and from a chair on which his clothes were lying she picked up his little grey squirrel. It was frozen stiff with the cold and now quite dead, but he grasped it tightly and kissed it passionately, while big teardrops rolled on to his cheeks.

"Carino!" said the doctor again, taking the dead squirrel away, and after a while the boy lay quiet and was comforted.

"Italiano—si?"

"Si, Signore."

"From which province?"

"Campagna Romana, Signore."

"Where does he say he comes from, doctor?"

"From the country district outside Rome. And now you are living at Maccari's in Greek Street—isn't that so?"

"Yes, sir."

"How long have you been in England—one year, two years?"

PROLOGUE

"Two years and a half, sir."

"And what is your name, my son?"

"David Leone."

"A beautiful name, carino! David Le-o-ne," repeated the doctor, smoothing the curly hair.

"A beautiful boy, too! What will you do with him, doctor?"

"Keep him here to-night at all events, and to-morrow we'll see if some institution will not receive him. David Leone! Where have I heard that name before, I wonder? Your father is a farmer?"

But the boy's face had clouded like a mirror that has been breathed upon, and he made no answer.

"Isn't your father a farmer in the Campagna Romana, David?"

"I have no father," said the boy.

"Carino! But your mother is alive—yes?"

"I have no mother."

"Caro mio! Caro mio! You shall not go to the institution to-morrow, my son," said the doctor, and then the mirror cleared in a moment as if the sun had shone on it.

"Listen, father!"

Two little feet were drumming on the floor above.

"Baby hasn't gone to bed yet. She wouldn't sleep until she had seen the boy, and I had to promise she might come down presently."

"Let her come down now," said the doctor.

The boy was supping a basin of broth when the door burst open with a bang, and like a tiny cascade which leaps and bubbles in the sunlight, a little maid of three, with violet eyes, golden complexion, and glossy black hair, came bounding into the room. She was trailing behind her a train of white nightdress, hobbling on the portion in front, and carrying under her arm a cat, which, being held out by the neck, was coiling its body and kicking its legs like a rabbit.

But having entered with so fearless a front, the little woman drew up suddenly at sight of the boy, and, entrenching herself behind the doctor, began to swing by his coat-tails, and to take furtive glances at the stranger in silence and aloofness.

"Bless their hearts! what funny things they are, to be sure," said the mother. "Somebody seems to have been tell-

5

ing her she might have a brother some day, and when nurse said to Susanna, 'The doctor has brought a boy home with him to-night,' nothing was so sure as that this was the brother they had promised her, and yet now . . . Roma, you silly child, why don't you come and speak to the poor boy who was nearly frozen to death in the snow?"

But Roma's privateering fingers were now deep in her father's pocket, in search of a specimen of the sugar-stick which seemed to live and grow there. She found two sugar-sticks this time, and sight of a second suggested a bold adventure. Sidling up toward the couch, but still holding on to the doctor's coat-tails, like a craft that swings to anchor, she tossed one of the sugar-sticks on to the floor at the boy's side. The boy smiled and picked it up, and this being taken for sufficient masculine response, the little daughter of Eve proceeded to proper overtures.

" Oo a boy? "

The boy smiled again and assented.

" Oo me brodder? "

The boy's smile paled perceptibly.

" Oo lub me? "

The tide in the boy's eyes was rising rapidly.

" Oo lub me eber and eber? "

The tears were gathering fast, when the doctor, smoothing the boy's dark curls again, said:

" You have a little sister of your own far away in the Campagna Romana—yes? "

" No, sir."

" Perhaps it's a brother? "

" I . . . I have nobody," said the boy, and his voice broke on the last word with a thud.

" You shall not go to the institution at all, David," said the doctor softly.

" Doctor Roselli! " exclaimed his wife. But something in the doctor's face smote her instantly and she said no more.

" Time for bed, baby."

But baby had many excuses. There were the sugar-sticks, and the pussy, and the boy-brother, and finally her prayers to say.

" Say them here, then, sweetheart," said her mother, and with her cat pinned up again under one arm and the sugar-stick held under the other, kneeling face to the fire, but screwing her half-closed eyes at intervals in the direction of the couch, the little maid put her little waif-and-stray hands together and said:

"Our Fader oo art in Heben, alud be dy name. Dy kingum tum. Dy will be done on eard as it is in Heben. Gib us dis day our dayey bread, and forgib us our trelspasses as we forgib dem dat trelspass ayenst us. And lee us not into temstashuns, but deliber us from ebil . . . for eber and eber. Amen."

The house in Soho Square was perfectly silent an hour afterward. In the surgery the lamp was turned down, the cat was winking and yawning at the fire, and the doctor sat in a chair in front of the fading glow and listened to the measured breathing of the boy behind him. It dropped at length, like a pendulum that is about to stop, into the noiseless beat of innocent sleep, and then the good man got up and looked down at the little head on the pillow.

Even with the eyes closed it was a beautiful face; one of the type which great painters have loved to paint for their saints and angels—sweet, soft, wise, and wistful. And where did it come from? From the Campagna Romana, a scene of poverty, of squalor, of fever, and of death!

The doctor thought of his own little daughter, whose life had been a long holiday, and then of the boy whose days had been an unbroken bondage.

"Yet who knows but in the rough chance of life our little Roma may not some day . . . God forbid!"

The boy moved in his sleep and laughed the laugh of a dream that is like the sound of a breeze in soft summer grass, and it broke the thread of painful reverie.

"Poor little man! he has forgotten all his troubles."

Perhaps he was back in his sunny Italy by this time, among the vines and the oranges and the flowers, running barefoot with other children on the dazzling whiteness of the roads! . . . Perhaps his mother in heaven was praying her heart out to the Blessed Virgin to watch over her fatherless darling cast adrift upon the world!

The train of thought was interrupted by voices in the street, and the doctor drew the curtain of the window aside and looked out. The snow had ceased to fall, and the moon was shining; the leafless trees were casting their delicate black shadows on the whitened ground, and the yellow light of a lantern on the opposite angle of the square showed where a group of lads were singing a Christmas carol.

"While shepherds watched their flocks by night, all seated on the ground,
The angel of the Lord came down, and glory shone around."

Doctor Roselli closed the curtain, put out the lamp, touched with his lips the forehead of the sleeping boy, and went to bed.

PART ONE—THE HOLY ROMAN EMPIRE

I

IT was the last day of the century. In a Bull proclaiming a Jubilee the Pope had called his faithful children to Rome, and they had come from all quarters of the globe. To salute the coming century, and to dedicate it, in pomp and solemn ceremony, to the return of the world to the Holy Church, one and universal, the people had gathered in the great Piazza of St. Peter.

Boys and women were climbing up every possible elevation, and a bright-faced girl who had conquered a high place on the base of the obelisk was chattering down at a group of her friends who were listening to their cicerone.

"Yes, that is the Vatican," said the guide, pointing to a square building at the back of the colonnade, "and the apartments of the Pope are those on the third floor, just on the level of the Loggia of Raphael. The Cardinal Secretary of State used to live in the rooms below, opening on the grand staircase that leads from the Court of Damasus. There's a private way up to the Pope's apartment, and a secret passage to the Castle of St. Angelo."

"Say, has the Pope got that secret passage still?"

"No, sir. When the Castle went over to the King the connection with the Vatican was cut off. Ah, everything is changed since those days! The Pope used to go to St. Peter's surrounded by his Cardinals and Bishops, to the roll of drums and the roar of cannon. All that is over now. The present Pope is trying to revive the old condition seemingly, but what can he do? Even the Bull proclaiming the Jubilee laments the loss of the temporal power which would have permitted him to renew the enchantments of the Holy City."

"Tell him it's just lovely as it is," said the girl on the obelisk, "and when the illuminations begin . . ."

9

"Say, friend," said her parent again, "Rome belonged to the Pope—yes? Then the Italians came in and took it and made it the capital of Italy—so?"

"Just so, and ever since then the Holy Father has been a prisoner in the Vatican, going into it as a cardinal and coming out of it as a corpse, and to-day will be the first time a Pope has set foot in the streets of Rome!"

"My! And shall we see him in his prison clothes?"

"Lilian Martha! Don't you know enough for that? Perhaps you expect to see his chains and a straw of his bed in the cell? The Pope is a king and has a court—that's the way I am figuring it."

"True, the Pope is a sovereign still, and he is surrounded by his officers of state—Cardinal Secretary, Majordomo, Master of Ceremonies, Steward, Chief of Police, Swiss Guards, Noble Guard and Palatine Guard, as well as the Papal Guard who live in the garden and patrol the precincts night and day."

"Then where the nation . . . prisoner, you say?"

"Prisoner indeed! Not even able to look out of his windows on to this piazza on the 20th of September without the risk of insult and outrage—and Heaven knows what will happen when he ventures out to-day!"

"Well! this goes clear ahead of me!"

Beyond the outer cordon of troops many carriages were drawn up in positions likely to be favourable for a view of the procession. In one of these sat a Frenchman in a coat covered with medals, a florid, fiery-eyed old soldier with bristling white hair. Standing by his carriage door was a typical young Roman, fashionable, faultlessly dressed, pallid, with strong lower jaw, dark watchful eyes, twirled-up moustache and cropped black mane.

"Ah, yes," said the old Frenchman. "Much water has run under the bridge since then, sir. Changed since I was here? Rome? You're right, sir. 'When Rome falls, falls the world;' but it can alter for all that, and even this square has seen its transformations. Holy Office stands where it did, the yellow building behind there, but this palace, for instance—this one with the people in the balcony . . ."

The Frenchman pointed to the travertine walls of a prison-like house on the farther side of the piazza.

"Do you know whose palace that is?"

"Baron Bonelli's, President of the Council and Minister of the Interior."

"Precisely! But do you know whose palace it used to be?"

"Belonged to the English Wolsey, didn't it, in the days when he wanted the Papacy?"

"Belonged in my time to the father of the Pope, sir—old Baron Leone!"

"Leone! That's the family name of the Pope, isn't it?"

"Yes, sir, and the old Baron was a banker and a cripple. One foot in the grave, and all his hopes centred in his son. 'My son,' he used to say, 'will be the richest man in Rome some day—richer than all their Roman princes, and it will be his own fault if he doesn't make himself Pope.'"

"He has, apparently."

"Not that way, though. When his father died, he sold up everything, and having no relations looking to him, he gave away every penny to the poor. That's how the old banker's palace fell into the hands of the Prime Minister of Italy —an infidel, an Antichrist."

"So the Pope is a good man, is he?"

"Good man, sir? He's not a man at all, he's an angel! Only two aims in life—the glory of the Church and the welfare of the rising generation. Gave away half his inheritance founding homes all over the world for poor boys. Boys— that's the Pope's tender point, sir! Tell him anything tender about a boy and he breaks up like an old swordcut."

The eyes of the young Roman were straying away from the Frenchman to a rather shabby single-horse hackney carriage which had just come into the square and taken up its position in the shadow of the grim old palace. It had one occupant only—a man in a soft black hat. He was quite without a sign of a decoration, but his arrival had created a general commotion, and all faces were turning toward him.

"Do you happen to know who that is?" said the gay Roman. "That man in the cab under the balcony full of ladies? Can it be David Rossi?"

"David Rossi, the anarchist?"

"Some people call him so. Do you know him?"

"I know nothing about the man except that he is an enemy of his Holiness."

"He intends to present a petition to the Pope this morning, nevertheless."

11

"Impossible!"

"Haven't you heard of it? These are his followers with the banners and badges."

He pointed to the line of working-men who had ranged themselves about the cab, with banners inscribed variously, "Garibaldi Club," "Mazzini Club," "Republican Federation," and "Republic of Man."

"Your friend Antichrist," tipping a finger over his shoulder in the direction of the palace, "has been taxing bread to build more battleships, and Rossi has risen against him. But failing in the press, in Parliament and at the Quirinal, he is coming to the Pope to pray of him to let the Church play its old part of intermediary between the poor and the oppressed."

"Preposterous!"

"So?"

"To whom is the Pope to protest? To the King of Italy who robbed him of his Holy City? Pretty thing to go down on your knees to the brigand who has stripped you! And at whose bidding is he to protest? At the bidding of his bitterest enemy? Pshaw!"

"You persist that David Rossi is an enemy of the Pope?"

"The deadliest enemy the Pope has in the world."

II

THE subject of the Frenchman's denunciation looked harmless enough as he sat in his hackney carriage under the shadow of old Baron Leone's gloomy palace. A first glance showed a man of thirty-odd years, tall, slightly built, inclined to stoop, with a long, clean-shaven face, large dark eyes, and dark hair which covered the head in short curls of almost African profusion. But a second glance revealed all the characteristics that give the hand-to-hand touch with the common people, without which no man can hope to lead a great movement.

From the moment of David Rossi's arrival there was a tingling movement in the air, and from time to time people approached and spoke to him, when the tired smile struggled through the jaded face and then slowly died away. After a while, as if to subdue the sense of personal observation, he took a pen and oblong notepaper and began to write on his knees.

Meantime the quick-eyed facile crowd around him beguiled the tedium of waiting with good-humoured chaff. One great creature with a shaggy mane and a sanguinary voice came up, bottle in hand, saluted the downcast head with a mixture of deference and familiarity, then climbed to the box-seat beside the driver, and in deepest bass began the rarest mimicry. He was a true son of the people, and under an appearance of ferocity he hid the heart of a child. To look at him you could hardly help laughing, and the laughter of the crowd at his daring dashes showed that he was the privileged pet of everybody. Only at intervals the downcast head was raised from its writing, and a quiet voice of warning said:

" Bruno ! "

Then the shaggy head on the box-seat slewed round and bobbed downward with an apologetic gesture, and ten seconds afterwards plunged into wilder excesses.

" Pshaw ! " mopping with one hand his forehead under his tipped-up billicock, and holding the bottle with the other. " It's hot ! Dog of a Government, it's hot, I say ! Never mind ! here's to the exports of Italy, brother; and may the Government be the first of them."

" Bruno ! "

" Excuse me, sir; the tongue breaks no bones, sir ! All Governments are bad, and the worst Government is the best."

A feeble old man was at that moment crushing his way up to the cab. Seeing him approach, David Rossi rose and held out his hand. The old man took it, but did not speak.

" Did you wish to speak to me, father ? "

" I can't yet," said the old man, and his voice shook and his eyes were moist.

David Rossi stepped out of the cab, and with gentle force, against many protests, put the old man in his place.

" I come from Carrara, sir, and when I go home and tell them I've seen David Rossi, and spoken to him, they won't believe me. ' He sees the future clear,' they say, ' as an almanack made by God.' "

Just then there was a commotion in the crowd, an imperious voice cried, " Clear out," and the next instant David Rossi, who was standing by the step of his cab, was all but run down by a magnificent equipage with two high-stepping horses and a fat English coachman in livery of scarlet and gold.

His face darkened for a moment with some powerful emotion, then resumed its kindly aspect, and he turned back to the old man without looking at the occupant of the carriage.

It was a lady. She was tall, with a bold sweep of fulness in figure, which was on a large scale of beauty. Her hair, which was abundant and worn full over the forehead, was raven black and glossy, and it threw off the sunshine that fell on her face. Her complexion had a golden tint, and her eyes, which were violet, had a slight recklessness of expression. Her carriage drew up at the entrance of the palace, and the porter, with the silver-headed staff, came running and bowing to receive her. She rose to her feet with a consciousness of many eyes upon her, and with an unabashed glance she looked around on the crowd.

There was a sulky silence among the people, almost a sense of antagonism, and if anybody had cheered there might have been a counter demonstration. At the same time, there was a certain daring in that marked brow and steadfast smile which seemed to say that if anybody had hissed she would have stood her ground.

She lifted from the blue silk cushions of the carriage a small half-clipped black poodle with a bow of blue ribbon on its forehead, tucked it under her arm, stepped down to the street, and passed into the courtyard, leaving an odour of ottar of roses behind her.

Only then did the people speak.

" Donna Roma! "

The name seemed to pass over the crowd in a breathless whisper, soundless, supernatural, like the flight of a bat in the dark.

III

THE Baron Bonelli had invited certain of his friends to witness the Pope's procession from the windows and balconies of his palace overlooking the piazza, and they had begun to arrive as early as half-past nine.

In the green courtyard they were received by the porter in the cocked hat, on the dark stone staircase by lackeys in knee-breeches and yellow stockings, in the outer hall, intended for coats and hats, by more lackeys in powdered wigs, and in the first reception-room, gorgeously decorated in the yellow and gold of the middle ages, by Felice, in a dress coat, the Baron's solemn personal servant, who said, in sepulchral tones:

"The Baron's excuses, Excellency! Engaged in the Council-room with some of the Ministers, but expects to be out presently. Sit in the Loggia, Excellency?"

"So our host is holding a Cabinet Council, General?" said the English Ambassador.

"A sort of scratch council, seemingly. Something that concerns the day's doings, I guess, and is urgent and important."

"A great man, General, if half one hears about him is true."

"Great?" said the American. "Yes, and no, Sir Evelyn, according as you regard him. In the opinion of some of his followers the Baron Bonelli is the greatest man in the country —greater than the King himself—and a statesman too big for Italy. One of those commanding personages who carry everything before them, so that when they speak even monarchs are bound to obey. That's one view of his picture, Sir Evelyn."

"And the other view?"

General Potter glanced in the direction of a door hung with curtains, from which there came at intervals the deadened drumming of voices, and then he said:

"A man of implacable temper and imperious soul, an infidel of hard and cynical spirit, a sceptic and a tyrant."

"Which view do the people take?"

"Can you ask? The people hate him for the heavy burden of taxation with which he is destroying the nation in his attempt to build it up."

"And the clergy, and the Court, and the aristocracy?"

"The clergy fear him, the Court detests him, and the Roman aristocracy are rancorously hostile."

"Yet he rules them all, nevertheless?"

"Yes, sir, with a rod of iron—people, Court, princes, Parliament, King as well—and seems to have only one unsatisfied desire, to break up the last remaining rights of the Vatican and rule the old Pope himself."

"And yet he invites us to sit in his Loggia and look at the Pope's procession."

"Perhaps because he intends it shall be the last we may ever see of it."

"The Princess Bellini and Don Camillo Murelli," said Felice's sepulchral voice from the door.

An elderly aristocratic beauty wearing nodding white plumes came in with a pallid young Roman noble dressed in the English fashion.

"*You* come to church, Don Camillo?"

"Heard it was a service which happened only once in a hundred years, dear General, and thought it mightn't be convenient to come next time," said the young Roman.

"And you, Princess! Come now, confess, is it the perfume of the incense which brings you to the Pope's procession, or the perfume of the promenaders?"

"Nonsense, General!" said the little woman, tapping the American with the tip of her lorgnette. "Who comes to a ceremony like this to say her prayers? Nobody whatever, and if the Holy Father himself were to say . . ."

"Oh! oh!"

"Which reminds me," said the little lady, "where is Donna Roma?"

"Yes, indeed, where is Donna Roma?" said the young Roman.

"*Who* is Donna Roma?" said the Englishman.

"Santo Dio! the man doesn't know Donna Roma!"

The white plumes bobbed up, the powdered face fell back, the little twinkling eyes closed, and the company laughed and seated themselves in the Loggia.

"Donna Roma, dear sir," said the young Roman, "is a type of the fair lady who has appeared in the history of every nation since the days of Helen of Troy."

"Has a woman of this type, then, identified herself with the story of Rome at a moment like the present?" said the Englishman.

The young Roman smiled.

"Why did the Prime Minister appoint so-and-so?— Donna Roma! Why did he dismiss such-and-such?—Donna Roma! What feminine influence imposed upon the nation this or that?—Donna Roma! Through whom come titles, decorations, honours?—Donna Roma! Who pacifies intractable politicians and makes them the devoted followers of the Ministers?—Donna Roma! Who organises the great

charitable committees, collects funds and distributes them?
—Donna Roma! Always, always Donna Roma!"

"So the day of the petticoat politician is not over in
Italy yet?"

"Over? It will only end with the last trump. But dear
Donna Roma is hardly that. With her light play of grace
and a whole artillery of love in her lovely eyes, she only in-
toxicates a great capital and "—with a glance towards the curtained door—"takes captive a great Minister."

"Just that," and the white plumes bobbed up and down.

"Hence she defies conventions, and no one dares to question her actions on her scene of gallantry."

"Drives a pair of thoroughbreds in the Corso every afternoon, and threatens to buy an automobile."

"Has debts enough to sink a ship, but floats through life
as if she had never known what it was to be poor."

"And has she?"

The voices from behind the curtained door were louder
than usual at that moment, and the young Roman drew his
chair closer.

"Donna Roma, dear sir, was the only child of Prince Volonna. Nobody mentions him now, so speak of him in a
whisper. The Volonnas were an old papal family, holding
office in the Pope's household, but the young Prince of the
house was a Liberal, and his youth was cast in the stormy
days of the middle of the century. As a son of the revolution
he was expelled from Rome for conspiracy against the papal
Government, and when the Pope went out and the King came
in, he was still a republican, conspiring against the reigning
sovereign, and, as such, a rebel. Meanwhile he had wandered over Europe, going from Geneva to Berlin, from Berlin
to Paris. Finally he took refuge in London, the home of all
the homeless, and there he was lost and forgotten. Some say
he practised as a doctor, passing under another name; others
say that he spent his life as a poor man in your Italian
quarter of Soho, nursing rebellion among the exiles from his
own country. Only one thing is certain: late in life he
came back to Italy as a conspirator—enticed back, his friends
say—was arrested on a charge of attempted regicide, and
deported to the island of Elba without a word of public report
or trial."

"Domicilio Coatto—a devilish and insane device," said
the American Ambassador.

"Was that the fate of Prince Volonna?"

"Just so," said the Roman. "But ten or twelve years after he disappeared from the scene a beautiful girl was brought to Rome and presented as his daughter."

"Donna Roma?"

"Yes. It turned out that the Baron was a kinsman of the refugee, and going to London he discovered that the Prince had married an English wife during the period of his exile, and left a friendless daughter. Out of pity for a great name he undertook the guardianship of the girl, sent her to school in France, finally brought her to Rome, and established her in an apartment on the Trinità de' Monti, under the care of an old aunt, poor as herself, and once a great coquette, but now a faded rose which has long since seen its June."

"And then?"

"Then? Ah, who shall say what then, dear friend? We can only judge by what appears—Donna Roma's elegant figure, dressed in silk by the best milliners Paris can provide, queening it over half the women of Rome."

"And now her aunt is conveniently bedridden," said the little Princess, "and she goes about alone like an English-woman; and to account for her extravagance, while every-body knows her father's estate was confiscated, she is by way of being a sculptor, and has set up a gorgeous studio, full of nymphs and cupids and limbs."

"And all by virtue of—what?" said the Englishman.

"By virtue of being—the good friend of the Baron Bonelli!"

"Meaning by that?"

"Nothing—and everything!" said the Princess with another trill of laughter.

"In Rome, dear friend," said Don Camillo, "a woman can do anything she likes as long as she can keep people from talking about her."

"Oh, you never do that apparently," said the Englishman. "But why doesn't the Baron make her a Baroness and have done with the danger?"

"Because the Baron has a Baroness already."

"A wife living?"

"Living and yet dead—an imbecile, a maniac, twenty years a prisoner in his castle in the Alban hills."

THE HOLY ROMAN EMPIRE

IV

THE curtain parted over the inner doorway, and three gentlemen came out. The first was a tall, spare man, about fifty years of age, with an intellectual head, features cut clear and hard like granite, glittering eyes under overhanging brows, black moustaches turned up at the ends, and iron-grey hair cropped very short over a high forehead. It was the Baron Bonelli.

One of the two men with him had a face which looked as if it had been carved by a sword or an adze, good and honest but blunt and rugged; and the other had a long, narrow head, like the head of a hen—a lanky person with a certain mixture of arrogance and servility in his expression.

The company rose from their places in the Loggia, and there were greetings and introductions.

" Sir Evelyn Wise, gentlemen, the new British Ambassador—General Morra, our Minister of War; Commendatore Angelelli, our Chief of Police. A thousand apologies, ladies! A Minister of the Interior is one of the human atoms that live from minute to minute and are always at the mercy of events. You must excuse the Commendatore, gentlemen; he has urgent duties outside."

The Prime Minister spoke with the lucidity and emphasis of a man accustomed to command, and when Angelelli had bowed all round he crossed with him to the door.

" If there is any suspicion of commotion, arrest the ringleaders at once. Let there be no trifling with disorder, by whomsoever begun. The first to offend must be the first to be arrested, whether he wears cap or cassock."

" Good, your Excellency," and the Chief of Police went out.

" Commotion! Disorder! Madonna mia! " cried the little Princess.

" Calm yourselves, ladies. It's nothing! Only it came to the knowledge of the Government that the Pope's procession this morning might be made the excuse for a disorderly demonstration, and of course order must not be disturbed even under the pretext of liberty and religion."

" So that was the public business which deprived us of your society? " said the Princess.

19

" And left my womanless house the duty of receiving you in my absence," said the Baron.

The Baron bowed his guests to their seats, stood with his back to a wide ingle, and began to sketch the Pope's career.

" His father was a Roman banker—lived in this house, indeed—and the young Leone was brought up in the Jesuit schools and became a member of the Noble Guard: handsome, accomplished, fond of society and social admiration, a man of the world. This was a cause of disappointment to his father, who had intended him for a great career in the Church. They had their differences, and finally a mission was found for him and he lived a year abroad. The death of the old banker brought him back to Rome, and then, to the astonishment of society, he renounced the world and took holy orders. Why he gave up his life of gallantry did not appear . . ."

" Some affair of the heart, dear Baron," said the little Princess, with a melting look.

" No, there was no talk of that kind, Princess, and not a whisper of scandal. Some said the young soldier had married in England, and lost his wife there, but nobody knew for certain. There was less doubt about his religious vocation, and when by help of his princely inheritance he turned his mind to the difficult task of reforming vice and ministering to the lowest aspects of misery in the slums of Rome, society said he had turned Socialist. His popularity with the people was unbounded, but in the midst of it all he begged to be removed to London. There he set up the same enterprises, and tramped the streets in search of his waifs and outcasts, night and day, year in, year out, as if driven on by a consuming passion of pity for the lost and fallen. In the interests of his health he was called back to Rome—and returned here a white-haired man of forty."

" Ah! what did I say, dear Baron? The apple falls near the tree, you know! "

" By this time he had given away millions, and the Pope wished to make him President of his Academy of Noble Ecclesiastics, but he begged to be excused. Then Apostolic Delegate to the United States, and he prayed off. Then Nuncio to Spain, and he went on his knees to remain in the Campagna Romana, and do the work of a simple priest among a simple people. At last, without consulting him they made him Bishop, and afterwards Cardinal, and, on the death of the Pope, he was Scrutator to the Conclave, and fainted when he read out his own name as that of Sovereign Pontiff of the Church."

The little Princess was wiping her eyes.

" Then—all the world was changed. The priest of the future disappeared in a Pope who was the incarnation of the past. Authority was now his watchword. What was the highest authority on earth? The Holy See! Therefore, the greatest thing for the world was the domination of the Pope. If anybody should say that the power conferred by Christ on his Vicar was only spiritual, let him be accursed! In Christ's name the Pope was sovereign—supreme sovereign over the bodies and souls of men—acknowledging no superior, holding the right to make and depose kings, and claiming to be supreme judge over the consciences and crimes of all—the peasant that tills the soil, and the prince that sits on the throne!"

" Tre-men-jous!" said the American.

" But, dear Baron," said the little Princess, " don't you think there was an affair of the heart after all?" and the little plumes bobbed sideways.

The Baron laughed again. " The Pope seems to have half of humanity on his side already—he has the women apparently."

All this time there had risen from the piazza into the room a humming noise like the swarming of bees, but now a shrill voice came up from the crowd with the sudden swish of a rocket.

" Look out!"

The young Roman, who had been looking over the balcony, turned his head back and said:

" Donna Roma, Excellency."

But the Baron had gone from the room.

" He knew her carriage wheels apparently," said Don Camillo, and the lips of the little Princess closed tight as if from sudden pain.

V

THE return of the Baron was announced by the faint rustle of a silk under-skirt and a light yet decided step keeping pace with his own. He came back with Donna Roma on his arm, and over his coolness and calm dignity he looked pleased and proud.

The lady herself was brilliantly animated and happy. A certain swing in her graceful carriage gave an instant impression of perfect health, and there was physical health also in the brightness of her eyes and the gaiety of her expression. Her face was lighted up by a smile which seemed to pervade her whole person and make it radiant with overflowing joy. A vivacity which was at the same time dignified and spontaneous appeared in every movement of her harmonious figure, and as she came into the room there was a glow of health and happiness that filled the air like the glow of sunlight through a veil of soft red gauze.

She saluted the Baron's guests with a smile that fascinated everybody. There was a modified air of freedom about her, as of one who has a right to make advances, a manner which captivates all women in a queen and all men in a lovely woman.

"Ah, it is you, General Potter? And my dear General Morra? Camillo mio!" (The Italian had rushed upon her and kissed her hand.) "Sir Evelyn Wise, from England, isn't it? I'm half an Englishwoman myself, and I'm very proud of it."

She had smiled frankly into Sir Evelyn's face, and he had smiled back without knowing it. There was something contagious about her smile. The rosy mouth with its pearly teeth seemed to smile of itself, and the lovely eyes had their separate art of smiling. Her lips parted of themselves, and then you felt your own lips parting.

"You were to have been busy with your fountain to-day . . ." began the Baron.

"So I expected," she said in a voice that was soft yet full, "and I did not think I should care to see any more spectacles in Rome, where the people are going in procession all the year through—but what do you think has brought me?"

"The artist's instinct, of course," said Don Camillo.

"No, just the woman's—to see a man!"

"Lucky fellow, whoever he is!" said the American. "He'll see something better than you will, though," and then the golden complexion gleamed up at him under a smile like sunshine.

"But who is he?" said the young Roman.

"I'll tell you. Bruno—you remember Bruno?"

"Bruno!" cried the Baron.

" Oh! Bruno is all right," she said, and, turning to the others, " Bruno is my man in the studio—my marble pointer, you know. Bruno Rocco, and nobody was ever so rightly named. A big, shaggy, good-natured bear, always singing or growling or laughing, and as true as steel. A terrible Liberal, though; a socialist, an anarchist, a nihilist, and everything that's shocking."

" Well? "

" Well, ever since I began my fountain . . . I'm making a fountain for the Municipality—it is to be erected in the new part of the Piazza Colonna. I expect to finish it in a fortnight. You would like to see it? Yes? I'll send you cards—a little private view, you know."

" But Bruno? "

" Ah! yes, Bruno! Well, I've been at a loss for a model for one of my figures . . . figures all round the dish, you know. They represent the Twelve Apostles, with Christ in the centre giving out the water of life."

" But Bruno! Bruno! Bruno! "

She laughed, and the merry ring of her laughter set them all laughing.

" Well, Bruno has sung the praises of one of his friends until I'm crazy . . . crazy, that's English, isn't it? I told you I was half an Englishwoman. American? Thanks, General! I'm ' just crazy ' to get him in."

" Simple enough—hire him to sit to you," said the Princess.

" Oh," with a mock solemnity, " he is far too grand a person for that! A member of Parliament, a leader of the Left, a prophet, a person with a mission, and I daren't even dream of it. But this morning, Bruno tells me, his friend, his idol, is to stop the Pope's procession, and present a petition, so I thought I would kill two birds with one stone—see my man and see the spectacle—and here I am to see them! "

" And who is this paragon of yours, my dear? "

" The great David Rossi! "

" *That* man! "

The white plumes were going like a fan.

" The man is a public nuisance and ought to be put down by the police," said the little Princess, beating her foot on the floor.

" He has a tongue like a sword and a pen like a dagger," said the young Roman.

23

Donna Roma's eyes began to flash with a new expression.

"Ah, yes, he is a journalist, isn't he, and libels people in his paper?"

"The creature has ruined more reputations than anybody else in Europe," said the little Princess.

"I remember now. He made a terrible attack on our young old women and our old young men. Declared they were meddling with everything—called them a museum of mummies, and said they were symbolical of the ruin that was coming on the country. Shameful, wasn't it? Nobody likes to be talked about, especially in Rome, where it's the end of everything. But what matter? The young man has perhaps learned freedom of speech in some free country. We can afford to forgive him, can't we? And then he is so interesting and so handsome!"

"An attempt to stop the Pope's procession might end in tumult," said the American General to the Italian General. "Was that the danger the Baron spoke about?"

"Yes," said General Morra. "The Government have been compelled to tax bread, and of course that has been a signal for the enemies of the national spirit to say that we are starving the people. This David Rossi is the worst Roman in Rome. He opposed us in Parliament and lost. Petitioned the King and lost again. Now he intends to petition the Pope—with what hope, Heaven knows."

"With the hope of playing on public opinion, of course," said the Baron cynically.

"Public opinion is a great force, your Excellency," said the Englishman.

"A great pestilence," said the Baron warmly.

"What is David Rossi?"

"An anarchist, a republican, a nihilist, anything as old as the hills, dear friend, only everything in a new way," said the young Roman.

"David Rossi is the politician who proposes to govern the world by the precepts of the Lord's Prayer," said the American.

"The Lord's Prayer!"

The Baron paraded on the hearthrug. "David Rossi," he said compassionately, "is a creature of his age. A man of generous impulses and wide sympathies, moved to indignation at the extremes of poverty and wealth, and carried away by the promptings of the eternal religion in the human soul. A dreamer, of course, a dreamer like the Holy Father himself, only his dream is different, and neither could succeed without destroying the other. In the millennium Rossi looks for, not only are kings and princes to disappear, but popes and prelates as well."

"And where does this unpractical politician come from?" said the Englishman.

"We must ask you to tell us that, Sir Evelyn, for though he is supposed to be a Roman, he seems to have lived most of his life in your country. As silent as an owl and as inscrutable as a sphinx. Nobody in Rome knows certainly who his father was, nobody knows certainly who his mother was. Some say his father was an Englishman, some say a Jew, and some say his mother was a gipsy. A self-centred man, who never talks about himself, and cannot be got to lift the veil which surrounds his birth and early life. Came back to Rome eight years ago, and made a vast noise by propounding his platonic scheme of politics—was called up for his term of military service, refused to serve, got himself imprisoned for six months and came out a mighty hero—was returned to Parliament for no fewer than three constituencies, sat for Rome, took his place on the Extreme Left, and attacked every Minister and every measure which favoured the interest of the army—encouraged the workmen not to pay their taxes and the farmers not to pay their rents—and thus became the leader of a noisy faction, and is now surrounded by the degenerate class throughout Italy which dreams of reconstructing society by burying it under ruins."

"Lived in England, you say?"

"Apparently, and if his early life could be traced it would probably be found that he was brought up in an atmosphere of conspiracy—perhaps under the influence of some vile revolutionary living in London under the protection of your too liberal laws."

Donna Roma sprang up with a movement full of grace and energy. "Anyhow," she said, "he is young and good-looking and romantic and mysterious, and I'm head over ears in love with him already."

"Well, every man is a world," said the American.

"And what about woman?" said Roma.

He threw up his hands, she smiled full into his face, and they laughed together.

VI

A FANFARE of trumpets came from the piazza, and with a cry of delight Roma ran into the balcony, followed by all the women and most of the men.

"Only the signal that the cortège has started," said Don Camillo. "They'll be some minutes still."

"Santo Dio!" cried Roma. "What a sight! It dazzles me; it makes me dizzy!"

Her face beamed, her eyes danced, and she was all aglow from head to foot. The American Ambassador stood behind her, and, as permitted by his greater age, he tossed back the shuttlecock of her playful talk with chaff and laughter.

"How patient the people are! See the little groups on camp-stools munching biscuits and reading the journals. 'La Vera Roma!'" (mimicking the cry of the newspaper sellers). "Look at that pretty girl—the fair one with the young man in the Homburg hat! She has climbed up the obelisk, and is inviting him to sit on an inch and a half of corbel beside her."

"Ah, those who love take up little room!"

"Don't they? What a lovely world it is! I'll tell you what this makes me think about—a wedding! Glorious morning, beautiful sunshine, flowers, wreaths, bridesmaids ready; coachman all a posy, only waiting for the bride!"

"A wedding is what you women are always dreaming about—you begin dreaming about it in your cradles—it's in a woman's bones, I do believe," said the American.

"Must be the ones she got from Adam, then," said Roma.

Meantime the Baron was still parading the hearthrug inside and listening to the warnings of his Minister of War.

"You are resolved to arrest the man?"

"If he gives us an opportunity—yes."

"You do not forget that he is a Deputy?"

"It is because I remember it that my resolution is fixed. In Parliament he is a privileged person; let him make half as much disorder outside and you shall see where he will be."

"Anarchists!" said Roma. "That group below the balcony? Is David Rossi among them? Yes? Which of them? Which? Which? Which? The tall man in the black hat with his back to us? Oh! why doesn't he turn his face? Should I shout?"

" Roma! " from the little Princess.

" I know; I'll faint, and you'll catch me, and the Princess will cry ' Madonna mia! ' and then he'll turn round and look up."

" My child! "

" He'll see through you, though, and then where will you be? "

" See through me, indeed! " and she laughed the laugh a man loves to hear, half-raillery, half-caress.

" Donna Roma Volonna, daughter of a line of princes, making love to a nameless nobody! "

" Shows what a heavenly character she is, then! See how good I am at throwing bouquets at myself? "

" Well, what is love, anyway? A certain boy and a certain girl agree to go for a row in the same boat to the same place, and if they pull together, what does it matter where they come from? "

" What, indeed? " she said, and a smile, partly serious, played about the parted mouth.

" Could *you* think like that? "

" I could! I could! I could! "

The clock struck eleven. Another fanfare of trumpets came from the direction of the Vatican, and then the confused noises in the square suddenly ceased and a broad " Ah! " passed over it, as of a vast living creature taking breath.

" They're coming! " cried Roma. " Baron, the cortège is coming."

" Presently," the Baron answered from within.

Roma's dog, which had slept on a chair through the tumult, was awakened by the lull and began to bark. She picked it up, tucked it under her arm and ran back to the balcony, where she stood by the parapet, in full view of the people below, with the young Roman on one side, the American on the other, and the ladies seated around.

By this time the procession had begun to appear, issuing from a bronze gate under the right arm of the colonnade, and passing down the channel which had been kept open by the cordon of infantry.

Roma abandoned herself to the fascinations of the scene, and her gaiety infected everybody.

" Camillo, you must tell me who they all are. There now —those men who come first in black and red? "

" Laymen," said the young Roman. " They're called the

Apostolic Cursori. When a Cardinal is nominated they take him the news, and get two or three thousand francs for their trouble."

"And these little fat folk in white lace pinafores?"

"Singers of the Sistine Chapel. That's the Director, old Maestro Mustafa—used to be the greatest soprano of the century."

"And this dear old friar with the mittens and rosary and the comfortable linsey-woolsey sort of face?"

"That's Father Pifferi of San Lorenzo, confessor to the Pope. He knows all the Pope's sins."

"Oh!" said Roma.

At that moment her dog barked furiously, and the old friar looked up at her, whereupon she smiled down on him, and then a half-smile played about his good-natured face.

"He is a Capuchin, and those Frati in different colours coming behind him . . ."

"I know them; see if I don't," she cried, as there passed under the balcony a double file of friars and monks. "The brown ones—Capuchins and Franciscans! Brown and white —Carmelites! Black—Augustinians and Benedictines! Black with a white cross—Passionists! And the monks all white are Trappists. I know the Trappists best, because I drive out to Tre Fontane to buy eucalyptus and flirt with Father John."

"Shocking!" said the American.

"Why not? What are their vows of celibacy but conspiracies against us poor women? Nearly every man a woman wants is either mated or has sworn off in some way. Oh, how I should love to meet one of those anchorites in real life and make him fly!"

"Well, I dare say the whisk of a petticoat would be more frightening than all his doctors of divinity."

"Listen!"

From a part of the procession which had passed the balcony there came the sound of harmonious voices.

"The singers of the Sistine Chapel! They're singing a hymn."

"I know it. '*Veni, Creator!*' How splendid! How glorious! I feel as if I wanted to cry!"

All at once the singing stopped, the murmuring and speaking of the crowd ceased too, and there was a breathless moment, such as comes before the first blast of a storm. A nerv-

ous quiver, like the shudder that passes over the earth at
sundown, swept across the piazza, and the people stood motionless, every neck stretched, and every eye turned in the
direction of the bronze gate, as if God were about to reveal
Himself from the Holy of Holies. Then in that grand silence
there came the clear call of silver trumpets, and at the next
instant the Presence itself.

"The Pope! Baron, the Pope!"

The atmosphere was charged with electricity. A great
roar of cheering went up from below like the roaring of surf,
and it was followed by a clapping of hands like the running
of the sea off a shingly beach after the boom of a tremendous
breaker.

An old man, dressed wholly in white, carried shoulder-
high on a chair glittering with purple and crimson, and having a canopy of silver and gold above him. He wore a triple
crown, which glistened in the sunlight, and but for the delicate white hand which he upraised to bless the people, he
might have been mistaken for an image.

His face was beautiful, and had a ray of beatified light
on it—a face of marvellous sweetness and great spirituality.

It was a thrilling moment, and Roma's excitement was intense. "There he is! All in white! He's on a gilded chair
under the silken canopy! The canopy is held up by prelates,
and the chairmen are in knee-breeches and red velvet. Look
at the great waving plumes on either side!"

"Peacock's feathers!" said a voice behind her, but she
paid no heed.

"Look at the acolytes swinging incense, and the golden
cross coming before! What thunders of applause—I can
hardly hear myself speak. It's like standing on a cliff while
the sea below is running mountains high. No, it's like no
other sound on earth; it's human—fifty thousand unloosed
throats of men! That's the clapping of ladies—listen to the
weak applause of their white-gloved fingers. Now they're
waving their handkerchiefs. Look! Like the wings of ten
thousand butterflies fluttering up from a meadow."

Roma's abandonment was by this time complete; she was
waving her handkerchief and crying "*Viva il Papa Re!*"

"They're bearing him slowly along. He's coming this
way. Look at the Noble Guard in their helmets and jack-
boots. And there are the Swiss Guard in Joseph's coat of
many colours! We can see him plainly now. Do you smell

the incense? It's like the ribbon of Bruges. The pluviale? That gold vestment? It's studded on his breast with precious stones. How they blaze in the sunshine! He is blessing the people, and they are falling on their knees before him."

"Like the grass before the scythe!"

"How tired he looks! How white his face is! No, not white—ivory! No, marble—Carrara marble! He might be Lazarus who was dead and has come back from the tomb! No humanity left in him! A saint! An angel!"

"The spiritual autocrat of the world!"

"*Viva il Papa Re!* He's going by! *Viva il Papa Re!* He has gone. . . . Well!"

She was rising from her knees and wiping her eyes, trying to cover up with laughter the confusion of her rapture.

"What is that?"

There was a sound of voices in the distance chanting dolorously.

"The cantors intoning *Tu es Petrus,*" said Don Camillo.

"No, I mean the commotion down there. Somebody is pushing through the Guard."

"It's David Rossi," said the American.

"Is that David Rossi? Oh, dear me! I had forgotten all about him." She moved forward to see his face. "Why . . . where have I . . . I've seen him before somewhere."

A strange physical sensation tingled all over her at that moment, and she shuddered as if with sudden cold.

"What's amiss?"

"Nothing! But I like him. Do you know, I really like him."

"Women are funny things," said the American.

"They're nice, though, aren't they?" And two rows of pearly teeth between parted lips gleamed up at him with gay raillery.

Again she craned forward. "He is on his knees to the Pope! Now he'll present the petition. No . . . yes . . . the brutes! They're dragging him away! The procession is going on! Disgraceful!"

"Long live the Workmen's Pope!" came up from the piazza, and under the shrill shouts of the pilgrims were heard the monotonous voices of the monks as they passed through the open doors of the Basilica intoning the praises of God.

"They're lifting him on to a car," said the American.

" David Rossi ? "

" Yes; he is going to speak."

" How delightful! Shall we hear him? Good! How glad I am that I came! He is facing this way! Oh, yes; those are his own people with the banners! Baron, the Holy Father has gone on to St. Peter's, and David Rossi is going to speak."

" Hush! "

A quivering, vibrating voice came up from below, and in a moment there was a dead silence.

VII

" BROTHERS, when Christ Himself was on the earth going up to Jerusalem, He rode on the colt of an ass, and the blind and the lame and the sick came to Him, and He healed them. Humanity is sick and blind and lame to-day, brothers, but the Vicar of Christ goes on."

At the words an audible murmur came from the crowd, such as goes before the clapping of hands in a Roman theatre, a great upheaval of the heart of the audience to the actor who has touched and stirred it.

" Brothers, in a little Eastern village a long time ago, there arose among the poor and lowly a great Teacher, and the only prayer He taught His followers was the prayer ' Our Father who art in Heaven.' It was the expression of man's utmost need, the expression of man's utmost hope. And not only did the Teacher teach that prayer—He lived according to the light of it. All men were His brothers, all women His sisters; He was poor, He had no home, no purse, and no second coat; when He was smitten He did not smite back, and when He was unjustly accused He did not defend Himself. Nineteen hundred years have passed since then, brothers, and the Teacher who arose among the poor and lowly is now a great Prophet. All the world knows and honours Him, and civilised nations have built themselves upon the religion He founded. A great Church calls itself by His name, and a mighty kingdom, known as Christendom, owes allegiance to His faith. But what of His teaching? He said: ' Resist not evil,' yet all Christian nations maintain standing armies. He said: ' Lay not up for yourselves treasures upon earth,' yet the wealthiest men are Christian men, and the richest organisation in the world is the Christian Church. He said: 'Our Father who art in Heaven,' yet men who ought to be brothers are divided into states, and hate each other as enemies. He said: 'Thy kingdom come, Thy will be done on earth as it is done in Heaven,' yet he who believes it ever will come is called a fanatic and a fool."

Some murmurs of dissent were drowned in cries of "Go on!" "Speak!" "Silence!"

"Foremost and grandest of the teachings of Christ are two inseparable truths—the fatherhood of God and the brotherhood of man. But in Italy, as elsewhere, the people are starved that king may contend with king, and when we appeal to the Pope to protest in the name of the Prince of Peace, he remembers his temporalities and passes on!"

At these words the emotion of the crowd broke into loud shouts of approval, with which some groans were mingled.

Roma had turned her face aside from the speaker, and her profile was changed—the gay, sprightly, airy, radiant look had given way to a serious, almost a melancholy expression.

"We have two sovereigns in Rome, brothers, a great State and a great Church, with a perishing people. We have soldiers enough to kill us, priests enough to tell us how to die, but no one to show us how to live."

"Corruption! Corruption!"

"Corruption indeed, brothers; and who is there among us to whom the corruptions of our rulers are unknown? Who cannot point to the wars made that should not have been made? to the banks broken that should not have broken? And who in Rome cannot point to the Ministers who allow their mistresses to meddle in public affairs and enrich themselves by the ruin of all around?"

The little Princess on the balcony was twisting about.

"What! Are you deserting us, Roma?"

And Roma answered from within the house, in a voice that sounded strange and muffled:

"It was cold on the balcony, I think."

The little Princess laughed a bitter laugh, and David Rossi heard it and misunderstood it, and his nostrils quivered like the nostrils of a horse, and when he spoke again his voice shook with passion.

"Who has not seen the splendid equipages of these privileged ones of fortune—their gorgeous liveries of scarlet and gold—emblems of the acid which is eating into the public organs? Has Providence raised this country from the dead only to be dizzied in a whirlpool of scandal, hypocrisy, and fraud—only to fall a prey to an infamous traffic without a name between high officials of low desires and women whose reputations are long since lost? It is men and women like these who destroy their country for their own selfish ends. Very well, let them destroy her; but before they do so, let them hear what one of her children says: The Government you are building up on the whitened bones of the people shall be overthrown—the King who countenances you, and the Pope who will not condemn you, shall be overthrown, and then—and not till then—will the nation be free."

At this there was a terrific clamour. The square resounded with confused voices. "Bravo!" "Dog!" "Dog's murderer!" "Traitor!" "Long live David Rossi!" "Down with the Vampire!"

The ladies had fled from the balcony back to the room with cries of alarm. "There will be a riot." "The man is inciting the people to rebellion!" "This house will be first to be attacked!"

"Calm yourselves, ladies. No harm shall come to you," said the Baron, and he rang the bell.

There came from below a babel of shouts and screams.

"Madonna mia! What is that?" cried the Princess, wringing her hands; and the American Ambassador, who had remained on the balcony, said:

"The Carabineers have charged the crowd and arrested David Rossi."

"Thank God!"

"They're going through the Borgo," said Don Camillo, "and kicking and cuffing and jostling and hustling all the way."

"Don't be alarmed! There's the Hospital of Santo Spirito round the corner, and stations of the Red Cross Society everywhere," said the Baron, and then Felice answered the bell.

"See our friends out by the street at the back, Felice. Good-bye, ladies! Have no fear! The Government does not mean to blunt the weapons it uses against the malefactors who insult the doctrines of the State."

"Excellent Minister!" said the Princess. "Such canaglia are not fit to have their liberty, and I would lock them all up in prison."

And then Don Camillo offered his arm to the little lady with the white plumes, and they came almost face to face with Roma, who was standing by the door hung with curtains, fanning herself with her handkerchief, and parting from the English Ambassador.

"Donna Roma," he was saying, "if I can ever be of use to you, either now or in the future, I beg of you to command me."

"Look at her!" whispered the Princess. "How agitated she is! A moment ago she was finding it cold in the Loggia! I'm so happy!"

At the next instant she ran up to Roma and kissed her. "Poor child! How sorry I am! You have my sympathy, my dear! But didn't I tell you the man was a public nuisance, and ought to be put down by the police?"

"Shameful, isn't it?" said Don Camillo. "Calumny is a little wind, but it raises such a terrible tempest."

"Nobody likes to be talked about," said the Princess, "especially in Rome, where it is the end of everything."

"But what matter? Perhaps the young man has learned freedom of speech in a free country!" said Don Camillo.

"And then he is so interesting and so handsome," said the Princess.

Roma made no answer. There was a slight drooping of the lovely eyes and a trembling of the lips and nostrils. For a moment she stood absolutely impassive, and then with a flash of disdain she flung round into the inner room.

VIII

Roma had taken refuge in the council-room. There had been much business that morning, and a copy of the constitutional statute lay open on a large table, which had a plate-glass top with photographs under the surface.

In this passionless atmosphere, so little accustomed to such scenes, Roma sat in her wounded pride and humiliation, with her head down, and her beautiful white hands over her face.

She heard measured footsteps approaching, and then a hand touched her on the shoulder. She looked up and drew back as if the touch stung her. Her lips closed sternly, and she got up and began to walk about the room, and then she burst into a torrent of anger.

"Did you hear them? The cats! How they loved to claw me, and still purr and purr! Before the sun is set the story will be all over Rome! It has run off already on the hoofs of that woman's English horses. To-morrow morning it will be in every newspaper in the kingdom. Olga and Lena and every woman of them all who lives in a glass house will throw stones. 'The new Pompadour! Who is she?' Oh, I could die of vexation and shame!"

The Baron leaned against the table and listened, twisting the ends of his moustache.

"The Court will turn its back on me now. They only wanted a good excuse to put their humiliations upon me. It's horrible! I can't bear it. I won't. I tell you, I won't!"

But the lips, compressed with scorn, began to quiver visibly, and she threw herself into a chair, took out her handkerchief, and hid her face on the table.

At that moment Felice came into the room to say that the Commendatore Angelelli had returned and wished to speak with his Excellency.

"I will see him presently," said the Baron, with an impassive expression, and Felice went out silently, as one who had seen nothing.

The Baron's calm dignity was wounded. "Be so good as to have some regard for me in the presence of my servants," he said. "I understand your feelings, but you are much too excited to see things in their proper light. You have been publicly insulted and degraded, but you must not talk to me as if it were my fault."

"Then whose is it? If it is not your fault, whose fault is it?" she said, and the Baron thought her red eyes flashed up at him with an expression of hate. He took the blow full in the face, but made no reply, and his silence broke her answer.

"No, no, that was too bad," she said, and she reached over to him, and he kissed her and then sat down beside her and took her hand and held it. At the next moment her brilliant eyes had filled with tears and her head was down and the hot drops were falling on to the back of his hand.

"I suppose it is all over," she said.

"Don't say that," he answered. "We don't know what a day may bring forth. Before long I may have it in my power to silence every slander and justify you in the eyes of all."

At that she raised her head with a smile and seemed to

look beyond the Baron at something in the vague distance, while the glass top of the table, which had been clouded by her breath, cleared gradually, and revealed a large house almost hidden among trees. It was a photograph of the Baron's castle in the Alban hills.

"Only," continued the Baron, "you must get rid of that man Bruno."

"I will discharge him this very day—I will! I will! I will!"

There was an intense bitterness in the thought that what David Rossi had said must have come of what her own servant told him—that Bruno had watched her in her own house day by day, and that time after time the two men had discussed her between them.

"I could kill him," she said.

"Bruno Rocco?"

"No, David Rossi."

"Have patience; he shall be punished," said the Baron.

"How?"

"He shall be put on his trial."

"What for?"

"Sedition. The law allows a man to say what he will about a Prime Minister, but he must not foretell the overthrow of the King. The fellow has gone too far at last. He shall go to Santo Stefano."

"What good will that do?"

"He will be silenced—and crushed."

She looked at the Baron with a sidelong smile, and something in her heart, which she did not understand, made her laugh at him.

"Do you imagine you can crush a man like that by trying and condemning him?" she said. "He has insulted and humiliated me, but I'm not silly enough to deceive myself. Try him, condemn him, and he will be greater in his prison than the King on his throne."

The Baron twisted the ends of his moustache again.

"Besides," she said, "what benefit will it be to me if you put him on trial for inciting the people to rebellion against the King? The public will say it was for insulting yourself, and everybody will think he was punished for telling the truth."

The Baron continued to twist the ends of his moustache.

"Benefit!" She laughed ironically. "It will be a

double injury. The insult will be repeated in public again and again. First the advocate for the crown will read it aloud, then the advocate for the defence will quote it, and then it will be discussed and dissected and telegraphed until everybody in court knows it by heart and all Europe has heard of it."

The Baron made no answer, but watched the beautiful face, now very pale, behind which conflicting thoughts seemed to wriggle like a knot of vipers. Suddenly she leaped up with a spring.

"I know!" she cried. "I know! I know! I know!"

"Well?"

"Give the man to me, and I will show you how to escape from this humiliating situation."

"Roma?" said the Baron, but he had read her thought already.

"If you punish him for this speech you will injure both of us and do no good to the King."

"It's true."

"Take him in a serious conspiracy, and you will be doing us no harm and the King some service."

"No doubt."

"You say there is a mystery about David Rossi, and you want to know who he is, who his father was, and where he spent the years he was away from Rome."

"I would certainly give a good deal to know."

"You want to know what vile refugee in London filled him with his fancies, what conspiracies he is hatching, what secret societies he belongs to, and, above all, what his plans and schemes are, and whether he is in league with the Vatican."

She spoke so rapidly that the words sputtered out of her quivering lips.

"Well?"

"Well, I will find it all out for you."

"My dear Roma!"

"Leave him to me, and within a month you shall know" —she laughed, a little ashamed—"the inmost secrets of his soul."

She was walking to and fro again, to prevent the Baron from looking into her face, which was now red over its white, like a rose moon in a stormy sky.

The Baron thought. "She is going to humble the man by her charms—to draw him on and then fling him away, and thus pay him back for what he has done to-day. So much the better for me if I may stand by and do nothing. A strong Minister should be unmoved by personal attacks. He should appear to regard them with contempt."

He looked at her, and the brilliancy of her eyes set his heart on fire. The terrible attraction of her face at that moment stirred in him the only love he had for her. At the same time it awakened the first spasm of jealousy.

"I understand you, Roma," he said. "You are splendid! You are irresistible! But remember—the man is one of the incorruptible."

She laughed.

"No woman who has yet crossed his path seems to have touched him, and it is the pride of all such men that no woman ever can."

"I've seen him," she said.

"Take care! As you say, he is young and handsome."

She tossed her head and laughed again.

The Baron thought: "Certainly he has wounded her in a way no woman can forgive."

"And what about Bruno?" he said.

"He shall stay," she answered. "Such men are easy enough to manage."

"You wish me to liberate David Rossi and leave you to deal with him?"

"I do! Oh, for the day when I can turn the laugh against him as he has turned the laugh against me! At the top of his hopes, at the height of his ambitions, at the moment when he says to himself, 'It is done'—he shall fall."

The Baron touched the bell. "Very well!" he said. "One can sometimes catch more flies with a spoonful of honey than with a hogshead of vinegar. We shall see."

A moment later the Chief of Police entered the room. "The Honourable Rossi is safely lodged in prison," he said.

"Commendatore," said the Baron, pointing to the book lying open on the table, "I have been looking again at the statute, and now I am satisfied that a Deputy can be arrested by the authorisation of Parliament alone."

"But, Excellency, if he is taken in the act, according to the forty-fifth article, the parliamentary immunity ceases."

"Commendatore, I have given you my opinion, and now it is my wish that the Honourable David Rossi should be set at liberty."

" Excellency ! "

" Be so good as to liberate him instantly, and let your officers see him safely through the streets to his home in the Piazza Navona."

The little head like a hen's went down like a hatchet, and Commendatore Angelelli backed out of the room.

PART TWO—THE REPUBLIC OF MAN

I

THE Piazza Navona is the heart and soul of old Rome. In other quarters of the living city you feel tempted to ask: "Is this London?" or, "Is this Paris?" or, "Is this New York or Berlin?" but in the Piazza Navona you can only tell yourself, "This is Rome!"

In an apartment-house of the Piazza Navona, David Rossi had lived during the seven years since he became Member of Parliament for Rome. The ground floor is a Trattoria, half eating-house and half wine-shop, with rude frescoes on its distempered walls, representing the Bay of Naples with Vesuvius in eruption. A passage running by the side of the Trattoria leads to the apartments overhead, and at the foot of the staircase there is a porter's lodge, a closet always lighted by a lamp, which burns down the dark passage day and night, like a bloodshot eye.

In this lodge lived a veteran Garibaldian, in his red shirt and pork-pie hat, with his old wife, wrinkled like a turkey, and wearing a red handkerchief over her head, fastened by a silver pin. David Rossi's apartments consisted of three rooms on the fourth floor, two to the front, the third to the back, and a lead flat opening out of them on to the roof.

In one of the front rooms on the afternoon of the Pope's Jubilee, a young woman sat knitting with an open book on her lap, while a boy of six knelt by her side, and pretended to learn his lesson. She was a comely but timid creature, with liquid eyes and a soft voice, and he was a shock-headed little giant, like the cub of a young lion.

"Go on, Joseph," said the woman, pointing with her knitting-needle to the line on the page. "'And it came to pass . . .'"

But Joseph's little eyes were peering first at the clock on the mantel-piece, and then out at the window and down the square.

"Didn't you say they were to be here at two, mamma?"

"Yes, dear. Mr. Rossi was to be set free immediately, and papa, who ran home with the good news, has gone back to fetch him."

"Oh! 'And it came to pass afterward that he loved a woman in the Valley of Sorek, whose name was Delilah. And the lords of the Philistines came unto her, and said unto her, Entice him and see wherein his great strength lieth . . .' But, mamma . . .'"

"Go on with your lesson, Joseph. 'And she made him sleep . . .'"

"'And she made him sleep upon her knees, and she called for a man, and she caused him to shave off the seven locks of his head . . .'"

At that moment there came a knock at the door, whereupon the boy uttered a cry of delight, and with a radiant face went plunging and shouting out of the room.

"Uncle David! It's Uncle David!"

The tumultuous voice rolled like baby thunder through the apartment until it reached the door, and then it dropped to a dead silence.

"Who is it, Joseph?"

"A gentleman," said the boy.

II

IT was the fashionable young Roman with the watchful eyes and twirled-up moustache, who had stood by the old Frenchman's carriage in the Piazza of St. Peter.

"I wish to speak with Mr. Rossi. I bring him an important message from abroad. He is coming along with the people, but to make sure of an interview I hurried ahead. May I wait?"

"Certainly! Come in, sir! You say he is coming? Yes? Then he is free?"

The woman's liquid eyes were glistening visibly, and the man's watchful ones seemed to notice everything.

"Yes, madam, he is free. I saw him arrested, and I also saw him set at liberty."

"Really? Then you can tell me all about it? That's good! I have heard so little of all that happened, and my boy and I have not been able to think of anything else. Sit down, sir!"

"As the police were taking him to the station-house in the Borgo," said the stranger, "the people made an attempt to rescue him, and it seemed as if they must certainly have succeeded if it had not been for his own intervention."

"He stopped them, didn't he? I'm sure he stopped them!"

"He did. The delegate had given his three warnings, and the Brigadier was on the point of ordering his men to fire, when the prisoner threw up his hands before the crowd."

"I knew it! Well?"

"'Brothers,' he said, 'let no blood be shed for my sake. We are in God's hands. Go home!'"

"How like him! And then, sir?"

"Then the crowd broke up like a bubble, and the officer who was in charge of him uncovered his head. 'Room for the Honourable Rossi!' he cried, and the prisoner went into the prison."

The liquid eyes were running over by this time, and the soft voice was trembling: "You say you saw him set at liberty?"

"Yes! I was in the public service myself until lately, so they allowed me to enter the police station, and when the order for release came I was present and heard all. 'Deputy,' said the officer, 'I have the honour to inform you that you are free.' 'But before I go I must say something,' said the Deputy. 'My only orders are that you are to be set at liberty,' said the officer. 'Nevertheless, I must see the Minister,' said Mr. Rossi. But the crowd had pressed in and surrounded him, and in a moment the flood had carried him out into the street, with shouts and the waving of hats and a whirlwind of enthusiasm. And now he is being drawn by force through the city in a mad, glad, wild procession."

"But he deserves it all, and more—far, far more!"

The stranger looked at the woman's beaming eyes, and said, "You are not his wife—no?"

"Oh, no! I'm only the wife of one of his friends," she answered.

"But you live here?"

"We live in the rooms on the roof."

"Perhaps you keep house for the Deputy?"

"Yes—that is to say—yes, we keep house for Mr. Rossi."

At that moment the room, which had been gloomy, was suddenly lighted by a shaft of sunshine, and there came from some unseen place a musical noise like the rippling of waters in a fountain.

"It's the birds," said the woman, and she threw open a window that was also a door and led to a flat roof on which some twenty or thirty canaries were piping and shrilling their little swollen throats in a gigantic bird-cage.

"Mr. Rossi's?"

"Yes, and he is fond of animals also—dogs and cats and rabbits and squirrels, especially squirrels."

"Squirrels?"

"He has a grey one in a cage on the roof now. But he is not like some people who love animals—he loves children, too. He loves all children, and as for Joseph . . ."

"The little boy who cried 'Uncle David' at the door?"

"Yes, sir. One day my husband said 'Uncle David' to Mr. Rossi, and he has been Uncle David to my little Joseph ever since."

"This is the dining-room, no doubt," said the stranger.

"Unfortunately, yes, sir."

"Why unfortunately?"

"Because here is the hall, and here is the table, and there's not even a curtain between, and the moment the door is opened he is exposed to everybody. People know it, too, and they take advantage. He would give the chicken off his plate if he hadn't anything else. I have to scold him a little sometimes—I can't help it. And as for father, he says he has doubled his days in purgatory by the lies he tells, turning people away."

"That will be his bedroom, I suppose," said the stranger, indicating a door which the boy had passed through.

"No, sir, his sitting-room. That is where he receives his colleagues in Parliament, and his fellow-journalists, and his electors and printers and so forth. Come in, sir."

The walls were covered with portraits of Mazzini, Garibaldi, Kossuth, Lincoln, Washington, and Cromwell, and the room, which had been furnished originally with chairs covered in chintz, was loaded with incongruous furniture.

"Joseph, you've been naughty again! My little boy is all for being a porter, sir. He has got the butt-end of his father's fishing-rod, you see, and torn his handkerchief into shreds to make a tassel for his mace." Then with a sweep of the arm, " All presents, sir. He gets presents from all parts of the world. The piano is from England, but nobody plays, so it is never opened; the books are from Germany, and the bronze is from France, but the strangest thing of all, sir, is this."

" A phonograph ? "

" It was most extraordinary. A week ago a cylinder came from the island of Elba."

" Elba ? From some prisoner, perhaps ? "

" ' A dying man's message,' Mr. Rossi called it. ' We must save up for an instrument to reproduce it, Sister,' he said. But, look you, the very next day the carriers brought the phonograph."

" And then he reproduced the message ? "

" I don't know—I never asked. He often turns on a cylinder to amuse the boy, but I never knew him try that one. This is the bedroom, sir; you may come in."

It was a narrow room, very bright and lightsome, with its white counterpane, white bed curtains, and white veil over the looking-glass to keep it from the flies.

" How sweet ! " said the stranger.

" It would be but for these," said the woman, and she pointed to the other end of the room, where a desk stood between two windows, amid heaps of unopened newspapers, which lay like fishes as they fall from the herring net.

" I presume this is a present also ? " said the stranger. He had taken from the desk a dagger with a lapis-lazuli handle, and was trying its edge on his finger-nail.

" Yes, sir, and he has turned it to account as a paper-knife. A six-chamber revolver came yesterday, but he had no use for that, so he threw it aside, and it lies under the newspapers."

" And who is this ? " said the stranger. He was looking at a faded picture in an ebony frame which hung by the side of the bed. It was the portrait of an old man with a beautiful forehead and a patriarchal face.

" Some friend of Mr. Rossi's in England, I think."

" An English photograph, certainly, but the face seems to me Roman for all that."

At that moment a thousand lusty voices burst on the air, as a great crowd came pouring out of the narrow lanes into the broad piazza. At the same instant the boy shouted from the adjoining room, and another voice that made the walls vibrate came from the direction of the door.

"They're coming! It's my husband! Bruno!" said the woman, and the ripple of her dress told the stranger she had gone.

III

LAUGHING, crying, cheering, chaffing, singing, David Rossi's people had brought him home in triumph, and now they were crowding upon him to kiss his hand, the big-hearted, baby-headed, beloved children of Italy.

The object of this aurora of worship stood with his back to the table in the dining-room, looking down and a little ashamed, while Bruno Rocco, six feet three in his stockings, hoisted the boy on to his shoulder, and shouted as from a tower to everybody as they entered by the door:

"Come in, sonny, come in! Don't stand there like the Pope between the devil and the deep sea. Come in among the people," and Bruno's laughter rocked through the room to where the crowd stood thick on the staircase.

"The Baron has had a lesson," said a man with a sheet of white paper in his hand. "He dreamed of getting the Collar of the Annunziata out of this."

"The pig dreamed of acorns," said Bruno.

"It's a lesson to the Church as well," said the man with the paper. "She wouldn't have anything to do with us. 'I alone strike the hour of the march,' says the Church."

"And then she stands still!" said Bruno.

"The mountains stand still, but men are made to walk," said the man with the paper, "and if the Pope doesn't advance with the people, the people must advance without the Pope."

"The Pope's all right, sonny," said Bruno, "but what does he know about the people? Only what his black-gowned beetles tell him!"

"The Pope has no wife and children," said the man with the paper.

"Old Vampire could find him a few," said Bruno, and then there was general laughter.

"Brothers," said David Rossi, "let us be temperate. There's nothing to be gained by playing battledore and shuttlecock with the name of an old man who has never done harm to any one. The Pope hasn't listened to us to-day, but he is a saint all the same, and his life has been a lesson in well-doing."

"Anybody can sail with a fair wind, sir," said Bruno.

"Let us be prudent. There's no need for violence, whether of the hand or of the tongue. You've found that out this morning. If you had rescued me from the police, I should have been in prison again by this time, and God knows what else might have happened. I'm proud of your patience and forbearance; and now go home, boys, and God bless you."

"Stop a minute!" said the man with the paper. "Something to read before we go. While the Carabineers kept Mr. Rossi in the Borgo, the Committee of Direction met in a café and drew up a proclamation."

"Read it, Luigi," said David Rossi, and the man opened his paper and read:

"Having appealed in vain to Parliament and to the King against the tyrannical tax which the Government has imposed upon bread in order that the army and navy may be increased, and having appealed in vain to the Pope to intercede with the civil authorities, and call back Italy to its duty, it now behoves us, as a suffering and perishing people, to act on our own behalf. Unless annulled by royal decree, the tax will come into operation on the 1st of February. On that day let every Roman remain indoors until an hour after Ave Maria. Let nobody buy so much as one loaf of bread, and let no bread be eaten, except such as you give to your children. Then, at the first hour of night, let us meet in the Coliseum, tens of thousands of fasting people, of one mind and heart, to determine what it is our duty to do next, that our bread may be sure and our water may not fail."

"Good!" "Beautiful!" "Splendid!"

"Only wants the signature of the president," said the reader, and Bruno called for pen and ink.

"Before I sign it," said Rossi, "let it be understood that none come armed. There is nothing our enemies would like better than to fix on us the names of rioters and rebels. We must defeat them. We must show the world that we alone are the people of law and order. Therefore I call on you to promise that none come armed."

"We promise," cried several voices.

"And now go home, boys, and God bless you."

THE REPUBLIC OF MAN

After a moment there was only one man left in the room. It was the fashionable young Roman with the watchful eyes and twirled-up moustache.

"For you, sir!" said the young man, taking a letter from a pocket inside his waistcoat.

David Rossi opened the letter and read: "The bearer of this, Charles Minghelli, is one of ourselves. He has determined upon the accomplishment of a great act, and wishes to see you with respect to it."

"You come from London?"

"Yes, sir."

"You wish to speak to me?"

"I do."

"You may speak freely."

The young man glanced in the direction of Bruno and of Bruno's wife, who stood beside him.

"It is a delicate matter, sir," he said.

"Come this way," said David Rossi, and he took the stranger into his bedroom.

IV

DAVID ROSSI took his seat at the desk between the windows, and made a sign to the man to take a chair that stood near.

"Your name is Charles Minghelli?" said David Rossi.

"Yes. I have come to propose a dangerous enterprise."

"What is it?"

"That somebody on behalf of the people should take the law into his own hands."

The man had spoken with perfect calmness, and after a moment of silence David Rossi replied as calmly:

"I will ask you to explain what you mean."

The man smiled, made a deferential gesture, and answered, "You will permit me to speak plainly?"

"Certainly."

"Thanks! I have read your Creed and Charter. I have even signed my name to it. It is beautiful as a theory— most beautiful! And the Republic of Man is beautiful too. Beautiful!"

"Well?"

"But more beautiful than practical, dear sir, and the

47

ideal thread that runs through your plan will break the moment the rough world begins to tug at it."

"I will ask you to be more precise," said David Rossi.

"With pleasure. You have called a meeting in the Coliseum to protest against the bread-tax. What if the Government prohibits it? Your principle of passive resistance will not permit you to rebel, and without the right of public meeting your association is powerless. Then where are you?"

David Rossi had taken up his paper-knife dagger and was drawing lines with the point of it on the letter of introduction which now lay open on the desk. The man saw the impression he had produced, and went on with more vigour.

"If the Governments of the world deny you the right of meeting, where are your weapons of warfare? On the one side armies on armies of men marshalled and equipped with all the arts and engines of war; on the other side a helpless multitude with their hands in their pockets, or paying a penny a week subscription to the great association that is to overcome by passive suffering the power of the combined treasuries of the world!"

David Rossi had risen from his seat, and was walking backward and forward with a step that was long and slow.

"Well, and what do *you* say we ought to do?" he said.

A flash came from the man's eyes, and he said in a thick voice:

"Remove the one man in Rome whose hand crushes the nation."

"The Prime Minister?"

"Yes."

There was silence.

"You expect me to do that?"

"No! I will do it for you. . . . Why not? If violence is wrong, it is right to resist violence."

David Rossi returned to his seat at the desk, touched the letter of introduction, and said:

"That is the great act referred to in this letter from London?"

"Yes."

"Why do you come to me?" he said.

"Because you can help me to accomplish this act. You are a Member of Parliament, and can give me cards to the

Chamber. You can show me the way to the Prime Minister's room in Monte Citorio, and tell me the moment when he is to be found alone."

"I do not deny that the Prime Minister deserves death."

"A thousand deaths, sir, and everybody would hail them with delight."

"I do not deny that his death would be a relief to the people."

"On the day he dies, sir, the people will live."

"Or that crimes—great crimes—have been the means of bringing about great reforms."

"You are right, sir—but it would be no crime."

The stranger's face flushed up, his eyes seemed to burn, and he leaned over to the desk and took up the dagger.

"See! Give me this! It's exactly what I want. I'll put it in a bouquet of flowers, and pretend to offer them. Only a way to do it, sir! Say the word—may I take it?"

"But the man who assumes such a mission," said David Rossi, "must know himself free from every thought of personal vengeance."

The dagger trembled in the stranger's hand.

"He must be prepared to realise the futility of what he has done—to know that even when he succeeds he only changes the persons, not the things; the actors, not the parts."

The man stood like one who had been stunned, with his mouth partly open, and balancing the dagger on one hand.

"More than that," said David Rossi; "he must be prepared to be told by every true friend of freedom that the man who uses force is not worthy of liberty—that the conflict of intellects alone is human, and to fight otherwise is to be on the level of the brute."

The man threw the dagger back on the desk and laughed.

"I knew you talked like that to the people—statesmen do sometimes—that's all right—it's pretty, and it keeps the people quiet—but *we* know . . ."

David Rossi rose with a sovereign dignity, but he only said:

"Mr. Minghelli, our interview is at an end."

"So you dismiss me?"

"I do," said David Rossi. "It is such men as you who put back the progress of the world and make it possible for the upholders of authority to describe our efforts as devilish machinations for the destruction of all order, human and divine. Besides that, you speak as one who has not only a perverted political sentiment, but a personal quarrel against an enemy."

The man faced round sharply, came back with a quick step, and said:

"You say I speak as one who has a personal quarrel with the Prime Minister. Perhaps I have! I heard your speech this morning about his mistress, with her livery of scarlet and gold. You meant the woman who is known as Donna Roma Volonna. What if I tell you she is not a Volonna at all, but a girl the Minister picked up in the streets of London, and has palmed off on Rome as the daughter of a noble house, because he is a liar and a cheat?"

David Rossi gave a start, as if an invisible hand had smitten him.

"Her name is Roma, certainly," said the man; "that was the first thing that helped me to seize the mysterious thread."

David Rossi's face grew pale, and he scarcely breathed.

"Oh, I'm not talking without proof," said the man. "I was at the Embassy in London ten years ago when the Ambassador was consulted by the police authorities about an Italian girl who had been found at night in Leicester Square. Mother dead, father gone back to Italy—she had been living with some people her father gave her to as a child, but had turned out badly and run away."

David Rossi had fixed his eyes on the stranger with a kind of glassy stare.

"I went with the Ambassador to Bow Street, and saw the girl in the magistrate's office. She pleaded that she had been ill-treated, but we didn't believe her story, and gave her back to her guardians. A month later we heard that she had run away once more and disappeared entirely."

David Rossi was breathing audibly, and shrinking like an old man into his shoulders.

"I never saw that girl again until a week ago, and where do you think I saw her?"

David Rossi swallowed his saliva, and said:

"Where?"

"In Rome. I had trouble at the Embassy, and came back to appeal to the Prime Minister. Everybody said I must reach him through Donna Roma, and one of my relatives took me to her rooms. The moment I set eyes on her I knew who she was. Donna Roma Volonna is the girl Roma Roselli, who was lost in the streets of London."

David Rossi seemed suddenly to grow taller.

"You scoundrel!" he said, in a voice that was hollow and choked.

The man staggered back and stammered:

"Why . . . what . . ."

"I knew that girl. Until she was seven years of age she was my constant companion—she was the same as my sister —and her father was the same as my father—and if you tell me she is the mistress . . . You infamous wretch! You calumniator! You villain! I could confound you with one word, but I won't. Out of my house this moment! And if ever you cross my path again I'll denounce you to the police as a cut-throat and an assassin."

Stunned and stupefied, the man opened the door and fled.

V

DAVID ROSSI came out with his long slow step, looking pale but calm, and tearing a letter into small pieces, which he threw into the fire.

"What was amiss, sir? They could hear you across the street," said Bruno.

"A man whose room was better than his company, that's all."

"What's his name?" said Bruno.

"Charles Minghelli."

"Why, that must be the secretary who was suspected of forgery at the Embassy in London, and got dismissed."

"I thought as much!" said David Rossi. "No doubt the man attributed his dismissal to the Prime Minister, and wanted to use me for his private revenge."

"That was his game, was it? Why didn't you let me know, sir? He would have gone downstairs like a falling star. Now that I remember, he's the nephew of old Polomba, the Mayor, and I've seen him at Donna Roma's."

A waiter in a white smock, with a large tin box on his head, entered the hall, and behind him came the old woman from the porter's lodge, with the wrinkled face and the red cotton handkerchief.

"Come in," cried Bruno. "I ordered the best dinner in the Trattoria, sir, and thought we might perhaps dine together for once."

"Good," said David Rossi.

"Here it is, a whole basketful of the grace of God, sir! Out with it, Riccardo," and while the women laid the table, Bruno took the dishes smoking hot from their temporary oven with its charcoal fire.

"Artichokes—good. Chicken—good again. I must be a fox—I was dreaming of chicken all last night! *Gnocchi!* (potatoes and flour baked). *Agradolce!* (sour and sweet). *Fagioletti!* (French beans boiled) and—a half-flask of Chianti! Who said the son of my mother couldn't order a dinner? All right, Riccardo; come back at Ave Maria."

The waiter went off, and the company sat down to their meal, Bruno and his wife at either end of the table, and David Rossi on the sofa, with the boy on his right, and the cat curled up into his side on the left, while the old woman stood in front, serving the food and removing the plates.

"Look at him!" said the old woman, who was deaf, pointing to David Rossi, with his two neighbours. "Now, why doesn't the Blessed Virgin give him a child of his own?"

"She has, mother, and here he is," said David Rossi.

"You'll let her give him a woman first, won't you?" said Bruno.

"Ah! that will never be," said David Rossi.

"What does he say?" said the old woman with her hand at her ear like a shell.

"He says he won't have any of you," bawled Bruno.

"What an idea! But I've heard men say that before, and they've been married sooner than you could say 'Hail Mary.'"

"It isn't an incident altogether unknown in the history of this planet, is it, mother?" said Bruno.

"A heart to share your sorrows and joys is something, and the man is not wise who wastes the chance of it," said the old woman. "Does he think parliaments will make up for it when he grows old and wants something to comfort him?"

"Hush, mother!" said Elena, but Bruno made mouths at her to let the old woman go on.

"As for me, I'll want somebody of my own about me

to close my eyes when the time comes to put the sacred oil on them," said the old woman.

"If a man has dedicated his life to work for humanity," said David Rossi, "he must give up many things—father, mother, wife, child."

The corner of Elena's apron crept up to the corner of her eye, but the old woman, who thought the subject had changed, laughed and said:

"That's just what I say to Tommaso. 'Tommaso,' I say, 'if a man is going to be a policeman he must have no father, or mother, or wife, or child—no, nor bowels neither,' I say. And Tommaso says, 'Francesca,' he says, 'the whole tribe of gentry they call statesmen are just policemen in plain clothes, and I do believe they've only liberated Mr. Rossi as a trap to catch him again when he has done something.'"

"They won't catch *you* though, will they, mother?" shouted Bruno.

"That they won't! I'm deaf, praise the saints, and can't hear them."

A knock came to the door, and seizing his mace the boy ran and opened it. An old man stood on the threshold. He was one of David Rossi's pensioners. Ninety years of age, his children all dead, he lived with his grandchildren, and was one of the poor human rats who stay indoors all day and come out with a lantern at night to scour the gutters of the city for the refuse of cigar-ends.

"Come another night, John," said Bruno.

But David Rossi would not send him away empty, and he was going off with the sparkling eyes of a boy, when he said:

"I heard you in the piazza this morning, Excellency! Grand! Only sorry for one thing."

"And what was that, sonny?" asked Bruno.

"What his Excellency said about Donna Roma. She gave me a half-franc only yesterday—stopped the carriage to do it, sir."

"So that's your only reason . . ." began Bruno.

"Good reason, too. Good-night, John!" said David Rossi, and Joseph closed the door.

"Oh, she has her virtues, like every other kind of spider," said Bruno.

"I'm sorry I spoke of her," said David Rossi.

"You needn't be, though. She deserved all she got. I

haven't been two years in her studio without knowing what she is."

" It was the man I was thinking of, and if I had remembered that the woman must suffer . . ."

" Tut! She'll have to make her Easter confession a little earlier, that's all."

" If she hadn't laughed when I was speaking . . ."

" You're on the wrong track now, sir. That wasn't Donna Roma. It was the little Princess Bellini. She is always stretching her neck and screeching like an old gandery goose."

Dinner was now over, and the boy called for the phonograph. David Rossi went into the sitting-room to fetch it, and Elena went in at the same time to light the fire. She was kneeling with her back to him, blowing on to the wood, when she said in a trembling voice:

" I'm a little sorry myself, sir, if I may say so. I can't believe what they say about the mistress, but even if it's true we don't know *her* story, do we?"

Then the phonograph was turned on, and Joseph marched to the tune of " Swannee River " and the strains of Sousa's band.

" Mr. Rossi," said Bruno, between a puff and a blow.

" Yes?"

" Have you tried the cylinder that came first?"

" Not yet."

" How's that, sir?"

" The man who brought it said the friend who had spoken into it was dead." And then with a shiver, " It would be like a voice from the grave—I doubt if I dare hear it."

" Like a ghost speaking to a man, certainly—especially if the friend was a close one."

" He was the closest friend I ever had, Bruno—he was my father."

" Father?"

" Foster-father, anyway. For four years he clothed and fed and educated me, and I was the same as his own son."

" Had he no children of his own?"

" One little daughter, no bigger than Joseph when I saw her last—Roma."

" Roma?"

" Yes, her father was a Liberal, and her name was Roma."

" What became of her?"

" When the doctor came to Italy on the errand which ended in his imprisonment he gave her into the keeping of some Italian friends in London. I was too young to take charge of her then. Besides, I left England shortly afterward and went to America."

" Where is she now ? " said Elena.

" When I returned to England . . . she was dead."

" Well, there's nothing new under the sun of Rome— Donna Roma came from London," said Bruno.

David Rossi felt the muscles of his face quiver.

" Her father was an exile in England, too, and when he came back on the errand that ended in Elba, he gave her away to some people who treated her badly—I've heard old Teapot, the Countess, say so when she's been nagging her poor niece."

David Rossi breathed painfully.

" Strange if it should be the same," said Bruno.

" But Mr. Rossi's Roma is dead," said Elena.

" Ah, of course, certainly! What a fool I am!" said Bruno.

David Rossi had a sense of suffocation, and he went out on to the lead flat.

VI

THE Ave Maria was ringing from many church towers, and the golden day was going down with the sun behind the dark outline of the dome of St. Peter's, while the blue night was rising over the snow-capped Apennines in a premature twilight with one twinkling star.

David Rossi's ears buzzed as with the sound of a mighty wind rushing through trees at a distance. Bruno's last words on top of Charles Minghelli's had struck him like an alarum bell heard through the mists of sleep, and his head was stunned and his eyes were dizzy. He buttoned his coat about him, and walked quickly to and fro on the lead flat by the side of the cage, in which the birds were already bunched up and silent.

Before he was aware of the passing of time, the church bells were tolling the first hour of night. Presently he became aware of flares burning in the Piazza of St. Peter, and of the shadows of giant heads cast up on the walls of the vast Basilica. It was the crowd gathering for the last ceremonial of the Pope's Jubilee, and at the sound of a double rocket, which went up as with the crackle of musketry, little Joseph came running on to the roof, followed by his mother and Bruno.

David Rossi took the boy into his arms and tried to dispel the gloom of his own spirits in the child's joy at the illuminations.

"Ever see 'luminations before, Uncle David?" said Joseph.

"Once, dear, but that was long ago and far away. I was a boy myself in those days, and there was a little girl with me then who was no bigger than you are now. But it's growing cold, there's frost in the air, besides it's late, and little boys must go to bed."

"Well, God is God, and the Pope is His Prophet," said Bruno, when Elena and Joseph had gone indoors. "It was like day! You could see the lightning conductor over the Pope's apartment! Pshew!" blowing puffs of smoke from his twisted cigar. "Won't keep the lightning off, though."

"Bruno!"

"Yes, sir?"

"Donna Roma's father would be Prince Volonna?"

"Yes, the last prince of the old papal name. When the Volonna estates were confiscated, the title really lapsed, but old Vampire got the lands."

"Did you ever hear that he bore any other name during the time he was in exile?"

"Sure to, but there was no trial and nothing was known. They all changed their names, though."

"Why . . . what . . ." said David Rossi in an unsteady voice.

"Why?" said Bruno. "Because they were all condemned in Italy, and the foreign countries were told to turn them out. But what am I talking about? You know all that better than I do, sir. Didn't your old friend go under a false name?"

"Very likely—I don't know," said David Rossi, in a voice that testified to jangled nerves.

"Did he ever tell you, sir?"

"I can't say that he ever . . . Certainly the school of revolution has always had villains enough, and perhaps to prevent treachery . . ."

"You may say so! The devil has the run of the world,

even in England. But I'm surprised your old friend, being like a father to you, didn't tell you—at the end anyway . . ."

"Perhaps he intended to—and then perhaps . . ."

David Rossi put his hand to his brow as if in pain and perplexity, and began again to walk backward and forward.

A screamer in the piazza below cried "*Trib-un-a!*" and Bruno said:

"That's early! What's up, I wonder? I'll go down and get a paper."

Darkness had by this time re-invaded the sky, and the stars looked down from their broad dome, clear, sweet, white, and serene, putting to shame by their immortal solemnity the poor little mimes, the paltry puppet-shows of the human jackstraws who had just been worshipping at their self-made shrine.

As David Rossi returned to the house, Elena, who was undressing the boy, saw a haggard look in his eyes, but Bruno, who was reading his evening journal, saw nothing, and cried out:

"Helloa! Listen to this, sir. It's Olga. She's got a pen, I can tell you. 'Madame de Pompadour. Hitherto we have had the pleasure of having Madame ——, whose pressure on the State and on Italy's wise counsellors was only incidental, but now that the fates have given us a Madame Pompadour . . .' Then there's a leading article on your speech in the piazza. Praises you up to the skies. Look! 'Thank God we have men like the Honourable Rossi, who at the risk of . . .'"

But with a clouded brow David Rossi turned away from him and passed into the sitting-room, and Bruno looked around in blank bewilderment.

"Shall you want the lamp, sir?" said Elena.

"Not yet, thank you," he answered through the open door.

The wood fire was glowing on the hearth, and in the acute state of his nerves he shuddered involuntarily as its reflection in the window opposite looked back at him like a fiery eye. He opened the case of the phonograph, which had been returned to its place on the piano, and then from a drawer in the bureau he took a small cardboard box. The wood in the fire flickered at that moment and started some ghastly shadows on the ceiling, but he drew a cylinder from the box and slid it on to the barrel of the phonograph. Then he stepped to the door, shut and locked it.

VII

" WELL!" said Bruno. " If that isn't enough to make a man feel as small as a sardine!"

There was only one thing to do, but to conceal the nature of it Bruno flourished the newspaper and said:

" Elena, I must go down to the lodge and read these articles to your father. Poor Donna Roma, she'll have to fly, I'm afraid. Bye-bye, Garibaldi-Mazzini! Early to bed, early to rise, and time enough to grow old, you know! . . . As for Mr. Rossi, he might be a sinner and a criminal instead of the hero of the hour! It licks me to little bits." And Bruno carried his dark mystery down to the café to see if it might be dispelled by a litre of autumnal light from sunny vineyards.

Meantime, Joseph, being very tired, was shooting out a pettish lip because he had to go to bed without saying goodnight to Uncle David; and his mother, making terms with this pretence, consented to bring down his nightdress, thinking Rossi might be out of the sitting-room by that time, and the boy be pacified. But when she returned to the diningroom the sitting-room door was still closed, and Joseph was pleading to be allowed to lie on the sofa until Uncle David carried him to bed.

" I'm not asleep, mamma," came in a drowsy voice from the sofa, but almost at the same moment the measured breath slowed down, the watch-lights blinked themselves out, and the little soul slid away into the darksome kingdom of unconsciousness.

Suddenly, in the silence of the room, Elena was startled by a voice. It came from the sitting-room. Was it Mr. Rossi's voice? No! The voice was older and feebler than Mr. Rossi's, and less clear and distinct. Could it be possible that somebody was with him? If so, the visitor must have arrived while she was in the bedroom above. But why had she not heard the knock? How did it occur that Joseph had not told her? And then the lamp was still on the diningroom table, and save for the firelight the sitting-room must be dark.

THE REPUBLIC OF MAN

A chill began to run through her blood, and she tried to hear what was said, but the voice was muffled by its passage through the wall, and she could only catch a word or two. Presently the strange voice, without stopping, was broken in upon by a voice that was clear and familiar, but now faltering with the note of pain: "I swear to God I will!"

That was Mr. Rossi's voice, and Elena's head began to go round. Whom was he speaking to? Who was speaking to him? He went into the room alone, he was sitting in the dark, and yet there were two voices.

A light dawned on Elena, and she could have laughed. What had terrified her as a sort of supernatural thing was only the phonograph! But after a moment a fresh tremor struck upon her in the agony of the exclamations with which David Rossi broke in upon the voice that was being reproduced by the machine. She could hear his words distinctly, and he was in great trouble. Hardly knowing what she did, she crept up to the door and listened. Even then, she could only follow the strange voice in passages, which were broken and submerged by the whirring of the phonograph, like the flight of a sea-bird which dips at intervals and leaves nothing but the wash of the waves.

"David," said the voice, "when this shall come to your hands . . . in my great distress of mind . . . do not trifle with my request . . . but whatever you decide to do . . . be gentle with the child . . . remember that . . . Adieu, my son . . . the end is near . . . if death does not annihilate . . . those who remain on earth . . . a helper and advocate in heaven . . . Adieu!" And interrupting these broken words were half-smothered cries and sobs from David Rossi, repeating again and again: "I will! I swear to God I will!"

Elena could bear the pain no longer, and mustering up her courage she tapped at the door. It was a gentle tap, and no answer was returned. She knocked louder, and then an angry voice said:

"Who's there?"

"It's I—Elena," she answered timidly. "Is anything the matter? Aren't you well, sir?"

"Ah, yes," came back in a calmer voice, and after a shuffling sound as of the closing of drawers, David Rossi opened the door and came out.

As he crossed the threshold he cast a backward glance into the dark room, as if he feared that some invisible hand would touch him on the shoulder. His face was pale and beads of perspiration stood on his forehead, but he smiled, and in a voice that was a little hoarse, yet fairly under control, he said:

"I'm afraid I've frightened you, Elena."

"You're not well, sir. Sit down, and let me run for some cognac."

"No! It's nothing! Only . . ."

"Take this glass of water, sir."

"That's good! I'm better now, and I'm ashamed. Elena, you mustn't think any more of this, and whatever I may do in the future that seems to you to be strange, you must promise me never to mention it."

"I needn't *promise* you that, sir," said Elena.

"Bruno is a brave, bright, loyal soul, Elena, but there are times . . ."

"I know—and I'll never mention it to anybody. But you've taken a chill on the roof at sunset looking at the illuminations—that's all it is! The nights are frosty now, and I was to blame that I didn't send out your cloak."

Then she tried to be cheerful, and turning to the sleeping boy, said:

"Look! He was naughty again and wouldn't go to bed until you came out to carry him."

"The dear little man!" said David Rossi. He stepped up to the couch, but his pale face was pre-occupied, and he looked at Elena again and said:

"Where does Donna Roma live?"

"Trinità de' Monti—eighteen," said Elena.

"Is it late?"

"It must be half-past eight at least, sir."

"We'll take Joseph to bed then."

He was putting his arms about the boy to lift him when a slippery-sloppery step was heard on the stairs, followed by a hurried knock at the door.

It was the old Garibaldian porter, breathless, bareheaded, and in his slippers.

"Father!" cried Elena.

"It's she. She's coming up."

At the next moment a lady in evening dress was standing in the hall. It was Donna Roma. She had unclasped her ermine cloak, and her bosom was heaving with the exertion of the ascent.

"May I speak to Mr. Rossi?" she began, and then looking beyond Elena and seeing him, where he stood above the sleeping child, a qualm of faintness seemed to seize her, and she closed her eyes for a moment.

David Rossi's face flushed to the roots of his hair, but he stepped forward, bowed deeply, led the way to the sitting-room, and, with a certain incoherency in his speech, said:

"Come in! Elena will bring the lamp. I shall be back presently."

Then, lifting little Joseph in his arms, he carried him up to bed, tucked him in his cot, smoothed his pillow, made the sign of the cross over his forehead, and came back to the sitting-room with the air of a man walking in a dream.

VIII

BEING left alone, Roma looked around, and at a glance she took in everything—the thin carpet, the plain chintz, the prints, the incongruous furniture. She saw the photograph on the piano, still standing open, with a cylinder exposed, and in the interval of waiting she felt almost tempted to touch the spring. She saw herself, too, in the mirror above the mantel-piece, with her glossy black hair rolled up like a tower, from which one curly lock escaped on to her forehead, and with the ermine cloak on her shoulders over the white silk muslin which clung to her full figure.

Then she heard David Rossi's footsteps returning, and though she was now completely self-possessed she was conscious of a certain shiver of fear, such as an actress feels in her dressing-room at the tuning-up of the orchestra. Her back was to the door and she heard the whirl of her skirt as he entered, and then he was before her, and they were alone.

He was looking at her out of large, pensive eyes, and she saw him pass his hand over them and then bow and motion her to a seat, and go to the mantel-piece and lean on it. She was tingling all over, and a certain glow was going up to her face, but when she spoke she was mistress of herself, and her voice was soft and natural.

"I am doing a very unusual thing in coming to see you," she said, "but you have forced me to it, and I am quite helpless."

'A faint sound came from him, and she was aware that he was leaning forward to see her face, so she dropped her eyes, partly to let him look at her, and partly to avoid meeting his gaze.

"I heard your speech in the piazza this morning. It would be useless to disguise the fact that some of its references were meant for me."

He did not speak, and she played with the glove in her lap, and continued in the same soft voice:

"If I were a man, I suppose I should challenge you. Being a woman, I can only come to you and tell you that you are wrong."

"Wrong?"

"Cruelly, terribly, shamefully wrong."

"You mean to tell me . . ."

He was stammering in a husky voice, and she said quite calmly:

"I mean to tell you that in substance and in fact what you implied was false."

There was a dry glitter in her eyes which she tried to subdue, for she knew that he was looking at her still.

"If . . . if . . ."—his voice was thick and indistinct— "if you tell me that I have done you an injury . . ."

"You have—a terrible injury."

She could hear his breathing, but she dared not look up, lest he should see something in her face.

"Perhaps you think it strange," she said, "that I should ask you to accept my assurance only. But though you have done me a great wrong I believe you will accept it."

"If . . . if you give me your solemn word of honour that what I said—what I implied—was false, that rumour and report have slandered you, that it is all a cruel and baseless calumny . . ."

She raised her head, looked him full in the face.

"I *do* give it," she said.

"Then I believe you," he answered. "With all my heart and soul, I believe you."

She dropped her eyes again, and turning with her thumb an opal ring on her finger, she began to use the blandishments which had never failed with other men.

"I do not say that I am altogether without blame," she said. "I may have lived a thoughtless life amid scenes of poverty and sorrow. If so, perhaps it has been partly the fault of the men about me. When is a woman anything but what the men around have made her?"

She dropped her voice almost to a whisper, and added: "You are the first man who has not praised and flattered me."

"I was not thinking of you," he said. "I was thinking of another, and perhaps of the poor working women who, in a world of luxury, have to struggle and starve."

She looked up, and a half-smile crossed her face.

"I honour you for that," she said. "And perhaps if I had earlier met a man like you my life might have been different. I used to hope for such things long ago—that a man of high aims and noble purposes would come to meet me at the gate of life. Perhaps you have felt like that—that some woman, strong and true, would stand beside you for good or for ill, in your hour of danger and your hour of joy?"

Her voice was not quite steady—she hardly knew why.

"A dream! We all have our dreams," he said.

"A dream indeed! Men came—he was not among them. They pampered every wish, indulged every folly, loaded me with luxuries, but my dream was dispelled. I respected few of them and reverenced none. They were my pastime, my playthings. And they have revenged themselves by saying in secret . . . what you said in public this morning."

He was looking at her constantly with his wistful eyes, the eyes of a child, and through all the joy of her success she was conscious of a spasm of pain at the expression of his sad face and the sound of his tremulous voice.

"We men are much to blame," he said. "In the battle of man with man we deal out blows and think we are fighting fair, but we forget that behind our foe there is often a woman —a wife, a mother, a sister, a friend—and, God forgive us, we have struck her, too."

The half-smile that had gleamed on Roma's face was wiped out of it by these words, and an emotion she did not understand began to surge in her throat.

"You speak of poor women who struggle and starve," she said. "Would it surprise you to hear that *I* know what it is to do that? Yes, and to be friendless and alone—quite, quite alone in a cruel and wicked city."

She had lost herself for a moment, and the dry glitter in her eyes had given way to a moistness and a solemn expression. But at the next instant she had regained her self-control, and went on speaking to avoid a painful silence.

"I have never spoken of this to any other man," she said. "I don't know why I should mention it to you—to you of all men."

She had risen to her feet, and he stepped up to her, and looking straight into her eyes he said:

"Have you ever seen me before?"

"Never," she answered.

"Sit down," he said. "I have something to say to you."

She sat down, and a peculiar expression, almost a crafty one, came into her face.

"You have told me a little of your life," he said. "Let me tell you something of mine."

She smiled again. These big children called men were almost to be pitied. She had expected a fight, but the man had thrown up the sponge from the outset, and now he was going to give himself into her hands. Only for that pathetic look in his eyes and that searching tone in his voice she could have found it in her heart to laugh.

She let her cape drop back from her shoulders, revealing her round bust and swanlike arms, and crossing one leg over the other she displayed the edge of a lace skirt and the point of a red slipper. Then she coughed a little behind a perfumed lace handkerchief and prepared to listen.

"You are the daughter of an ancient family," he said, "older than the house it lived in, and prouder than a line of kings. And whatever sorrows you may have seen, you knew what it was to have a mother who nursed you and a father who loved you, and a home that was your own. Can you realise what it is to have known neither father nor mother, to be homeless, nameless, and alone?"

She looked up—a deep furrow had crossed his brow, which she had not seen there before.

"Happy the child," he said, "though shame stands beside his cradle, who has one heart beating for him in a cruel world. That was not my case. I never knew my mother."

The mocking fire had died out of Roma's face, and she uncrossed her knees.

"My mother was the victim of a heartless man and a cruel law. She tied to her baby's wrist a paper on which she had written its father's name, placed it in the rota at the Foundling of Santo Spirito, and flung herself into the Tiber."

THE REPUBLIC OF MAN

Roma drew the cape over her shoulders.

"She lies in an unnamed pauper's grave in the Campo Verano."

"*Your* mother?"

"Yes. My earliest memory is of being put out to nurse at a farmstead in the Campagna. It was the time of revolution; the treasury of the Pope was not yet replaced by the treasury of the King, the nuns at Santo Spirito had no money with which to pay their pensions; and I was like a child forsaken by its own, a fledgling in a foreign nest."

"Oh!"

"Those were the days when scoundrels established abroad traded in the white slavery of poor Italian boys. They scoured the country, gathered them up, put them in railway trucks like cattle, and despatched them to foreign countries. My foster-parents parted with me for money, and I was sent to London."

Roma's bosom was heaving, and tears were gathering in her eyes.

"My next memory is of living in a large half-empty house in Soho—fifty foreign boys crowded together. The big ones were sent out into the streets with an organ, the little ones with a squirrel or a cage of white mice. We had a cup of tea and a piece of bread for breakfast, and were forbidden to return home until we had earned our supper. Then— then the winter days and nights in the cold northern climate, and the little southern boys with their organs and squirrels, shivering and starving in the darkness and the snow."

Roma's eyes were filling frankly, and she was allowing the tears to flow.

"Thank God, I have another memory," he continued. "It is of a good man, a saint among men, an Italian refugee, giving his life to the poor, especially to the poor of his own people."

Roma's labouring breath seemed to be arrested at that moment.

"On several occasions he brought their masters to justice in the English courts, until, finding they were watched, they gradually became less cruel. He opened his house to the poor little fellows, and they came for light and warmth between nine and ten at night, bringing their organs with them. He taught them to read, and on Sunday evenings he talked to them of the lives of the great men of their country. He is dead, but his spirit is alive—alive in the souls he made to live."

Roma's eyes were blinded with the tears that sprang to them, and her throat was choking, but she said:

"What was he?"

"A doctor."

"What was his name?"

David Rossi passed his hand over the furrow in his forehead, and answered:

"They called him Joseph Roselli."

Roma half rose from her seat, then sank back, and the lace handkerchief dropped from her hand.

"But I heard afterwards—long afterwards—that he was a Roman noble, one of the fearless few who had taken up poverty and exile and an unknown name for the sake of liberty and justice."

Roma's head had fallen into her bosom, which was heaving with an emotion she could not conceal.

"One day a letter came from Italy, telling him that a thousand men were waiting for him to lead them in an insurrection that was to dethrone an unrighteous king. It was the trick of a scoundrel who has since been paid the price of a hero's blood. I heard of this only lately—only to-night."

There was silence for a moment. David Rossi had put one arm over his eyes.

"Well?"

"He was enticed back from England to Italy; an English minister violated his correspondence with a friend, and communicated its contents to the Italian Government; he was betrayed into the hands of the police, and deported without trial."

"Was he never heard of again?"

"Once—only once—by the friend I speak about."

Roma felt dizzy, as if she were coming near to some deep places; but she could not stop—something compelled her to go on.

"Who was the friend?" she asked.

"One of his poor waifs—a boy who owed everything to him, and loved and revered him as a father—loves and reveres him still, and tries to follow in the path he trod."

"What—what was his name?"

"David Leone."

She looked at him for a moment without being able to speak. Then she said:

" What happened to him? "

" The Italian courts condemned him to death, and the English police drove him from England."

" Then he has never been able to return to his own country? "

" He has never been able to visit his mother's grave except by secret and at night, and as one who was perpetra:ing a crime."

" What became of him? "

" He went to America."

" Did he ever return? "

" Yes! Love of home in him, as in all homeless ones, was a consuming passion, and he came back to Italy."

" Where—where is he *now?* "

David Rossi stepped up to her, and said:

" In this room."

She rose:

" Then *you* are David Leone! "

He raised one hand:

" *David Leone is dead!* "

There was silence for a moment. She could hear the thumping of her heart. Then she said in an almost inaudible whisper:

" I understand. David Leone is dead, but David Rossi is alive."

He did not speak, but his head was held up and his face was shining.

" Are you not afraid to tell me this? "

" No."

Her eyes glistened and her lips quivered.

" You insulted and humiliated me in public this morning, yet you think I will keep your secret? "

" I *know* you will."

She felt a sensation of swelling in her throbbing heart, and with a slow and nervous gesture she held out her hand.

" May I . . . may I shake hands with you? " she said.

There was a moment of hesitation, and then their hands seemed to leap at each other and clasp with a clasp of fire.

At the next instant he had lifted her hand to his lips and was kissing it again and again.

A sensation of triumphant joy flashed through her, and

instantly died away. She wished to cry out, to confess, to say something, she knew not what. But *David Leone is dead* rang in her ears, and at the same moment she remembered what the impulse had been which brought her to that house.

Then her eyes began to swim and her heart to fail, and she wanted to fly away without uttering another word. *She* could not speak, *he* could not speak; they stood together on a precipice where only by silence could they hold their heads.

"Let me go home," she said in a breaking voice, and with downcast head and trembling limbs she stepped to the door.

IX

Reaching the door, she stopped, as if reluctant to leave, and said in a voice still soft, but coming more from within:

"I wished to meet you face to face, but now that I have met you, you are not the man I thought you were."

"Nor you," he said, "the woman I pictured you."

A light came into her eyes at that, and she looked up and said:

"Then you had never seen me before?"

And he answered after a moment:

"I had never seen Donna Roma Volonna until to-day."

"Forgive me for coming to you," she said.

"I thank you for doing so," he replied, "and if I have sinned against you, from this hour onward I am your friend and champion. Let me try to right the wrong I have done you. What I said was the result of a mistake—let me ask your forgiveness."

"You mean publicly?"

"Yes!"

"You are very good, very brave," she said; "but no, I will not ask you to do that."

"Ah! I understand. I know it is impossible to overtake a lie. Once started it goes on and on, like a stone rolling down-hill, and even the man who started can never stop it. Tell me what better I can do—tell me, tell me."

Her face was still down, but it had now a new expression of joy.

"There is one thing you can do, but it is difficult."

"No matter! Tell me what it is."

By courtesy of Liebler & Co.; from photographs by Byron.

THEY STOOD TOGETHER ON A PRECIPICE.

"I thought when I came here . . . but it is no matter."

"Tell me, I beg of you."

He was trying to look into her face again, and she was eluding his gaze as before, but now for another, a sweeter reason.

"I thought if—if you would come to my house when my friends are there, your presence as my guest, in the midst of those in whose eyes you have injured me, might be sufficient of itself to wipe out everything. But . . ."

"Is that *all?*" he said.

"Then you are not afraid?"

"Afraid?"

For one moment they looked at each other, and their eyes were shining.

"I have thought of something else," she said.

"What is it?"

"You have heard that I am a sculptor. I am making a fountain for the Municipality, and if I might carve your face into it . . ."

"It would be coals of fire on my head."

"You would need to sit to me."

"When shall it be?"

"To-morrow morning to begin with, if that is not too soon."

"It will be years on years till then," he said.

She bent her head and blushed. He tried again to look at her beaming eyes and golden complexion, and for sheer joy of being followed up she turned her face away.

"Forgive me if I have stayed too long," she said, making a feint of opening the door.

"I should have grudged every moment if you had gone sooner," he answered.

"I only wished that you should not think of me with hatred and bitterness."

"If I ever had such a feeling it is gone."

"Mine has gone too," she said softly, and again she prepared to go.

One hook of her cape had got entangled in the silk muslin at her shoulder, and while trying to free it she looked at him, and her look seemed to say, "Will you?" and his look replied, "May I?" and at the physical touch a certain impalpable bridge seemed in an instant to cross the space that had divided them.

"Let me see you to the door?" he said, and her eyes said openly, "Will you?"

They walked down the staircase side by side, going step by step, and almost touching.

"I forgot to give you my address—eighteen Trinità de' Monti," she said.

"Eighteen Trinità de' Monti," he repeated.

They had reached the second storey. "I am trying to remember," she said. "After all, I think I have seen you before somewhere."

"In a dream, perhaps," he answered.

"Yes," she said. "Perhaps in the dream I spoke about."

They had reached the street, and Roma's carriage, a hired *coupé*, stood waiting a few yards from the door.

They shook hands, and at the electric touch she raised her head and gave him in the darkness the look he had tried to take in the light.

"Until to-morrow then," she said.

"To-morrow morning," he replied.

"To-morrow morning," she repeated, and again in the eye-asking between them she seemed to say, "Come early, will you not?—there is still so much to say."

He looked at her with his shining eyes, and something of the boy came back to his world-worn face as he closed the carriage door.

"Adieu!"

"Adieu!"

She drew up the window, and as the carriage moved away she smiled and bowed through the glass.

PART THREE—ROMA

I

THE Piazza of Trinità de' Monti takes its name from a church and convent which stand on the edge of the Pincian Hill.

A flight of travertine steps, twisted and curved to mask the height, goes down from the church to a diagonal piazza, the Piazza di Spagna, which is always bright with the roses of flower-sellers, who build their stalls around a fountain.

At the top of these steps there stands a house, four-square to all winds, and looking every way over Rome. The sun rises and sets on it, the odour of the flowers comes up to it from the piazza, and the music of the band comes down to it from the Pincio. Donna Roma occupied two floors of this house. One floor, the lower one, built on arches and entered from the side of the city, was used as a studio, the other was as a private apartment.

Donna Roma's home consisted of ten or twelve rooms on the second floor, opening chiefly out of a central drawing-room, which was furnished in red and yellow damask, papered with velvet wall-papers, and lighted by lamps of Venetian glass representing lilies in rose-colour and violet. Her bed-room, which looked to the Quirinal, was like the nest of a bird in its pale-blue satin, with its blue silk counterpane and its embroidered cushion at the foot of the bed; and her boudoir, which looked to the Vatican, was full of vases of malachite and the skins of wild animals, and had a bronze clock on the chimney-piece set in a statue of Mephistopheles. The only other occupant of her house, besides her servants, was a distant kinswoman, called her aunt, and known to familiars as the Countess Betsy; but in the studio below, which was connected with the living rooms by a circular staircase, and hung round with masks, busts, and weapons, there was Bruno Rocco, her marble-pointer, the friend and housemate of David Rossi.

THE ETERNAL CITY

On the morning after Donna Roma's visit to the Piazza Navona a letter came from the Baron. He was sending Felice to be her servant. "The man is a treasure and sees nothing," he wrote. And he added in a footnote: "Don't look at the newspapers this morning, my child; and if any of them send to you say nothing."

But Roma had scarcely finished her coffee and roll when a lady journalist was announced. It was Lena, the rival of Olga both in literature and love.

"I'm 'Penelope,'" she said. "'Penelope' of the *Day*, you know. Come to see if you have anything to say in answer to the Deputy Rossi's speech yesterday. Our editor is anxious to give you every opportunity; and if you would like to reply through me to Olga's shameful libels . . . Haven't you seen her article? Here it is. Disgraceful insinuations. No lady could allow them to pass unnoticed."

"Nevertheless," said Roma, "that is what I intend to do. Good-morning!"

Lena had barely crossed the doorstep when a more important person drove up. This was the Senator Palomba, Mayor of Rome, a suave, oily man, with little twinkling eyes.

"Come to offer you my sympathy, my dear! Scandalous libels. Liberty of the press, indeed! Disgraceful! It's in all the newspapers—I've brought them with me. One journal actually points at you personally. See—'A lady sculptor who has recently secured a commission from the Municipality through the influence of a distinguished person.' Most damaging, isn't it? The elections so near, too! We must publicly deny the statement. Ah, don't be alarmed! Only way out of a nest of hornets. Nothing like diplomacy, you know. Of course the Municipality will buy your fountain just the same, but I thought I would come round and explain before publishing anything."

Roma said nothing, and the great man backed himself out with the air of one who had conferred a favour, but before going he had a favour to ask in return.

"It's rumoured this morning, my dear, that the Government is about to organise a system of secret police—and quite right, too. You remember my nephew, Charles Minghelli? I brought him here when he came from Paris. Well, Charles would like to be at the head of the new force. The very man! Finds out everything that happens, from the fall of a pin to an attempt at revolution, and if Donna Roma

72

will only say a word for him. . . . Thanks! . . . What a beautiful bust! Yours, of course? A masterpiece! Fit to put beside the masterpieces of old Rome."

The Mayor was not yet out of the drawing-room when a third visitor was in the hall. It was Madame Sella, a fashionable modiste, with social pretensions, who contrived to live on terms of quasi-intimacy with her aristocratic customers.

"Trust I am not *de trop!* I knew you wouldn't mind my calling in the morning. What a scandalous speech of that agitator yesterday! Everybody is talking about it. In fact, people say you will go away. It isn't true, is it? No? So glad! So relieved! . . . By the way, my dear, don't trouble about those stupid bills of mine, but . . . I'm giving a little reception next week, and if the Baron would only condescend . . . you'll mention it? A thousand thanks! Good-morning!"

"Count Mario," announced Felice, and an effeminate old dandy came tripping into the room. He was Roma's landlord and the Italian Ambassador at St. Petersburg.

"So good of you to see me, Donna Roma. Such an uncanonical hour, too, but I *do* hope the Baron will not be driven to resign office on account of these malicious slanders. You think not? So pleased!"

Then stepping to the window, "What a lovely view! The finest in Rome, and that's the finest in Europe! I'm always saying if it wasn't Donna Roma I should certainly turn out my tenant and come to live here myself. . . . That reminds me of something. I'm . . . well, I'm tired of Petersburg, and I've written to the Minister asking to be transferred to Paris, and if somebody will only whisper a word for me. . . . How sweet of you! Adieu!"

Roma was sick of all this insincerity, and feeling bitter against the person who had provoked it, when an unseen hand opened the door of a room on the Pincio side of the drawing-room, and the testy voice of her aunt called to her from within.

The old lady, who had just finished her morning toilet and was redolent of scented soap, reclined in a white robe on a bed-sofa with a gilded mirror on one side of her and a little shrine on the other. Her bony fingers were loaded with loose rings, and a rosary hung at her wrist. A cat was sitting at her feet, with a gold cross suspended from its ribbon.

THE ETERNAL CITY

"Ah, is it you at last? You come to me sometimes. Thanks!" she said in a withering whimper. "I thought you might have looked in last night, and I lay awake until after midnight."

"I had a headache and went to bed," said Roma.

"I never have anything else, but nobody thinks of me," said the old lady, and Roma went over to the window.

"I suppose you are as headstrong as ever, and still intend to invite that man in spite of all my protests?"

"He is to sit to me this morning, and may be here at any time."

"Just so! It's no use speaking. I don't know what girls are coming to. When I was young a man like that wouldn't have been allowed to cross the threshold of any decent house in Rome. He would have been locked up in prison instead of sitting for his bust to the ward of the Prime Minister."

"Aunt Betsy," said Roma, "I want to ask you a question."

"Be quick, then. My head is coming on as usual. Natalina! Where's Natalina?"

"Was there any quarrel between my father and his family before he left home and became an exile?"

"Certainly not! Who said there was? Quarrel indeed! His father was broken-hearted, and as for his mother, she closed the gate of the palace, and it was never opened again to the day of her death. Natalina, give me my smelling salts. And why haven't you brought the cushion for the cat?"

"Still, a man has to live his own life, and if my father thought it right . . ."

"Right? Do you call it right to break up a family, and, being an only son, to let a title be lost and estates go to the dogs?"

"I thought they went to the Baron, auntie."

"Roma, aren't you ashamed to sneer at me like that? At the Baron, too, in spite of all his goodness! As for your father, I'm out of patience. He wasted his wealth and his rank, and left his own flesh and blood to the mercy of others —and all for what?"

"For country, I suppose."

"For fiddlesticks! For conceit and vanity and vainglory. Go away! My head is fit to split. Natalina, why haven't you given me my smelling salts? And why will you always forget to . . ."

Roma left the room, but the voice of her aunt scolding the maid followed her down to the studio.

Her dog was below, and the black poodle received her with noisy demonstrations, but the humorous voice which usually saluted her with a cheery welcome she did not hear. Bruno was there, nevertheless, but silent and morose, and bending over his work with a sulky face.

She had no difficulty in understanding the change when she looked at her own work. It stood on an easel in a compartment of the studio shut off by a glass partition, and was a head of David Rossi which she had roughed out yesterday. Not yet feeling sure which of the twelve apostles around the dish of her fountain was the subject that Rossi should sit for, she had decided to experiment on a bust. It was only a sketch, but it was stamped with the emotions that had tortured her, and it showed her that unconsciously her choice had been made already. Her choice was Judas.

Last night she had laughed when looking at it, but this morning she saw that it was cruel, impossible, and treacherous. A touch or two at the clay obliterated the sinister expression, and, being unable to do more until the arrival of her sitter, she sat down to write a letter.

"MY DEAR BARON,—Thanks for Cardinal Felice. He will be a great comfort in this household if only he can keep the peace with Monsignor Bruno, and live in amity with the Archbishop of Porter's Lodge. Senator Tom-tit has been here to suggest some astonishing arrangement about my fountain, and to ask me to mention his nephew, Charles Minghelli, as a fit and proper person to be chief of your new department of secret police. Madame de Trop and Count Signorina have also been, but of their modest messages more anon.

"As for D. R., my barometer is 'set fair,' but it is likely to be a stormier time than I expected. Last night I decked myself in my best bib and tucker, and, in defiance of all precedent, went down to his apartment. But the strange thing was that, whereas I had gone to find out all about *him*, I hadn't been ten minutes in his company before he told all about *me*—about my father, at all events, and his life in London. I believe he knew me in that connection and expected to appeal to my filial feelings. Did too, so strong is the force of nature, and then and thereafter, and all night long, I was like somebody who had been shaken in an earthquake and wanted to cry out and confess. It was not until I remembered what my father had been—or rather hadn't—and that he was no more to me than a name, representing exposure to the cruellest fate a girl ever passed through, that I recovered from the shock of D. R.'s dynamite.

"He has promised to sit to me for his bust, and is to come this morning!—Affectionately,   ROMA.

"P. S.—My gentleman has good features, fine eyes, and a wonderful voice, and though I truly believe he trembles at the sight of a woman and has never been in love in his life, he has an astonishing way of getting at one. But I could laugh to think how little execution his fusillade will make in this direction."

"Honourable Rossi!" said Felice's sepulchral voice behind her, and at that moment David Rossi stepped into the studio.

II

In spite of her protestations, Roma was nervous and confused. Putting David Rossi to sit in the armchair on the platform for sitters, she rattled on about everything—her clay, her tools, her sponge, and the water they had forgotten to change for her. He must not mind if she stared at him—that wasn't nice, but it was necessary—and he must promise not to look at her work while it was unfinished—children and fools, you know—the proverb was musty.

And while she talked she told herself that Thomas was the apostle he must stand for. These anarchists were all doubters, and the chief of doubters was the figure that would represent them.

David Rossi did not speak much at first, and he did not join in Roma's nervous laughter. Sometimes he looked at her with a steadfast gaze, which would have been disconcerting if it had not been so simple and childlike. At length he looked out of the window to where the city lay basking in the sunshine, and birds were swirling in the clear blue sky, and began to talk of serious subjects.

"How beautiful!" he said. "No wonder the English and Americans who come to Italy for health and the pleasure of art think it a paradise where every one should be content. And yet . . ."

"Yes?"

"Under the smile of this God-blessed land there is suffering such as can hardly be found in any other country of the world. Sometimes I think I cannot bear it any longer, and must go away, as others do."

"A little more this way, please—thank you! That doesn't do much for them, does it?"

"For them? No! God comfort the poor exiles—their path is a bridge of sighs! Poor, friendless, forgotten, huddled together in some dingy quarter of a foreign city, one a music-master, another a teacher of languages, a third a supernumerary at a theatre, a fourth an organ-man or even a beggar in the streets, yet weapons in the hand of God and shaking the thrones of the world!"

"*You* have seen something of that, haven't you?"

"I have."

"In London?"

"Yes. There's an old quarter on the fringe of the fashionable district. It is called Soho. Densely populated, infested with vice, the very sewer of the city, yet an asylum of liberty for all that. The refugees of Europe fly to it. Its criminals, too, perhaps; for misery, like poverty, has many bedfellows."

"You lived there?"

"Yes."

Roma was wiping her fingers with the sponge, and looking sideways out of the window. "And your old friend, Doctor Roselli—he lived in Soho?"

"In Soho Square when I knew him first. The house faced to the north, and had a porch and trees in front of it."

The sponge had dropped to the floor, but Roma did not observe it. She took up a tooth-tool and began to work on the clay again.

"A little more that way, please—thanks! Do you think your friend had a right to renounce his rank and to break up his family in Italy? Think of his father—he would be broken-hearted."

"He was—I've heard my old friend say so. He cursed him at last and forbade him to call himself his son."

"There!"

"But he would never hear a word against the old man. 'He's my father—that's enough,' he would say."

The tooth-tool, like the sponge, dropped out of Roma's fingers.

"How stupid! But his mother . . ."

"That was sadder still. In the early years of his exile she would pray him to come home. 'You are the best of mothers,' he would answer, 'but I cannot do so.'"

"He never saw her again?"

"Never, but he worshipped her very name and she was a tower of strength to him. 'Mothers!' he used to say, 'if you only knew your power! God be merciful to the wayward one who has no mother!'"

Roma's throat was throbbing. "He . . . he was married?"

"Yes. His wife was an Englishwoman, almost as friendless as himself."

"Eyes the other way, at the window—thank you! . . . Did she know who he was?"

"Nobody knew. He was only a poor Italian doctor to all of us in Soho."

"They . . . they were . . . happy?"

"As happy as love and friendship could make them. And even when poverty came . . ."

"He became poor—very poor?"

"Very! It got known that Doctor Roselli was a revolutionary, and then his English patients began to be afraid. The house in Soho Square had to be given up at last, and we went into a side street. Only two rooms now, one to the front, the other to the back, and four of us to live in them, but the misery of that woman's outward circumstances never dimmed the radiance of her sunny soul."

Roma's bosom was heaving and her voice was growing thick. "She . . . died?"

David Rossi bent his head and spoke in short, jerky sentences. "Her death came at the bitterest moment of want. It was Christmas time. Very cold and raw. We hadn't too much at home to keep us warm. She caught a cold and it settled on her chest. Pneumonia! Only three or four days altogether. She lay in the back room; it was quieter. The doctor nursed her constantly. How she fought for life! She was thinking of her little daughter. Just six years of age at that time, and playing with her doll on the floor."

His voice had enough to do to control itself.

"When it was all over we went into the front room and made our beds on a blanket spread out on the bare boards. Only three of us now—the child with her father, weeping for the mother lying cold the other side of the wall."

His eyes were still looking out at the window. In Roma's eyes the tears were gathering.

"We were nearly penniless, but our good angel was buried somehow. Oh, the poor are the richest people in the world! I love them! I love them!"

Roma could not look at him any longer.

"It was in the cemetery of Kensal Green. There was a London fog and the grave-diggers worked by torches, which smoked in the thick air. But the doctor stood all the time with his head uncovered. The child was there too, and driving home she looked out of the window and sometimes laughed at the sights in the streets. Only six—and she had never been in a coach before!"

At that moment was heard the boom of the gun that is fired from the Castle of St. Angelo at midday, and Roma put down her tools.

"If you don't mind, I'll not try to do any more to-day," she said in a husky voice. "Somehow it isn't coming right this morning. It's like that sometimes. But if you can come at this time to-morrow . . ."

"With pleasure," said David Rossi, and a moment later he was gone.

She looked at her work and obliterated the expression again.

"Not Thomas," she thought. "John—the beloved disciple! That would fit him exactly."

As she went upstairs to dress for lunch, Felice gave her an envelope bearing the seal of the Prime Minister, and told her the dog was missing.

"He must have followed Mr. Rossi," said Roma, and without ado she read the letter.

"DEAR ROMA,—A thousand thanks for suggesting Charles Minghelli. I sent for him, saw him, and appointed him immediately. Thanks, too, for the clue about your father. Highly significant! I mentioned it to Minghelli, and the dark fire in his eyes shone out instantly. Adieu, my dear! You are on the right track! I will observe your request and not come near you.—Affectionately,

"BONELLI."

III

NEXT morning Roma found herself dressing with extraordinary care.

After coffee she went into the Countess's room as usual. The old lady had made her toilette, and her cat was purring on a cushion by her side.

"Aunt Betsy, is it true that my father was decoyed back to Italy by the police?"

"How do I know that? But if he was, it was no more than he might have expected. He had been breeding sedition at the safe distance of a thousand miles, and it was time he was brought to justice. Besides . . ."

"Well?"

"There were the estates, and naturally the law could not assign them to anybody else while there was no judgment against your father."

"So my father was enticed back to Italy in the interests of the next of kin."

"Roma! How dare you talk like that? About your best friend, too!"

"I didn't say anything against the Baron, did I?"

"You would be an ungrateful girl if you did. As for your father, I'm tired of talking. Only for his exile you would have had possession of your family estates at this moment, and been a princess in your own right."

"Only for this exile I shouldn't have been here at all, auntie, and somebody else would have been the princess, it seems to me."

The old lady dropped the perfumed handkerchief that was at her nose and said:

"What do you talk about downstairs all day long, miss? Pretty thing if you allow a man like that to fill you with his fictions. He is a nice person to take your opinions from, and you are a nice girl to stand up for a man who sold you into slavery, as I might say! Have you forgotten the baker's shop in London—or was it a pastry cook's, or what?—where they made you a drudge and a scullery-maid, after your father had given you away?"

"Don't speak so loud, Aunt Betsy."

"Then don't worry me by defending such conduct. Ah, how my head aches! Natalina, where are my smelling salts? Natalina!"

"I'm not defending my father, but still . . ."

"Should think not, indeed! If it hadn't been for the Baron, who went in search of you, and found you after you had run away and been forced to go back to your slave-master, and then sent you to school in Paris, and now permits you to enjoy half the revenue of your father's estates, and forbids us to say a word about his generosity, where would you be? Madonna mia! In the streets of London, perhaps, to which your father had consigned you!"

The Princess Bellini was waiting for Roma when she returned to the drawing-room. The little lady was as friendly as if nothing unusual had occurred.

"Just going for a walk in the Corso, my dear. You'll come? No? Ah, work, work, work!"

The little lady tapped Roma's arm with her pince-nez and laughed.

"Everybody has heard that *he* is sitting to you, and everybody understands. That reminds me—I've a box at the new opera to-morrow night:—'Samson' at the Costanzi, you know. Only Gi-gi and myself, but if you would like me to take you and to ask your own particular Samson . . ."

"Honourable Rossi," said Felice at the door, and David Rossi entered the room, with the black poodle bounding before him.

"I must apologise for not sending back the dog," he said. "It followed me home yesterday, but I thought as I was coming to-day . . ."

"Black has quite deserted me since Mr. Rossi appeared," said Roma, and then she introduced the deputy to the Princess.

The little lady was effusive. "I was just saying, Honourable Rossi, that if you would honour my box at the opera to-morrow night . . ."

David Rossi glanced at Roma.

"Oh yes, Donna Roma is coming, and if you will . . ."

"With pleasure, Princess."

THE ETERNAL CITY

"That's charming! After the opera we'll have supper at the Grand Hotel. Good-day!" said the Princess, and then in a low voice at the door, "I leave you to your delightful duties, my dear. You are not looking so well, though. Must be the scirocco. My poor dear husband used to suffer from it shockingly. Adieu!"

Roma was less confused but just as nervous when she settled to her work afresh.

"I've been thinking all night long of the story you told me yesterday," she said. "No, that way, please—eyes as before—thank you! About your old friend, I mean. He was a good man—I don't doubt that—but he made everybody suffer. Not only his father and mother, but his wife also. Has anybody a right to sacrifice his flesh and blood to a work for the world?"

"When a man has taken up a mission for humanity his kindred must reconcile themselves to that," said Rossi.

"Yes, but a child, one who cannot be consulted. Your friend's daughter, for example. She was to lose everything —her father himself at last. How could he love her? I suppose you would say he did love her."

"Love her? He lived for her. She was everything on earth to him, except the one thing to which he had dedicated his life."

A half-smile parted her lovely lips.

"When her mother was gone he was like a miser who had been robbed of all his jewels but one, and the love of father, mother, and wife seemed to gather itself up in the child."

The lovely lips had a doubtful curve.

"How bright she was, too! I can see her still in the dingy London house with her violet eyes and coal-black hair and happy ways—a gleam of the sun from our sunny Italy."

She looked at him. His face was calm and solemn. Did he really know her after all? She felt her cheeks flush and tingle.

"And yet he left her behind to come to Italy on a hopeless errand," she said.

"He did."

"How could he know what would happen?"

"He couldn't, and that troubled him most of all. He lived in constant fear of being taken away from his daugh-

ter before her little mind was stamped with the sense of
how much he loved her. Delicious selfishness! Yet it was
not altogether selfish. The world was uncharitable and
cruel, and in the rough chance of life it might even happen
that she would be led to believe that because her father gave
her away, and left her, he did not love her."

Roma looked up again. His face was still calm and
solemn.

"He gave her away, you say?"

"Yes. When the treacherous letter came from Italy he
could not resist it. It was like a cry from the buried-alive
calling upon him to break down the door of their tomb. But
what could he do with the child? To take her with him was
impossible. A neighbour came—a fellow-countryman—he
kept a baker's shop in the Italian quarter. 'I'm only a poor
man,' he said, 'but I've got a little daughter of the same age
as yours, and two sticks will burn better than one. Give the
child to me and do as your heart bids you!' It was like a
light from heaven. He saw his way at last."

Roma listened with head aside.

"One day he took the child and washed her pretty face
and combed her glossy hair, telling her she was going to see
another little girl and would play with her always. And
the child was in high glee and laughed and chattered and
knew no difference. It was evening when we set out for the
stranger's house, and in the twilight of the little streets
happy-hearted mothers were calling to their children to come
in to go to bed. The doctor sent me into a shop to buy a
cake for the little one, and she ate it as she ran and skipped
by her father's side."

Roma was holding her breath.

"The baker's shop was poor but clean, and his own little
girl was playing on the hearthrug with her cups and sau-
cers. And before we were aware of it two little tongues were
cackling and gobbling together, and the little back-parlour
was rippling over with a merry twitter. The doctor stood
and looked down at the children, and his eyes shone with a
glassy light. 'You are very good, sir,' he said, 'but she is
good too, and she'll be a great comfort and joy to you always.'
And the man said, 'She'll be as right as a trivet, doctor,
and you'll be right too—you'll be made triumvir like Mazzini, when the republic is proclaimed, and then you'll send
for the child, and for me too, I daresay.' But I could see

that the doctor was not listening. 'Let us slip away now,' I said, and we stole out somehow."

Roma's eyes were moistening, and the little tool was trembling in her hand.

There was silence for some moments, and then from without, muffled by the walls it passed through, there came the sound of voices. The nuns and children of Trinità de' Monti were singing their Benediction—*Ora pro nobis!*

"I don't think I'll do any more to-day," said Roma. "The light is failing me, and my eyes . . ."

"The day after to-morrow, then," said Rossi, rising.

"But do you really wish to go to the opera to-morrow night?"

He looked steadfastly into her face and answered "Yes."

She understood him perfectly. He had sinned against her and he meant to atone. She could not trust herself to look at him, so she took the damp cloth and turned to cover up the clay. When she turned back he was gone.

After dinner she replied to the Baron's letter of the day before.

"DEAR BARON,—I have misgivings about being on the right track, and feel sorry you have set Minghelli to work so soon. Do Prime Ministers appoint people at the mere mention of their names by wards, second cousins, and lady friends generally? Wouldn't it have been wise to make inquiries? What was the fault for which Minghelli was dismissed in London?

"As for D. R., I must have been mistaken about his knowing me. He doesn't seem to know me at all, and I believe his shot at me by way of my father was a fluke. At all events, I'm satisfied that it is going in the wrong direction to set Minghelli on his trail. *Leave him to me alone.*— Yours, ROMA.

"P.S.—Princess Potiphar and Don Saint Joseph are to take me to the new opera to-morrow night. D. R. is also to be there, so he will be seen with me in public!

"I have begun work on King David for a bust. He is not so wonderfully good-looking when you look at him closely."

IV

THE little Princess called for Roma the following night, and they drove to the opera in her magnificent English carriage. Already the theatre was full and the orchestra was tuning up. With the movement of people arriving and recognising each other there was an electrical atmosphere which affected everybody. Don Camillo came, oiled and perfumed, and when he had removed the cloaks of the ladies and they took their places in the front of the box, there was a slight tingling all over the house. This pleased the little Princess immensely, and she began to sweep the place with her opera-glass.

"Crowded already!" she said. "And every face looking up at my box! That's what it is to have for your companion the most beautiful and the most envied girl in Rome. What a sensation! Nothing to what it will be, though, when your illustrious friend arrives."

At that moment David Rossi appeared at the back, and the Princess welcomed him effusively.

"So glad! So honoured! Gi-gi, let me introduce you—Honourable Rossi, Don Camillo Luigi Murelli."

Roma looked at him—he had an air of distinction in a dress coat such as comes to one man in a thousand. He looked at Roma—she wore a white gown with violets on one shoulder and two rows of pearls about her beautiful white throat. The Princess looked at both of them, and her little eyes twinkled.

"Never been here before, Mr. Rossi? Then you must allow me to explain everything. Take this chair between Roma and myself. No, you must not sit back. *You* can't mind observation—so used to it, you know."

Without further ado David Rossi took his place in front of the box, and then a faint commotion passed over the house. There were looks of surprise and whispered comments, and even some trills of laughter.

He bore it without flinching, as if he had come for it and expected it, and was taking it as a penance.

Roma dropped her head and felt ashamed, but the little Princess went on talking. "These boxes on the first tier are occupied by Roman society generally, those on the second tier mainly by the diplomatic corps, and the stalls are filled by all sorts and conditions of people—political people, literary people, even trades-people if they're rich enough or can pretend to be."

" And the upper circles ? " asked Rossi.

" Oh," in a tired voice, " professional people, I think—Collegio Romano and University of Rome, you know."

" And the gallery ? "

" Students, I suppose." Then eagerly, after bowing to somebody below, " Gi-gi, there's Lu-lu. Don't forget to ask him to supper. . . . All the beautiful young men of Rome are here to-night, Mr. Rossi, and presently they'll pay a round of calls on the ladies in the boxes."

The voice of the Princess was suddenly drowned by the sharp tap of the conductor, followed by the opening blast of the overture. Then the lights went down and the curtain rose, but still the audience kept up a constant movement in the lower regions of the house, and there was an almost unbroken chatter.

The curtain fell on the first act without anybody knowing what the opera had been about, except that Samson loved a woman named Delilah, and the lords of the Philistines were tempting her to betray him. Students in the gallery, recognisable by their thin beards, shouted across at each other for the joy of shouting, and spoke by gestures to their professors below. People all over the house talked gaily on social subjects, and there was much opening and shutting of the doors of boxes. The beautiful young man called Lu-lu came to pay his respects to the Princess, and there was a good deal of gossip and laughter.

The second act was more dramatic than the first, showing Samson in his character as a warrior, and when the curtain came down again, General Morra, the Minister of War, visited the Princess's box.

" So you're taking lessons in the art of war from the professor who slew an army with the jaw-bone of an ass ? " said Don Camillo.

" Wish we could enlist a few thousands of him—jaw-bones as well," said the General. " The gentleman might be worth having at the War Office, if it was only as a *jetta-tura*." And then in a low voice to the Princess, with a glance at Roma, " Your beautiful young friend doesn't look so well to-night."

The Princess shrugged her shoulders. "Of the pains of love one suffers but does not die," she whispered.

"You surely cannot mean . . ."

The Princess put the tip of her fan to his lips and laughed.

Roma was conscious of a strange conflict of feelings. The triumph she had promised herself by David Rossi's presence with her in public—the triumph over the envious ones who would have rejoiced in her downfall—brought her no pleasure.

The third act dealt with the allurements of Delilah, and was received with a good deal of laughter.

"Ah, these sweet, round, soft things—they can do anything they like with the giants," said Don Camillo.

The Baron, who had dined with the King, came round at the end of the next act, wearing a sash diagonally across his breast, with crosses, stars, and other decorations. He bowed to David Rossi with ceremonious politeness, greeted Don Camillo familiarly, kissed the hand of the Princess, and offered his arm to Roma to take her into the corridor to cool —she was flushed and overheated.

"I see you are getting on, my child! Excellent idea to bring him here! Everybody is saying you cannot be the person he intended, so his trumpet has brayed to no purpose."

"You received my letters?" she said in a faltering voice.

"Yes, but don't be uneasy. I'm neither the prophet nor the son of a prophet if we are not on the right track. What a fortunate thought about the man Minghelli! An inspiration! You asked what his fault was in London—forgery, my dear!"

"That's serious enough, isn't it?"

"In a Secretary of Legation, yes, but in a police agent . . ."

He laughed significantly, and she felt her skin creep.

"Has he found out anything?" she asked.

"Not yet, but he is clearly on the track of great things. It is nearly certain that your King David is a person wanted by the law."

Her hand twitched at his arm, but they were turning at the end of the corridor and she pretended to trip over her train.

" Some clues missing still, however, and to find them we are sending Minghelli to London."

" London? Anything connected with my father?"

" Possibly! We shall see. But there's the orchestra and here's your box! You're wonderful, my dear! Already you've undone the mischief he did you, and one half of your task is accomplished. Diplomatists! Pshaw! We'll all have to go to school to a girl. Adieu!"

All through the next act Roma seemed to feel a sting on her arm where the Baron had touched it, and she was conscious of colouring up when the Princess said:

" Everybody is looking this way, my dear! See what it is to be the most talked-of girl in Rome!"

And then she felt David Rossi's hand on the back of her chair, and heard his soft voice saying:

" The light is in your eyes, Donna Roma. Let me change places with you for a while."

After that everything passed in a kind of confusion. She heard somebody say:

" He's putting a good deal of heart into it, poor thing!"

And somebody answered, " Yes, of broken heart apparently."

Then there was a crash and the opera was over, and she was going out in a crowd on David Rossi's arm, and feeling as if she would fall if she dropped it.

The magnificent English carriage drew up under the portico and all four of them got into it.

" Grand Hotel!" cried Don Camillo. Then dropping back to his place he laughed and chanted:

" And the dead he slew at his death were more than he slew in his life . . . and he judged Israel twenty years."

V

A MARSHY air from the Campagna shrouded the city as with a fog, and pierced through the closed windows of the carriage, but there was warmth and glow in the Grand Hotel.

One woman after another came in clothed in diamonds under the fur cloak which hung over her bare arms and shoulders, until the room was a dazzling blaze of jewels.

People caught each other's eyes through lorgnettes and eye-glasses, and there were constant salutations. The men chattered, the women laughed, and there was an affectation of baby-talk at nearly every table. Then supper was served, glasses were held up as signals, and bright eyes began to play about the room, until the atmosphere was tingling with electric currents and heated by human passion.

Roma sat facing the Princess. She was still confused and preoccupied, but when rallied upon her silence she brightened up for a moment and tried to look buoyant and happy. David Rossi, who was on her left, was still quiet and collected, but bore the same air as before, of a man going through a penance.

This was observed by Don Camillo, who sat on the right of the Princess, and led to various little scenes.

"Very good company here, Mr. Rossi. Always sure of seeing some beautiful young women," said Don Camillo.

"And beautiful young men, apparently," said David Rossi.

The beautiful young man called Lu-lu was there, and reaching over to Don Camillo, and speaking in a whisper between the puff of a cigarette and a sip of coffee, he said:

"Why doesn't the Minister buy the man up? Easy enough to buy the press these days."

"He's doing better than that," said Don Camillo. "He's drawing him from opposition by the allurements of . . ."

"Office?"

"No, the lady," whispered Don Camillo, but Roma heard him.

She was ashamed. The innuendoes which belittled David Rossi were belittling herself as well, and she wanted to get up and fly.

Rossi himself seemed to be unconscious of anything hurtful. Although silent, he was calm and cheerful, and his manner was natural and polite. The wife of one of the royal aides-de-camp sat next to him, and talked constantly of the King.

Roma found herself listening to every word that was said to David Rossi, but she also heard a conversation that was going on at the other end of the table.

"Wants to be another Cola di Rienzi, doesn't he?" said Lu-lu.

"Another Christ," said Don Camillo. "He'll be asking for a crown of thorns by-and-by, and calling on the world to immolate him for the sake of humanity. Look! He's talking to the little Baroness, but he is fifteen thousand miles above the clouds at this moment."

"Where does he come from, I wonder?" said Lu-lu, and then the two hands of Don Camillo played the invisible accordion.

"Madame de Trop says his father was Master of the House to Prince Petrolium—vice-prince, you know, and brought up in the little palace," said the Princess.

"Don't believe a word of it," said Don Camillo, "and I'll wager he never supped at a decent hotel before."

"I'll ask him! Listen now! Some fun," said the Princess. "Honourable Rossi!"

"Yes, Princess," said David Rossi.

The eyes of the little Princess swept the table with a sparkling light.

"Beautiful room, isn't it?"

"Beautiful."

"Never been here before, I suppose?"

David Rossi looked steadfastly into her eyes and answered, "Oh yes, Princess. When I first returned to Italy eight years ago I was a waiter in this house for a month."

The sparkling face of the little Princess broke up like a snowball in the sun, and the two other men dropped their heads.

Roma hardly knew what her own feelings were. Humiliation, shame, confusion, but above all, pride—pride in David Rossi's courage and strength.

The white mist from the Campagna pierced to the bone as they came out by the glass-covered hall, and an old woman with an earthenware scaldino, crouching by the marble pillars in the street, held out a chill, damp hand and cried:

"A penny for God's sake! May I die unconfessed if I've eaten anything since yesterday! . . . God bless you, my daughter! and the Holy Virgin and all the saints!"

At the door of her house Roma parted from the Princess, and said to Rossi, as the carriage drove away, "Come early to-morrow. I've not yet been able to work properly somehow."

She was restless and feverish, and she would have gone to bed immediately, but crossing the drawing-room she heard the fretful voice of her aunt saying, "Is that you, Roma?" and she had no choice but to go into the Countess's bedroom.

ROMA

A red lamp burned before the shrine, and the old lady was in an embroidered nightdress, but she was wide awake, and her eyes flashed and her lips trembled.

"Ah, it's you at last! Sit down! I want to speak to you. Natalina!" cried the Countess. "Oh, dear me, the girl has gone to bed. Give me the cognac. There it is—on the dressing-table."

She sipped the brandy, fidgeted with her cambric handkerchief, and said:

"Roma, I'm surprised at you! You hadn't used to be so stupid! How? Don't you see what that woman is doing? What woman? The Princess, of course. Inviting you to share her box at the opera so that you may be seen in public with that man. She hates him like poison, but she would swallow anything to throw you and this Rossi together. Do you expect the Baron to approve of that? His enemy, and you on such terms with the man? Here, take back this cognac. I feel as if I would choke—Natalina . . ."

"You're quite mistaken, Aunt Betsy," said Roma. "The Baron was at the opera and came into the box himself, and he approved of everything."

"Tut! Don't tell me! Because he has some respect for himself and keeps his own counsel you are simple enough to think he will not be offended."

The old lady's voice was dying down to a choking whisper, but she went on without a pause.

"If you've no thought for yourself, you might have some for me. You are young, and anything may come to you. but I'm old and I'm tied down to this mattress, and what is to happen if the Baron takes offence? The income he allows us from your father's estates is under his own control still. He can cut it off at any moment, and if he does, what is to become of me?"

Roma's bosom was swelling under her heavy breathing, her heart was beating violently and her head was dizzy. All the bitterness of the evening was boiling in her throat, and it burst out at length in a flood.

"So that is all your moral protestations come to, is it?" she said. "Because the Baron is necessary to you and you cannot exist without him, you expect me to buy and sell myself according to your necessities."

"Roma! What are you saying? Aren't you ashamed . . ."

"Aren't *you* ashamed? You've been trying to throw me

7   91

into the arms of the Baron, and you haven't cared what would happen so long as I kept up appearances."

"Oh, dear! I see what it is. You want to be the death of me! You will, too, before you've done. Natalina! Where is . . ."

"More than that, you've poisoned my mind against my father, and because I couldn't remember him, you've brought me up to think of him as selfish and vain and indifferent to his own daughter But my father wasn't that kind of man at all."

"Who told you that, miss?"

"Never mind who told me. My father was a saint and a martyr, and a great man, and he loved me with all his heart and soul."

"Oh, my head! My poor head! . . . A martyr indeed! A socialist, a republican, a rebel, an anarchist, you mean!"

"Never mind what his politics were. He was my father —that is enough—and you had no right to make *me* think ill of him, whatever the world might do."

Roma was superb at that moment, with her head thrown back, her eyes flaming, and her magnificent figure swelling and heaving under her clinging gown.

"You'll kill me, I tell you. The cognac . . . Natalina . . ." cried the Countess, but Roma was gone.

Before going to bed Roma wrote to the Baron:

"Certain you are wrong. Why waste time sending Charles Minghelli to London? Why? Why? Why? The forger will find out nothing, and if he does, it will only be by exercise of his Israelitish art of making bricks without straw. Stop him at once if you wish to save public money and spare yourself personal disappointment. Stop him! Stop him! Stop him!

"P.S.—To show you how far astray your man has gone, D. R. mentioned to-night that he was once a waiter at the Grand Hotel!"

VI

NEXT morning David Rossi arrived early.

"Now we must get to work in earnest," said Roma. "I think I see my way at last."

ROMA

It was not John the beloved disciple, John who lay in the bosom of his Lord. It was Peter, the devoted, stalwart, brave individual, human, erring but glorious Peter. "Thou art Peter, and on this rock I build my church."

"Same position as before. Eyes the other way. Thank you!. . . Afraid you didn't enjoy yourself last night—no?"

"At the theatre? I was interested. But the human spectacle was perhaps more to me than the artistic one. I am no artist, you see. . . . How did *you* become a sculptor?"

"Oh, I studied a little in the studios of Paris, where I went to school, you see."

"But you were born in London?"

"Yes."

"Why did you come to Rome?"

"Rome was the home of my people, you know. And then there was my name—Roma!"

"I knew a Roma long ago."

"Really? Another Roma?"

There was a tremor in her voice.

"It was the little daughter of the friend I've spoken about."

"How interest . . . No, at the window, please—that will do."

Roma was choking with a sense of duplicity, but save for a turn of the head David Rossi gave no sign.

"She was only seven when I saw her last."

"That was long ago, you say?"

"Seventeen years ago."

"Then she will be the same age as . . ."

"The first time I saw her she was only three, and she was in her nightdress ready for bed."

Roma laughed a little, but she knew that every note in her voice was confused and false.

"She said her prayers with a little lisp at that time. 'Our Fader oo art in heben, alud be dy name.'"

He laughed a little now, as he mimicked the baby voice. They laughed together, then they looked at each other, and then with serious eyes they turned away.

"You'll think it strange, but I date my first conscious and definite aspiration to the memory of that hour."

"Really?"

"Ten years afterward, when I was in America, the words

93

of that prayer came back to me in Roma's little lisp. 'Dy kingum tum. Dy will be done on eard as it is in heben.'"

For some time after that Roma worked on without speaking, feeling feverish and restless. But just as the silence was becoming painful, and she could bear it no longer, Felice came to announce lunch.

"You'll stay? I want so much to work on while I'm in the mood," she said.

"With pleasure," he replied.

She ate hardly at all, for she was troubled by many misgivings. Did he know her? He did; he must; every word, every tone seemed to tell her that. Then why did he not speak out plainly? Because, having revealed himself to her, he was waiting for her to reveal herself to him. And why had she not done so? Because she was enmeshed in the nets of the society she lived in; because she was ashamed of the errand that had brought them together; and most of all because she had not dared to lay bare that secret of his life which, like an escaped convict, dragged behind it the broken chain of the prison-house.

David Leone is dead! To uncover, even to their own eyes only, the fact that lay hidden behind those words was like personating the priest and listening at the grating of the confessional!

No matter! She must do it! She must reveal herself as her heart and instinct might direct. She must claim the parentage of the noblest soul that ever died for liberty, and David Rossi must trust his secret to the bond of blood which would make it impossible for her to betray the foster-son of her own father.

Having come to this conclusion, the light seemed to break in her heavy sky, but the clouds were charged with electricity. As they returned to the studio she was excited and a little hysterical, for she thought the time was near. At that moment a regiment of soldiers passed along under the ilex trees to the Pincio, with their band of music playing as they marched.

"Ah, the dear old days!" said David Rossi. "Everything reminds me of them! I remember that when she was six . . ."

"Roma?"

"Yes—a regiment of troops returned from a glorious campaign, and the doctor took us to see the illuminations and rejoicings. We came to a great piazza almost as large as the piazza of St. Peter's, with fountains and a tall column in the middle of it."

" I know—Trafalgar Square!"

" Dense crowds covered the square, but we found a place on the steps of a church."

" I remember—St. Martin's Church. You see, I know London."

" The soldiers came in by the big railway station close by . . ."

" Charing Cross, isn't it."

" And they marched to the tune of the 'British Grenadiers' and the thunder of fifty thousand throats. And as their general rode past, a beacon of electric lights in the centre of the square blazed out like an aureole about the statue of a great Englishman who had died long ago for the cause which had then conquered."

" Gordon!" she cried—she was losing herself every moment.

" 'Look, darling!' said the doctor to little Roma. And Roma said, 'Papa, is it God?' I was a tall boy then, and stood beside him. 'She'll never forget that, David,' he said."

" And she didn't . . . she couldn't . . . I mean . . . Have you ever told me what became of her?"

She would reveal herself in a moment—only a moment—after all, it was delicious to play with this sweet duplicity.

" Have you?" she said in a tremulous voice.

His head was down. " Dead!" he answered, and the tool dropped out of her hand on to the floor.

" I was five years in America after the police expelled me from London, and when I returned to England I went back to the little shop in Soho."

She was staring at him and holding her breath. He was looking out of the window.

" The same people were there, and their own daughter was a grown-up girl, but Roma was gone."

She could hear the breath in her nostrils.

" They told me she had been missing for a week, and then . . . her body had been found in the river."

She felt like one struck dumb.

" The man took me to the grave. It was the grave of her mother in Kensal Green, and under her mother's name I read her own inscription—'Sacred also to the memory of

Roma Roselli, found drowned in the Thames, aged twelve years.'"

The warm blood which had tingled through her veins was suddenly frozen with horror.

"Not to-day," she thought, and at that moment a faint sound of the band on the Pincio came floating in by the open window.

"I must go," said David Rossi, rising.

Then she recovered herself and began to talk on other subjects. When would he come again? He could not say. The parliamentary session opened soon. He would be very busy.

When David Rossi was gone Roma went upstairs, and Natalina met her carrying two letters. One of them was going to the post—it was from the Countess to the Baron. The other was from the Baron to herself.

"MY DEAREST ROMA,—A thousand thanks for the valuable clue about the Grand Hotel. Already we have followed up your lead, and we find that the only David Rossi who was ever a waiter there gave as reference the name of an Italian baker in Soho. Minghelli has gone to London, and I am sending him this further information. Already he is fishing in strange waters, and I am sure you are dying to know if he has caught anything. So am I, but we must possess our souls in patience.

"But, my dearest Roma, what is happening to your handwriting? It is so shaky nowadays that I can scarcely decipher some of it.—With love.   "B."

VII

"DEAR GUARDIAN,—But I'm not—I'm not! I'm not in the least anxious to hear of what Mr. Minghelli is doing in London, because I know he is doing nothing, and whatever he says, either through his own mouth or the mouth of his Italian baker in Soho, I shall never believe a word he utters. As to Mr. Rossi, I am now perfectly sure that he does not identify me at all. He believes my father's daughter is dead, and he has just been telling me a shocking story of how the body of a young girl was picked out of the Thames (about the time you took me away from London) and buried in the name of Roma Roselli. He actually saw the grave and the tombstone! Some scoundrel has been at work somewhere. Who is it, I wonder?—Yours,   "R. V."

Having written this letter in the heat and haste of the first moment after David Rossi's departure, she gave it to Bruno to post immediately.

"Just so!" said Bruno to himself, as he glanced at the superscription.

Next morning she dressed carefully, as if expecting David Rossi as usual, but when he did not come she told herself she was glad of it. Things had happened too hurriedly; she wanted time to breathe and to think.

All day long she worked on the bust. It was a new delight to model by memory, to remember an expression and then try to reproduce it. The greatest difficulty lay in the limitation of her beautiful art. There were so many memories, so many expressions, and the clay would take but one of them.

The next day after that she dressed herself as carefully as before, but still David Rossi did not come. No matter! It would give her time to think of all he had said, to go over his words and stories.

Did he know her? Certainly he knew her! He must have known from the first that she was her father's daughter, or he would never have put himself in her power. His belief in her was such a sweet thing. It was delicious.

Next day also David Rossi did not come, and she began to torture herself with misgivings. Was he indifferent? Had all her day-dreams been delusions? Little as she wished to speak to Bruno, she was compelled to do so.

Bruno hardly lifted his eyes from his chisel and soft iron hammer. "Parliament is to meet soon," he said, "and when a man is leader of a party he has enough to do, you know."

"Ask him to come to-morrow. Say I wish for one more sitting—only one."

"I'll tell him," said Bruno, with a bob of his head over the block of marble.

But David Rossi did not come the next day either, and Bruno had no better explanation.

"Busy with his new 'Republic' now, and no time to waste, I can tell you."

"He will never come again," she thought, and then everything around and within her grew dark and chill.

She was sleeping badly, and to tire herself at night she went out to walk in the moonlight along the path under the convent wall. She walked as far as the Pincio gates, where the path broadens to a circular space under a table of clipped ilexes, beneath which there is a fountain and a path going down to the Piazza di Spagna. The night was soft and very quiet, and standing under the deep shadows of the trees, with only the cruel stars shining through, and no sound in the air save the sobbing of the fountain, she heard a man's footstep on the gravel coming up from below.

It was David Rossi. He passed within a few yards, yet he did not see her. She wanted to call to him, but she could not do so. For a moment he stood by the deep wall that overlooks the city, and then turned down the path which she had come by. A trembling thought that was afraid to take shape held her back and kept her silent, but the stars beat kindly in an instant and the blood in her veins ran warm. She watched him from where she stood, and then with a light foot she followed him at a distance.

It was true! He stopped at the parapet before the church, and looked up at her windows. There was a light in one of them, and his eyes seemed to be steadfastly fixed on it. Then he turned to go down the steps. He went down slowly, sometimes stopping and looking up, then going on again. Once more she tried to call to him. "Mr. Rossi." But her voice seemed to die in her throat. After a moment he was gone, the houses had hidden him, and the church clock was striking twelve.

When she returned to her bedroom and looked at herself in the glass, her face was flushed and her eyes were sparkling. She did not want to sleep at all that night, for the beating of her heart was like music, and the moon and stars were singing a song.

"If I could only be quite, quite sure!" she thought, and next morning she tackled Bruno.

Bruno was no match for her now, but he put down his shaggy head, like a bull facing a stone fence.

"Tell you the honest truth, Donna Roma," he said, "Mr. Rossi is one of those who think that when a man has taken up a work for the world it is best if he has no ties of family."

"Really? Is that so?" she answered. "But I don't understand. He can't help having father and mother, can he?"

"He can help having a wife, though," said Bruno, "and Mr. Rossi thinks a public man should be like a priest, giving up home and love and so forth, that others may have them more abundantly."

"So for that reason . . ."

"For that reason he doesn't throw himself in the way of temptation."

"And you think that's why . . ."

"I think that's why he keeps out of the way of women."

"Perhaps he doesn't care for them—some men don't, you know."

"Care for them! Mr. Rossi is one of the men who think pearls and diamonds of women, and if he had to be cast on a desert island with anybody, he would rather have one woman than a hundred thousand men."

"Ah, yes, but perhaps there's no 'one woman' in the world for him yet, Bruno."

"Perhaps there is, perhaps there isn't," said Bruno, and his hammer fell on the chisel and the white sparks began to fly.

"*You* would soon see if there were, wouldn't you, Bruno?"

"Perhaps I would, perhaps I wouldn't," said Bruno, and then he wagged his wise head and growled, "In the battle of love he wins who flies."

"Does *he* say that, Bruno?"

"He does. One day our old woman was trying to lead him on a bit. 'A heart to share your joys and sorrows is something in this world,' says she."

"And what did Mr. Rossi say?"

"'A woman's love is the sweetest thing in the world,' he said; 'but if I found myself caring too much for anybody I should run away.'"

"Did Mr. Rossi really say that, Bruno?"

"He did—upon my life he did!"

Bruno had the air of a man who had achieved a moral victory, and Roma, whose eyes were dancing with delight, wanted to fall on his stupid, sulky face and kiss and kiss it.

During the afternoon of the day following, the Princess Bellini came in with Don Camillo. "Here's Gi-gi!" she cried. "He comes to say there's to be a meet of the fox-hounds on the Campagna to-morrow. If you'd like to come I'll take you, and if you think Mr. Rossi will come too . . ."

"If he rides and has time to spare," said Roma.

"Precisely," said Don Camillo. "The worst of being a prophet is that it gives one so much trouble to agree with one's self, you know. Rumour says that our illustrious Deputy has been a little out of odour with his own people lately, and is now calling a meeting to tell the world what his 'Creed and Charter' doesn't mean. Still a flight into the country might do no harm even to the stormy petrel of politics, and if any one could prevail with him . . ."

"Leave that to Roma, and see to everything else yourself," said the Princess. "On the way to that tiresome tea-room in the Corso, my dear. Charity and Work,' you know. Committee for the protection of poor girls, or something. But we must see the old aunt first, I suppose. Come in, Gi-gi!"

Three minutes afterwards Roma was dressed for the street, and her dog was leaping and barking beside her.

"Carriage, Eccellenza?"

"Not to-day, thank you! Down, Black, down! Keep the dog from following me, Felice."

As she passed the lodge the porter handed her an envelope bearing the seal of the Minister, but she did not stop to open it. With a light step she tripped along the street, hailed a *coupé*, cried "Piazza Navona," and then composed herself to read her letter.

When the Princess and Don Camillo came out of the Countess's room Roma was gone, and the dog was scratching at the inside of the outer door.

"Now where can she have gone to so suddenly, I wonder? And there's her poor dog trying to follow her!"

"Is that the dog that goes to the Deputy's apartment?"

"Certainly it is! His name is Black. I'll hold him while you open the door, Felice. There! Good dog! Good Black! Oh, the brute, he has broken away from me."

"Black! Black! Black!"

"No use, Felice. He'll be half way through the streets by this time."

And going down the stairs the little Princess whispered to her companion: "Now, if Black comes home with his mistress this evening it will be easy to see where *she* has been."

Meantime Roma in her *coupé* was reading her letter—

"DEAREST,—Been away from Rome for a few days, and hence the delay in answering your charming message. Don't trouble a moment about the dead-and-buried nightmare. If the story is true, so much the better. R. R. *is* dead, thank God, and her unhappy wraith will haunt your path no more. But if Dr. Roselli knew nothing about David Rossi, how comes it that David Rossi knows so much about Dr. Roselli? It looks like another clue. Thanks again. A thousand thanks!

"Still no news from London, but though I pretend neither to knowledge nor foreknowledge, I am still satisfied that we are on the right track.

"Dinner-party to-night, dearest, and I shall be obliged to you if I may borrow Felice. Your Princess Potiphar, your Don Saint Joseph, your Count Signorina, your Senator Tom-tit, and—will you believe it?—your Madame de Trop! I can deny you nothing, you see, but I am cruelly out of luck that my dark house must lack the light of all drawing-rooms, the sunshine of all Rome!

"How clever of you to throw dust in the eyes of your aunt herself! And these red-hot prophets in petticoats, how startled they will soon be! Adieu!   "BONELLI."

As the *coupé* turned into the Piazza Navona, Roma was tearing the letter into shreds and casting them out of the window.

VIII

WHILE Roma climbed the last flight of stairs to David Rossi's apartment, with the slippery-sloppery footsteps of the old Garibaldian going before her, Bruno's thunderous voice was rocking through the rooms above.

"Look at him, Mr. Rossi! Republican, democrat, socialist, and rebel! Upsets the government of this house once a day regularly—dethrones the King and defies the Queen! Catch the piggy-wiggy, Uncle David! Here goes for it—one, two, three, and away!"

Then shrieks and squeals of childish laughter, mingled with another man's gentler tones, and a woman's frightened remonstrance. And then sudden silence and the voice of the Garibaldian in a panting whisper, saying, "She's here again, sir!"

"Donna Roma?"

"Yes."

"Come in," cried David Rossi, and from the threshold of the open hall she saw him, in the middle of the floor, with a little boy pitching and heaving like a young sea-lion in his arms.

He slipped the boy to his feet and said, "Run to the lady and kiss her hand, Joseph." But the boy stood off shyly, and, stepping into the room, Roma knelt to the child and put her arms about him.

"What a big little man, to be sure! His name is Joseph, is it? And what's his age? Six! Think of that! Have I seen him before, Mrs. Rocco? Yes? Perhaps he was here the day I called before? Was he? So? How stupid of me to forget! Ah, of course, now I remember, he was in his night-dress and asleep, and Mr. Rossi was carrying him to bed."

The mother's heart was captured in a moment. "Do you love children, Donna Roma?"

"Indeed, I do!"

During this passage between the women Bruno had grunted his way out of the room, and was now sidling down the staircase, being suddenly smitten by his conscience with the memory of a message he had omitted to deliver.

"Come, Joseph," said Elena. But Joseph, who had recovered from his bashfulness, was in no hurry to be off, and Roma said:

"No, no! I've only called for a moment. It is to say," turning to David Rossi, "that there's a meet of the foxhounds on the Campagna to-morrow, and to tell you from Don Camillo that if you ride and would care to go . . ."

"*You* are going?"

"With the Princess, yes! But there will be no necessity to follow the hounds all day long, and perhaps coming home . . ."

"I will be there."

"How charming! That's all I came to say, and so . . ."

She made a pretence of turning to go, but he said:

"Wait! Now that you are here I have something to show to you."

"To me?"

"Come in," he cried, and, blowing a kiss to the boy, Roma followed Rossi into the sitting-room.

"One moment," he said, and he left her to go into the bedroom.

When he came back he had a small parcel in his hands wrapped in a lace handkerchief.

"We have talked so much of my old friend Roselli that I thought you might like to see his portrait."

"His portrait? Have you really got his portrait?"

"Here it is," and he put into her hands the English photograph which used to hang by his bed.

She took it eagerly and looked at it steadfastly, while her lips trembled and her eyes grew moist. There was silence for a moment, and then she said, in a voice that struggled to control itself: "So this was the father of little Roma?"

"Yes."

"Is it very like him?"

"Very."

"What a beautiful face! What a reverend head! Did he look like that on the day . . . the day he was at Kensal Green?"

"Exactly."

The excitement she laboured under could no longer be controlled, and she lifted the picture to her lips and kissed it. Then catching her breath, and looking up at him with swimming eyes, she laughed through her tears and said:

"That is because he was your friend, and because . . . because he loved my little namesake."

David Rossi did not reply, and the silence was too audible, so she said with another nervous laugh:

"Not that I think she deserved such a father. He must have been the best father a girl ever had, but she . . ."

"She was a child," said David Rossi.

"Still, if she had been worthy of a father like that . . ."

"She was only seven, remember."

"Even so, but if she had not been a little selfish . . . wasn't she a little selfish?"

"You mustn't abuse my friend Roma."

Her eyes beamed, her cheeks burned, her nerves tingled. It would be a sweet delight to egg him on, but she dare not go any farther.

"I beg your pardon," she said in a soft voice. "Of course you know best. And perhaps years afterward when she came to think of what her father had been to her . . . that is to say if she lived . . ."

Their eyes met again, and now hers fell in confusion.

"I want to give you that portrait," he said.

"Me?"

"You would like to have it?"

"More than anything in the world. But you value it yourself?"

"Beyond anything I possess."

"Then how can I take it from you?"

"There is only one person in the world I would give it to. She has it, and I am contented."

It was impossible to bear the strain any longer without crying out, and to give physical expression to her feelings she lifted the portrait to her lips again and kissed and kissed it.

He smiled at her, she smiled back; the silence was hard to break, but just as they were on the edge of the precipice the big shock-head of the little boy looked in on them through the chink of the door and cried:

"You needn't ask me to come in, 'cause I won't!"

By the blessed instinct of the motherhood latent in her, Roma understood the boy in a moment. "If I were a gentleman, I would, though," she said.

"*Would* you?" said Joseph, and in he came, with a face shining all over.

"Hurrah! A piano!" said Roma, leaping up and seating herself at the instrument. "What shall I play for you, Joseph?"

Joseph was indifferent so long as it was a song, and with head aside, Roma touched the keys and pretended to think. After a moment of sweet duplicity she struck up the air she had come expressly to play.

It was the "British Grenadiers." She sang a verse of it. She sang in English and with the broken pronunciation of a child—

"Some talk of Allisander, and some of Hergoles;
    Of Hector and Eyesander, and such gate names as these . . ."

Suddenly she became aware that David Rossi was looking at her through the glass on the mantel-piece, and to keep herself from crying she began to laugh, and the song came to an end.

At the same moment the door burst open with a bang, and the dog came bounding into the room. Behind it came Elena, who said:

"It was scratching at the staircase door, and I thought it must have followed you."

"Followed Mr. Rossi, you mean. He has stolen my dog's heart away from me," said Roma.

"That is what I say about my boy's," said Elena.

"But Joseph is going for a soldier, I see."

"It's a porter he wants to be."

"Then so he shall—he shall be my porter some day," said Roma, whereupon Joseph was frantic with delight, and Elena was saying to herself, "What wicked lies they tell of her—I wonder they are not ashamed!"

The fire was going down and the twilight was deepening.

"Shall I bring you the lamp, sir?" said Elena.

"Not for me," said Roma. "I am going immediately." But even when mother and child had gone she did not go. Unconsciously they drew nearer and nearer to each other in the gathering darkness, and as the daylight died their voices softened and there were quiet questions and low replies. The desire to speak out was struggling in the woman's heart with the delight of silence. But she would reveal herself at last.

"I have been thinking a great deal about the story they told you in London—of Roma's death and burial, I mean. Had you no reason to think it might be false?"

"None whatever."

"It never occurred to you that it might be to anybody's advantage to say that she was dead while she was still alive?"

"How could it? Who was to perpetrate a crime for the sake of the daughter of a poor doctor in Soho—a poor prisoner in Elba?"

"Then it was not until afterward that you heard that the poor doctor was a great prince?"

"Not until the night you were here before."

"And you had never heard anything of his daughter in the interval?"

"Once I had! It was on the same day, though. A man came here from London on an infamous errand . . ."

"What was his name?"

"Charles Minghelli."

"What did he say?"

"He said Roma Roselli was not dead at all, but worse than dead—that she had fallen into the hands of an evil man, and turned out badly."

"Did you . . . did you believe that story?"

"Not one word of it! I called the man a liar, and flung him out of the house."

"Then you . . . you think . . . if she is still living . . ."

"My Roma is a good woman."

Her face burned up to the roots of her hair. She choked

with joy, she choked with pain. His belief in her purity stifled her. She could not speak now—she could not reveal herself. There was a moment of silence, and then in a tremulous voice she said:

"Will you not call *me* Roma, and try to think I am your little friend?"

When she came to herself after that she was back in her own apartment, in her aunt's bedroom, and kissing the old lady's angular face. And the Countess was breaking up the stupefaction of her enchantment with sighs and tears and words of counsel.

"I only want you to preserve yourself for your proper destiny, Roma. You are the *fiancée* of the Baron, as one might say, and the poor maniac can't last long."

Before dressing for dinner Roma replied to the Minister:—

"DEAR BARON BONELLI,—Didn't I tell you that Minghelli would find out nothing? I am now more than ever sure that the whole idea is an error. Take my advice and drop it. Drop it! Drop it! I shall, at all events!—Yours,

"ROMA VOLONNA.

"Success to the dinner! Am sending Felice. He will give you this letter.—R. V."

IX

IT was the sweetest morning of the Roman winter. The sun shone with a gentle radiance, and the motionless air was fragrant with the odour of herbs and flowers. Outside the gate which leads to the old Appian Way grooms were waiting with horses, blanketed and hooded, and huntsmen in red coats, white breeches, pink waistcoats, and black boots, were walking their mounts to the place appointed for the meet. In a line of carriages were many ladies, some in riding-habits, and on foot there was a string of beggars, most of them deformed, with here and there, at little villages, a group of rosy children watching the procession as it passed.

The American and English Ambassadors were riding side by side behind a magnificent carriage with coachman and tiger in livery of scarlet and gold.

"Who would think, to look on a scene like this, that the city is seething with dissatisfaction?" said the Englishman.

"Rome?" said the American. "Its aristocratic indifference will not allow it to believe that here, as everywhere else in the world, great and fatal changes are going on all the time. These lands, for example—to whom do they belong? Nominally to the old Roman nobility, but really to the merchants of the Campagna—a company of middlemen who grew rich by leasing them from the princes and subletting them to the poor."

"And the nobles themselves—how are they faring?"

"Badly! Already they are of no political significance, and the State knows them not."

"They don't appear to go into the army or navy—what do they go into?"

"Love!"

"And meantime the Italian people?"

"Meantime the great Italian people, like the great English people, the great German people, and the people of every country where the privileged classes still exist, are rising like a mighty wave to sweep all this sea-wrack high and dry on to the rocks."

"And this wave of the people," said the Englishman, inclining his head toward the carriage in front, "is represented by men like friend Rossi?"

"Would be, if he could keep himself straight," said the American.

"And where is the Tarpeian rock of friend Rossi's politics?"

The American slapped his glossy boot with his whip, lowered his voice, and said, "There!"

"Donna Roma?"

"A fortnight ago you heard his speech on the liveries of scarlet and gold, and look! He's under them himself already."

"You think there is no other inference?"

The American shook his head. "Always the way with these leaders of revolution. It's Samson's strength with Samson's weakness in every mother's son of them."

"Good-morning, General Potter!" said a cheerful voice from the carriage in front.

It was Roma herself. She sat by the side of the little Princess, with David Rossi on the seat before them. Her eyes were bright, there was a glow in her cheeks, and she looked lovelier than ever in her close-fitting riding-habit.

At the meeting-place there was a vast crowd of on-lookers, chiefly foreigners, in cabs and carriages and four-in-hand coaches from the principal hotels. The Master of the Hunt was ready, with his impatient hounds at his feet, and around him was a brilliant scene. Officers in blue, huntsmen in red, ladies in black, jockeys in jackets, a sea of feathers and flowers and sunshades, with the neighing of the horses and yapping of the dogs, the vast undulating country, the smell of earth and herbs, and the morning sunlight over all.

Don Camillo was waiting with horses for his party, and they mounted immediately. The horse for Roma was a quiet bay mare with limpid eyes. General Potter helped her to the saddle, and she went cantering through the long lush grass.

"What has your charming young charge been doing with herself, Princess?" said the American. "She was always beautiful, but to-day she's lovely."

"She's like Undine after she had found her soul," said the Englishman.

The little Princess laughed. "Love and a cough cannot be hidden, gentlemen," she whispered, with a look toward David Rossi.

"You don't mean . . ."

"Hush!"

Meantime Rossi, in ordinary walking dress, was approaching the horse he was intended to ride. It was a high strong-limbed sorrel with wild eyes and panting nostrils. The English groom who held it was regarding the rider with a doubtful expression, and a group of booted and spurred huntsmen were closing around.

To everybody's surprise, the deputy gathered up the reins and leaped lightly to the saddle, and at the next moment he was riding at Roma's side. Then the horn was sounded, the pack broke into music, the horses beat their hoofs on the turf and the hunt began.

There was a wall to jump first, and everybody cleared it easily until it came to David Rossi's turn, when the sorrel refused to jump. He patted the horse's neck and tried it again, but it shied and went off with its head between its legs. A third time he brought the sorrel up to the wall, and a third time it swerved aside.

ROMA

The hunters had waited to watch the result, and as the horse came up for a fourth trial, with its wild eyes flashing, its nostrils quivering, and its forelock tossed over one ear, it was seen that the bridle had broken and Rossi was riding with one rein.

"He'll be lucky if he isn't hurt," said some one.

"Why doesn't he give it the whip over its quarters?" said another.

But David Rossi only patted his horse until it came to the spot where it had shied before. Then he reached over its neck on the side of the broken rein, and with open hand struck it sharply across the nose. The horse reared, snorted, and jumped, and at the next moment it was standing quietly on the other side of the wall.

Roma, on her bay mare, was ashen pale, and the American Ambassador turned to her and said:

"Never knew but one man to do a thing like that, Donna Roma."

Roma swallowed something in her throat and said: "Who was it, General Potter?"

"The present Pope when he was a Noble Guard."

"He can ride, by Jove!" said Don Camillo.

"That sort of stuff has to be in a man's blood. Born in him—must be!" said the Englishman.

And then David Rossi came up with a new bridle to his sorrel, and Sir Evelyn added: "You handle a horse like a man who began early, Mr. Rossi."

"Yes," said David Rossi; "I was a stable-boy two years in New York, your Excellency."

At that moment the huntsman who was leading with two English terriers gave the signal that the fox was started, whereupon the hounds yelped, the whips whistled, and the horses broke into a canter.

Two hours afterwards the poor little creature that had been the origin of the holiday was tracked to earth and killed. Its head and tail were cut off, and the rest of its body was thrown to the dogs. After that flasks were taken out, healths were drunk, cheers were given, and then the hunt broke up, and the hunters began to return at an easy trot.

Roma and David Rossi were riding side by side, and the Princess was a pace or two behind them.

"Roma!" cried the Princess, "what a stretch for a gallop!"

109

"Isn't it?" said Roma, and in a moment she was off.

"I believe her mare has mastered her," said the Princess, and at the next instant David Rossi was gone too.

"Peace be with them! They're a lovely pair!" said the Princess, laughing. "But we might as well go home. They are like Undine, and will return no more."

X

MEANTIME, with the light breeze in her ears, and the beat of her horse's hoofs echoing among the aqueducts and tombs, Roma galloped over the broad Campagna. After a moment she heard some one coming after her, and for joy of being pursued she whipped up and galloped faster. Without looking back she knew who was behind, and as her horse flew over the hillocks her heart leaped and sang. When the strong-limbed sorrel came up with the quiet bay mare, they were nearly two miles from their starting-place, and far out of the track of their fellow-hunters. Both were aglow from head to foot, and as they drew rein they looked at each other and laughed.

"Might as well go on now, and come out by the English cemetery," said Roma.

"Good!" said David Rossi.

"But it's half-past two," said Roma, looking at her little watch, "and I'm as hungry as a hunter."

"Naturally," said David Rossi, and they laughed again. There was an osteria somewhere in that neighbourhood. He had known it when he was a boy. They would dine on yellow beans and macaroni.

Presently they saw a house smoking under a scraggy clump of eucalyptus. It was the osteria, half farmstead and half inn. A timid lad took their horses, an evil-looking old man bowed them into the porch, and an elderly woman, with a frightened expression and a face wrinkled like the bark of a cedar, brought them a bill of fare.

They laughed at everything—at the unfamiliar menu, because it was soiled enough to have served for a year; at the food, because it was so simple; and at the prices, because they were so cheap.

Roma looked over David Rossi's shoulder as he read out the bill of fare, and they ordered the dinner together.

"Macaroni — threepence! Right! Trout — fourpence! Shall we have fourpennyworth of trout? Good! Lamb— sixpence! We'll take two lambs—I mean two sixpenny-worths," and then more laughter.

While the dinner was cooking they went out to walk among the eucalyptus, and came upon a beautiful dell surrounded by trees and carpeted with wild flowers.

"Carnival!" cried Roma. "Now if there was anybody here to throw a flower at one!"

He picked up a handful of violets and tossed them over her head.

"When I was a boy this was where men fought duels," said David Rossi.

"The brutes! What a lovely spot! Must be the place where Pharaoh's daughter found Moses in the bulrushes!"

"Or where Adam found Eve in the garden of Eden?"

They looked at each other and smiled.

"What a surprise that must have been to him," said Roma. "Whatever did he think she was, I wonder?"

"An angel who had come down in the moonlight and forgotten to go up in the morning!"

"Nonsense! He would know in a moment she was a woman."

"Think of it! She was the only woman in the world for him!"

"And fancy! He was the only man!"

The dinner was one long delight. Even its drawbacks were no disadvantage. The food was bad, and it was badly cooked and badly served, but nothing mattered.

"Only one fork for all these dishes?" asked David Rossi.

"That's the best of it," said Roma. "You only get one dirty one."

Suddenly she dropped knife and fork, and held up both hands. "I forgot!"

"What?"

"I was to be little Roma all day to-day."

"Why, so you are, and so you have been."

"That cannot be, or you would call her by her name, you know."

"I'll do so the moment she calls me by mine."

"That's not fair," said Roma, and her face flushed up, for the wine of life had risen to her eyes.

In a vineyard below a girl working among the orange-trees was singing *stornelli*. It was a song of a mother to her son. He had gone away from the old roof-tree, but he would come back some day. His new home was bright and big, but the old hearthstone would draw him home. Beautiful ladies loved him, but the white-haired mother would kiss him again.

They listened for a short dreaming space, and their laughter ceased and their eyes grew moist. Then they called for the bill, and the old man with the evil face came up with a forced smile from a bank that had clearly no assets of that kind to draw upon.

"You've been a long time in this house, landlord," said David Rossi.

"Very long time, Excellency," said the man.

"You came from the Ciociaria."

"Why, yes, I did," said the man, with a look of surprise. "I was poor then, and later on I lived in the caves and grottoes of Monte Parioli."

"But you knew how to cure the phylloxera in the vines, and when your master died you married his daughter and came into his vineyard."

"Angelica! Here's a gentleman who knows all about us," said the old man, and then, grinning from ear to ear, he added:

"Perhaps your Excellency was the young gentleman who used to visit with his father at the Count's palace on the hill twenty to thirty years ago?"

David Rossi looked him steadfastly in the face and said: "Do you remember the poor boy who lived with you at that time?"

The forced smile was gone in a moment. "We had no boy then, Excellency."

"He came to you from Santo Spirito and you got a hundred francs with him at first, and then you built this pergola."

"If your Excellency is from the Foundling, you may tell them again, as I told the priest who came before, that we never took a boy from there, and we had no money from the people who sent him to London."

"You don't remember him, then?"

"Certainly not."

"Nor you?"

The old woman hesitated, and the old man made mouths at her.

"No, Excellency."

David Rossi took a long breath. "Here is the amount of your bill, and something over. Good-bye!"

The timid lad brought round the horses and the riders prepared to mount. Roma was looking at the boy with pitying eyes.

"How long have you been here?" she asked.

"Ten years, Excellency," he replied.

He was just twelve years of age and both his parents were dead.

"Poor little fellow!" said Roma, and before David Rossi could prevent her she was emptying her purse into the boy's hand.

They set off at a trot, and for some time they did not exchange a word. The sun was sinking and the golden day was dying down. Over the broad swell of the Campagna, treeless, houseless, a dull haze was creeping like a shroud, and the long knotted grass was swept by the chill breath of evening. Nothing broke the wide silence of the desolate space except the lowing of cattle, the bleat of sheep that were moving in masses like the woolly waves of a sea, the bark of big white dogs, the shouts of cowherds carrying long staves, and of shepherds riding on shaggy ponies. Here and there were wretched straw huts, with groups of fever-stricken people crouching over the embers of miserable fires, and here and there were dirty pothouses, which alternated with wooden crosses of the Christ and grass-covered shrines of the Madonna.

The rhythm of the saddles ceased and the horses walked.

"Was that the place where you were brought up?" said Roma.

"Yes."

"And those were the people who sold you into slavery, so to speak?"

"Yes."

"And you could have confounded them with one word, and did not!"

"What was the use? Besides, they were not the first offenders."

"No; your father was more to blame. Don't you feel sometimes as if you could hate him for what he has made you suffer?"

David Rossi shook his head. "I was saved from that bitterness by the saint who saved me from so much besides.

THE ETERNAL CITY

'Don't try to find out who your father is, David,' he said,
'and if by chance you ever do find out, don't return evil for
evil, and don't avenge yourself on the world. By-and-bye
the world will know you for what you are yourself, not for
what your father is. Perhaps your father is a bad man, perhaps he isn't. Leave him to God!'"

"It's a terrible thing to think evil of one's own father,
isn't it?" said Roma, but David Rossi did not reply.

"And then—who knows?—perhaps some day you may discover that your father deserved your love and pity after all."

"Perhaps!"

They had drawn up at another house under a thick clump
of eucalyptus trees. It was the Trappist Monastery of Tre
Fontane. Silence was everywhere in this home of silence.

They went up on to the roof. From that height the whole
world around seemed to be invaded by silence.

It was the silence of all sacred things, the silence of the
mass; and the undying paganism in the hearts of the two
that stood there had its eloquent silence also.

Roma was leaning on the parapet with David Rossi behind her, when suddenly she began to weep. She wept violently and sobbed.

"What is it?" he asked, but she did not answer.

After a while she grew calm and dried her eyes, called
herself foolish, and began to laugh. But the heart-beats
were too audible without saying something, and at length she
tried to speak.

"It was the poor boy at the inn," she said; "the sight of
his sweet face brought back a scene I had quite forgotten,"
and then, in a faltering voice, turning her head away, she
told him everything.

"It was in London, and my father had found a little Roman boy in the streets on a winter's night, carrying a squirrel
and playing an accordion. He wore a tattered suit of velveteens, and that was all that sheltered his little body from
the cold. His fingers were frozen stiff, and he fainted when
they brought him into the house. After a while he opened
his eyes, and gazed around at the fire and the faces about
him, and seemed to be looking for something. It was his
squirrel, and it was frozen dead. But he grasped it tight
and big tears rolled on to his cheeks, and he raised himself
as if to escape. He was too weak for that, and my father
comforted him and he lay still. That was when I saw him

first; and looking at the poor boy at the inn I thought . . .
I thought perhaps he was another . . . perhaps my little
friend of long ago . . ."

Her throat was throbbing, and her faltering voice was
failing like a pendulum that is about to stop.

"Roma!" he cried over her shoulder.

"David!"

Their eyes met, their hands clasped, their pent-up secret
was out, and in the dim-lit catacombs of love two souls stood
face to face.

"How long have you known it?" she whispered.

"Since the night you came to the Piazza Navona. And
you?"

"Since the moment I heard your voice." And then she
shuddered and laughed.

When they left the house of silence a blessed hush had
fallen on them, a great wonder which they had never known
before, the wonder of the everlasting miracle of human
hearts.

The sun was sitting behind Rome in a glorious blaze of
crimson, with the domes of churches glistening in the hori-
zontal rays, and the dark globe of St. Peter's hovering over
all. The mortal melancholy which had been lying over the
world seemed to be lifted away, and the earth smiled with
flowers and the heavens shone with gold.

Only the rhythmic cadence of the saddles broke the silence
as they swung to the movement of the horses. Sometimes
they looked at each other, and then they smiled, but they
did not speak.

The sun went down, and there was a far-off ringing of
bells. It was Ava Maria. They drew up the horses for a
moment and dropped their heads. Then they started again.

The night chills were coming, and they rode hard. Roma
bent over the mane of her horse and looked proud and happy.

Grooms were waiting for them at the gate of St. Paul,
and, giving up their horses, they got into a carriage. When
they reached Trinità de' Monti the lamplighter was lighting
the lamps on the steps of the piazza, and Roma said in a low
voice, with a blush and a smile:

"Don't come in to-night—not to-night, you know."

She wanted to be alone.

XI

FELICE met Roma at the door of her own apartment, and in more than usually sepulchral tones announced that the Countess had wished to see her as soon as she came home. Without waiting to change her riding-habit, Roma turned into her aunt's room.

The old lady was propped up with pillows, and Natalina was fussing about her. Her eyes glittered, her thin lips were compressed, and regardless of the presence of the maid, she straightway fell upon Roma with bitter reproaches.

"Did you wish to see me, aunt?" said Roma, and the old lady answered in a mocking falsetto:

"Did I wish to see you, miss? Certainly I wished to see you, although I'm a broken-hearted woman and sorry for the day I saw you first."

"What have I done now?" said Roma, and the radiant look in her face provoked the old lady to still louder denunciations.

"What have you done? Mercy me! . . . Give me my salts, Natalina!"

"Natalina," said Roma quietly, "lay out my studio things, and if Bruno has gone, tell Felice to light the lamps and see to the stove downstairs."

The old lady fanned herself with her embroidered handkerchief and began again.

"I thought you meant to mend your ways when you came in yesterday, miss—you were so meek and modest. But what was the fact? You had come to me straight from that man's apartments. You had! You know you had! Don't try to deny it."

"I don't deny it," said Roma.

"Holy Virgin! She doesn't deny it! Perhaps you admit it?"

"I do admit it."

"Madonna mia! She admits it! Perhaps you made an appointment?"

"No, I went without an appointment."

"Merciful heavens! She is on such terms with the man that she can go to his apartments without even an appointment! Perhaps you were alone with him, miss?"

"Yes, we were quite alone," said Roma.

ROMA

The old lady, who was apparently about to faint right away, looked up at her little shrine, and said:

"Goodness! A girl! Not even a married woman! And without a maid, too!"

Trying not to lose control of herself, Roma stepped to the door, but her aunt followed her up.

"A man like that, too! Not even a gentleman! The hypocrite! The impostor! With his airs of purity and pretence!"

"Aunt Betsy," said Roma, "I was sorry I spoke to you as I did the other night, not because anything I said was wrong, but because you are weak and bedridden and suffering. Don't provoke me to speak again as I spoke before. I did go to Mr. Rossi's rooms yesterday, and if there is any fault in that, I alone am to blame."

"Are you indeed?" said the old lady, with a shrill, piping cry. "Holy Saints! she admits so much! Do you know what people will call you when they hear of it? A hussy! A shameless hussy!"

Roma was flaming up, but she controlled herself and put her hand on the door-handle.

"They *will* hear of it, depend on that," cried the Countess. "Last night at dinner the women were talking of nothing else. Felice heard all their chattering. That woman let the dog out to follow you, knowing it would go straight to the man's rooms. 'Whom did it come home with, Felice?' 'Donna Roma, your Excellency.' 'Then it's clear where Donna Roma had been.' Ugh! I could choke to think of it. My head is fit to split! Is there any cognac . . . ?"

Roma's bosom was visibly stirred by her breathing, but she answered quietly:

"No matter! Why should I care what is thought of my conduct by people who have no morality of their own to judge me by?"

"Really now?" said the Countess, twisting the wrinkles of her old face into skeins of mock courtesy. "Upon my word, I didn't think you were so simple. Understand, miss, it isn't the opinion of the Princess Bellini I am thinking about, but that of the Baron Bonelli. He has his dignity to consider, and when the time comes and he is free to take a wife, he is not likely to marry a girl who has been talked of with another man. Don't you see what that woman is doing? She has been doing it all along, and like a simpleton you've been helping her. You've been flinging away your chances with this Rossi and making yourself impossible to the Minister."

Roma tossed her head and answered:

"I don't care if I have, Aunt Betsy. I'm not of the same mind as I used to be, and I think no longer that the holiest things are to be bought and sold like so much merchandise."

The old lady, who had been bending forward in her vehemence, fell back on the pillow.

"You'll kill me!" she cried. "Where did you learn such folly? Goodness knows I've done my best by you. I have tried to teach you your duty to the baron and to society. But all this comes of admitting these anarchists into the house. You can't help it, though. It's in your blood. Your father before you . . ."

Crimson and trembling from head to foot, Roma turned suddenly and left the room. Natalina and Felice were listening on the other side of the door.

But not even this jarring incident could break the spell of Roma's enchantment, and when dinner was over, and she had gone to the studio and closed the door, the whole world seemed to be shut out, and nothing was of the slightest consequence.

Taking the damp cloth from the bust, she looked at her work again. In the light of the aurora she now lived in, the head she had wrought with so much labour was poor and inadequate. It did not represent the original. It was weak and wrong.

She set to work again, and little by little the face in the clay began to change. Not Peter any longer, Peter the disciple, but Another. It was audacious, it was shocking, but no matter. She was not afraid.

Time passed, but she did not heed it. She was working at lightning speed, and with a power she had never felt before.

Night came on, and the old Rome, the Rome of the Popes, repossessed itself of the Eternal City. The silent streets, the dark patches, the luminous piazzas, the three lights on the loggia of the Vatican, the grey ghost of the great dome, the kind stars, the sweet moon, and the church bells striking one by one during the noiseless night.

At length she became aware of a streak of light on the

floor. It was coming through the shutters of the window. She threw them open, and the breeze of morning came up from the orange trees in the garden below. The day was dawning over the sleepy city. Convent bells were ringing for matins, but all else was still, and the silence was sweet and deep.

She turned back to her work and looked at it again. It thrilled her now. She walked to and fro in the studio and felt as if she were walking on the stars. She was happy, happy, happy!

Then the city began to sound on every side. Cabs rattled, electric trams tinkled, vendors called their wares in the streets, and the new Rome, the Rome of the Kings, awoke.

Somebody was singing as he came upstairs. It was Bruno, coming to his work. He looked astonished, for the lamps were still burning, although the sunlight was streaming into the room.

" Been working all night, Donna Roma ? "

" Fear I have, Bruno, but I'm going to bed now."

She had an impulse to call him up to her work and say, " Look ! I did that, for I am a great artist." But no ! Not yet ! Not yet !

She had covered up the clay, and turned the key of her own compartment, when the bell rang on the floor above. It was the porter with the post, and Natalina, in curl papers, met her on the landing with the letters.

One of them was from the Mayor, thanking her for what she had done for Charles Minghelli; another was from her landlord, thanking her for his translation to Paris; a third was from the fashionable modiste, thanking her for an invitation from the Minister. A feeling of shame came over her as she glanced at these letters. They brought the implication of an immoral influence, the atmosphere of an evil life.

There was a fourth letter. It was from the Minister himself. She had seen it from the first, but a creepy sense of impending trouble had made her keep it to the last. Ought she to open it ? She ought, she must !

" MY DARLING CHILD,—News at last, too, and success within hail ! Minghelli, the Grand Hotel, the reference in London, and the dead-and-buried nightmare have led up to and compassed everything ! Prepare for a great surprise—

David Rossi is *not* David Rossi, but a *condemned man who has no right to live in Italy!* Prepare for a still greater surprise—*he has no right to live at all!*

"So you are avenged! The man humiliated and degraded you. He insulted me also, and did his best to make me resign my portfolio and put my private life on its defence. You set out to undo the effects of his libel and to punish him for his outrage. You've done it! You have avenged yourself for both of us! It's all your work! You are magnificent! And now let us draw the net closer . . . let us hold him fast . . . let us go on as we have begun . . ."

Her sight grew dim. The letter seemed to be full of blotches. It dropped out of her helpless fingers. She sat a long time looking out on the sunlit city, and all the world grew dark and chill. Then she rose, and her face was pale and rigid.

"No, I will *not* go on!" she thought. "I will *not* betray him! I will *save* him! He insulted me, he humiliated me, he was my enemy, but . . . I love him! I love him!"

PART FOUR—DAVID ROSSI

I

DAVID ROSSI was in his bedroom writing his leader for next morning's paper. A lamp with a dark shade burned on the desk, and the rest of the room was in shadow. It was late, and the house was quiet.

The door opened softly, and Bruno, in shirt-sleeves and slippered feet, came on tiptoe into the room. He brought a letter in a large violet envelope with a monogram on the front of it, and put it down on the desk by Rossi's side. It was from Roma.

"DEAR DAVID ROSSI,—Without rhyme or reason I have been expecting to see you here to-day, having something to say which it is important that you should hear. May I expect you in the morning? Knowing how busy you are, I dare not bid you come, yet the matter is of great consequence and admits of no delay. It is not a subject on which it is safe or proper to write, and how to speak of it I am at a loss to decide. But you shall help me. Therefore come without delay! There! I have bidden you come in spite of myself. Judge from that how eager is my expectation.—In haste,

"ROMA V.

"P.S.—I open my envelope, to wonder if you can ever forgive me the humiliations you have suffered for my sake. To think that *I* threw you into the way of them! And merely to wipe out an offence that is not worth considering! I am ashamed of myself. I am also ashamed of the people about me. You will remember that I told you they were pitiless and cruel. They are worse—they are heartless and without mercy. But how bravely you bore their insults and innuendoes! I almost cry to think of it, and if I were a good Catholic I should confess and do penance. See? I do confess, and if you want me to do penance you will come yourself and impose it."

121

THE ETERNAL CITY

It was the first letter that David Rossi had received from Roma, and as he read it the air seemed to him to be filled with the sweet girlish voice. He could see the play of her large, bright, violet eyes. The delicate fragrance of the scented paper rose to his nostrils, and without being conscious of what he was doing he raised the letter to his lips.

Then he became aware that Bruno was still in the room. The good fellow was in the shadow behind him, pushing things about under some pretext and trying to make a noise.

"Don't let me keep you up, Bruno."

"Sure you don't want anything, sir?" said Bruno with confusion.

David Rossi rose and walked about the room with his slow step.

"You have something to say to me?"

"Well, yes, sir—yes, I have."

"What is it?"

Bruno scratched his shock head and looked about as if for help. His eyes fell on the letter lying open in the light on the desk.

"It's about that, sir. I knew where it came from by the colour and the monogram."

"Well?"

Bruno began to look frightened, and then in a louder voice, that bubbled out of his mouth like water from the neck of a bottle, he said:

"Tell you the truth, sir, people are talking about you."

"What are they saying, Bruno?"

"Saying? . . . Ever heard the proverb, 'Sun in the eyes, the battle lost'? Sun in the eyes—that's what they're saying, sir."

"So they're saying that, are they?"

"They are. And doesn't it look like it, sir? You'll allow it looks like it, anyway. When you started the Republic, sir, the people had hopes of you. But a month is gone and you haven't done a thing."

David Rossi, with head down, continued to pace to and fro.

"'Patience,' I'm saying. 'Go slow and sure,' says I. That's all right, sir, but the Government is going fast enough. Forty thousand men called out to keep the people quiet, and when the bread-tax begins on the first of the month the blessed saints know what will happen. Next week we hold our meeting in the Coliseum. You called it yourself, sir, yet they're laying odds you won't be there. Where will you be? In the house of a bad woman?"

"Bruno!" cried Rossi in a stern voice, "what right have you to talk to me like this?"

Bruno was frightened at what he had said, but he tried to carry it off with a look of passion.

"Right? The right of a friend, sir, who can't stand by and see you betrayed. Yes, betrayed, that's the word for it. Betrayed! Betrayed! It's a plot to ruin the people through the weakness of their leader. A woman drawn across a man's trail. The trick is as old as the ages. Never heard what we say in Rome?—'The man is fire, the woman is tow; then comes the devil and puts them together.'"

David Rossi was standing face to face with Bruno, who was growing hot and trying to laugh bitterly.

"Oh, I know what I'm saying, sir. The Prime Minister is at the bottom of everything. David Rossi never goes to Donna Roma's house but the Baron Bonelli knows all about it. They write to each other every day, and I've posted her letters myself. *Her* house is *his* house. Carriages, horses, servants, liveries—how else could she support it? By her art, her sculpture?"

Bruno was frightened to the bottom of his soul, but he continued to talk and to laugh bitterly.

"She's deceiving you, sir. Isn't it as plain as daylight? You hit her hard, and old Vampire too, in your speech on the morning of the Pope's Jubilee, and she's paying you out for both of them."

"That's enough, Bruno."

"All Rome knows it, and everybody will be laughing at you soon."

"You've said enough, I tell you. Go to bed."

"Oh, I know! The heart has its reasons, but it listens to none."

"Go to bed, I tell you! Isn't it sufficient that by your tittle-tattle you caused me to wrong the lady?"

"*I* did?"

"*You* did."

"I did not."

"You did, and if it hadn't been for the tales you told me before I knew her, or had ever seen her, I should never have spoken of her as I did."

"She deserved all you said of her."

"She didn't deserve one word of it, and it was your lies that made me slander her."

Bruno's eyes flinched as if a blow had fallen on them. Then he tried to laugh.

"Hit me again. The skin of the ass is used to blows. Only don't go too far with me, David Rossi."

"Then don't *you* go too far with your falsehoods and suspicion."

"Suspicion! Holy Virgin! Is it suspicion that she has had you at her studio to make a Roman holiday for her friends and cronies? By the saints! Suspicion!"

"Go on, if it becomes you."

"If what becomes me?"

"To eat her bread and talk against her."

"That's a lie, David Rossi, and you know it. It's my own bread I'm eating. My labour belongs to me, and I sell it to my employer. But my conscience belongs to God, and she cannot buy it."

David Rossi's white and angry face broke up like a snowflake in the sun.

"I was wrong when I said that, Bruno, and I ask your pardon."

"Do you say that, sir? And after I've insulted you?"

David Rossi held out his hand, and Bruno clasped it.

"I had no right to be angry with you, Bruno, but you are wrong about Donna Roma. Believe me, dear friend, cruelly, awfully, terribly wrong."

"You think she is a good woman."

"I know she is, and if I said otherwise, I take it back and am ashamed."

"Beautiful! If I could only believe in her as you do, sir. But I've known her for two years."

"And I've known her for twenty."

"*You* have?"

"I have. Shall I tell you who she is? She is the daughter of my old friend in England."

"The one who died in Elba?"

"Yes."

"The good man who found you and fed you, and educated you when you were a boy in London?"

"That was the father of Donna Roma."

"Then he was Prince Volonna, after all?"

"Yes, and they lied to me when they told me she was dead and buried."

Bruno was silent for a moment, and then in a choking voice he said:

"Why didn't you strike me dead when I said she was deceiving you? Forgive me, sir!"

"I do forgive you, Bruno, but not for myself—for her."

Bruno turned away with a dazed expression.

"Forget what I said about going to Donna Roma's, sir."

Rossi sat down and took up his pen.

"No, I cannot forget it," he said. "I *will not* forget it. I will go to her house no more."

Bruno was silent for a moment, and then he said in a thick voice:

"I understand! God help you, David Rossi. It's a lonely road you mean to travel."

Rossi drew a long breath and made ready to write.

"Good-night, Bruno."

"Good-night," said Bruno, and the good fellow went out with wet eyes.

II

THE night was far gone, and the city lay still, while Rossi replied to Roma.

"MY DEAR R.,—You have nothing to reproach yourself with in regard to my poor doings, or tryings-to-do. They were necessary, and if the penalties had been worse a hundredfold I should not chew the cud of my bargain now. Besides your wish, I had another motive, a secret motive, and perhaps, if I were a good Catholic, I should confess too, although not with a view to penance. Apparently, it has come out well, and now that it seems to be all over, both your scheme and mine, now that the wrong I did you is to some extent undone, and my own object is in some measure achieved, I find myself face to face with a position in which it is my duty to you as well as to myself to bring our intercourse to an end.

"The truth is that we cannot be friends any longer, for the reason that I love some one in whom you are, unhappily, too much interested, and because there are obstacles between that person and myself which are decisive and insurmountable. This alone puts it on me as a point of honour that you and I should never see each other again. Each of my visits adds to my embarrassment, to the feeling that I am doing wrong in paying them, and to the certainty that I must give them up altogether.

"Thank you again and again for the more than pleasant hours we have spent together. It is not your fault that I must bury the memory of them in oblivion. This does not mean that it is any part of the painful but unavoidable result of circumstances I cannot explain, that we should not write to each other as occasion may arise. Continue to think of me as your brother—your brother far away—to be called upon for counsel in your hour of need and necessity. And whenever you call, be sure I shall be there.

"What you say of an important matter suggests that something has come to your knowledge which concerns myself and the authorities; but when a man has spent all his life on the edge of a precipice, the most urgent perils are of little moment, and I beg of you not to be alarmed for my sake. Whatever it is, it is only a part of the atmosphere of danger I have always lived in—the glacier I have always walked upon—and 'if it is not now, it is to come; if it is not to come, it will be now—the readiness is all.' Good-bye!—Yours, dear R——, D."

III

Next day brought Roma's reply.

"My dear D.,—Your letter has thrown me into the wildest state of excitement and confusion. I have done no work all day long, and when Black has leapt upon me and cried, 'Come out for a walk, you dear, dear dunce,' I have hardly known whether he barked or talked.

"I am sorry our charming intercourse is to be interrupted, but you can't mean that it is to be broken off altogether. You can't, you can't, or my eyes would be red with crying, instead of dancing with delight.

"Yet why they should dance I don't really know, seeing you are so indefinite, and I have no right to understand anything. If you cannot write by post, or even send messages by hand, if my man F. is your enemy, and your housemate B. is mine, isn't that precisely the best reason why you should come and talk matters over? Come at once. I bid you come! In a matter of such inconceivable importance, surely a sister has a right to command.

"In that character, I suppose, I ought to be glad of the news you give me. Well, I *am* glad! But being a daughter of Eve, I have a right to be curious. I want to ask questions. You say I know the lady, and am, unhappily, too deeply interested in her—who is she? Does she know of your love for her? Is she beautiful? Is she charming? Give me one initial of her name—only one—and I will be good. I am so much in the dark, and I cannot commit myself until I know more.

"You speak of obstacles, and say they are decisive and insurmountable. That's terrible, but perhaps you are only thinking of what the poets call the 'cruel madness' of love, as if its madness and cruelty were sufficient reason for flying away from it. Or perhaps the obstacles are those of circumstances; but in that case, if the woman is the right one, she will be willing to wait for such difficulties to be got over, or even to find her happiness in sharing them.

"See how I plead for my unknown sister! Which is sweet of me, considering that you don't tell me who she is, but leave me to find out if she is likely to suit me. But why not let me help you? Come at once and talk things over.

"Yet how vain I am! Even while I proffer assistance with so loud a voice, I am smitten cold with the fear of an impediment which you know a thousand times better than I do how to measure and to meet. Perhaps the woman you speak of is unworthy of your friendship and love. I can understand that to be an insurmountable obstacle. You stand so high, and have to think about your work, your aims, your people. And perhaps it is only a dream and a delusion, a mirage of the heart, that love lifts a woman up to the level of the man who loves her.

"Then there may be some fault—some grave fault. I can understand that too. We do not love because we should, but because we must, and there is nothing so cruel as the inequality of man and woman in the way the world regards their conduct. But I am like a bat in the dark, flying at gleams of light from closely-curtained windows. Will you not confide in me? Do! Do! Do!

"Besides, I have the other matter to talk about. You remember telling me how you kicked out the man M——?

He turned spy as the consequence, and has been sent to England. You ought to know that he has been making inquiries about you, and appears to have found out various particulars. Any day may bring urgent news of him, and if you will not come to me I may have to go to you in spite of every protest.

"To-morrow is the day for your opening of Parliament, and I have a ticket for the Court tribune, so you may expect to see me floating somewhere above you in an atmosphere of lace and perfume. Good-night!—Your poor bewildered sister, ROMA."

IV

NEXT morning David Rossi put on evening dress, in obedience to the etiquette of the opening day of Parliament. Before going to the ceremony he answered Roma's letter of the night before.

"DEAR R.,—If anything could add to the bitterness of my regret at ending an intercourse which has brought me the happiest moments of my life, it would be the tone of your sweet and charming letter. You ask me if the woman I love is beautiful. She is more than beautiful, she is lovely. You ask me if she knows that I love her. I have never dared to disclose my secret, and if I could have believed that she had ever so much as guessed at it, I should have found some consolation in a feeling which is too deep for the humiliations of pride. You ask me if she is worthy of my friendship and love. She is worthy of the love and friendship of a better man than I am or can ever hope to be.

"Yet even if she were not so, even if there were, as you say, a fault in her, who am I that I should judge her harshly? I am not one of those who think that a woman is fallen because circumstances and evil men have conspired against her. I reject the monstrous theory that while a man may redeem the past, a woman never can. I abhor the judgment of the world by which a woman may be punished because she is trying to be pure, and dragged down because she is rising from the dirt. And if she had sinned as I have sinned, and suffered as I have suffered, I would pray for strength enough to say, 'Because I love her we are one, and we stand or fall together.'

"But she is sweet, and pure, and true, and brave, and

noble-hearted, and there is no fault in her, or she would not be the daughter of her father, who was the noblest man I ever knew or ever expect to know. No, the root of the separation is in myself, in myself only, in my circumstances and the personal situation I find myself in.

" And yet it is difficult for me to state the obstacle which divides us, or to say more about it than that it is permanent and insurmountable. I should deceive myself if I tried to believe that time would remove or lessen it, and I have contended in vain with feelings which have tempted me to hold on at any price to the only joy and happiness of my life.

" To go to her and open my heart is impossible, for personal intercourse is precisely the peril I am trying to avoid. How weak I am in her company! Even when her dress touches me at passing, I am thrilled with an emotion I cannot master; and when she lifts her large bright eyes to mine, I am the slave of a passion which conquers all my will.

" No, it is not lightly and without cause that I have taken a step which sacrifices love to duty. I love her, with all my heart and soul and strength I love her, and that is why she and I, for her sake more than mine, should never meet again.

" I note what you say about the man M——, but you must forgive me if I cannot be much concerned about it. There is nobody in London who knows me in the character I now bear, and can link it to the one you are thinking of. Good-bye, again! God be with you and keep you always! D."

Having written this letter, David Rossi sealed it carefully and posted it with his own hand on his way to the opening of Parliament.

V

THE day was fine, and the city was bright with many flags in honour of the King. All the streets leading from the royal palace to the Hall of the Deputies were lined with people. The square in front of the Parliament House was kept clear by a cordon of Carabineers, but the open windows of the hotels and houses round about were filled with faces.

David Rossi entered the house by the little private door for deputies in the side street. The chamber was already thronged, and as full of movement as a hive of bees. Ladies in light dresses, soldiers in uniform, diplomatists wearing decorations, senators and deputies in white cravats and gloves, were moving to their places and saluting each other with bows and smiles.

Rossi slipped into the place he usually occupied among the deputies. It was the corner seat by the door on the left of the royal canopy, immediately facing the section which had been apportioned to the Court tribune. He did not lift his eyes as he entered, but he was conscious of a tall, well-rounded yet girlish figure in a grey dress that glistened in a ray of sunshine, with dark hair under a large black hat, and flashing eyes that seemed to pierce into his own like a shaft of light.

Beautiful ladies with big oriental eyes were about her, and young deputies were using their opera-glasses upon them with undisguised curiosity. There was much gossip, some laughter, and a good deal of gesticulation. The atmosphere was one of light spirits, approaching gaiety, the atmosphere of the theatre or the ballroom.

The clock over the reporters' gallery showed seven minutes after the hour appointed, when the walls of the chamber shook with the vibration of a cannon-shot. It was a gun fired at the Castle of St. Angelo to announce the King's arrival. At the same moment there came the muffled strains of the royal hymn played by the band in the piazza. The little gales of gossip died down in an instant, and in dead silence the assembly rose to its feet.

A minute afterwards the King entered amid a fanfare of trumpets, the shouts of many voices, and the clapping of hands. He was a young man, in the uniform of a general, with a face that was drawn into deep lines under the eyes by ill-health and anxiety. Two soldiers, carrying their brass helmets with waving plumes, walked by his side, and a line of his Ministers followed. His Queen, a tall and beautiful girl, came behind, surrounded by many ladies.

The King took his seat under the baldacchino, with his Ministers on his left. The Queen sat on his right hand, with her ladies beside her. They bowed to the plaudits of the assembly, and the drawn face of the young King wore a painful smile.

The Baron Bonelli, in court dress and decorations, stood at the King's elbow, calm, dignified, self-possessed—the one strong face and figure in the group under the canopy. After the cheering and the shouting had subsided he requested the assembly, at the command of His Majesty, to resume their seats. Then he handed a paper to the King.

It was the King's speech to his Parliament, and he read it nervously in a voice that had not learned to control itself. But the speech was sufficiently emphatic, and its words were grandiose and even florid.

It consisted of four clauses. In the first clause the King thanked God that his country was on terms of amity with all foreign countries, and invoked God's help in the preservation of peace. The second clause was about the increase of the army.

" The army," said the King, " is very dear to me, as it has always been dear to my family. My illustrious grandfather, who granted freedom to the kingdom, was a soldier; my honoured father was a soldier, and it is my pride that I am myself a soldier also. The army was the foundation of our liberty and it is now the security of our rights. On the strength and stability of the army rest the power of our nation abroad and the authority of our institutions at home. It is my firm resolve to maintain the army in the future as my illustrious ancestors have maintained it in the past, and therefore my Government will propose a bill which is intended to increase still further its numbers and its efficiency."

This was received with a great outburst of applause and the waving of many handkerchiefs. It was observed that some of the ladies shed tears.

The third clause was about the growth and spread of anarchism.

" My house," said the King, " gave liberty to the nation, and now it is my duty and my hope to give security and strength. It is known to Parliament that certain subversive elements, not in Italy alone, but throughout Europe, throughout the world, have been using the most devilish machinations for the destruction of all order, human and divine. Cold, calculating criminals have perpetrated crimes against the most innocent and the most highly placed, which have sent a thrill of horror into all humane hearts. My Government asks for an absolute power over such criminals, and if we are to bring security to the State, we must reinvigorate the authority to which society trusts the high mandate of protecting and governing."

A still greater outburst of cheering interrupted the young King, who raised his head amid the shouts, the clapping of hands, and the fluttering of handkerchiefs, and smiled his painful smile.

" More than that," continued the King, " I have to deplore the spread of associations, sodalities, and clubs, which, by an erroneous conception of liberty, are disseminating the germs of revolt against the State. Under the most noble propositions about the moral and economical redemption of the people is hidden a propaganda for the conquest of the public powers.

" My aim is to gain the affection of my people, and to interest them in the cause of order and public security, and therefore my Government will present an urgent bill, which is intended to stop the flowering of these parasitic organisations, by revising these laws of the press and of public meeting, in whose defects agitators find opportunity for their attacks on the doctrines of the State."

A prolonged outburst of applause followed this passage, mingled with a tumult of tongues, which went on after the King had begun to read again, rendering his last clause— an invocation of God's blessing on the deliberations of Parliament—almost inaudible.

The end of the speech was a signal for further cheering, and when the King left the hall, bowing as before, and smiling his painful smile, the shouts of " Long live the King," the clapping of hands, and the waving of handkerchiefs followed him to the street. The entire ceremony had occupied twelve minutes.

Then the clamour of voices drowned the sound of the royal hymn outside. Deputies were climbing about to join their friends among the ladies, whose light laughter was to be heard on every side.

David Rossi rose to go. Without lifting his head, he had been conscious that during the latter part of the King's speech many eyes were fixed upon him. Playing with his watch-chain, he had struggled to look calm and impassive. But his heart was sick, and he wished to get away quickly.

A partition, shielding the door of the corridor, stood near to his seat, and he was trying to get round it. He heard his name in the air around him, mingled with significant trills and unmistakable accents. All at once he was conscious of a perfume he knew, and of a girlish figure facing him.

" Good-day, Honourable," said a voice that thrilled him like the strings of a harp drawn tight.

DAVID ROSSI

He lifted his head and answered. It was Roma. Her face was lighted up with a fire he had never seen before. Only one glance he dared to take, but he could see that at the next instant those flashing eyes would burst into tears.

The tide was passing out by the front doors where the carriages and the reporters waited, but Rossi stepped round to the back. He was on the way to the office of his newspaper, and dipping into the Corso from a lane that crossed it, he came upon the King's carriage returning to the Quirinal. It was entirely surrounded by soldiers, the military commander of Rome on the right, the commander of the Carabineers on the left, and the Cuirassiers, riding two deep, before and behind, so that the King and Queen were scarcely visible to the cheering crowd. Last in the royal procession came an ordinary cab containing two detectives in plain clothes.

The office of the *Sunrise* was in a narrow lane out of the Corso. It was a dingy building of three floors, with the machine-rooms on the ground-level, the composing-rooms at the top, and the editorial rooms between. Rossi's office was a large apartment, with three desks, that were intended for the editor and his day and night assistants.

His day assistant received him with many bows and compliments. He was a small man with an insincere face.

Rossi drank a cup of coffee and settled to his work. It was an article on the day's doings, more fearless and outspoken than he had ever published before. Such a day as they had just gone through, with the flying of flags and the playing of royal hymns, was not really a day of joy and rejoicing, but of degradation and shame. If the people had known what they were doing, they would have hung their flags with crape and played funeral marches.

" Such a scene as we have witnessed to-day," he wrote, " like all such scenes throughout the world, whether in Germany, Russia, and England, or in China, Persia, and the darkest regions of Africa, is but proof of the melancholy fact that while man, as the individual, has been nineteen hundred years converted to Christianity, man, as the nation, remains to this day for the most part utterly pagan."

The assistant editor, who had glanced over the pages of manuscript as Rossi threw them aside, looked up at last and said:

" Are you sure, sir, that you wish to print this article? "

" Quite sure."

The man made a shrug of his shoulders, and took the copy upstairs.

The short day had closed in when Rossi was returning home. Screamers in the streets were crying early editions of the evening papers, and the cafés in the Corso were full of officers and civilians, sipping vermouth and reading glowing accounts of the King's enthusiastic reception. Pitiful! Most pitiful! And the man who dared to tell the truth must be prepared for any consequences.

David Rossi told himself that he *was* prepared. Henceforth he would devote himself to the people, without a thought of what might happen. Nothing should come between him and his work—nothing whatever—not even . . . but, no, he could not think of it!

VI

Two letters were awaiting David Rossi in his rooms at home.

One was a circular from the President of the Chamber of Deputies summoning Parliament for the day after tomorrow to elect officials and reply to the speech of the King.

The other was from Roma, and the address was in a large, hurried hand. David Rossi broke the seal with nervous fingers.

"MY DEAR FRIEND,—I know! I know! I know now what the obstacle is. B. gave me the hint of it on one of the days of last week, when I was so anxious to see you and you did not come. It is your unflinching devotion to your mission and to your public duties. You are one of those who think that when a man has dedicated his life to work for the world, he should give up everything else—father, mother, wife, child—and live like a priest, who puts away home, and love, and kindred, that others may have them more abundantly. I can understand that, and see a sort of nobility in it too, especially in days when the career of a statesman is only a path to vainglory of every kind. It is great, it is glorious, it thrills me to think of it.

"But I am losing faith in my unknown sister that is to be, in spite of all my pleading. You say she is beautiful—

that's well enough, but it comes by nature. You say she is sweet, and true, and charming—and I am willing to take it all on trust. But when you say she is noble-hearted I respectfully refuse to believe it. If she were that, you would be sure that she would know that friendship is the surest part of love, and to be the friend of a great man is to be a help to him, and not an impediment.

"My gracious! What does she think you are? A *cavaliere servente* to dance attendance on her ladyship day and night? Give me the woman who wants her husband to be a man, with a man's work to do, a man's burdens to bear, and a man's triumphs to win.

"Yet perhaps I am too hard on my unknown sister that is to be, or ought to be, and it is only your own distrust that wrongs her. If she is the daughter of one brave man and really loves another, she knows her place and her duty. It is to be ready to follow her husband wherever he must go, to share his fate whatever it may be, and to live his life, because it is now her own.

"And since I am in the way of pleading for her again, let me tell you how simple you are to suppose that because you have never disclosed your secret she may never have guessed it. Goodness me! To think that men who can make women love them to madness itself can be so ignorant as not to know that a woman can always tell if a man loves her, and even fix the very day, and hour, and minute when he looked into her eyes and loved her first.

"And if my unknown sister that ought to be knows that you love her, be sure that she loves you in return. Then trust her. Take the counsel of a woman and go to her. Remember, that if you are suffering by this separation, perhaps she is suffering too, and if she is worthy of the love and friendship of a better man than you are, or ever hope to be (which, without disparaging her ladyship, I respectfully refuse to believe), let her at least have the refusal of one or both of them.

"Good-night! I go to the Chamber of Deputies again the day after to-morrow, being so immersed in public matters (and public men) that I can think of nothing else at present. Happily my bust is out of hand, and the caster (not B. this time) is hard at work on it.

"You won't hear anything about the M—— doings, yet I assure you they are a most serious matter. Unless I am much mistaken there is an effort on foot to connect you with my father, which is surely sufficiently alarming. M—— is returning to Rome, and I hear rumours of an intention to bring pressure on some one *here* in the hope of leading to identification. Think of it, I beg, I pray!—Your friend,

"R."

VII

Next day Rossi's editorial assistant came with a troubled face. There was bad news from the office. The morning's edition of the *Sunrise* had been confiscated by the police owing to the article on the King's speech and procession. The proprietors of the paper were angry with their editor, and demanded to see him immediately.

"Tell them I'll be at the office at four o'clock, as usual," said Rossi, and he sat down to write a letter.

It was to Roma. The moment he took up the pen to write to her the air of the room seemed to fill with a sweet feminine presence that banished everything else. It was like talking to her. She was beside him. He could hear her soft replies.

"If it were possible to heighten the pain of my feelings when I decided to sacrifice my best wishes to my sense of duty, a letter like your last would be more than I could bear. The obstacle you deal with is not the one which chiefly weighs with me, but it is a very real impediment, not altogether disposed of by the sweet and tender womanliness with which you put it aside. In that regard what troubles me most is the hideous inequality between what the man gives and what he gets, and the splendid devotion with which the woman merges her life in the life of the man she marries only quickens the sense of his selfishness in allowing himself to accept so great a prize.

"In my own case, the selfishness, if I yielded to it, would be greater far than anybody else could be guilty of, and of all men who have sacrificed women's lives to their own career, I should feel myself to be the most guilty and inexcusable. My dear and beloved girl is nobly born, and lives in wealth and luxury, while I am poor—poor by choice, and therefore poor for ever, brought up as a foundling, and without a name that I dare call my own.

"What then? Shall such a man as I am ask such a woman

as she is to come into the circle of his life, to exchange her riches for his poverty, her comfort for his suffering? No.

"Besides, what woman could do it if I did? Women can be unselfish, they can be faithful, they can be true; but—don't ask me to say things I do not want to say—women love wealth and luxury and ease, and shrink from pain and poverty and the forced marches of a hunted life. And why shouldn't they? Heaven spare them all such sufferings as men alone should bear!

"Yet all this is still outside the greater obstacle which stands between me and the dear girl from whom I must separate myself now, whatever it may cost me, as an inexorable duty. I entreat you to spare me the pain of explaining further. Believe that for her sake my resolution, in spite of all your sweet and charming pleading, is strong and unalterable.

"Only one thing more. If it is as you say it may be, that she loves me, though I had no right to believe so, that will only add to my unhappiness in thinking of the wrench that she must suffer. But she is strong, she is brave, she is the daughter of her father, and I have faith in the natural power of her mind, in her youth and the chances of life for one so beautiful and so gifted, to remove the passing impression that may have been made.

"Good-bye yet again! And God bless you!   D.

"P. S.—I am not afraid of M——, and come when he may, I shall certainly stand my ground. There is only one person in Rome who could be used against me in the direction you indicate, and I could trust her with my heart's blood."

VIII

BEFORE two o'clock next day the Chamber of Deputies was already full. The royal chair and baldacchino had been removed, and their place was occupied by the usual bench of the President.

When the Prime Minister took his place, cool, collected, smiling, faultlessly dressed and wearing a flower in his button-hole, he was greeted with some applause from the members, and the dry rustle of fans in the ladies' tribune was distinctly heard. The leader of the Opposition had a less marked reception, and when David Rossi glided round the partition to his place on the extreme Left, there was a momentary hush, followed by a buzz of voices.

Then the President of the Chamber entered, with his secretaries about him, and took his seat in a central chair under a bust of the young King. Ushers, wearing a linen band of red, white, and green on their arms, followed with portfolios, and with little trays containing water-bottles and glasses. Conversation ceased, and the President rang a hand-bell that stood by his side, and announced that the sitting was begun.

The first important business of the day was the reply to the speech of the King, and the President called on the member who had been appointed to undertake this duty. A young Deputy, a man of letters, then made his way to a bar behind the chairs of the Ministers and read from a printed paper a florid address to the sovereign.

Having read his printed document, the Deputy proceeded to move the adoption of the reply.

With the proposal of the King and the Government to increase the army he would not deal. It required no recommendation. The people were patriots. They loved their country, and would spend the last drop of their blood to defend it. The only persons who were not with the King in his desire to uphold the army were the secret foes of the nation and the dynasty—persons who were in league with their enemies.

"That," said the speaker, "brings us to the next clause of our reply to His Majesty's gracious speech. We know that there exists among the associations aimed at a compact between strangely varying forces—between the forces of socialism, republicanism, unbelief, and anarchy, and the forces of the Church and the Vatican."

At this statement there was a great commotion. Members on the Left protested with loud shouts of "It is not true," and in a moment the tongues and arms of the whole assembly were in motion. The President rang his bell, and the speaker concluded.

"Let us draw the teeth of both parties to this secret conspiracy, that they may never again use the forces of poverty and discontent to disturb public order."

When the speaker sat down, his friends thronged around him to shake hands with him and congratulate him.

Then the eyes of the House and of the audience in the gallery turned to David Rossi. He had sat with folded arms and head down while his followers screamed their protests. But passing a paper to the President, he now rose and said:

"I ask permission to propose an amendment to the reply to the King's speech."

"You have the word," said the President.

David Rossi read his amendment. At the feet of His Majesty it humbly expressed an opinion that the present was not a time at which fresh burdens should be laid upon the country for the support of the army, with any expectation that they could be borne. Misfortune and suffering had reached their climax. The cup of the people was full.

At this language some of the members laughed. There were cries of "Order" and "Shame," and then the laughter was resumed. The President rang his bell, and at length silence was secured. David Rossi began to speak, in a voice that was firm and resolute.

"If," he said, "the statement that members of this House are in alliance with the Pope and the Vatican is meant for me and mine, I give it a flat denial. And, in order to have done with this calumny once and for ever, permit me to say that between the Papacy and the people, as represented by us, there is not, and never can be, anything in common. In temporal affairs, the theory of the Papacy rejects the theory of the democracy. The theory of the democracy rejects the theory of the Papacy. The one claims a divine right to rule in the person of the Pope because he is Pope. The other denies all divine right except that of the people to rule themselves."

This was received with some applause mingled with laughter, and certain shouts flung out in a shrill hysterical voice. The President rang his bell again, and David Rossi continued.

"The proposal to increase the army," he said, "in a time of tranquillity abroad but of discord at home, is the gravest impeachment that could be made of the Government of a country. Under a right order of things Parliament would be the conscience of the people, Government would be the servant of that conscience, and rebellion would be impossible. But this Government is the master of the country and is keeping the people down by violence and oppression. Parliament is dead. Fod God's sake let us bury it!"

Loud shouts followed this outburst, and some of the Deputies rose from their seats, and crowding about the speaker in the open space in front, yelled and screamed at him like a pack of hounds. He stood calm, playing with his watch-chain, while the President rang his bell and called for silence. The interruptions died down at last, and the speaker went on:

"If you ask me what is the reason of the discontent which produces the crimes of anarchism, I say, first, the domination of a Government which is absolute, and the want of liberty of speech and meeting. In other countries the discontented are permitted to manifest their woes, and are not punished unless they commit deeds of violence; but in Italy alone, except Russia, a man may be placed outside the law, torn from his home, from the bedside of his nearest and dearest, and sent to *domicilio coatto* to live or die in a silence as deep as that of the grave. Oh, I know what I am saying. I have been in the midst of it. I have seen a father torn from his daughter, and the motherless child left to the mercy of his enemies."

This allusion quieted the House, and for a moment there was a dead silence. Then through the tense air there came a strange sound, and the President demanded silence from the galleries, whereupon the reporters rose and made a negative movement of the hand with two fingers upraised, pointing at the same time to the ladies' tribune.

One of the ladies had cried out. David Rossi heard the voice, and, when he began again, his own voice was softer and more tremulous.

"Next, I say that the cause of anarchism in Italy, as everywhere else, is poverty. Wait until the 1st of February, and you shall see such an army enter Rome as never before invaded it. I assert that within three miles of this place, at the gates of this capital of Christendom, human beings are living lives more abject than that of savage man.

"Housed in huts of straw, sleeping on mattresses of leaves, clothed in rags or nearly nude, fed on maize and chestnuts and acorns, worked eighteen hours a day, and sweated by the tyranny of the overseers, to whom landlords lease their lands while they idle their days in the *salons* of Rome and Paris, men and women and children are being treated worse than slaves, and beaten more than dogs."

At that there was a terrific uproar, shouts of "It's a lie!" and "Traitor!" followed by a loud outbreak of jeers and laughter. Then, for the first time, David Rossi lost control of himself, and, turning upon Parliament with flaming eyes and quivering voice, he cried:

" You take these statements lightly—you that don't know what it is to be hungry, you that have food enough to eat, and only want sleep to digest it. But *I* know these things by bitter knowledge—by experience. Don't talk to me, you who had fathers and mothers to care for you, and comfortable homes to live in. I had none of these. I was nursed in a poorhouse and brought up in a hut on the Campagna. Because of the miserable laws of your predecessors my mother drowned herself in the Tiber, and I knew what it was to starve. And I am only one of many. At the very door of Rome, under a Christian Government, the poor are living lives of moral anæmia and physical atrophy more terrible by far than those which made the pagan poet say two thousand years ago—*Paucis vivit humanum genus*—the human race exists for the benefit of the few."

The silence was breathless while the speaker made this personal reference, and when he sat down, after a denunciation of the militarism which was consuming the heart of the civilised world, the House was too dazed to make any manifestation.

In the dead hush that followed, the President put the necessary questions, but the amendment fell through without a vote being taken, and the printed reply was passed.

Then the Minister of War rose to give notice of his bill for increased military expenditure, and proposed to hand it over to the general committee of the budget.

The Baron Bonelli rose next as Minister of the Interior, and gave notice of his bill for the greater security of the public, and the remodelling of the laws of the press and of association.

He spoke incisively and bitterly, and he was obviously excited, but he affected his usual composure.

" After the language we have heard to-day," he said, " and the knowledge we possess of mass meetings projected, it will not surprise the House that I treat this measure as urgent, and propose that we consider it on the principle of the three readings, taking the first of them in four days."

At that there were some cries from the Left, but the Minister continued:

" It will also not surprise the House that, to prevent the obstruction of members who seem ready to sing their Miserere without end, I will ask the House to take the readings without debate."

Then in a moment the whole House was in an uproar and members were shaking their fists in each other's faces. In vain the President rang his bell for silence. At length he put on his hat and left the Chamber, and the sitting was at an end.

IX

THE last post that night brought Rossi a letter from Roma.

"MY DEAR, DEAR FRIEND,—It's all up! I'm done with her! My unknown and invisible sister that is to be, or rather isn't to be and oughtn't to be, is not worth thinking about any longer. You tell me that she is good and brave and noble-hearted, and yet you would have me believe that she loves wealth, and ease, and luxury, and that she could not give them up even for the sweetest thing that ever comes into a woman's life. Out on her! What does she think a wife is? A pet to be pampered, a doll to be dressed up and danced on your knee? If that's the sort of woman she is, I know what I should call her. A name is on the tip of my tongue, and the point of my finger, and the end of my pen, and I'm itching to have it out, but I suppose I must not write it. Only don't talk to me any more about the bravery of a woman like that.

" The wife I call brave is a man's friend, and if she knows what that means, to be the friend of her husband to all the limitless lengths of friendship, she thinks nothing about sacrifices between him and her, and differences of class do not exist for either of them. Her pride died the instant love looked out of her eyes at him, and if people taunt her with his poverty, or his birth, she answers and says: ' It's true he is poor, but his glory is, that he was a workhouse boy who hadn't father or mother to care for him, and now he is a great man, and I'm proud of him, and not all the wealth of the world shall take me away.'

" One thing I will say, though, for the sister that isn't to be, and that is, that you are deceiving yourself if you suppose that she is going to reconcile herself to your separation while she is kept in the dark as to the cause of it.

It is all very well for you to pay compliments to her beauty and youth and the natural strength of her mind to remove passing impressions, but perhaps the impressions are the reverse of passing ones, and if you go out of her life, what is to become of her? Have you thought of that? Of course you haven't.

"No, no, no! My poor sister! you shall not be so hard on her! In my darkness I could almost fancy that I personate her, and I am she and she is I. Conceited, isn't it? But I told you it wasn't for nothing I was a daughter of Eve. Anyhow I have fought hard for her and beaten you out and out, and now I don't say: 'Will you go to her?' You will—I know you will.

"My bust is out of the caster's hand, and ought to be under mine, but I've done no work again to-day. Tried, but the glow of soul was not there, and I was injuring the face at every touch.

"No further news of M——, and my heart's blood is cold at the silence. But if you are fearless, why should I be afraid?—Your friend's friend,   R."

X

BEFORE going to bed that night, Rossi replied to Roma.

"MY DEAREST,—Bruno will take this letter, and I will charge him on his soul to deliver it safely into your hands. When you have read it, you will destroy it immediately, both for your sake and my own.

"From this moment onward I throw away all disguises. The duplicities of love are sweet and touching, but I cannot play hide-and-seek with you any longer.

"You are right—it is you that I love, and little as I understand and deserve it, I see now that you love me with all your soul and strength. I cannot keep my pen from writing it, and yet it is madness to do so, for the obstacles to our union are just as insurmountable as before.

"It is not only my unflinching devotion to public work that separates us, though that is a serious impediment; it is not only the inequality of our birth and social conditions, though that is an honest difficulty. The barrier between us is not merely a barrier made by man, it is a barrier made by God—it is death.

"Think what that would be in the ordinary case of death by disease. A man is doomed to die by cancer or consumption, and even while he is engaged in a desperate struggle with the mightiest and most relentless conqueror, love comes to him with its dreams of life and happiness. What then? Every hour of joy is poisoned for him henceforth by visions of the end that is so near, in every embrace he feels the arms of death about him, and in every kiss the chill breath of the tomb.

"Terrible tragedy! Yet not without relief. Nature is kind. Her miracles are never-ending. Hope lives to the last. The balm of God's healing hand may come down from heaven and make all things well. Not so the death I speak of. It is pitiless and inevitable, without hope or dreams.

"Remember what I told you in this room on the night you came here first. Had you forgotten it? Your father, charged with an attempt at regicide, as part of a plan of insurrection, was deported without trial, and I, who shared his views, and had expressed them in letters that were violated, being outside the jurisdiction of the courts, was tried in contumacy and condemned to death.

"I am back in Italy for all that, under another name, my mother's name, which is my name too, thanks to the merciless marriage laws of my country, with other aims and other opinions, but I have never deceived myself for a moment. The same doom hangs over me still, and though the court which condemned me was a military court, and its sentence would be modified by a Court of Assize, I see no difference between death in a moment on the gallows, and in five, ten, twenty years in a cell.

"What am I to do? I love you, you love me. Shall I, like the poor consumptive, to whom gleams of happiness have come too late, conceal everything and go on deluding myself with hopes, indulging myself with dreams? It would be unpardonable, it would be cruel, it would be wrong and wicked.

"No, it is impossible. You cannot but be aware that my life or liberty is in serious jeopardy, and that my place in Parliament and in public life is in constant and hourly peril. Every letter that you have written to me shows plainly that you know it. And when you say your heart's

144

blood runs cold at the thought of what may happen when Minghelli returns from England, you betray the weakness, the natural weakness, the tender and womanly weakness, which justifies me in saying that, as long as we love each other, you and I should never meet again.

"Don't think that I am a coward and tremble at the death that hangs over me. I neither fear the future nor regret the past. In every true cause some one is called to martyrdom. To die for the right, for humanity, to lay down all you hold most dear for the sake of the poor and the weak and the down-trodden and God's holy justice—it is a magnificent duty, a privilege! And I am ready. If my death is enough, let me give the last drop of my blood, and be dragged through the last degrees of infamy. Only don't let me drag another after me, and endanger a life that is a thousand times dearer to me than my own.

"I want you, dearest, I want you with my soul, but my doom is certain; it waits for me somewhere; it may be here, it may be there; *it may come to me to-morrow*, or next day, or next year, but it is coming, I feel it, I am sure of it, and I will not fly away. But if I go on until my beloved is my bride, and my name is stamped all over her, and she has taken up my fate, and we are one, and the world knows no difference, what then? Then death with its sure step will come in to separate us, and after death for me, danger, shame, poverty for you, all the penalties a woman pays for her devotion to a man who is down and done.

"I couldn't bear it. The very thought of it would unman me. It would turn heaven into hell. It would disturb the repose of the grave itself.

"Isn't it hard enough to do what is before me without tormenting myself with thoughts like these? It is true I have had my dreams like other men—dreams of the woman whom Heaven might give a man for his support—the anchor to which his soul might hold in storm and tempest, and in the very hour of death itself. But what woman is equal to a lot like that? Martyrdom is for man. God keep all women safe from it!

"Have I said sufficient? If this letter gives you half the pain on reading it that I have felt in writing it, you will be satisfied at last that the obstacles to our union are permanent and insuperable. The time is come when I am forced to tell you the secrets which I have never before revealed to any human soul. You know them now. *They are in your keeping, and it is enough.*

"Heaven be over you! And when you are reconciled to our separation, and both of us are strong, remember that if you want me I will come, and that as long as I live, as long as I am at liberty, I shall be always ready, always waiting, always near. God bless you, my dear one! Adieu!

"DAVID LEONE."

During the afternoon of the following day a letter came by a flying messenger on a bicycle. It was written in pencil in large and straggling characters.

"DEAR MR. ROSSI,—Your letter has arrived and been read, and, yes, it has been destroyed, too, according to your wish, although the flames that burnt it burnt my hand also, and scorched my heart as well.

"No doubt you have done wisely. You know better than I do what is best for both of use, and I yield, I submit. Only —and therefore—I must see you immediately. There is a matter of some consequence on which I wish to speak. It has nothing to do with the subject of your letter—nothing directly, at all events—or yet is it in any way related to the Minghelli mischief-making. So you may receive me without fear. And you will find me with a heart at ease.

"Didn't I tell you that if you wouldn't come to me I must go to you? Expect me this evening about Ave Maria, and arrange it that I may see you alone.   ROMA V."

XI

As Ave Maria approached, David Rossi became still more agitated. The sky had darkened, but there was no wind; the air was empty, and he listened with strained attention for every sound from the staircase and the street. At length he heard a cab stop at the door, and a moment afterwards a light hurrying footstep in the outer room seemed to beat upon his heart.

The door opened and Roma came in quickly, with a scarcely audible salutation. He saw her with her golden complexion and her large violet eyes, wearing a black hat and an astrachan

DAVID ROSSI

coat, but his head was going round and his pulses were beating violently, and he could not control his eyes.

"I have come for a minute only," she said. "You received my letter?"

Rossi bent his head.

"David, I want the fulfilment of your promise."

"What promise?"

"The promise to come to me when I stand in need of you. I need you now. My fountain is practically finished, and to-morrow afternoon I am to have a reception to exhibit it. Everybody will be there, and I want you to be present also."

"Is that necessary?" he asked.

"For my purposes, yes. Don't ask me why. Don't question me at all. Only trust me and come."

She was speaking in a firm and rapid voice, and looking up he saw that her brows were contracted, her lips were set, her cheeks were slightly flushed, and her eyes were shining. He had never seen her like that before. "What is the secret of it?" he asked himself, but he only answered, after a brief pause:

"Very well, I will be there."

"That's all. I might have written, but I was afraid you might object, and I wished to make quite certain. Adieu!"

He had only bowed to her as she entered, and now she was going away without offering her hand.

"Roma," he said, in a voice that sounded choked.

She stopped but did not speak, and he felt himself growing hot all over.

"I'm relieved—so much relieved—to hear that you agree with what I said in my letter."

"The last—in which you wish me to forget you?"

"It is better so—far better. I am one of those who think that if either party to a marriage"—he was talking in a constrained way—"entertains beforehand any rational doubt about it, he is wiser to withdraw, even at the church door, rather than set out on a lifelong voyage under doubtful auspices."

"Didn't we promise not to speak of this?" she said impatiently. Then their eyes met for a moment, and he knew that he was false to himself and that his talk of renunciation was a mockery.

"Roma," he said again, "if you want me in the future you must write."

Her face clouded over.

"For your own sake, you know . . ."

"Oh, that! That's nothing at all—nothing now."

"But people are insulting me about you, and . . ."

"Well—and you?"

The colour rushed to his cheeks and he smote the back of a chair with his clenched fist.

"I tell them . . ."

"I understand," she said, and her eyes began to shine again. But she only turned away, saying: "I'm sorry you are angry that I came."

"Angry!" he cried, and at the sound of his voice as he said the word their love for each other went thrilling through and through them.

The rain had begun to fall, and it was beating with smart strokes on the window panes.

"You can't go now," he said, "and since you are never to come here again there is something you ought to hear."

She took a seat immediately, unfastened her coat, and slipped it back on to her shoulders.

The thick-falling drops were drenching the piazza, and its pavement was bubbling like a lake.

"The rain will last for some time," said Rossi, looking out, "and the matter I speak of is one of some urgency, therefore it is better that you should hear it now."

Taking the pins out of her hat, Roma lifted it off and laid it in her lap, and began to pull off her gloves. The young head with its glossy hair and lovely face shone out with a new beauty.

Rossi hardly dared to look at her. He was afraid that if he allowed himself to do so he would fling himself at her feet. "How calm she is," he thought. "What is the meaning of it?"

He went to the bureau by the wall and took out a small round packet.

"Do you remember your father's voice?" he asked.

"That is all I do remember about my father. Why?"

"It is here in this cylinder."

She rose quickly and then slowly sat down again.

"Tell me," she said.

"When your father was deported to the Island of Elba, he was a prisoner at large, without personal restraint but under police supervision. The legal term of *domicilio coatto* is from one year to five, but excuses were found and his banishment was made perpetual. He saw prisoners come and go, and in the sealed chamber of his tomb he heard echoes of the world outside."

" Did he ever hear of me? "

" Yes, and of myself as well. A prisoner brought him news of one David Rossi, and under that name and the opinions attached to it he recognised David Leone, the boy he had brought up and educated. He wished to send me a message."

" Was it about . . ."

" Yes. The letters of prisoners are read and copied, and to smuggle out by hand a written document is difficult or impossible. But at length a way was discovered. Some one sent a phonograph and a box of cylinders to one of the prisoners, and the little colony of exiled ones used to meet at your father's house to hear the music. Among the cylinders were certain blank ones. Your father spoke on to one of them, and when the time came for the owner of the phonograph to leave Elba, he brought the cylinder back with him. This is the cylinder your father spoke on to."

With an involuntary shudder she took out of his hands a circular cardboard-box, marked in print on the outside : " Selections from Faust," and in pencil on the inside of the lid : " For the hands of D. L. only—to be destroyed if Deputy David Rossi does not know where to find him."

The heavy rain had darkened the room, but by the red light of a dying fire he could see that her face had turned white.

" And this contains my father's voice? " she said.

" His last message."

" He is dead—two years dead—and yet . . ."

" Can you bear to hear it? "

" Go on," she said, hardly audibly.

He took back the cylinder, put it on the phonograph, wound up the instrument, and touched the lever. Through the strokes of the rain, lashing the window like a hundred whips, the whizzing noise of the machine began.

He was standing by her side, and he felt her hand on his arm.

Then through the sound of the rain and of the phonograph there came a clear, full voice:

" David Leone—your old friend Doctor Roselli sends you his dying message . . ."

The hand on Rossi's arm clutched it convulsively, and, in a choking whisper, Roma said:

"Wait! Give me one moment."

She was looking around the darkening room as if almost expecting a ghostly presence.

She bowed her head. Her breath came quick and fast.

"I am better now. Go on," she said.

The whirring noise began again, and after a moment the clear voice came as before:

"My son, the promise I made when we parted in London I fulfilled faithfully, but the letter I wrote you never came to your hands. It was meant to tell you who I was, and why I changed my name. That is too long a story now, and I must be brief. I am Prospero Volonna. My father was the last prince of that name. Except the authorities and their spies, nobody in Italy knows me as Roselli and nobody in England as Volonna—nobody but one, my poor dear child, my daughter Roma."

The hand tightened on Rossi's arm, and his head began to swim.

"Little by little, in this grave of a living man, I have heard what has happened since I was banished from the world. The treacherous letter which called me back to Italy and decoyed me into the hands of the police was the work of a man who now holds my estates as the payment for his treachery."

"The Baron?"

Rossi had stopped the phonograph.

"Can you bear it?" he said.

The pale young face flushed with resolution.

"Go on," she said.

When the voice from the phonograph began again it was more tremulous and husky than before.

"After he had betrayed the father, what impulse of fear or humanity prompted him to take charge of the child, God alone, who reads all hearts, can say. He went to England to look for her, found her in the streets to which she had been abandoned by the faithlessness of the guardians to whom I left her, and shut their mouths by buying them to the perjury of burying the unknown body of an unfortunate being in the name of my beloved child."

The hand on Rossi's arm trembled feebly, and slipped down to his own hand. It was cold as ice. The voice from the phonograph was growing faint.

" She is now in Rome, living in the name that was mine in Italy, amid an atmosphere of danger and perhaps of shame. My son, save her from it. The man who betrayed the father may betray the daughter also. Take her from him. Rescue her. It is my dying prayer."

The hand in Rossi's hand was holding it tightly, and his blood was throbbing at his heart.

" David," the voice from the phonograph was failing rapidly, " when this shall come to your hands the darkness of the grave will be over me. . . . In my great distress of mind I torture myself with many terrors. . . . Do not trifle with my request. But whatever you decide to do . . . be gentle with the child. . . . I dream of her every night, and send my heart's heart to her on the swelling tides of love. . . . Adieu, my son. The end is near. God be with you in all you do that I did ill or left undone. And if death's great sundering does not annihilate the memory of those who remain on earth, be sure you have a helper and an advocate in heaven."

The voice ceased, the whirring of the instrument came to an end, and an invisible spirit seemed to fade into the air. The pattering of the rain had stopped, and there was the crackle of cab wheels on the pavement below. Roma had dropped Rossi's hand, and was leaning forward on her knees with both hands over her face. After a moment, she wiped her eyes with her handkerchief and began to put on her hat.

" How long is it since you received this message? " she said.

" On the night you came here first."

" And when I asked you to come to my house on that . . . that useless errand, you were thinking of . . . of my father's request as well? "

" Yes."

" You have known all this about the Baron for a month, yet you have said nothing. *Why* have you said nothing? "

" You wouldn't have believed me at first, whatever I had said against him."

" But afterwards? "

" Afterwards I had another reason."

" Did it concern me? "

" Yes."

" And now? "

" Now that I have to part from you I am compelled to tell you what he is."

"But if you had known that all this time he has been trying to use somebody against you . . ."

"That would have made no difference."

She lifted her head, and a look of fire, almost of fierceness, came into her face, but she only said, with a little hysterical cry, as if her throat were swelling:

"Come to me to-morrow, David! Be sure you come! If you don't come I shall never, never forgive you! But you will come! You will! You will!"

And then, as if afraid of breaking out into sobs, she turned quickly and hurried away.

"She can never fall into that man's hands now," he thought. And then he lit his lamp and sat down to his work, but the light was gone, and the night had fallen on him.

XII

NEXT morning David Rossi had not yet risen when some one knocked at his door. It was Bruno. The great fellow looked nervous and troubled, and he spoke in a husky whisper.

"You're not going to Donna Roma's to-day, sir?"

"Why not, Bruno?"

"Have you seen her bust of yourself?"

"Hardly at all."

"Just so. My case, too. She has taken care of that—locking it up every night, and getting another caster to cast it. But I saw it the first morning after she began, and I know what it is."

"What is it, Bruno?"

"You'll be angry again, sir."

"What is it?"

"Judas—that's what it is, sir; the study for Judas in the fountain for the Municipality."

"Is that all?"

"All? . . . But it's a caricature, a spiteful caricature! And you sat four days and never even looked at it! I tell you it's disgusting, sir. Simply disgusting. It's been done on purpose, too. When I think of it I forget all you said, and I hate the woman as much as ever. And now she is to have a reception, and you are going to it, just to help her to have her laugh. Don't go, sir! Take the advice of a fool, and don't go!"

"Bruno," said Rossi, lying with his head on his arm, "understand me once for all. Donna Roma may have used my head as a study for Judas—I cannot deny that since you say it is so—but if she had used it as a study for Satan, I would believe in her the same as ever."

"You would?"

"Yes, by God! So now, like a good fellow, go away and leave her alone."

The streets were more than usually full of people when Rossi set out for the reception. Thick groups were standing about the hoardings, reading a yellow placard, which was still wet with the paste of the bill-sticker. It was a proclamation, signed by the Minister of the Interior, and it ran:

"ROMANS,—It having come to the knowledge of the Government that a set of misguided men, the enemies of the throne and of society, known to be in league with the republican, atheist, and anarchist associations of foreign countries, are inciting the people to resist the just laws made by their duly elected Parliament, and sanctioned by their King, thus trying to lead them into outbreaks that would be unworthy of a cultivated and generous race, and would disgrace us in the view of other nations—the Government hereby give notice that they will not allow the laws to be insulted with impunity, and therefore they warn the public against the holding of all such mass meetings in public buildings, squares, and streets, as may lead to the possibility of serious disturbances."

XIII

THE little Piazza of Trinità de' Monti was full of carriages, and Roma's rooms were thronged. David Rossi entered with the calmness of a man who is accustomed to personal observation, but Roma met him with an almost extravagant salutation.

"Ah, you have come at last," she said in a voice that was intended to be heard by all. And then, in a low tone, she added, "Stay near me, and don't go until I say you may."

Her face had the expression that had puzzled him the day before, but with the flushed cheeks, the firm mouth and the shining eyes, there was now a strange look of excitement, almost of hysteria.

The company was divided into four main groups. The

first of them consisted of Roma's aunt, powdered and perfumed, propped up with cushions on an invalid chair, and receiving the guests by the door, with the Baron Bonelli, silent and dignified, but smiling his icy smile, by her side. A second group consisted of Don Camillo and some ladies of fashion, who stood by the window and made little half-smothered trills of laughter. The third group included Lena and Olga, the journalists, with Madame Sella, the modiste; and the fourth group was made up of the English and American Ambassadors, Count Mario, and some other diplomatists.

The conversation was at first interrupted by the little pauses that follow fresh arrivals; and after it had settled down to the dull buzz of a beehive, when the old brood and her queen are being turned out, it consisted merely of hints, giving the impression of something in the air that was scandalous and amusing, but could not be talked about.

"Have you heard that" . . . "Is it true that" . . . "No?" "Can it be possible?" "How delicious!" and then inaudible questions and low replies, with tittering, tapping of fans, and insinuating glances.

But Roma seemed to hear everything that was said about her, and constantly broke in upon a whispered conversation with disconcerting openness.

"That man here!" said one of the journalists at Rossi's entrance. "In the same room with the Prime Minister!" said another. "After that disgraceful scene in the House, too!"

"I hear that he was abominably rude to the Baron the other day," said Madame Sella.

"Rude? He has blundered shockingly, and offended everybody. They tell me the Vatican is now up in arms against him, and is going to denounce him and all his ways."

"No wonder! He has made himself thoroughly disagreeable, and I'm only surprised that the Prime Minister . . ."

"Oh, leave the Prime Minister alone. He has something up his sleeve. . . . Haven't you heard why we are invited here to-day? No? Not heard that . . ."

"Really! So that explains . . . I see, I see!" and then more tittering and tapping of fans.

"Certainly, he is an extraordinary man, and one of the first statesmen in Europe."

"It's so unselfish of you to say that," said Roma, flashing

round suddenly, "for the Minister has never been a friend of journalists, and I've heard him say that there wasn't one of them who wouldn't sell his mother's honour if he thought he could make a sensation."

"Love?" said the voice of Don Camillo in the silence that followed Roma's remark. "What has marriage to do with love except to spoil it?" And then, amidst laughter, and the playful looks of the ladies by whom he was surrounded, he gave a gay picture of his own poverty, and the necessity of marrying to retrieve his fortunes.

"What would you have? Look at my position! A great name, as ancient as history, and no income. A gorgeous palace, as old as the pyramids, and no cook!"

"Don't be so conceited about your poverty, Gi-gi," said Roma. "Some of the Roman ladies are as poor as the men. As for me, Madame Sella could sell up every stick in my house to-morrow, and if the Municipality should throw up my fountain . . ."

"Senator Palomba," said Felice's sepulchral voice from the door.

The suave, oily little Mayor came in, twinkling his eyes and saying:

"Did I hear my name as I entered?"

"I was saying," said Roma, "that if the Municipality should throw up my fountain . . ."

The little man made an amusing gesture, and the constrained silence was broken by some awkward laughter.

"Roma," said the testy voice of the Countess, "I think I've done my duty by you, and now the Baron will take me back. Natalina! Where's Natalina?"

But half-a-dozen hands took hold of the invalid chair, and the Baron followed it into the bedroom.

"Wonderful man!" "Wonderful!" whispered various voices as the Minister's smile disappeared through the door.

The conversation had begun to languish when the Princess Bellini arrived, and then suddenly it became lively and general.

"I'm late, but do you know, my dear," she said, kissing Roma on both cheeks, "I've been nearly torn to pieces in coming. My carriage had to plough its way through crowds of people."

"Crowds?"

"Yes, indeed, and the streets are nearly impassable. Another demonstration, I suppose! The poor must always be demonstrating."

"Ah! yes," said Don Camillo. "Haven't you heard the news, Roma?"

"I've been working all night and all day, and I have heard nothing," said Roma.

"Well, to prevent a recurrence of the disgraceful scene of yesterday, the King has promulgated the Public Security Act by royal decree, and the wonderful crisis is at an end."

"And now?"

"Now the Prime Minister is master of the situation, and has begun by proclaiming the mass meeting which was to have been held in the Coliseum."

"Good thing too," said Count Mario. "We've heard enough of liberal institutions lately."

"And of the scandalous speeches of professional agitators," said Madame Sella.

"And of the liberty of the press," said Senator Palómba. And then the effeminate old dandy, the fashionable dressmaker, and the oily little Mayor exchanged significant nods.

"Wait! Only wait!" said Roma, in a low voice, to Rossi, who was standing in silence by her side.

"Unhappy Italy!" said the American Ambassador. "With the largest array of titled nobility and the largest army of beggars. The one class sipping iced drinks in the piazzas during the playing of music, and the other class marching through the streets and conspiring against society."

"You judge us from a foreign standpoint, dear friend," said Don Camillo, "and forget our love of a pageant. The Princess says our poor are always demonstrating. We are all always demonstrating. Our favourite demonstration is a funeral, with drums beating and banners waving. If we cannot have a funeral we have a wedding, with flowers and favours and floods of tears. And when we cannot have either, we put up with a revolution, and let our Radical orators tell us of the wickedness of taxing the people's bread."

"Always their bread," said the Princess, with a laugh.

"In America, dear General, you are so tragically sincere, but in Italy we are a race of actors. The King, the Parliament, the Pope himself . . ."

"Shocking!" said the little Princess. "But if you had said as much of our professional agitators . . ."

"Oh, they are the most accomplished and successful actors, Princess. But we are all actors in Italy, from the greatest to the least, and the 'curtain' is to him who can score off everybody else."

"So," began the American, "to be Prime Minister in Rome . . ."

"Is to be the chief actor in Europe, and his leading part is that in which he puts an end to his adversary amidst a burst of inextinguishable laughter."

"What is he driving at?" said the English to the American Ambassador.

"Don't you know? Haven't you heard what is coming?" And then some further whispering.

"Wait, only wait!" said Roma.

"Gi-gi," said the Princess, "how stupid you are! You're all wrong about Roma. Look at her now. To think that men can be so blind! And the Baron is no better than the rest of you. He's too proud to believe what I tell him, but he'll learn the truth some day. He is here, of course? In the Countess's room, isn't he? . . . How do you like my dress?"

"It's perfect."

"Really? The black and the blue make a charming effect, don't they? They are the Baron's favourite colours. How agitated our hostess is! She seems to have all the world here. When are we to see the wonderful work? What's she waiting for? Ah, there's the Baron coming out at last!"

"They're all here, aren't they?" said Roma, looking round with flushed cheeks and flaming eyes at the jangling, slandering crew, who had insulted and degraded David Rossi.

"Take care," he answered, but she only threw up her head and laughed.

Then the company went down the circular iron staircase to the studio. Roma walked first with her rapid step, talking nervously and laughing frequently.

The fountain stood in the middle of the floor, and the guests gathered about it.

"Superb!" they exclaimed one after another. "Superb!" "Superb!"

The little Mayor was especially enthusiastic. He stood near the Baron, and holding up both hands he cried:

"Marvellous! Miraculous! Fit to take its place beside the masterpieces of old Rome!"

"But surely this is 'Hamlet' without the prince," said

the Baron. "You set out to make a fountain representing Christ and His twelve apostles, and the only figure you leave unfinished is Christ Himself."

He pointed to the central figure above the dish, which was merely shaped out and indicated.

"Not only one, your Excellency," said Don Camillo. "Here is another unfinished figure—intended for Judas, apparently."

"I left them to the last on purpose," said Roma. "They were so important, and so difficult. But I have studies for both of them in the boudoir, and you shall give me your advice and opinion."

"The saint and the satyr, the God and the devil, the betrayed and the betrayer—what subjects for the chisel of the artist!" said Don Camillo.

"Just so," said the Mayor. "She must do the one with all the emotions of love, and the other with all the faculties of hate."

"Not that art," said Don Camillo, "has anything to do with life—that is to say, real life . . ."

"Why not?" said Roma sharply. "The artist has to live in the world, and he isn't blind. Therefore, why shouldn't he describe what he sees around him?"

"But is that art? If so, the artist is at liberty to give his views on religion and politics, and by the medium of his art he may even express his private feelings—return insults and wreak revenge."

"Certainly he may," said Roma; "the greatest artists have often done so." Saying this, she led the way upstairs, and the others followed with a chorus of hypocritical approval.

"It's only human, to say the least." "Of course it is!" "If she's a woman and can't speak out, or fight duels, it's a lady-like way, at all events." And then further tittering, tapping of fans, and significant nods at Rossi when his back was turned.

Two busts stood on pedestals in the boudoir. One of them was covered with a damp cloth, the other with a muslin veil. Going up to the latter first, Roma said, with a slightly quavering voice:

"It was so difficult to do justice to the Christ that I am almost sorry I made the attempt. But it came easier when I began to think of some one who was being reviled and humiliated and degraded because he was poor and wasn't ashamed of it, and who was always standing up for the weak and the down-trodden, and never returning anybody's insult, however shameful and false and wicked, because he wasn't thinking of himself at all. So I got the best model I could in real life, and this is the result."

With that she pulled off the muslin veil and revealed the sculptured head of David Rossi, in a snow-white plaster cast. The features expressed pure nobility, and every touch was a touch of sympathy and love.

A moment of chilling silence was followed by an underbreath of gossip. "Who is it?" "Christ, of course." "Oh, certainly, but it reminds me of some one." "Who can it be?" "The Pope?" "Why, no; don't you see who it is?" "Is it really?" "How shameful!" "How blasphemous!"

Roma stood looking on with a face lighted up by two flaming eyes. "I'm afraid you don't think I've done justice to my model," she said. "That's quite true. But perhaps my Judas will please you better," and she stepped up to the bust that was covered by the wet cloth.

"I found this a difficult subject also, and it was not until yesterday evening that I felt able to begin on it."

Then, with a hand that trembled visibly, she took from the wall the portrait of her father, and offering it to the Minister, she said:

"Some one told me a story of duplicity and treachery—it was about this poor old gentleman, Baron—and then I knew what sort of person it was who betrayed his friend and master for thirty pieces of silver, and listened to the hypocrisy, and flattery, and lying of the miserable group of parasites who crowded round him because he was a traitor, and because he kept the purse."

With that she threw off the damp cloth, and revealed the clay model of a head. The face was unmistakable, but it expressed every baseness—cunning, arrogance, cruelty, and sensuality.

The silence was freezing, and the company began to turn away, and to mutter among themselves, in order to cover their confusion. "It's the Baron!" "No?" "Yes." "Disgraceful!" "Disgusting!" "Shocking!" "A scarecrow!"

Roma watched them for a moment, and then said: "You don't like my Judas? Neither do I. You're right—it *is* disgusting."

And taking up in both hands a piece of thin wire, she cut the clay across, and the upper part of it fell face downward with a thud on to the floor.

The Princess, who stood by the side of the Baron, offered him her sympathy, and he answered in his icy smile:

"But these artists are all slightly insane, you know. That is an evil which must be patiently endured, without noticing too much the ludicrous side of it."

Then, stepping up to Roma, and handing back the portrait, the Baron said, with a slight frown:

"I must thank you for a very amusing afternoon, and bid you good-day."

The others looked after him, and interpreted his departure according to their own feelings. "He is done with her," they whispered. "He'll pay her out for this." And without more ado they began to follow him.

Roma, flushed and excited, bowed to them as they went out one by one, with a politeness that was demonstrative to the point of caricature. She was saying farewell to them for ever, and her face was lighted up with a look of triumphant joy. They tried to bear themselves bravely as they passed her, but her blazing eyes and sweeping curtseys made them feel as if they were being turned out of the house.

When they were all gone, she shut the door with a bang, and then turning to David Rossi, who alone remained, she burst into a flood of hysterical tears, and threw herself on to her knees at his feet.

XIV

"David!" she cried.

"Don't do that. Get up," he answered.

His thoughts were in a whirl. He had been standing aside, trembling for Roma as he had never trembled for himself in the hottest moments of his public life. And now he was alone with her, and his blood was beating in his breast in stabs.

"Haven't I done enough?" she cried. "You taunted me with my wealth, but I am as poor as you are now. Every penny I had in the world came from the Baron. He allowed me to use part of the revenues of my father's estates, but the income was under his control, and now he will stop it altogether. I am in debt. I have always been in debt. That was my benefactor's way of reminding me of my dependence on his bounty. And now all I have will be sold to satisfy my creditors, and I shall be turned out homeless."

"Roma . . ." he began, but her tears and passion bore down everything.

"House, furniture, presents, carriages, horses, everything will go soon, and I shall have nothing whatever! No matter! You said a woman loved ease and wealth and luxury. Is that all a woman loves? Is there nothing else in the world for any of us? Aren't you satisfied with me at last?"

"Roma," he answered, breathing hard, "don't talk like that. I cannot bear it."

But she did not listen. "You taunted me with being a woman," she said through a fresh burst of tears. "A woman was incapable of friendship and sacrifices. She was intended to be a man's plaything. Do you think I want to be my husband's mistress? I want to be his wife, to share his fate, whatever it may be, for good or bad, for better or worse."

"For God's sake, Roma!" he cried. But she broke in on him again.

"You taunted me with the dangers you had to go through, as if a woman must needs be an impediment to her husband, and try to keep him back. Do you think I want my husband to do nothing? If he were content with that he would not be the man I had loved, and I should despise him and leave him."

"Roma! . . ."

"Then you taunted me with the death that hangs over you. When you were gone I should be left to the mercy of the world. But that can never happen. Never! Do you think a woman can outlive the man she loves as I love you? . . . There! I've said it. You've shamed me into it."

He could not speak now. His words were choking in his throat, and she went on in a torrent of tears:

"The death that threatens you comes from no fault of yours, but only from your fidelity to my father. Therefore I have a right to share it, and I will not live when you are dead."

"If I give way now," he thought, "all is over."

And clenching his hands behind his back to keep himself from throwing his arms around her, he began in a low voice:

"Roma, you have broken your promise to me."

"I don't care," she interrupted. "I would break ten

thousand promises. I deceived you. I confess it. I pretended to be reconciled to your will, and I was not reconciled. I wanted you to see me strip myself of all I had, that you might have no answer and excuse. Well, you have seen me do it, and now . . . what are you going to do *now?*"

"Roma," he began again, trembling all over, "there have been two men in me all this time, and one of them has been trying to protect you from the world and from yourself, while the other . . . the other has been wanting you to despise all his objections, and trample them under your feet. . . . If I could only believe that you know all you are doing, all the risk you are running, and the fate you are willing to share . . . but no, it is impossible."

"David," she cried, "you love me! If you didn't love me, I should know it now—at this moment. But I am braver than you are . . ."

"Let me go. I cannot answer for myself."

"I am braver than you are, for I have not only stripped myself of all my possessions, and of all my friends . . . I have even compromised myself again and again, and been daring and audacious, and rude to everybody for your sake. . . . I, a woman . . . while you, a man . . . you are afraid . . . yes, afraid . . . you are a coward—that's it, a coward! . . . No, no, no! What am I saying? . . . David Leone!"

And with a cry of passion and remorse she flung both arms about his neck.

He had stood, during this fierce struggle of love and pain, holding himself in until his throbbing nerves could bear the strain no longer.

"Come to me, then—come to me," he cried, and at the moment when she threw herself upon him he stretched out his arms to receive her.

"You do love me?" she said.

"Indeed, yes! And you?"

"Yes, yes, yes!"

He clasped her in his arms with redoubled ardour, and pressed her to his breast and kissed her. The love so long pent up was bursting out like a liberated cataract that sweeps the snow and the ice before it.

All at once the girl who had been so brave in the great battle of her love became weak and womanish in the moment of her victory. Under the warmth of his tenderness she dropped her head on to his breast to conceal her face in her shame.

"You will never think the worse of me?" she faltered.

"The worse of you! For loving me?"

"For telling you so and forcing myself into your life?"

"My darling, no!"

She lifted her head, and he kissed away the tears that were shining in her eyes.

"But tell me," he said, "are you sure—quite sure? Do you know what is before you?"

"I only know I love you."

He folded her afresh in his strong embrace, and kissed her head as it lay on his breast.

"Think again," he said. "A man's enemies can be merciless. They may watch you and put pressure upon you, and even humiliate you for my sake."

"No matter, I am not afraid," she answered, and again he tightened his arms about her in a passionate embrace, and covered her hair and her neck and her hands and her finger-tips with kisses.

They did not speak for a long time after that. There was no need for words. He was conquered, yet he was conqueror, and she was happy and at peace. The long fight was over, and everything was well.

He put her to sit in a chair, and sat himself on the arm of it, with his face to her face, and her arms still round his neck. It was like a dream. She could scarcely believe it. He whom she had looked up to with adoration was caressing her. She was like a child in her joy, blushing and half afraid.

He ran his hand through her hair and kissed her forehead. She threw back her head that she might put her lips to his forehead in return, and he kissed her full, round throat.

Then they exchanged rings as the sign of their eternal union. When she put her diamond ring, set in gold, on to his finger, he looked grave and even sad; but when he put his plain silver one on to hers, she lifted up her glorified hand to the light, and kissed and kissed it.

They began to talk in low tones, as if some one had been listening. It was the whispering of their hearts, for the angel of happy love has no voice louder than a whisper. She asked him to say again that he loved her, but as soon as he began to say it she stopped his mouth with a kiss.

They talked of their love. She was sure she had loved him before he loved her, and when he said that he had loved her always, she protested in that case he did not love her at all.

They rose at length to close the windows, and side by side, his arm about her waist, her head leaning lightly on his shoulder, they stood for a moment looking out. The mother of cities lay below in its lightsome whiteness, and over the ridge of its encircling hills the glow of the departing sun was rising in vaporous tints of amber and crimson into the transparent blue, with the dome of St. Peter's, like a balloon ready to rise into a celestial sky.

"A storm is coming," he said, looking at the colours in the sunset.

"It has come and gone," she whispered, and then his arm folded closer about her waist.

It took him half-an-hour to say adieu. After the last kiss and the last handshake, their arms would stretch out to the utmost limit, and then close again for another and another and yet another embrace.

XV

WHEN at length Rossi was gone, Roma ran into her bedroom to look at her face in the glass. The golden complexion was heightened by a bright spot on either cheek, and a teardrop was glistening in the corner of each of her eyes.

She went back to the boudoir. David Rossi was no longer there, but the room seemed to be full of his presence. She sat in the chair again, and again she stood by the window. At length she opened her desk and wrote a letter:—

"DEAREST,—You are only half-an-hour gone, and here I am sending this letter after you, like a handkerchief you had forgotten. I have one or two things to say, quite matter-of-fact and simple things, but I cannot think of them sensibly for joy of the certainty that you love me. Of course I knew it all the time, but I couldn't be at ease until I had heard it from your own lips; and now I feel almost afraid of my great happiness. How wonderful it seems! And, like all events that are long expected, how suddenly it has happened in the end. To think that a month ago—only a little month

164

—you and I were both in Rome, within a mile of each other, breathing the same air, enclosed by the same cloud, kissed by the same sunshine, and yet we didn't know it!

"Soberly, though, I want you to understand that I meant all I said so savagely about going on with your work, and not letting your anxiety about my welfare interfere with you. I am really one of the women who think that a wife should further a man's aims in life if she can; and if she can't do that, she should stand aside and not impede him. So go on, dear heart, without fear for me. I will take care of myself, whatever occurs. Don't let one hour or one act of your life be troubled by the thought of what would happen to me if you should fall. Dearest, I am your beloved, but I am your soldier also, ready and waiting to follow where my captain calls:

> "'Teach me, only teach, Love!
>   As I ought
> I will speak thy speech, Love!
>   Think thy thought.'

"And if I was not half afraid that you would think it bolder than is modest in your bride to be, I would go on with the next lines of my sweet quotation.

"Another thing. You went away without saying you forgive me for the wicked duplicity I practised upon you. It was very wrong, I suppose, and yet for my life I cannot get up any real contrition on the subject. There's always some duplicity in a woman. It is the badge of every daughter of Eve, and it must come out somewhere. In my case it came out in loving you to all the lengths and ends of love, and drawing you on to loving me. I ought to be ashamed, but I'm not—I'm glad.

"I *did* love first, and, of course, I knew you from the beginning, and when you wrote about being in love with some one else, I knew quite well you meant me. But it was so delicious to pretend not to know, to come near and then to sheer off again, to touch and then to fly, to tempt you and then to run away, until a strong tide rushed at me and overwhelmed me, and I was swooning in your arms at last.

"Dearest, don't think I made light of the obstacles you urged against our union. I knew all the time that the risks of marriage were serious, though perhaps I am not in a position even yet to realise how serious they may be. Only I knew also that the dangers were greater still if we kept apart, and that gave me courage to be bold and to defy conventions.

"Which brings me to my last point, and please prepare to be serious, and bend your brow to that terrible furrow which comes when you are fearfully in earnest. What you said of your enemies being merciless, and perhaps watching me and putting pressure upon me to injure you, is only too imminent a danger. The truth is that I have all along known more than I had courage to tell, but I was hoping you would understand, and now I tremble to think how I have suffered myself to be silent.

"The Minghelli matter is an alarming affair, for I have reason to believe that the man has lit on the name you bore in England, and that when he returns to Rome he will try to fix it upon you by means of me. This is fearful to contemplate, and my heart quakes to think of it. But happily there is a way to checkmate such a devilish design, and it is within your own power to save me from lifelong remorse.

"I don't think the laws of any civilized country compel a man's *wife* to compromise him, and thinking of this gives me courage to be unmaidenly and say: Don't let it be long, dearest! I could die to bring it to pass in a moment. With all my great, great happiness, I shall have the heartache until it is done, and only when it is over shall I begin to live."

"There! You didn't know what a forward hussy I could be if I tried, and really I have been surprised at myself since I began to be in love with you. For weeks and weeks I have been thin and haggard and ugly, and only to-day I begin to be a little beautiful. I couldn't be anything but beautiful to-day, and I've been running to the glass to look at myself, as the only way to understand why you love me at all. And I'm glad—so glad for your sake.

"Good-bye, dearest! You cannot come to-morrow or the next day, and what a lot I shall have to live before I see you again! Shall I look older? No, for thinking of you makes me feel younger and younger every minute. How old are you? Thirty-four? I'm twenty-four and a half, and that is just right, but if you think I ought to be nearer your age I'll wear a bonnet and fasten it with a bow.

"ROMA.

"P.S.—Don't delay the momentous matter. Don't! Don't! Don't!"

She dined alone that night that she might be undisturbed in her thoughts of Rossi. Ordinary existence had almost disappeared from her consciousness, and every time Felice spoke as he served the dishes his voice seemed to come from far away.

She went to bed early, but it was late before she slept. For a long time she lay awake to think over all that had happened, and, when the night was far gone, and she tried to fall asleep in order to dream of it also, she could not do so for sheer delight of the prospect. But at last amid the gathering clouds of sleep she said " Good-night," with the ghost of a kiss, and slept until morning.

When she awoke it was late, and the sun was shining into the room. She lay on her back and stretched out both arms for sheer sweetness of the sensation of health and love. Everything was well, and she was very happy. Thinking of yesterday, she was even sorry for the Baron, and told herself she had been too bold and daring.

But that thought was gone in a moment. Body and soul were suffused with joy, and she leapt out of bed with a spring.

A moment afterwards Natalina came with a letter. It was from the Baron himself, and it was dated the day before:—

" Minghelli has returned from London, and therefore I must see you to-morrow at eleven o'clock. Be so good as to be at home, and give orders that for half-an-hour at least we shall be quite undisturbed."

Then the sun went out, the air grew dull, and darkness fell over all the world.

PART FIVE—THE PRIME MINISTER

I

It was Sunday. The storm threatened by the sunset of the day before had not yet come, but the sun was struggling through a veil of clouds, and a black ridge lay over the horizon.

At eleven o'clock to the moment the Baron arrived. As usual, he was faultlessly dressed, and he looked cool and tranquil.

"I am to show you into this room, Excellency," said Felice, leading the way to the boudoir.

"Thanks! . . . Anything to tell me, Felice?"

"Nothing, Excellency," said Felice. Then, pointing to the plaster bust on its pedestal in the corner, he added in a lower tone, "*He* remained last night after the others had gone, and . . ."

But at that moment there was the rustle of a woman's dress outside, and, interrupting Felice, the Baron said in a high-pitched voice:

"Certainly; and please tell the Countess I shall not forget to look in upon her before I go."

Roma came into the room with a gloomy and firm-set face. The smile that seemed always to play about her mouth and eyes had given place to a slight frown and an air of defiance. But the Baron saw in a moment that behind the lips so sternly set, and the straight look of the eyes, there was a frightened expression which she was trying to conceal. He greeted her with his accustomed calm and naturalness, kissed her hand, offered her the flower from his button-hole, put her to sit in the arm-chair with its back to the window, took his own seat on the couch in front of it, and leisurely drew off his spotless gloves.

Not a word about the scene of yesterday, not a look of pain or reproof. Only a few casual pleasantries, and then a quiet gliding into the business of his visit,

THE PRIME MINISTER

"What an age since we were here alone before! And what changes you've made! Your pretty nest is like a cell! Well, I've obeyed your mandate, you see. I've stayed away for a month. It was hard to do—bitterly hard—and many a time I've told myself it was imprudent. But you were a woman. You were inexorable. I was forced to submit. And now, what have you got to tell me?"

"Nothing," she answered, looking straight before her.

"Nothing whatever?"

"Nothing whatever."

She did not move or turn her face, and he sat for a moment watching her. Then he rose, and began to walk about the room.

"Let us understand each other, my child," he said gently. "Will you forgive me if I recall facts that are familiar?"

She did not answer, but looked fixedly into the fire, while he leaned on the stove and stood face to face with her.

"A month ago, a certain Deputy, an obstructionist politician, who has for years made the task of government difficult, uttered a seditious speech, and brought himself within the power of the law. In that speech he also attacked me, and—shall I say?—grossly slandered you. Parliament was not in session, and I was able to order his arrest. In due course, he would have been punished, perhaps by imprisonment, perhaps by banishment, but you thought it prudent to intervene. You urged reasons of policy which were wise and far-seeing. I yielded, and, to the bewilderment of my officials, I ordered the Deputy's release. But he was not therefore to escape. You undertook his punishment. In a subtle and more effectual way, you were to wipe out the injury he had done, and requite him for his offence. The man was a mystery—you were to find out all about him. He was suspected of intrigue—you were to discover his conspiracies. Within a month, you were to deliver him into my hands, and I was to know *the inmost secrets of his soul.*"

It was with difficulty that Roma maintained her calmness while the Baron was speaking, but she only shook a stray lock of hair from her forehead, and sat silent.

"Well, the month is over. I have given you every opportunity to deal with our friend as you thought best. Have you found out anything about him?"

She put on a bold front and answered, "No."

"So your effort has failed?"

"Absolutely."

"Then you are likely to give up your plan of punishing the man for defaming and degrading you?"

"I have given it up already."

"Strange! Very strange! Very unfortunate also, for we are at this moment at a crisis when it is doubly important to the Government to possess the information you set out to find. Still, your idea was a good one, and I can never be sufficiently grateful to you for suggesting it. And although *your* efforts have failed, you need not be uneasy. You have given us the clues by which *our* efforts are succeeding, and you shall yet punish the man who insulted you so publicly and so grossly."

"How is it possible for me to punish him?"

"By identifying David Rossi as one who was condemned in contumacy for high treason sixteen years ago."

"That is ridiculous," she said. "Sixteen months ago I had never heard the name of David Rossi."

The Baron stooped a little and said:

"Had you ever heard the name of David Leone?"

She dropped back in her chair, and again looked straight before her.

"Come, come, my child," said the Baron caressingly, and moving across the room to look out of the window, he tapped her lightly on the shoulder:

"I told you that Minghelli had returned from London."

"That forger!" she said hoarsely.

"No doubt! One who spends his life ferreting out crime is apt to have the soul of a criminal. But civilisation needs its scavengers, and it was a happy thought of yours to think of this one. Indeed, everything we've done has been done on your initiative, and when our friend is finally brought to justice, the deed will really be due to you, and you alone."

The defiant look was disappearing from her eyes, and she rose with an expression of pain.

"Why do you torture me like this?" she said. "After what has happened, isn't it quite plain that I am his friend, and not his enemy?"

"Perhaps," said the Baron. His face assumed a death-like rigidity. "Sit down and listen to me."

She sat down, and he returned to his place by the stove.

THE PRIME MINISTER

"I say you gave us the clues we have worked upon. Those clues were three. First, that David Rossi knew the life-story of Doctor Roselli in London. Second, that he knew the story of Doctor Roselli's daughter, Roma Roselli. Third, that he was for a time a waiter at the Grand Hotel in Rome. Two minor clues came independently, that David Rossi was once a stable-boy in New York, that his mother drowned herself in the Tiber, and he was brought up in a Foundling. By these five clues the authorities have discovered eight facts. Permit me to recite them."

Leaning his elbow on the stove and opening his hand, the Baron ticked off the facts one by one on his fingers.

"Fact one. Some thirty odd years ago a woman carrying a child presented herself at the office in Rome for the registry of births. She gave the name of Leonora Leone, and wished her child, a boy, to be registered as David Leone. But the officer in attendance discovered that the woman's name was Leonora Rossi, and that she had been married according to the religious rites of the Church, but not according to the civil regulations of the State. The child was therefore registered as David Rossi, son of Leonora Rossi and of a father unknown."

"Shameful!" cried Roma. "Shameful! shameful!"

"Fact two," said the Baron, without the change of a tone. "One night a little later the body of a woman found drowned in the Tiber was recognised as the body of Leonora Rossi, and buried in the pauper part of the Campo Verano under that name. The same night a child was placed by an unknown hand in the *rota* of Santo Spirito, with a paper attached to its wrist, giving particulars of its baptism and its name. The name given was David Leone."

The Baron ticked off the third of his fingers and continued:

"Fact three. Fourteen years afterwards a boy named David Leone, fourteen years of age, was living in the house of an Italian exile in London. The exile was a Roman prince under the incognito of Doctor Roselli; his family consisted of his wife and one child, a daughter named Roma, four years of age. David Leone had been adopted by Doctor Roselli, who had picked him up in the street."

Roma covered her face with her hands.

"Fact four. Four years later a conspiracy to assassinate the King of Italy was discovered at Milan. The chief conspirator turned out to be, unfortunately, the English exile known as Doctor Roselli. By the good offices of a kinsman, jealous of the honour of his true family name, he was not brought to public trial, but deported by one of the means adopted by all Governments when secrecy or safety is in question. But his confederates and correspondents were shown less favour, and one of them, still in England, being tried in contumacy by a military court which sat during a state of siege, was condemned for high treason to the military punishment of death. The name of that confederate and correspondent was David Leone."

Roma's slippered foot was beating the floor fast, but the Baron went on in his cool and tranquil tone.

" Fact five. Our extradition treaty excluded the delivery of political offenders, but after representations from Italy, David Leone left England. He went to America. There he was first employed in the stables of the Tramway Company in New York, and lived in the Italian quarter of the city, but afterwards he rose out of his poverty and low position and became a journalist. In that character he attracted attention by a new political and religious propaganda. Jesus Christ was lawgiver for the nation as well as for the individual, and the redemption of the world was to be brought to pass by a constitution based on the precepts of the Lord's Prayer. The creed was sufficiently sentimental to be seized upon by fanatics in that country of countless faiths, but it cut at the roots of order, of poverty, even of patriotism, and being interpreted into action, seemed likely to lead to riot."

The Baron twisted the ends of his moustache, and said, with a smile, " David Leone disappeared from New York. From that time forward no trace of him has yet been found. He was as much gone as if he had ceased to exist. *David Leone was dead.*"

Roma's hands had come down from her face, and she was picking at the buttons of her blouse with twitching fingers.

" Fact six," said the Baron, ticking off the thumb of his other hand. " Twenty-five or six years after the registration of the child David Rossi in Rome, a man, apparently twenty-five or six years of age, giving the name of David Rossi, arrived in England from America. He called at a baker's shop in Soho to ask for Roma Roselli, the daughter of Doctor Roselli, left behind in London when the exile returned to

Italy. They told him that Roma Roselli was dead and buried."

Roma's face, which had been pale until now, began to glow like a fire on a gloomy night, and her foot beat faster and faster.

"Fact seven. David Rossi appeared in Rome, first as a waiter at the Grand Hotel, but soon afterwards as a journalist and public lecturer, propounding precisely the same propaganda as that of David Leone in New York, and exciting the same interest."

"Well? What of it?" said Roma. "David Leone was David Leone, and David Rossi is David Rossi—there is no more in it than that."

The Baron clasped his hands so tight that his knuckles cracked, and said, in a slightly exalted tone:

"Eighth and last fact. About that time a man called at the office of the Campo Santo to know where he was to find the grave of Leonora Leone, the woman who had drowned herself in the Tiber twenty-six years before. The pauper trench had been dug up over and over again in the interval, but the officials gave him their record of the place where she had once been buried. He had the spot measured off for him, and he went down on his knees before it. Hours passed, and he was still kneeling there. At length night fell, and the officers had to warn him away."

Roma's foot had ceased to beat on the floor, and she was rising in her chair.

"That man," said the Baron, "the only human being who ever thought it worth while to look up the grave of the poor suicide, Leonora Rossi, the mother of David Leone, was David Rossi! Who was David Leone?—David Rossi! Who was David Rossi?—David Leone! The circle had closed around him—the evidence was complete."

"Oh! oh! oh!"

Roma had leapt up and was moving about the room. Her lips were compressed with scorn, her eyes were flashing, and she burst into a torrent of words, which spluttered out of her quivering lips.

"Oh, to think of it! To think of it! You are right! The man who spends his life looking for crime must have the soul of a criminal! He has no conscience, no humanity, no mercy, no pity. And when he has tracked and dogged a man to his mother's grave—*his mother's grave*—he can dine, he can laugh, he can go to the theatre! Oh, I hate you! There, I've told you! Now, do with me as you please!"

The deathlike rigidity in the Baron's face decomposed into an expression of intense pain, but he only passed his hand over his brow, and said, after a moment of silence:

"My child, you are not only offending me, you are offending the theory and principle of Justice. Justice has nothing to do with pity. In the vocabulary of Justice there is but one word—duty. Duty called upon me to fix this man's name upon him, that his obstructions, his slanders, and his evil influence might be at an end. And now Justice calls upon you to do the same."

The Baron leaned against the stove, and spoke in a calm voice, while Roma in her agitation continued to walk about the room.

"Being a Deputy, and Parliament being in session, David Rossi can only be arrested by the authorisation of the Chamber. In order to obtain that authorisation, it is necessary that the Attorney-General should draw up a statement of the case. The statement must be presented by the Attorney-General to the Government, by the Government to the President, by the President to a Committee, and by the Committee to Parliament. Towards this statement the police have already obtained important testimony, and a complete chain of circumstantial evidence has been prepared. But they lack one link of positive proof, and until that link is obtained the Attorney-General is unable to proceed. It is the keystone of the arch, the central fact, without which all other facts fall to pieces—the testimony of somebody who can swear, if need be, that she knew both David Leone and David Rossi, and can identify the one with the other."

"Well?"

The Baron, who had stopped, continued in a calm voice: "My dear Roma, need I go on? Dead as a Minister is to all sensibility, I had hoped to spare you. There is only one person known to me who can supply that link. That person is yourself."

Roma's eyes were red with anger and terror, but she tried to laugh over her fear.

"How simple you are, after all!" she said. "It was Roma Roselli who knew David Leone, wasn't it? Well, Roma Roselli is dead and buried. Oh, I know all the story. You did that yourself, and now it cuts the ground from under you."

"My dear Roma," said the Baron, with a hard and angry face, "if I did anything in that matter, it was done for your welfare, but whatever it was, it need not disturb me now. Roma Roselli is *not* dead, and it would be easy to bring people from England to say so."

"You daren't! You know you daren't! It would expose them to persecution for perpetrating a crime."

"In England, not in Italy."

Roma's red eyes fell, and the Baron began to speak in a caressing voice:

"My child, don't fence with me. It is so painful to silence you. . . . It is perhaps natural that you should sympathise with the weaker side. That is the sweet and tender if illogical way of all women. But you must not imagine that when David Rossi has been arrested he will be walked off to his death. As a matter of fact, he must go through a new trial, he must be defended, his sentence would in any case be reduced to imprisonment, and it may even be wiped out altogether. That's all."

"All? And you ask me to help you to do that?"

"Certainly."

"I won't!"

"Then you could if you would?"

"I can't!"

"Your first word was the better one, my child."

"Very well, I won't! I won't! Aren't you ashamed to ask me to do such a thing? According to your own story, David Leone was my father's friend, yet you wish me to give him up to the law that he may be imprisoned, perhaps for life, and at least turned out of Parliament. Do you suppose I am capable of treachery like that? Do you judge of everybody by yourself? . . . Ah, I know that story too! For shame! For shame!"

The Baron was silent for a moment, and then said in an impassive voice:

"I will not discuss that subject with you now, my child —you are excited, and don't quite know what you are saying. I will only point out to you that even if David Leone was your father's friend, David Rossi was your own enemy."

"What of that? It's my own affair, isn't it? If I choose to forgive him, what matter is it to anybody else? I *do* forgive him! Now, whose business is it except my own?"

"My dear Roma, I might tell you that it's mine also, and

that the insult that went through you was aimed at me. But I will not speak of myself. . . . That you should change your plans so entirely, and setting out a month ago to . . . to . . . shall I say betray . . . this man Rossi, you are now striving to save him, is a problem which admits of only one explanation, and that is that . . . that you . . ."

"That I love him—yes, that's the truth," said Roma boldly, but flushing up to the eyes and trembling with fear.

There was a death-like pause in the duel. Both dropped their heads, and the silent face in the bust seemed to be looking down on them. Then the Baron's icy cheeks quivered visibly, and he said in a low, hoarse voice:

"I'm sorry! Very sorry! For in that case I may be compelled to justify your conclusion that a Minister has no humanity and no pity. If David Rossi cannot be arrested by the authorisation of Parliament, he must be arrested when Parliament is not in session, and then his identity will have to be established in a public tribunal. In that event you will be forced to appear, and having refused to make a private statement in the secrecy of a magistrate's office, you will be compelled to testify in the Court of Assize."

"Ah, but you can't make me do that!" cried Roma excitedly, as if seized by a sudden thought.

"Why not?"

"Never mind why not. You can't do it, I tell you," she cried excitedly.

He looked at her as if trying to penetrate her meaning, and then said:

"We shall see."

At that moment the fretful voice of the Countess was heard calling to the Baron from the adjoining room.

II

ROMA went to her bedroom when the Baron left her, and remained there until late in the afternoon. In spite of the bold front she had put on, she was quaking with terror and tortured by remorse. Never before had she realised David Rossi's peril with such awful vividness, and seen her own position in relation to him in its hideous nakedness.

Was it her duty to confess to David Rossi that at the beginning of their friendship she had set out to betray him?

Only so could she be secure, only so could she be honest, only so could she be true to the love he gave her and the trust he reposed in her.

Yet why should she confess? The abominable impulse was gone. Something sweet and tender had taken its place. To confess to him now would be cruel. It would wound his beautiful faith in her.

And yet the seeds she had sown were beginning to fructify. They might spring up anywhere at any moment, and choke the life that was dearer to her than her own. Thank God, it was still impossible to injure him except by her will and assistance. But her will might be broken and her assistance might be forced, unless the law could be invoked to protect her against itself. It could and it should be invoked! When she was married to David Rossi no law in Italy would compel her to witness against him.

But if Rossi hesitated from any cause, if he delayed their marriage, if he replied unfavourably to the letter in which she had put aside all modesty and asked him to marry her soon—what then? How was she to explain his danger? How was she to tell him that he must marry her before Parliament rose, or she might be the means of expelling him from the Chamber, and perhaps casting him into prison for life? How was she to say: "I was Delilah; I set out to betray you, and unless you marry me the wicked work is done!"

The afternoon was far spent; she had eaten nothing since morning, and was lying face down on the bed, when a knock came to the door.

"The person in the studio to see you," said Felice

It was Bruno in Sunday attire, with little Joseph in top-boots, and more than ever like the cub of a young lion.

"A letter from him," said Bruno.

It was from Rossi. She took it without a word of greeting, and went back to her bedroom. But when she returned a moment afterwards her face was transformed. The clouds had gone from it and the old radiance had returned. All the brightness and gaiety of her usual expression were there as she came swinging into the drawing-room and filling the air with the glow of health and happiness.

"*That's* all right," she said. "Tell Mr. Rossi I shall expect to see him soon . . . or no, don't say that . . . say that as he is over head and ears in work this week, he is not to think it necessary. . . . Oh, say anything you like," she said, and the pearly teeth and lovely eyes broke into an aurora smiles.

Bruno, whose bushy face and shaggy head had never once been raised since he came into the room, said:

"He's busy enough, anyway—what with this big meeting coming off on Wednesday, and the stairs to his room as full of people as the Santa Scala."

"So you've brought little Joseph to see me at last?" said Roma.

"He has bothered my life out to bring him ever since you said he was to be your porter some day."

"And why not? Gentlemen ought to call on the ladies, oughtn't they, Joseph?"

And Joseph, whose curly poll had been hiding behind the leg of his father's trousers, showed half of a face that was shining all over.

"See! See here—do you know who *this* is? This gentleman in the bust?"

"Uncle David," said the boy.

"What a clever boy you are, Joseph!"

"Doesn't want much cleverness to know that, though," said Bruno. "It's wonderful! it's magnificent! And it will shut up all their damned . . . excuse me, miss, excuse *me*."

"And Joseph still intends to be a porter?"

"Dead set on it, and says he wouldn't change his profession to be a king."

"Quite right, too! And now let us look at something a little birdie brought me the other day. Come along, Joseph. Here it is. Down on your knees, gentleman, and help me to drag it out. One—two—and away!"

From the knee-hole of the desk came a large cardboard box, and Joseph's eyes glistened like big black beads.

"Now, what do you think is in this box, Joseph? Can't guess? Give it up? Sure? Well, listen! Are you listening? Which do you think you would like best—a porter's cocked hat, or a porter's long coat, or a porter's mace with a gilt hat and a tassel?"

Joseph's face, which had gleamed at every item, clouded and cleared, cleared and clouded at the cruel difficulty of choice, and finally looked over at Bruno for help.

"Choose now—which?"

But Joseph only sidled over to his father, and whispered something which Roma could not hear.

"What does he say?"

"He says it is his birthday on Wednesday," said Bruno.

"Bless him! He shall have them all, then," said Roma, and Joseph's legs as well as his eyes began to dance.

The cords were cut, the box was opened, the wonderful hat and coat and mace were taken out, and Joseph was duly invested. In the midst of this ceremony Roma's black poodle came bounding into the room, and when Joseph strutted out of the boudoir into the drawing-room the dog went leaping and barking beside him.

"Dear little soul!" said Roma, looking after the child; but Bruno, who was sitting with his head down, only answered with a groan.

"What is the matter, Bruno?" she asked.

Bruno brushed his coat-sleeve across his eyes, set his teeth, and said with a savage fierceness:

"What's the matter? Treason's the matter, telling tales and taking away a good woman's character—that's what is the matter! A man who has been eating your bread for years has been lying about you, and he is a rascal and a sneak and a damned scoundrel, and I would like to kick him out of the house."

"And who has been doing all this, Bruno?"

"Myself! It was I who told Mr. Rossi the lies that made him speak against you on the day of the Pope's Jubilee, and when you asked him to come here, I warned him against you, and said you were only going to pay him back and ruin him."

"So you said that, did you?"

"Yes, I did."

"And what did Mr. Rossi say to you?"

"Say to me? 'She's a good woman,' says he, 'and if I have ever said otherwise, I take it all back, and am ashamed.'"

Roma, who had turned to the window, heaved a sigh and said: "It has all come out right in the end, Bruno. If you hadn't spoken against me to Mr. Rossi, he wouldn't have spoken against me in the piazza, and then he and I should never have met and known each other and been friends. All's well that ends well, you know."

"Perhaps so, but the miracle doesn't make the saint, and you oughtn't to keep me any longer."

"Do you mean that I ought to dismiss you?"

"Yes."

"Bruno," said Roma, "I am in trouble just now, and I may be in worse trouble by-and-by. I don't know how long I may be able to keep you as a servant, but I may want you as a friend, and if you leave me now . . ."

"Oh, put it like that, miss, and I'll never leave you, and as for your enemies . . ."

Bruno was doubling up the sleeve of his right arm, when Joseph and the poodle came back to the room. Roma received them with a merry cry, and there was much noise and laughter. At length the gorgeous garments were taken off, the cardboard box was corded, and Bruno and the boy prepared to go.

"You'll come again, won't you, Joseph?" said Roma, and the boy's face beamed.

"I suppose this little man means a good deal to his mother, Bruno?"

"Everything! I do believe she'd die, or disappear, or drown herself if anything happened to that boy."

"And Mr. Rossi?"

"He's been a second father to the boy ever since the young monkey was born."

"Well, Joseph must come here sometimes, and let me try and be a second mother to him too. . . . What is he saying now?"

Joseph had dragged down his father's head to whisper something in his ear.

"He says he's frightened of your big porter downstairs."

"Frightened of *him!* He is only a man, my precious! Tell him you are a little Roman boy, and he'll *have* to let you up. Will you remember? You will? That's right! By-bye!"

Before going to sleep that night, Roma switched on the light that hung above her head and read her letter again. She had been hoarding it up for that secret hour, and now she was alone with it, and all the world was still.

"Saturday Night.

"MY DEAR ONE,—Your sweet letter brought me the intoxication of delight, and the momentous matter you speak of is under way. It is my turn to be ashamed of all the great to-do I made about the obstacles to our union when I see how courageous you can be. Oh, how brave women are—

every woman who ever marries a man! To take her heart into her hands, and face the unknown in the fate of another being, to trust her life into his keeping, knowing that if he falls she falls too, and will never be the same again! What *man* could do it? Not one who was ever born into the world. Yet some woman does it every day, promising some man that she will—let me finish your quotation—

> " 'Meet, if thou require it,
> Both demands,
> Laying flesh and spirit
> In thy hands.'

"Don't think I am too much troubled about the Minhelli matter, and yet it is pitiful to think how merciless the world can be even in the matter of a man's name. A name is only a word, but it is everything to the man who bears it— honour or dishonour, poverty or wealth, a blessing or a curse. If it is a good name, everybody tries to take it away from him, but if it's a bad name and he has attempted to drop it, everybody tries to fix it on him afresh.

"The name I was compelled to leave behind me when I returned to Italy was a bad name in nothing except that it was the name of my father, and if the spies and ferrets of authority ever fix it upon me God only knows what mischief they may do. But one thing *I* know—that if they do fix my father's name upon me, and bring me to the penalties which the law has imposed on it, it will not be by help of my darling, my beloved, my brave, brave girl with the heart of gold.

"Dearest, I wrote to the Capitol immediately on receiving your letter, and to-morrow morning I will go down myself to see that everything is in train. I don't yet know how many days are necessary to the preparations, but earlier than Thursday it would not be wise to fix the event, seeing that Wednesday is the day of the great mass meeting in the Coliseum, and, although the police have proclaimed it, I have told the people they are to come. There is some risk at the outset, which it would be reckless to run, and in any case the time is short.

"Good-night! I can't take my pen off the paper. Writing to you is like talking to you, and every now and then I stop and shut my eyes, and hear your voice replying. Only it is myself who make the answers, and they are not half so sweet as they would be in reality. Ah, dear heart, if you only knew how my life was full of silence until you came into it, and now it is full of music! Good-night, again!

"D. R.

"*Sunday Morning.*

"Just returned from the Capitol. The legal notice for the celebration of a marriage is longer than I expected. It seems that the ordinary term must be twelve days at least, covering two successive Sundays (on which the act of publication is posted on the board outside the office) and three days over. Only twelve days more, my dear one, and you will be mine, mine, mine, and all the world will know!"

It took Roma a good three-quarters of an hour to read this letter, for nearly every word seemed to be written out of a lover's lexicon, which bore secret meanings of delicious import, and imperiously demanded their physical response from the reader's lips. At length she put it between the pillow and her cheek, to help the sweet delusion that she was cheek to cheek with some one and had his strong, protecting arms about her. Then she lay a long time, with eyes open and shining in the darkness, trying in vain to piece together the features of his face. But in the first dream of her first sleep she saw him plainly, and then she ran, she raced, she rushed to his embrace.

Next day brought a message from the Baron:

"DEAR ROMA,—Come to the Palazzo Braschi to-morrow (Tuesday) morning at eleven o'clock. Don't refuse, and don't hesitate. If you do not come, you will regret it as long as you live, and reproach yourself for ever afterwards.—Yours,

"BONELLI."

III

THE Palazzo Braschi is a triangular palace, whereof one front faces to the Piazza Navona and the two other fronts to side streets. It is the official palace of the Minister of the Interior, usually the President of the Council and Prime Minister of Italy.

Roma arrived at eleven o'clock, and was taken to the Minister's room immediately, by way of an outer chamber, in which colleagues and secretaries were waiting their turn for an interview. The Baron was seated at a table covered with books and papers. There was a fur rug across his knees, and at his right hand lay a small ivory-handled revolver. He rose as Roma entered, and received her with his great but glacial politeness.

"How prompt! And how sweet you look to-day, my child! On a cheerless morning like this you bring the sun itself into a poor Minister's gloomy cabinet. Sit down."

"You wished to see me?" said Roma.

The Baron rested his elbow on the table, leaned his head on his hand, looked at her with his never-varying smile, and said:

"I hear you are to be congratulated, my dear."

She changed colour slightly.

"Are you surprised that I know?" he asked.

"Why should I be surprised?" she answered. "You know everything. Besides, this is published at the Capitol, and therefore common knowledge."

His smiling face remained perfectly impassive.

"Now I understand what you meant on Sunday. It is a fact that a wife cannot be called as a witness against her husband."

She knew he was watching her face as if looking into the inmost recesses of her soul.

"But isn't it a little courageous of you to think of marriage?"

"Why courageous?" she asked, but her eyes fell and the colour mounted to her cheek.

"*Why* courageous?" he repeated.

He allowed a short time to elapse, and then he said in a low tone, "Considering the past, and all that has happened . . ."

Her eyelids trembled and she rose to her feet.

"If this is all you wish to say to me . . ."

"No, no! Sit down, my child. I sent for you in order to show you that the marriage you contemplate may be difficult, perhaps impossible."

"I am of age—there can be no impediment."

"There may be the greatest of all impediments, my dear."

"What do you mean?"

"I mean . . . But wait! You are not in a hurry? A number of gentlemen are waiting to see me, and if you will permit me to ring for my secretary . . . Don't move. Colleagues merely! They will not object to *your* presence. My ward, you know—almost a member of my own household. Ah, here is the secretary. Who now?"

"The Minister of War, the Prefect, Commendatore Angelelli, and one of his delegates," replied the secretary.

"Bring the Prefect first," said the Baron, and a severe-looking man of military bearing entered the room.

"Come in, Senator. You know Donna Roma. Our business is urgent—she will allow us to go on. I am anxious to hear how things stand and what you are doing."

The Prefect began on his report. Immediately the new law was promulgated by royal decree, he had sent out a circular to all the Mayors in his province, stating the powers it gave the police to dissolve associations and forbid public meetings.

"But what can we expect in the provincial towns, your Excellency, while in the capital we are doing nothing? The chief of all subversive societies is in Rome, and the directing mind is at large among ourselves. Listen to this, sir."

The Prefect took a newspaper from his pocket and began to read:

"ROMANS,—The new law is an attempt to deprive us of liberties which our fathers made revolutions to establish. It is, therefore, our duty to resist it, and to this end we must hold our meeting on the 1st of February according to our original intention. Only thus can we show the Government and the King what it is to oppose the public opinion of the world. . . . Meet in the Piazza del Popolo at sundown and walk to the Coliseum by way of the Corso. Be peaceful and orderly, and God put it into the hearts of your rulers to avert bloodshed."

"That is from the *Sunrise?*"

"Yes, sir, the last of many manifestoes. And what is the result? The people are flocking into Rome from every part of the province."

"And how many political pilgrims are here already?"

"Fifty thousand, sixty, perhaps a hundred thousand. It cannot be allowed to go on, your Excellency."

"It is a *levée-en-masse* certainly. What do you advise?"

"That the enemies of the Government and the State,

whose erroneous conceptions of liberty have led to this burst of anarchist feelings, be left to the operation of the police laws."

The Baron glanced at Roma. Her face was flushed and her eyes were flashing.

"That," he said, "may be difficult, considering the number of the discontented. What is the strength of your police?"

"Seven hundred in uniform, four hundred in plain clothes, and five hundred and fifty municipal guards. Besides these, sir, there are three thousand Carabineers and eight thousand regular troops."

"Say twelve thousand five hundred armed men in all?"

"Precisely, and what is that against fifty, a hundred, perhaps a hundred and fifty thousand people?"

"You want the army at call?"

"Exactly! but above everything else we want the permission of the Government to deal with the greater delinquents, whether Deputies or not, according to the powers given us by the statute."

The Baron rose and held out his hand. "Thanks, Senator! The Government will consider your suggestions immediately. Be good enough to send in my colleague, the Minister of War."

When the Prefect left the room Roma rose to go.

"You cannot suppose this is very agreeable to me?" she said in an agitated voice.

"Wait! I shall not be long . . . Ah, General Morra! Roma, you know the General, I think. Sit down, both of you. . . . Well, General, you hear of this *levée-en-masse?*"

"I do."

"The Prefect is satisfied that the people are moved by a revolutionary organisation, and he is anxious to know what force we can put at his service to control it."

The General detailed his resources. There were sixteen thousand men always under arms in Rome, and the War Office had called up the old-timers of two successive years— perhaps fifty thousand in all.

"As a Minister of State and your colleague," said the General, "I am at one with you in your desire to safeguard the cause of order and protect public institutions, but as a man and a Roman I cannot but hope that you will not call upon me to act without the conditions required by law."

"Indeed, no," said the Baron; "and in order to make sure that our instructions are carried out with wisdom and humanity, let these be the orders you issue to your staff: First, that in case of disturbance to-morrow night, whether at the Coliseum or elsewhere, the officers must wait for the proper signal from the delegate of police."

"Good!"

"Next, that on receiving the order to fire, the soldiers must be careful that their first volley goes over the heads of the people."

"Excellent!"

"If that does not disperse the crowds, if they throw stones at the soldiers or otherwise resist, the second volley— I see no help for it—the second volley, I say, must be fired at the persons who are leading on the ignorant and deluded mob."

"Ah!"

The General hesitated, and Roma, whose breathing came quick and short, gave him a look of tenderness and gratitude.

"You agree, General Morra?"

"I'm afraid I see no alternative. But if the blood of their leader only infuriates the people, is the third volley . . ."

"That," said the Baron, "is a contingency too terrible to contemplate. My prediction would be that when their leader falls, the poor, misguided people will fly. But in all human enterprises the last word has to be left to destiny. Let us leave it to destiny in the present instance. Adieu, dear General! Be good enough to tell my secretary to send in the Chief of Police."

The Minister of War left the room, and once more Roma rose to go.

"You cannot possibly imagine that a conversation like this . . ." she began, but the Baron only interrupted her again.

"Don't go yet. I shall be finished presently. Angelelli cannot keep me more than a moment. Ah, here is the Commendatore."

The Chief of Police came bowing and bobbing at every step, with the extravagant politeness which differentiates the vulgar man from the well-bred.

"About this meeting at the Coliseum, Commendatore— has any authorisation been asked for it?"

"None whatever, your Excellency."

"Then we may properly regard it as seditious?"

"Quite properly, your Excellency."

"Listen! You will put yourself into communication with the Minister of War immediately. He will place fifty thousand men at the disposition of your Prefect. Choose your delegates carefully. Instruct them well. At the first overt act of resistance, let them give the word to fire. After that, leave everything to the military."

"Quite so, your Excellency."

"Be careful to keep yourself in touch with me until midnight to-morrow. It may be necessary to declare a state of siege, and in that event the royal decree will have to be obtained without delay. Prepare your own staff for a general order. Ask for the use of the cannon of St. Angelo as a signal, and let it be understood that if the gun is fired to-morrow night, every gate of the city is to be closed, every outward train is to be stopped, and every telegraph office is to be put under control. You understand me?"

"Perfectly, Excellency."

"After the signal has been given let no one leave the city, and let no telegraphic message of any kind be despatched. In short, let Rome from that hour onward be entirely under the control of the Government."

"Entirely, your Excellency."

"The military have already received their orders. After the call of the delegate of police, the first volley is to be fired over the heads of the people, and the second at the ringleaders. But if any of these should escape . . ."

The Baron paused, and then repeated in a low tone with the utmost deliberation:

"I say, *if* any of these should escape, Commendatore . . ."

"They shall not escape, your Excellency."

There was a moment of profound silence, in which Roma felt herself to be suffocating, and could scarcely restrain the cry that was rising in her throat.

"Let me go," she said, when the Chief of Police had backed and bowed himself out; but again the Baron pretended to misunderstand her.

"Only one more visitor! I shall be finished in a few minutes," and then Charles Minghelli was shown into the room.

The man's watchful eyes blinked perceptibly as he came

face to face with Roma, but he recovered himself in a moment, and began to brush with his fingers the breast of his frock-coat.

"Sit down, Minghelli. You may speak freely before Donna Roma. You owe your position to her generous influence, you may remember, and she is abreast of all our business. You know all about this meeting at the Coliseum?"

Minghelli bent his head.

"The delegates of police have received the strictest orders not to give the word to the military until an overt act of resistance has been committed. That is necessary as well for the safety of our poor deluded people as for our own credit in the eyes of the world. But an act of rebellion in such a case is a little thing, Mr. Minghelli."

Again Minghelli bent his head.

"A blow, a shot, a shower of stones, and the peace is broken and the delegate is justified."

A third time Minghelli bent his head.

"Unfortunately, in the sorrowful circumstances in which the city is placed, an overt act of resistance is quite sure to be committed."

Minghelli flecked a speck of dust from his spotless cuff and said:

"Quite sure, your Excellency."

There was another moment of profound silence, in which Roma felt her heart beat violently.

"Adieu, Mr. Minghelli. Tell my secretary as you pass out that I wish to dictate a letter."

The letter was to the Minister of Foreign Affairs.

"Dear colleague," dictated the Baron, "I entirely approve of the proposal you have made to the Governments of Europe and America to establish a basis on which anarchists should be suppressed by means of an international net, through which they can hardly escape. My suggestion would be the universal application of the Belgian clause in all existing extradition treaties, whereby persons guilty of regicide may be dealt with as common murderers. In any case please say that the Government of Italy intends to do its duty to the civilised world, and will look to the Governments of other countries to allow it to follow up and arrest the criminals who are attempting to reconstruct society by burying it under ruins."

Notwithstanding all her efforts to appear calm, Roma felt as if she must go out into the streets and scream. Now she knew why she had been sent for. It was in order that the Baron might talk to her in parables—in order that he might show her by means of an object lesson, as palpable as pitiless, what was the impediment which made her marriage with David Rossi impossible.

The marriage could not be celebrated until after eleven days, but the meeting at the Coliseum must take place to-morrow, and as surely as it did so it must result in riot and David Rossi must be shot.

The secretary gathered up his note-book and left the room, and then the Baron turned to Roma with beaming eyes and lips expanding to a smile.

"Finished at last! A thousand apologies, my dear! Twelve o'clock already! Let us go out and lunch some-where."

"Let me go home," said Roma.

She was trembling violently, and as she rose to her feet she swayed a little.

"My dear child! you're not well. Take this glass of water."

"It's nothing. Let me go home."

The Baron walked with her to the head of the staircase.

"I understand you perfectly," she said in a choking voice, "but there is something you have not counted upon, and you are quite mistaken."

And making a great call on her resolution, she threw up her head and walked firmly down the stairs.

Immediately on reaching home she wrote to David Rossi:

"I MUST see you to-night. Where can it be? To-night! Mind, to-night. To-morrow will be too late.   ROMA."

Bruno delivered the note by hand, and brought back an answer:

"DEAREST,—Come to the office at nine o'clock. Sorry I cannot go to you. It is impossible.   D. R.

"P.S.—You have converted Bruno, and he would die for you. As for the 'little Roman boy,' he is in the seventh heaven over your presents, and says he must go up to Trinità de' Monti to begin work at once."

THE ETERNAL CITY

IV

THE office of the *Sunrise* at nine o'clock that night tingled with excitement. A supplement had already gone to press, and the machines in the basement were working rapidly. In the business office on the first floor people were constantly coming and going, and the footsteps on the stairs of the composing-room sounded through the walls like the irregular beat of a hammer.

The door of the editor's room was frequently swinging open, as reporters with reports, messengers with telegrams, and boys with proofs came in and laid them on the desk at which the sub-editor sat at work.

David Rossi stood by his desk at the farther end of the room. This was the last night of his editorship of the *Sunrise,* and by various silent artifices the staff were showing their sympathy with the man who had made the paper and was forced to leave it.

The excitement within the office of the *Sunrise* corresponded to the commotion outside. The city was in a ferment, and from time to time unknown persons, the spontaneous reporters of tumultuous days, were brought in from the outer office to give the editor the latest news of the night. Another trainful of people had arrived from Milan! Still another from Bologna and Carrara! The storm was growing! Soon would be heard the crash of war! Their faces were eager and their tone was one of triumph. They pitched their voices high, so as to be heard above the reverberation of the machines, whose deep thud in the rooms below made the walls vibrate like the side of a ship at sea.

David Rossi did not catch the contagion of their joy. At every fresh announcement his face clouded. The unofficial head of the surging and straining democracy, which was filling itself hourly with hopes and dreams, was unhappy and perplexed. He was trying to write his last message to his people, and he could not get it clear because his own mind was confused.

" *Romans,*" he wrote first, " *your rulers are preparing to resist your right of meeting, and you will have nothing to oppose to the muskets and bayonets of their soldiers but the bare breasts of a brave but peaceful people. No matter. Fifty, a hundred, five hundred of you killed at the first volley, and the day is won! The reactionary Government of Italy —all the reactionary Governments of Europe—will be borne down by the righteous indignation of the world."*

It would not do! He had no right to lead the people to certain slaughter, and he tore up his manifesto and began again.

" *Romans,*" he wrote the second time, " *when reforms cannot be effected without the spilling of blood, the time for them has not yet come, and it is the duty of a brave and peaceful people to wait for the silent operation of natural law and the mighty help of moral forces. Therefore at the eleventh hour I call upon you, in the names of your wives and children . . ."*

It was impossible! The people would think he was afraid, and the opportune moment would be lost.

One man in the office of the *Sunrise* was entirely outside the circle of its electric currents. This was the former day-editor, who had been appointed by the proprietors to take Rossi's place, and was now walking about with a silk hat on his head, taking note of everything and exercising a premature and gratuitous supervision.

David Rossi was tearing up the second of his manifestoes when this person came to say that a lady in the outer office was asking to see him.

" Show her into the private waiting-room," said Rossi.

" But may I suggest," said the man, " that considering who the lady is, it would perhaps be better to see her elsewhere?"

" Show her into the private room, sir," said Rossi, and the man shrugged his shoulders and disappeared.

As David Rossi opened the door of a small room at his right hand, something rustled lightly in the corridor outside, and a moment afterwards Roma glided into his arms. She was pale and nervous, and after a moment she began to cry.

" Dear one," said Rossi, pressing her head against his breast, " what has happened? Tell me! Something has frightened you. You look anxious."

" No wonder," she said, and then she told him of her summons to the Palazzo Braschi, and of the business she saw done there.

There was to be a riot at the meeting at the Coliseum, because, if need be, the Government itself would provoke violence. The object was to kill *him*, not the people, and if he stayed in Rome until to-morrow night there would be no possibility of escape.

"You must fly," she said. "You are the victim marked out by all these preparations—you, you, nobody but you."

"It is the best news I've heard for days," he said. "If I am the only one who runs a risk . . ."

"Risk! My dearest, don't you understand? Your life is aimed at, and you must fly before it is quite impossible."

"It is already impossible," he answered.

He drew off one of her white gloves and kissed her finger-tips. "My dear one," he said, "if there were nothing else to think of, do you suppose I could go away and leave you behind me? That is just what somebody expected me to do when he permitted you to witness his preparations. But he was mistaken. I cannot and I will not leave you."

Her pale face was suddenly overspread by a burning blush, and she threw both arms about his neck.

"Very well," she said, "I will go with you."

"Darling!" he cried, and he clasped her to his breast again. "But no! That is impossible also. Our marriage cannot take place for ten days."

"No matter! I'll go without it."

"My dear child, you don't know what you are saying. You are too good, too pure . . ."

"Hush! Our marriage is nothing to anybody but ourselves, and if we choose to go without it . . ."

"My dear girl!"

"I can't hear you," she said. Loosening her hands from his neck, she had covered her ears.

"Dearest, I know what you are thinking of, but it must not be."

"I can't hear a word you're saying," she said, beating her hands over her ears. "I'm ready to go now, this very minute—and if you don't take me, it is because you love other things better than you love me."

"My darling, don't tempt me. If you only knew what it costs me . . . but I would rather die . . ."

"I don't want you to die. That's just it! I want you to live, and I am willing to risk everything—everything . . ."

Her warm and lovely form was quivering in his arms, and his heart was labouring wildly.

"Dearest," he whispered over her head, "you are so

good, so pure, so noble, that you don't know how evil tongues can wag at a woman because she is brave and true. But I must remember my mother—and if your poor father is to rest in his grave . . ."

His voice broke and he stopped.

"See how much I love you," he whispered again, "when I would rather lose you than see you lower yourself in your own esteem. . . . And then think of my people! my poor people who trust me and look up to me so much more than I deserve. I called them and they have come. They are here now, tens of thousands of them. And they will be here to-morrow wherever I may be. Shall I desert them in their hour of need, thinking of my own safety, my own happiness? No! You cannot wish it! You do not wish it! I know you too well!"

She lifted her head from his breast. "You are right," she said. "You must stay."

"My sweet girl!"

"Can you ever forgive me for being frightened at the first note of danger and telling you to fly?"

"I will always love you for it."

"And you will never think the worse of me for offering to go with you?"

"I will love you for that too."

"I must be brave," she said, drawing herself up proudly, though her lips were trembling, her voice was breaking, and her eyes were wet. "Whether you are right or wrong in what you are doing it is not for me to decide, but if your heart tells you to do it you *must* do it, and I must be your soldier, ready and waiting for my captain's call."

"My brave girl!"

"It is not for nothing that I am my father's daughter. *He* risked everything and so will I, and if they come to me to-morrow night and say that . . . that you . . . that you are . . ."

The proud face had fallen on his breast again. But after a moment it was raised afresh, and then it was shining all over.

"That's right! How beautiful your face is when it smiles, Roma! Roma, do you know what I'm going to do when this is all over? I'm going to spend my life in making you smile all the time."

She gave him a sudden kiss, and then broke out of his arms.

"I must be going. I've stayed too long. I may not see you before the meeting, but I won't say 'good-bye.' I've thought of something, and now I know what I'm going to do."

"What is it?"

"Don't ask me."

She opened the door.

"Come to me to-morrow night—I shall expect you," she whispered, and waving her glove to him over her head she disappeared from the room.

He stood a moment where she had left him, trying to think what she intended to do, and then he returned to his desk in the outer office. His successor was there, looking sour and stubborn.

"Mr. Rossi," he said, "this afternoon I was told at the Press Club that the authorities were watching for a plausible excuse for suppressing the paper; and considering the relations of this lady to the Minister of the Interior, and the danger of spies . . ."

"Listen to this carefully, sir," interrupted Rossi. "When you come into possession of the chair I occupy, you may do as you think well, but to-night it is mine, and I shall conduct the paper as I please."

"Still, you will allow me to say . . ."

"Not one word."

"Permit me to protest . . ."

"Leave the room immediately."

When the man was gone, David Rossi wrote a third and last version of his manifesto:

"ROMANS.—Have no fear. Do not allow yourselves to be terrified by the military preparations of your Government. Believe a man who has never deceived you—the soldiers will not fire upon the people! Violate no law. Assail no enemy. Respect property. Above all, respect life. Do not allow yourself to be pushed into the doctrine of physical force. If any man tries to provoke violence, think him an agent of your enemies and pay no heed. Be brave, be strong, be patient, and to-morrow night you will send up such a cry as will ring throughout the world. Romans, remember your fathers and be great."

Rossi was handing his manuscript to the sub-editor, that it might be sent upstairs, when all at once the air seemed to become empty and the world to stand still. The machine in the basement had ceased to work. There was a momentary pause, such as comes on a steamship at sea when the engines are suddenly stopped, and then a sound of frightened voices and the noise of hurrying feet. Somebody ran along the corridor outside and rapped sharply at the door.

At the next moment the door opened and four men entered the room. One of them was an inspector, another was a delegate, and the others were policemen in plain clothes.

" The journal is sequestered," said the inspector to David Rossi. And turning to one of his men, he said, " Go up to the composing-room and superintend the distribution of the type."

" Allow no one to leave the building," said the delegate to the other policeman.

" Gentlemen," said the inspector, " we are charged to make a perquisition, and must ask you for the keys of your desks."

" What is this? " said the delegate, taking the manifesto out of Rossi's fingers, and proceeding to read it.

At that moment the editor-elect came rushing into the room with a face like the rising sun.

" I demand to see a list of the things sequestered," he cried.

" You shall do so at the police-office," said the inspector.

" Does that mean that we are all arrested? "

" Not all. The Honourable Rossi, being a Deputy, is at liberty to leave."

" Thought as much," said the new editor, with a contemptuous snort. And turning to Rossi, and showing his teeth in a bitter smile, he said: " What did I say would happen? Has it followed quickly enough to satisfy you? "

The inspector and the delegate opened the editors' desks and were rummaging among their papers when David Rossi put on his hat and went home.

At the door of the lodge the old Garibaldian was waiting in obvious excitement.

" Old John has been here, sir," he said. " Something to tell you. Wouldn't tell me. But Bruno got it out of him at last. Must be something serious, for the big booby has been drinking ever since. Hear him in the café, sir. I'll send him up."

Half-an-hour afterwards Bruno staggered into Rossi's room. He had a tearful look in his drink-deadened eyes, and was clearly struggling with a desire to put his arms about Rossi's neck and weep over him.

"D'ye know wha'?" he mumbled in a maudlin voice. "Ole Vampire is a villain! Ole John—'member ole John?—well, ole John heard his grandson, the d'ective, say that if you go to the Coliseum to-morrow night . . ."

"I know all about it, Bruno. You may go to bed."

"Stop a minute, sir," said Bruno, with a melancholy smile. "You don't unnerstand. They're going t' shoot you. See? Ole John—'member ole John? Well, ole John . . ."

"I know, Bruno. But I'm going nevertheless."

Bruno fought with the vapour in his brain, and said: "You don' mean t' say you inten' t' let yourself be a target . . ."

"That's what I do mean, Bruno."

Bruno burst into a loud laugh. "Well, I'll be . . . wha' the devil . . . But you sha'n't go. "I'll . . . I'll see you damned first!"

"You're drunk, Bruno. Go and put yourself to bed."

The drink-deadened eyes flashed, and to grief succeeded rage. "Pu' mysel t' bed! D'ye know wha' I'd like t' do t' you for t' nex' twenty-four hours? I'd jus' like—yes, by Bacchus—I'd jus' like to punch you in t' belly and put *you t'* bed."

And straightening himself up with drunken dignity, Bruno stalked out of the room.

The Baron Bonelli in the Piazza Leone was rising from his late and solitary dinner when Felice entered the shaded dining-room and handed him a letter from Roma. It ran:

"This is to let you know that I intend to be present at the meeting in the Coliseum to-morrow night. Therefore, if any shots are to be fired by the soldiers at the crowd or their leader, you will know beforehand that they must also be fired at me."

As the Baron held the letter under the red shade of the lamp, the usual immobility of his icy face gave way to a rapturous expression.

"The woman is magnificent! And worth fighting for to the bitter end."

Then, turning to Felice, he told the man to ring up the Commendatore Angelelli and tell him to send for Minghelli without delay.

V

NEXT day began with heavy clouds lying low over the city, a cold wind coming down from the mountains, and the rumbling of distant thunder. Nevertheless the people who had come to Rome for the demonstration at the Coliseum seemed to be in the streets the whole day long. From early morning they gathered in the Piazza Navona, inquired for David Rossi, stood by the fountains, and looked up at his windows.

As the day wore on the crowds increased.

All the public squares seemed to be full of motley, ill-clad, ill-nourished, but formidable multitudes. Towards evening the tradesmen began to shut up their shops, and a regiment of cavalry paraded the principal streets with a band that played the royal march.

Meantime, the leader, to whom thousands were looking up, was miserable and alone. He had cried " Peace," but the perils of protest were so many and so near. A blow, a push, a quarrel at a street corner, and God knows what might happen!

Elena came with his coffee. The timid creature kept looking at him out of her liquid eyes as if struggling with a desire to speak, but when she did so it was only on indifferent subjects.

Bruno had got up with a headache and gone off to work. Little Joseph was very trying this morning, and she had threatened to whip him.

Her father had been upstairs to say that countless people were asking for the Deputy, and he wished to know if anybody was to come up.

" Tell him I wish to be quite alone to-day," said Rossi, and then the soft voice ceased, and the timid creature went out with a guilty look.

Like a man who is going on a long and perilous journey, David Rossi spent the morning in arranging his affairs. He looked over his letters and destroyed most of them. The letters from Roma were hard to burn, but he read each of them again, as if trying to stamp their words and characters on his brain, and with a deep sigh he committed them to the flames.

It was twelve o'clock by this time, and Francesca, in her red cotton handkerchief, brought up his lunch. The good old thing looked at him with a comical expression of pity on her wrinkled face, and he knew that Bruno had told his story.

"Come now, my son! Put away your papers and get something on your stomach. People eat even if they're going to the gallows, you know."

After lunch Rossi called upstairs for Joseph, and the shock-headed little cub was brought down, with his wet eyes twinkling and his petted lip beginning to smile.

"Joseph has been naughty, Uncle David," said Elena. "He is crying for the clothes Donna Roma gave him, and he says he must go out because it is his birthday."

"Does a man cry when he is seven?" said Uncle David.

Thereupon Joseph, keeping his eyes upon his mother, whispered something in Uncle David's ear, and straightway the gorgeous garments were produced.

"Joseph will promise not to go out to-day; won't you, Joseph?"

And Joseph rolled his fists into his eyes and was understood to say "Yes."

At four o'clock Bruno came home, looking grim and resolute.

"I was pretty drunk last night, sir," he said, "but if there's shooting to be done this evening I'm going to be there."

The time came for the two men to go, and everybody saw them to the door.

"Adieu!" said Rossi. "Thank you for all you've done for me, and may God bless you! Take care of my little Roman boy. Kiss me, Joseph! Again! For the last time! Adieu!"

"Ah, God is a good old saint. He'll take care of you, my son," said the old woman.

"Adieu, Uncle David! Adieu, papa!" cried Joseph over the banisters, and the brave little voice, with its manly falsetto, was the last the men heard as they descended the stairs.

The Piazza del Popolo was densely crowded, and seemed to be twice as large as usual. Bruno elbowed a way through for himself and Rossi until they came to the obelisk in the centre of the great circle. On the steps of the obelisk a company of artillery was stationed with a piece of cannon which commanded the three principal thoroughfares of the city, the Corso, the Ripetta, and the Babunio, which branch off from that centre like the ribs from the handle of a fan. Without taking notice of the soldiers, the people ranged themselves in order and prepared for their procession. At the ringing of Ave Maria the great crowd linked in files and turned their faces towards the Corso.

Bruno walked first, carrying from his stalwart breast a standard, on which was inscribed, under the title of the "Republic of Man," the words, "Give us this day our daily bread." Rossi had meant to walk immediately behind Bruno, but he found himself encircled by a group of his followers. No sovereign was ever surrounded by more watchful guards.

By the spontaneous consent of the public, traffic in the street was suspended, and crowds of the people of the city had turned out to look on. The four tiers of the Pincian Hill were packed with spectators, and every window and balcony in the Corso was filled with faces. All the shops were shut, and many of them were barricaded within and without. A regiment of infantry was ranged along the edge of the pavement, and the people passed between two lines of rifles.

As the procession went on it was constantly augmented, and the column, which had been four abreast when it started from the Popolo, was eight abreast before it reached the end of the Corso. There were no bands of music, and there was no singing, but at intervals some one at the head of the procession would begin to clap, and then the clapping of hands would run down the street like the rattle of musketry.

Going up the narrow streets beyond the Venezia, the people passed into the Forum—out of the living city of the present into the dead city of the past, with its desolation and its silence, its chaos of broken columns and cornices, of corbels and capitals, of wells and watercourses, lying in the waste where they had been left by the earthquake which had passed over them, the earthquake of the ages—and so on through the arch of Titus to the meeting-place in the Coliseum.

All this time David Rossi's restless eyes had passed nervously from side to side. Coming down the Corso he had been dimly conscious of eyes looking at him from windows and balconies. He was struggling to be calm and firm, but he was in a furnace of dread, and beneath his breath he was praying from time to time that God would prevent accident and avert bloodshed. He was also praying for strength of spirit and feeling like a guilty coward. His face was deadly pale, the fire within seemed to consume the grosser senses, and he walked along like a man in a dream.

VI

HALF-AN-HOUR before Ave Maria, Roma had put on an inconspicuous cloak, a plain hat, and a dark veil, and walked down to the Coliseum. Soldiers were stationed on all the high ground about the circus, and large numbers of persons were already assembled inside. The people were poor and ill-clad, and they smelt of garlic and uncleanness. "*His* people, though," thought Roma, and so she conquered her repulsion.

Three tiers encircle the walls of the Coliseum, like the galleries of a great theatre, and the lowest of these was occupied by a regiment of Carabineers. There was some banter and chaff at the expense of the soldiers, but the people were serious for all that, and the excitement beneath their jesting was deep and strong.

The low cloud which had hung over the city from early morning seemed to lie like a roof over the topmost circle of the amphitheatre, and as night came on the pit below grew dark and chill. Then torches were lit and put in prominent places—long pitch sticks covered with rags or brown paper. The people were patient and good-humoured, but to beguile the tedium of waiting they sang songs. They were songs of labour chiefly, but one man started the *Te Deum*, and the rest joined in with one voice. It was like the noise the sea makes on a heavy day when it breaks on a bank of sand.

After a while there was a deep sound from outside. The procession was approaching. It came on like a great tidal wave and flowed into the vast place in the gathering darkness with the light of a hundred fresh torches.

In less than half-an-hour the ruined amphitheatre was a moving mass of heads from the ground to its upmost storey. Long sinuous trails of blue smoke swept across the people's faces, and the great brown mass of circular stones was lit up in fitful gleams.

Roma was lifted off her feet by the breaker of human beings that surged around. At one moment she was conscious of some one behind who was pressing the people back and making room for her. At the next moment she was aware that through the multitudinous murmur of voices that rumbled as in a vault somebody near her was trying to speak.

The speaking ceased and there was a sharp crackle of applause which had the effect of producing silence. In this silence another voice, a clear, loud, vibrating voice, said, "Romans and brothers," and then there was a prolonged shout of recognition from ten thousand throats.

In a moment a dozen torches were handed up, and the speaker was in a circle of light and could be seen by all. It was Rossi. He was standing bareheaded on a stone, with a face of unusual paleness. He was wearing the loose cloak of the common people of Rome, thrown across his breast and shoulder. Bruno stood by his left side holding a standard above their heads. At his right hand were two other men who partly concealed him from the crowd. Roma found herself immediately below them, and within two or three paces.

After a moment the shouting died down, and there was no sound in the vast place but a soft, quick, indrawn hiss that was like the palpitating breath of an immense flock of sheep. Then Rossi began again.

"First and foremost," he said, "let me call on you to preserve the peace. One false step to-night and all is lost. Our enemies would like to fix on us the name of rebels. Rebels against whom? There is no rebellion except rebellion against the people. The people are the true sovereigns, and the only rebels are the classes who oppress them."

A murmur of assent broke from the crowd. Rossi paused, and looked around at the soldiers.

"Romans," he said, "do not let the armed rebels of the State provoke you to violence. It is to their interest to do so. Defeat them. You have come here in the face of their rifles and bayonets to show that you are not afraid of death. But I ask you to be afraid of doing an unrighteous thing. It is on my responsibility that you are here, and it would be an undying remorse to me if through any fault of yours one drop of blood were shed.

"I call on you as earnestly as if my nearest and dearest were among you, liable to be shot down by the rifles of the military, not to give any excuse for violence."

Roma turned to look at the soldiers. As far as she

could see in the uncertain light, they were standing passively in their circle, with their rifles by their sides.

"Romans," said Rossi again, "a month ago we protested against an iniquitous tax on the first necessary of life. The answer is sixty thousand men in arms around us. Therefore we are here to-night to appeal to the mightiest force on earth, mightier than any army, more powerful than any parliament, more absolute than any king—the force of moral sympathy and public opinion throughout the world."

At this there were shouts of "Bravo!" and some clapping of hands.

"Romans, if your bread is moistened by tears to-day, think of the power of suffering and be strong. Think of the history of these old walls. Think of the words of Christ, 'Which of the prophets have not your fathers stoned?' The prophets of humanity have all been martyrs, and God has marked you out to be the martyr nation of the world. Suffering is the sacred flame that sanctifies the human soul. Pray to God for strength to suffer, and He will bless you from the heights of Heaven."

People were weeping on every hand.

"Brothers, you are hungry, and I say these things to you with a beating heart. Your children are starving, and I swear before God that from this day forward I will starve with them. If I have eaten two meals a day hitherto, for the future I will eat but one. But leave it to the powers that are over you to do their worst. If they imprison you for resisting their tyrannies, others will take your place. If they kill your leader, God will raise up another who will be stronger than he. Swear to me in this old Coliseum, sacred to the martyrs, that, come what may, you will not yield to injustice and wrong."

There was something in Rossi's face at that last moment that seemed to transcend the natural man. He raised his right arm over his head and in a loud voice cried, "Swear!"

The people took the oath with uplifted hands and a great shout. It was terrible.

Rossi stepped down, and the excitement was overwhelming. The vast crowd seemed to toss to and fro under the smoking lights like a tumultuous sea. The simple-hearted Roman populace could not contain themselves.

The crowd began to break up, and the people went off singing. Rossi and his group of friends had disappeared when Roma turned to go. She found herself weeping and singing, too, but for another reason. The danger was passed, and all was over!

Going out by one of the arches, she was conscious of some-body walking beside her. Presently a voice said:

"You don't recognise me in the darkness, Donna Roma?"

It was Charles Minghelli. He had been told to take care of her. Could he offer her his escort home?

"No, thank you," she replied, and she was surprised at herself that she experienced no repulsion.

Her heart was light, a great weight had been lifted away, and she felt a large and generous charity. At the top of the hill she found a cab, and as it dipped down the broad avenue that leads out of the circle of the dead centuries into the world of living men, she turned and looked back at the Coli-seum. It was like a dream. The moving lights—the shadows of great heads on the grim old walls—the surging crowds—the cheers from hoarse throats. But the tinkle of the electric tram brought her back to reality, and then she noticed that it had begun to snow.

.   .   .   .

Bruno ploughed a way for David Rossi, and they reached home at last.

Elena was standing at the door of David Rossi's rooms, with an agitated face.

"Have you seen anything of Joseph?" she asked.

"Joseph?"

"I opened the window to look if you were coming, and in a moment he was gone. On a night like this, too, when it isn't too safe for anybody to be in the streets."

"Has he still got the clothes on?" said Bruno.

"Yes, and the naughty boy has broken his promise and must be whipped."

The men looked into each other's faces.

"Donna Roma?" said Rossi.

"I'll go and see," said Bruno.

"I must have a rod, whatever you say. I really must!" said Elena.

VII

ROMA reached home in a glow of joy. She told herself that Rossi would come to her in obedience to her command. He must dine with her to-night. Seven was now striking on all the clocks outside, and to give him time to arrive she put back the dinner until eight. Her aunt would dine in her own room, so they would be quite alone. The conventions of life had fallen absolutely away, and she considered them no more.

Meantime she must dress and perhaps take a bath. A certain sense of soiling which she could not conquer had followed her up from that glorious meeting. She felt a little ashamed of it, but it was there, and though she told herself " They were *his* people, poor things," she was glad to take off the clothes she had worn at the Coliseum.

She combed out the curls of her glossy black hair, put herself into a loose tea gown and red slippers, took one backward glance at herself in the glass, and then going into the drawing-room, she stood by the window to dream and wait. The snow still fell in thin flakes, but the city was humming on, and the piazza down below was full of people.

After a while the electric bell of the outer door was rung, and her heart beat against her breast. " It's he," she thought, and in the exquisite tumult of the moment she lifted her arms and turned to meet him.

But when the door was opened it was the Baron Bonelli who was shown into the room. He was in evening dress, with black tie and studs which had a chilling effect, and his manner was as cold and calm as usual.

" I regret," he said, " that we must enter on a painful interview."

" As you please," she answered, and sitting on a stool by the fire she rested her elbows on her knees, and looked straight before her.

" Your letter of last night, my dear, produced the result you desired. I sent for Commendatore Angelelli, invented some plausible excuses, and reversed my orders. I also sent for Minghelli and told him to take care of you on your reckless errand. The matter has thus far ended as you wished, and I trust you are satisfied."

She nodded her head without turning round, and bore herself with a certain air of defiance.

" But it is necessary that we should come to an understanding," he continued. " You have driven me hard, my child. With all the tenderness and sympathy possible, I am compelled to speak plainly. I wished to spare your feelings. You will not permit me to do so."

The incisiveness of his speech cut the air like ice dropping from a glacier, and Roma felt herself turning pale with a sense of something fearful whirling around her.

"According to your own plans, Rossi is to marry you within a week, although a month ago he spoke of you in public as an unworthy woman. Will you be good enough to tell me how this miracle has come to pass?"

She laughed, and tried to carry herself bravely.

"If it is a miracle, how can I explain it?" she said.

"Then permit me to do so. He is going to marry you because he no longer thinks as he thought a month ago; because he believes he was wrong in what he said, and would like to wipe it out entirely."

"He is going to marry me because he loves me," she answered hotly; "that's why he is going to marry me."

At the next moment a faintness came over her, and a misty vapour flashed before her sight. In her anger she had torn open a secret place in her own heart, and something in the past of her life seemed to escape as from a tomb.

"Then you have not told him?" said the Baron in so low a voice that he could scarcely be heard.

"Told him what?" she said.

"The truth—the fact."

She caught her breath and was silent.

"My child, you are doing wrong. There is a secret between you already. That is a bad basis to begin life upon, and the love that is raised on it will be a house built on the sand."

Her heart was beating violently, but she turned on him with a burning glance.

"What do you mean?" she said, while the colour increased in her cheeks and forehead. "I am a good woman. You know I am."

"To me, yes! The best woman in the world."

She had risen to her feet, and was standing by the chimney-piece.

"Understand me, my child," he said affectionately. "When I say you are doing wrong, it is only in keeping a secret from the man you intend to marry. Between you and me . . . there is no secret."

She looked at him with haggard eyes.

"For me you are everything that is sweet and good, but

for another who knows? When a man is about to marry a woman, there is one thing he can never forgive. Need I say what that is?"

The glow that had suffused her face changed to the pallor of marble, and she turned to the Baron and stood over him with the majesty of a statue.

"Is it you that tell me this?" she said. "You—you? Can a woman never be allowed to forget? Must the fault of another follow her all her life? Oh, it is cruel! It is merciless. . . . But no matter!" she said in another voice; and turning away from him she added, as if speaking to herself: "He believes everything I tell him. Why should I trouble?"

The Baron followed her with a look that pierced to the depths of her soul.

"Then you have told him a falsehood?" he said.

She pressed her lips together and made no answer.

"That was foolish. By-and-by somebody may come along who will tell him the truth."

"What can any one tell him that he has not heard already? He has heard everything, and put it all behind his back."

"Could nobody bring conviction to his mind? Nobody whatever? Not even one who had no interest in slandering you?"

"You don't mean that you . . ."

"Why not? He has come between us. What could be more natural than that I should tell him so?"

A look of dismay came over her face, and it was followed by an expression of terror.

"But you wouldn't do that," she stammered. "You couldn't do it. It is impossible. You are only trying me."

His face remained perfectly passive, and she seized him by the arm.

"Think! Only think! You would do no good for yourself. You might stop the marriage—yes! But you wouldn't carry out your political purpose. You couldn't! And while you would do no good for yourself, think of the harm you would do for me. He loves me, and you would hurt his beautiful faith in me, and I should die of grief and shame."

"You are cruel, my child," said the Baron, speaking with dignity. "You think *I* am hard and unrelenting, but *you* are selfish and cruel. You are so concerned about your own feelings that you don't even suspect that perhaps you are wounding mine."

"Ah, yes, it is too bad," she said, dropping to her knees at his feet. "After all, you have been very good to me thus far, and it was partly my own fault if matters ended as they did. Yes, I confess it. I was vain and proud. I wanted all the world. And when you gave me everything, being so tied yourself, I thought I might forgive you. . . . But I was wrong —I was to blame—nothing in the world could excuse you— I saw that the moment afterwards. I really hadn't thought at all until then—but then my soul awoke. And then . . ."

She turned her head aside that he might not see her face.

"And then love came, and I was like a woman who had married a man thirty years older than herself—married without love—just for the sake of her pride and vanity. But love, real love, drove all that away. It is gone now; I only wish to lead a good life, however simple and humble it may be. Let me do so! . . . Do not take him away from me! Do not . . ."

She stammered and stopped, with a sudden consciousness of what she was doing.

"What a fool I am!" she said, leaping to her feet. "What fresh story can you tell him that he is likely to believe?"

"I can tell him that, according to the law of nature and of reason, you belong to me," said the Baron.

"Very well! It will be your word against mine, will it not? Tell him, and he will fling your insult in your face."

The Baron rose and began to walk about the room, and there were some moments in which nothing could be heard but the slight creaking of his patent-leather boots. Then he said:

"In that case I should be compelled to challenge him."

"Challenge him!" She repeated the words with scorn. "Is it likely? Do you forget that duelling is a crime, that you are a Minister, that you would have to resign, and expose yourself to penalties?"

"If a man insults me grievously in my affections and my honour, I will challenge him," said the Baron.

"But he will not fight—it would be contrary to his principles," said Roma.

"In that event he will never be able to lift his head in Italy again. But make no mistake cn that point, my child.

The man who is told that the woman he is going to marry is secretly the wife of another must either believe it or he must not. If he believes it, he casts her off for ever. If he does not believe it, he fights for her name and his own honour. If he does neither, he is not a man."

Roma had returned to the stool, and was resting her elbows on her knees and gazing into the fire.

"Have you thought of that?" said the Baron. "If the man fights a duel, it will be in defence of what you have told him. In the blindness of his belief in your word he will be ready to risk his life for it. Are you going to stand by and see him fight for a lie?"

Roma hid her face in her hands.

"Say he is wounded—it will be for a lie! Say he wounds his adversary—that will be for a lie too! Say that David Rossi kills me—what then? He must fly from Italy, and his career is at an end. If he is alone, he is a miserable exile who has earned what he may not enjoy. If you are with him, you are both miserable, for a lie stands between you. Every hour of your life is poisoned by the secret you cannot share with him. You are afraid of blurting it out in your sleep. At last you go to him and confess everything. What then? The idol he worshipped has turned to clay. What he thought an act of retribution is a crime. The dead man had told the truth, and he committed murder on the word of a woman who was a deceiver—a drab."

Roma raised her hands to her head as if to avert a blow.

"Stop! stop!" she cried in a choking voice, and lifting her face, distorted with suffering, tears rose in her eyes. To see Roma cry touched the only tenderness of which his iron nature was capable. He patted the beautiful head at his feet, and said in a caressing tone:

"Why will you make me seem so hard, my child? There is really no need to talk of these things. They will not occur. How can I have any desire to degrade you since I must degrade myself at the same time? I have no wish to tell any one the secret which belongs only to you and me. In that matter you were not to blame either. It was all my doing. I was sweltering under the shameful law which tied me to a dead body, and I tried to attach you to me. And then your beauty—your loveliness . . ."

At that moment Felice announced Commendatore Angelelli. Roma walked over to the window and leaned her face against the glass. Snow was still falling, and there were some rumblings of thunder. Sheets of light shone here and there in the darkness, but the world outside was dark and drear. Would David Rossi come to-night? She almost hoped he would not.

VIII

BEHIND her the Prime Minister, who had apologised for turning her house into a temporary Ministry of the Interior, was talking to his Chief of Police.

"You were there yourself?"

"I was, Excellency. I went up into a high part and looked down. It was a strange and wild sight."

"How many would there be?"

"Impossible to guess. Inside and outside, Romans, country people, perhaps a hundred thousand."

"And Rossi's speech?"

"The usual appeal to the passions of the people, Excellency. An extraordinary exhibition of the art of flying between wind and water. We couldn't have found a word that was distinctly seditious, even if we hadn't had your Excellency's order to let the man go on."

"You have stopped the telegraph wires?"

"Yes."

"When the meeting was over, Rossi went home?"

"He did, Excellency."

"And the hundred thousand?"

"In their excitement they began to sing and to march through the streets. They are still doing so. After going down to the Piazza Navona, they are coming up by the Piazza del Popolo and along the Babuino with banners and torches."

"Men only?"

"Men, women, and children."

"You would say that their attitude is threatening?"

"Distinctly threatening, your Excellency."

"Let your delegates give the legal warning and say that the gathering of great mobs at this hour will be regarded as open rebellion. Allow three minutes' grace for the sake of the women and children, and then . . . let the military do their duty."

"Quite so, your Excellency."

" After that you may carry out the instructions I gave you yesterday."

" Certainly, your Excellency."

" Keep in touch with all the leaders. Some of them will find that the air of Rome is a little dangerous to their health to-night, and may wish to fly to Switzerland or England, where it would be impossible to follow them."

Roma heard behind her the thin cackle as of a hen over her nest, which always came when Angelelli laughed.

" Their meeting itself was illegal, and our license has been abused."

" Grossly abused, your Excellency."

" The action of the Government was too conciliatory, and has rendered them audacious, but the new law is clear in prohibiting the carrying of seditious flags and emblems."

" We'll deal with them according to Articles 134 and 252 of the Penal Code, your Excellency."

" You can go. But come back immediately if anything happens. I must remain here for the present, and in case of riot I may have to send you to the King."

Angelelli's thin voice fell to a whisper of awe at the mention of Majesty, and after a moment he bowed and backed out of the room.

Roma did not turn round, and the Minister, who had touched the bell and called for pen and paper, spoke to her from behind.

" I daresay you thought I was hard and inhuman at the Palazzo Braschi yesterday, but I was really very merciful. In letting you see the preparations to enclose your friend as in a net, I merely wished you to warn him to fly from the country. He has not done so, and now he must take the consequences."

Felice brought the writing materials, and the Baron sat down at the table. There was a long silence in which nothing could be heard but the scratching of the Minister's pen, the snoring of the poodle, and the deadened sound through the wall of the Countess's testy voice scolding Natalina.

Roma stepped into the boudoir. The room was dark, and from its unlit windows she could see more plainly into the streets. Masses of shadow lay around, but the untrodden steps were white with thin snow, and the piazza were alive with black figures which moved on the damp ground like worms on an upturned sod.

THE PRIME MINISTER

She was leaning her hot forehead against the glass and looking out with haggard eyes, when a deep rumble as of a great multitude came from below. The noise quickly increased to a loud uproar, with shouts, songs, whistles, and shrill sounds blown out of door-keys. Before she was aware of his presence the Baron was standing behind her, between the window and the pedestal with the plaster bust of Rossi.

"Listen to them," he said. "The proletariat indeed! . . . And this is the flock of bipeds to whom men in their senses would have us throw the treasures of civilisation and hand over the delicate machinery of government."

He laughed bitterly, and drew back the curtain with an impatient hand.

"Democracy! *Christian* Democracy! *Vox Populi vox Dei!* The sovereignty and infallibility of the people! Pshaw! I would as soon believe in the infallibility of the Pope!"

The crowds increased in the piazza until the triangular space looked like the rapids of a swollen river, and the noise that came up from it was like the noise of falling cliffs and uprooted trees.

"Fools! Rabble! Too ignorant to know what you really want, and at the mercy of every rascal who sows the wind and leaves you to reap the whirlwind."

Roma crept away from the Baron with a sense of physical repulsion, and at the next moment, from the other window, she heard the blast of a trumpet. A dreadful silence followed the trumpet blast, and then a clear voice cried:

"In the name of the law I command you to disperse."

It was the voice of a delegate of the police. Roma could see the man on the lowest stage of the steps with his tricoloured scarf of office about him. A second blast came from the trumpet, and again the delegate cried:

"In the name of the law I command you to disperse."

At that moment somebody cried, "Long live the Republic of Man!" and there was great cheering. In the midst of the cheering the trumpet sounded a third time, and then a loud voice cried "Fire!"

At the next moment a volley was fired from somewhere, a cloud of white smoke was coiling in front of the window at which Roma stood, and women and children in the vagueness below were uttering acute cries.

"Oh! oh! oh!"

211

"Don't be afraid, my child. Nothing has happened yet. The police had orders to fire first over the people's heads."

In her fear and agitation Roma ran back to the outer room, and a moment afterwards Angelelli opened the door and stood face to face with her.

"What have you done?" she demanded.

"An unfortunate incident, Excellency," said Angelelli, as the Baron appeared. "After the warning of the delegate the mob laughed and threw stones, and the Carabineers fired. They were in the piazza and fired up the steps."

"Well?"

"Unluckily there were a few persons on the upper flights at the moment, and some of them are wounded, and a child is dead."

Roma muttered a low moan and sank on to the stool.

"Whose child is it?"

"We don't yet know, but the father is there, and he is raging like a madman, and unless he is arrested he will provoke the people to frenzy, and there will be riot and insurrection."

The Baron took from the table a letter he had written and sealed.

"Take this to the Quirinal instantly. Ask for an immediate audience with the King. When you receive his written reply, call up the Minister of War and say you have the royal decree to declare a state of siege."

Angelelli was going out hurriedly.

"Wait! Send to the Piazza Navona and arrest Rossi. Be careful! You will arrest the Deputy under Articles 134 and 252 on a charge of using the great influence he has acquired over the people to urge the masses by speeches and writings to resist public authority and to change violently the form of government and the constitution of the State."

"Good!"

Angelelli disappeared, the acute cries outside died away, the scurrying of flying feet was no more heard, and Roma was still on the stool before the fire, moaning behind the hands that covered her face. The Baron came near to her and touched her with a caressing gesture.

"I'm sorry, my child, very sorry. Rossi is a dreamer, not a statesman, but he is none the less troublesome on that account. No wonder he has fascinated you, as he has fascinated the people, but time will wipe away an impression like that. The best thing that can happen for both of you is that he should be arrested to-night. It will save you so many ordeals and so much sorrow."

At that moment a cannon-shot boomed through the darkness outside, and its vibration rattled the windows and walls.

"The signal from St. Angelo," said the Baron. "The gates are closed and the city is under siege."

IX

WHEN, in the commotion of the household caused by the near approach of the crowd which brought Rossi home from the Coliseum, little Joseph slipped down the stairs and made a dash for the street, he chuckled to himself as he thought how cleverly he had eluded his mother, who had been looking out of the bedroom window, and those two old watch-dogs, his grandfather and grandmother, who were nearly always at the door.

It was not until he was fairly plunged into the great sea of the city, and had begun to be a little dazed by more lights than he ever saw when he closed his eyes in bed, that he remembered that he had disobeyed orders and broken his promise not to go out. But even then, he told himself, he was not responsible. He was Donna Roma's porter now. Therefore, he couldn't be Joseph, could he?

So, with his magic mace in hand, the serious man of seven marched on, and reconciled himself to his disobedience by thinking nothing more about it. People looked at him and smiled as he passed through the Piazza Madama, where the Senate House stands, and that made him lift his head and walk on proudly, but as he went through the Piazza of the Pantheon a boy who was coming out of a cookshop with a tray on his head cried, "Helloa, kiddy! playing Pulcinello?" and that dashed his worshipful dignity for several minutes.

It began to snow, and the white flakes on his gold braid clouded his soul at first, but when he remembered that porters had to work in all weathers, he wagged his sturdy head and strode on. He was going to Donna Roma's according to her invitation, and he found his way by his recollection of what he had seen when he made the same journey on Sunday

—here a tramcar coming round a corner, there a line of posts across a narrow thoroughfare, and there a fat man with a gruff voice shouting something at the door of a trattoria.

At the corner of a lane there was a shop window full of knives and revolvers. He didn't care for knives—they cut people's fingers—but he liked guns, and when he grew up to be a man he would buy one and kill somebody.

Coming to the Piazza Monte Citorio, he remembered the soldiers at the door of the House of Parliament, and the cellar full of long guns with knives (bayonets) stuck on the ends of their muzzles. One of the soldiers laughed, called him "Uncle," and asked him something about enlisting, but he only struck his mace firmly on the flags and marched on.

At the corner of the Piazza Colonna he had to wait some time before he could cross the Corso, for the crowds were coming both ways and the traffic frightened him. He had made various little sorties and had been driven back, when a soft hand was slipped into his fat palm and he was piloted across in safety. Then he looked up at his helper. It was a girl with big white feathers in her hat, and her face painted pink and white like the face of the little Jesus in the cradle in church at Christmas. She asked him what his name was, and he told her; also where he was going, and he told her that too. It was dark by this time, and the great little man was beginning to be glad of company.

"Aren't you tired of carrying that heavy stick?" she said.

It wasn't a stick, and he wasn't a bit tired of carrying it.

"But aren't you tired *yourself?*" she said, and he admitted that perhaps it was so.

So she picked him up, and carried him in her arms, while he carried the mace, and for some minutes both were satisfied. But presently some one in the Via Tritone cried out, "Helloa! here comes the Blessed Bambino," whereupon his worshipful dignity was again wounded, and he wriggled to the ground.

It began to thunder and there were some flashes of lightning, whereupon Joseph shuddered and crept closer to the girl's side.

"Are you afraid of lightning, Joseph?" she asked.

He wasn't. He often saw it at home when he went to bed. His mother held his hand and he covered up his head in the clothes, and then he liked it.

214

The girl took the wee, fat hand again, and the little feet toddled on.

After vain efforts to snatch a kiss, which were defeated by a proper withdrawal of the manly head in the cocked hat, the girl with the feathers and the doll's face left him in the Via due Macelli under a bright electric lamp that hung over the door of a café-chantant.

Joseph knew then that he was not far from Donna Roma's, and he began to think of what he would do when he got there. If the big porter at the door tried to stop him he would say, "I'm a little Roman boy," and the man would *have* to let him go up. Then he would take charge of the hall, and when he had not to open the door he would play with the dog, and sometimes with Donna Roma.

With sound practical sense he thought of his wages. Would it be a penny a week or twopence? He thought it would be twopence. Men didn't work for nothing nowadays. He had heard his father say so.

Then he remembered his mother, and his lip began to drop. But it rose again when he told himself that of course she would come every night to put him to bed as usual. "Good-night, mamma! See you in the morning," he would say, and when he opened his eyes it would be to-morrow.

He was feeling sleepy now, and do what he would he could hardly keep his eyes from closing. But he was in the Piazza di Spagna by this time, and his little feet in their top-boots began to patter up the snowy steps.

There are three principal landings to the Spanish Steps, and the great little man of seven had reached the second of them when a noise in the streets below made him stop and turn his head.

A great crowd, carrying hundreds of torches, was marching into the piazza. They were singing, shouting, and blowing whistles and trumpets. It was like *Befana* in the Piazza Navona, and when Joseph blinked his eyes he almost thought he was at home in bed.

All at once silence—then soldiers—then a jump all over his body like that which came to him when he was falling asleep—then a sense of something warm—then a buzzing noise—then a boom like that of the gun of St. Angelo at dinner-time . . . then a deep, familiar voice calling and calling to him, and his eyes opened for a moment and saw his father's face.

"Good-night, papa! So sleepy! See you in the morning!"

And then nothing more.

While Elena waited for Bruno's return with little Joseph, she went up and downstairs between David Rossi's apartment and her own on all manner of invented errands. Meantime she tried to keep down her anxiety by keeping up her anger. Joseph was so worrisome. When he came home he would have to be whipped and sent to bed without his supper. It was true his *verdura* was already on the stove, but he must not be allowed to touch it. You really must be strict with children. They would like you all the better for it when they grew up to be men and women.

But every moment broke down this brave severity, until the desire to punish Joseph for his disobedience was all gone. She stood at the head of the stairs and listened for his voice and his little pattering feet. If she had heard them, her anxious expression would have given way to a cross look and she would have scolded both father and son all the way up to bed. But they did not come, and she turned to the dining-room with a downcast face.

"Where can the boy be? If I could only have him back! I will never let him out of my sight again. Never!"

David Rossi, who was walking in the sitting-room to calm his nerves after a trying time, tried to comfort her. It would be all right. Depend upon it, Joseph had gone up to Donna Roma's. She was to remember what Bruno told them on Sunday. "The little Roman boy." Joseph had thought of nothing else for three days, and this being his birthday . . .

"You think so? You really think . . ."

"I'm sure of it. Bruno will be back presently, carrying Joseph on his back. Or perhaps Donna Roma will send the boy home in the carriage, and the great little man will come upstairs like the Mayor. Meantime she has kept him to play with, and . . ."

"Yes, that must be it," said Elena, with shining eyes. "The Signorina must have kept him to play with! He must be playing now with the Signorina!"

At that moment through the open door there came the sound of a heavy tread on the stairs, mingled with various voices. Elena's shining face suddenly clouded, and Rossi, who read her thought, went out on to the landing. Bruno was coming up the staircase with something in his arms, and behind him were the Garibaldian and his old wife and a line of strangers.

Rossi ran down two flights of stairs and met them. He saw everything as by a flash of lightning. The boy lay in his father's arms. He was white and cold, with his head fallen back, and his hair matted with flakes of snow. His gay coat was open, and his little stained shirt was torn out at the breast. A stranger behind was carrying the cocked hat and mace.

Elena, who was at the head of the stairs by this time, was screaming.

" Keep her away, sir," said Bruno. The poor fellow was trying to be brave and strong, but his voice was like a voice from the other side of an abyss.

They took the boy into the dining-room, and laid him on a sofa. There was no keeping the mother back. She forced her way through and laid hold of the child.

" Get away, he's mine," she cried fiercely.

And then she dropped on her knees before the boy, threw her arms about him and called on him by his name.

" Joseph! Speak to me! Open your eyes and speak! . . . What have you been doing with my child? He is ill. Why don't you send for a doctor? Don't stand there like fools. Go for a doctor, I tell you . . . Joseph! Only a word! . . . Have you carried him home without his hat on? And it's snowing too! He'll get his death of cold . . . what's this? Blood on his shirt? And a wound? Look at this red spot. Have they shot him? No, no, it's impossible! A child! Joseph! Joseph! Speak to me! . . . Yes, his heart is beating." She was pressing her ear to the boy's breast. " Or is it only the beating in my head? Oh, where is the doctor? Why don't you send for him?"

They could not tell her that it was useless, that a doctor had seen the child already, and that all was over. All they could do was to stand round her with awe in their faces. She understood them without words. Her hair fell from its knot, and her eyes began to blaze like the eyes of a maniac.

" They've killed my child!" she cried. " He's dead! My little boy is dead! Only seven, and it was his birthday! O God! My child! What had he done that they should kill him?"

And then Bruno, who was standing by with a wild lustre in his eyes, said between his teeth, "Done? Done nothing but live under a Government of murderers and assassins."

The room filled with people. Neighbours who had never before set foot in the rooms came in without fear, for death was among them. They stood silent for the most part, only handing round the table the little cocked hat and the mace, with sighs and deep breathing. But some one speaking to Rossi told him what had happened. It was at the Spanish Steps. The delegate gave the word, and the Carabineers fired over the people's heads. But they hit the child and made him cold. His little heart had burst.

"And I was going to whip him," said Elena. "Not a minute before I was talking about the rod, and not giving him his supper. O God! I can never forgive myself."

And then the blessed tears came and she wept bitterly.

David Rossi put his arms about her, and her head fell on his breast. All barriers were broken down, and she clung to him and cried.

Just then cries came from the piazza—"Hurrah for the Revolution!" and "Down with the destroyers of the people!"—the woolly tones of voices shouting in the snow. Somebody on the stairs explained that a young man was going about waving a bloody handkerchief, and that the sight of it was exasperating the people to frenzy. Women were marching through the streets, and the entire city was on the point of insurrection.

In the dining-room the stricken ones still stood around the couch. Presently there was a sound of singing outside. A great crowd was coming into the piazza singing the Garibaldi Hymn. Bruno heard it, and the wild lustre in his eyes gave place to a look of savage joy. An awful oath burst from his lips, and he ran out of the house. At the next moment he was heard in the street, singing in a thundering voice:

> "The tombs are uncovered,
> The dead arise,
> The martyrs are rising
> Before our eyes."

The old Garibaldian threw up his head like a warhorse at the call of battle, and his rickety limbs were going towards the door.

"Stay here, father," said Rossi, and the old man obeyed him.

Elena was quieter by this time. She was sitting by the child and stroking his little icy hand.

David Rossi, who had hardly spoken, went into his bedroom. His lips were tightly pressed together, his eyes were bloodshot, and his breath was labouring hard in his heaving breast.

He took up his dagger paper-knife, tried its point on his palm with two or three reckless thrusts and threw it back on the desk. Then he went down on his hands and knees and rummaged among the newspapers lying in heaps under the window. At last he found what he looked for. It was the six-chambered revolver which had been sent to him as a present. "I'll kill the man like a dog," he thought.

He loaded the revolver, put it in his breast-pocket, went back to the sitting-room, and made ready to go out.

X

TEN was striking on the different clocks of the city. Felice had lit the stove in the boudoir and the wood was burning in fitful blue and red flames. There was no other light in the room, and Roma lay with her body on the floor, and her face buried in the couch.

The world outside was full of fearful and unusual noises. Snow was still falling, and the voices heard through it had a peculiar sound of sobbing. The soft rolling of thunder came from a long way off, like the boom of a slow wave on a distant beach. At intervals there was the crackle of musketry, like the noise of rockets sent up in the night, and sometimes there were pitiful cries, smothered by the unreverberating snow, like the cries of a drowning man on a foundering ship at sea.

Roma, face downward, heard these sounds in the lapses of a terrible memory. She was seeing, as in a nightmare, the incidents of a night that was hardly six weeks past. One by one the facts flashed back upon her with a burning sense of shame, and she felt herself to be a sinner and a criminal.

It was the night of the royal ball at the Quirinal. The blaze of lights, the glitter of jewels, the brilliant throng of handsome men and lovely women, the clash of music, the whirl of dancing, and finally the smiles and compliments of the King. Then going home in the carriage in the early morning, swathed in furs over her thin white silk, with the Baron, in his decorations worn diagonally over his white breast, and through the glass the waning moon, the silent stars, the empty streets.

Then this room, this couch, sinking down on it, very tired, with eyes smiling and half closed, and nearly gone already into the mists of sleep. And then the Baron at her feet, pressing his lips to her wrist where the pulse was beating, kissing her arms and shoulders. . . . "Oh, dear! You are mad! I must not listen to you." And then burning words of love and passion: "My wife! My wife that is to be!" And then the call of her aunt from the adjoining chamber, "Roma!"

The sobbing sounds from outside broke in on Roma's nightmare, and when the chain of memory linked on again it was morning in her vision, and the Countess was comforting her in a whimpering voice:

"After all, God is merciful, and things that happen to everybody can be atoned for by prayer and penance. Besides, the Baron is a man of honour, and the poor maniac cannot last much longer."

The sobbing sounds in the snow, the cries far away, the crackle of the rifle-shots, the rumble of the thunder broke in again, and the elements outside seemed to whirl round her in the tempest of her trouble. For a moment she lifted her head and heard voices in the next room.

The Baron was still there, and from time to time, as he wrote his despatches, messengers came to take them away, to bring replies, and to deliver the latest news of the night. The populace had risen in all parts of the city, and the soldiers had charged them. There had been several misadventures and many arrests. The large house of detention by St. Andrea delle Frate was already full, but the people continued to hold out. They had disconnected the gas at the gasometer and cut the electric wires, and the city was plunged in darkness.

"Tell the electric light company to turn on the flashlight from Monte Mario," said the Baron.

And when the voices ceased in the drawing-room there came the deadened sound of the Countess's frightened treble behind the wall.

"O Holy Virgin, full of grace, save me! It would be a sin to let me die to-night! Holy Virgin, see! I have given thee two more candles. Art thou not satisfied? Save me from murder, Mother of God."

Roma saw another phase of her vision. It was filled with a new face, which made her at once happy and unhappy, proud and ashamed. Hitherto the only condition on which she had been able to live with the secret of her life was that she should think nothing about it. Now she was compelled to think, and she was asking herself if it was her duty to confess.

Before she married David Rossi she must tell him everything. She saw herself trying to do so. He was looking vacantly before him with the deep furrow that came to his forehead when he was strongly moved. She had sobbed out her story, telling all, excusing nothing, and now she was waiting for him to speak. He would take her side, he would tell her she had been more sinned against than sinning, that she had been young and alone at the mercy of an evil man, and that her will had not consented.

"No, no! It is impossible!" she cried aloud, and, startled by the sound of her voice, the Baron came into the room.

"My dear child!" he said, and he picked her up from the floor. "I shall never be able to forgive myself if you take things like this. Every tear you shed will burn my flesh like fire. Come now, dry these beautiful eyes and be calm."

She did not listen to him, but leaning on the stove and fingering with one hand the frame of her father's picture which hung above it, she said:

"I see now that happiness was not for me. There must be some punishment for every sin, however little one has been guilty of it, and perhaps this is God's way of asking for an expiation. It is very, very hard . . . it seems more than I deserve . . . and heavier than I can bear . . . but there is no help for it."

The tears she brushed from her eyes seemed to be gathering in her throat.

"The bitterest part of it is that I must make others suffer for it also. He must suffer who has loved and trusted me. His love for me, my love for him, this has been dragging him down since the first day I knew him. Perhaps he is in prison by this time."

Sobs interrupted her for a moment, and in a caressing tone the Baron tried to comfort her. It was natural that she should feel troubled, very natural and very womanly. But time was the great remedy for human ills. It would heal everything.

"Roma, you have wounded and humiliated and insulted me, but you are the only woman in the world I would give one straw to have. I will make you the wife of the Dictator of Italy, and when all these troubles are over and you are great, and have forgotten what has taken place . . ."

"I can never forget and I don't want to be great. I only want to be good. Leave me!"

"You *are* good. You have always been good. What happened was my fault alone, and you have nothing to reproach yourself with. I found you growing up to be a great woman, and passing out of my legal control, while I was bound down to a poor, helpless, living corpse. Some day you would meet a younger, freer man, and you would be lost to me for good. Wasn't it human to try to hold you to me until the time came when I could claim you altogether? And if meanwhile this man has interposed . . ."

He pointed to the bust on the pedestal. She looked up at it, and then dropped her head.

"Put the man out of your mind, my dear, and all will be well. Probably he is in the hands of the authorities already. God grant it may be so! No trouble about his arrest this time! It cannot be complicated by the danger of scandal. Nobody else's name and character will be concerned in it. And if it serves to dispose of a dangerous man and a subversive politician, I am willing to let everything else sleep."

He paused a moment, and then added in his most incisive accents: "But if not, the law must take its course, and Roma Roselli must complete what Roma Volonna has begun."

At that moment Felice's dark form stood against the light in the open door.

"Commendatore Angelelli and Charles Minghelli, Excellency."

As the Baron went back to the drawing-room Roma returned to the window. Scales of snow adhered to the glass, and it was difficult to see anything outside. But the masses of shadow and sheets of light were gone, and the city lay in utter darkness. The sobbing sounds, the crackle of musketry and the rumble of thunder were all gone, and the air was empty and void.

At one moment there was a soft patter as of a flock

of sheep passing under the window in the darkness. It was a company of riflemen going at a quick march over the snow, with torches and lanterns.

Voices came from the next room, and Roma found herself listening.

"Apparently the insurrection is suppressed, your Excellency."

"I congratulate you."

"The soldiers are patrolling the streets, and all is quiet."

"Good!"

"We have some hundreds of rioters in the house of detention, and the military courts will begin to sit to-morrow morning."

"Excellent!"

"The misadventures have been few and unimportant, the child I spoke of being the only one killed."

"You have discovered whose child it was?"

"Yes. Unluckily . . ."

Roma felt dizzy. A thought had flashed upon her.

"It is the child of Donna Roma's man, Bruno Rocco, and apparently . . ."

A choking cry rang through the room. Was it herself who made it?

"Go on, Commendatore. Apparently . . ."

"The child was dressed in some carnival costume, and apparently he was on his way to this house."

Roma's dizziness increased, and to save herself from falling she caught at a side-table that stood under the bust.

On this table were some sculptor's tools—a chisel and a small mallet, with which she had been working.

There was an interval in which the voices were deadened and confused. Then they became clear and sharp as before.

"But the most important fact you have not yet given me. I trust you are only saving it up for the last. The Deputy Rossi is arrested?"

"Unfortunately . . . Excellency . . ."

"No?"

"He left home immediately after the outbreak and has not been seen since. Presently the flashlight will be turned on by a separate battery from Monte Mario, and every corner of the city shall be searched. But we fear he is gone."

"Gone?"

"Perhaps by the train that left just before the signal."

Roma felt a cry rising to her throat again, but she put up her hand to keep it down.

"No matter! Commendatore, send telegrams after the train to all stations up to the frontier, with orders that nobody is to alight until every carriage has been overhauled. Minghelli, go to the Consulta immediately, and ask the Minister of Foreign Affairs to despatch a portrait of Rossi to every foreign Government."

"But no portrait exists, Excellency. It was a difficulty I found in England."

"Yes, there is a portrait. Come this way."

Roma felt the room going round as the Baron came into it and switched on the light.

"*There* is the only portrait of the illustrious Deputy, and our hostess will lend it to be photographed."

"Never!" said Roma, and taking up the mallet she struck the bust a heavy blow, and it fell in fragments to the floor.

Half-an-hour afterwards Roma was sitting amid the wreck of her work when the Baron, wearing his fur-lined overcoat and pulling on his gloves, came into the boudoir.

"I am compelled," he said, "to inflict my presence upon you for a moment longer in order to tell you what my attitude in the future is to be, and what feelings are to guide you. I shall continue to think of you as my wife according to the law of nature, and of the man who has come between us as your lover. I will not give you up to him, whatever happens; and if he tries to take you away, or if you try to go to him, you must be prepared to find that I offer every resistance. Two passions are now engaged against the man, and I will not shrink from any course that seems necessary to subdue either him or you, or both."

A moment afterwards she heard the patrol challenging him on the piazza. Then "Pardon, Excellency," and the soft swish of carriage wheels in the snow.

XI

WHEN Rossi left home he was like a raging madman. He made straight for the Palazzo Braschi at the other side of the piazza, and going up the marble staircase on limbs that could scarcely support him, his thoughts went back in a broken maze to the scene he had left behind.

THE PRIME MINISTER

"Our little boy dead! Dead in his mother's arms! O God! let me meet the man face to face! . . . Our innocent darling! The light of our eyes put out in a moment! Our sweet little Joseph! . . . Shall there be no retribution? God forbid! The man who has been the chief cause of this crime shall be the first to suffer punishment. No use wasting time on the hounds who executed his orders. They are only delegates of police, and over them is this Minister of the Interior. He alone is responsible, and he is here!"

When he reached the green baize door to the hall, he stopped to wipe away the perspiration which stood on his forehead although his face was flecked with snow. The messengers looked scared when he stepped inside, and they answered his questions with obvious hesitation. The Minister was not in his cabinet. He had not been there that night. It was possible the Honourable might find his Excellency at home.

Rossi turned on his heel instantly, and went hurriedly downstairs. He would go to the Palazzo Leone. There was no time to lose. Presently the man would hide himself in the darkness like a toad under a stone.

As he left the Ministry of the Interior he heard the singing of the Garibaldi Hymn in the distance, and turning into the Corso Victor Emmanuel, he came upon crowds of people and some noisy and tumultuous scenes.

One group had broken into a gun-shop and seized rifles and cartridges; another group had taken possession of two electric tram-cars, and tumbled them on their sides to make a barricade across the street; and a third group was tearing up the street itself to use the stones for missiles. "Our turn now," they were shouting, and there were screams of delirious laughter.

As Rossi crossed the bridge of St. Angelo the cannon was fired from the Castle, and he knew that it was meant for a signal. "No matter!" he thought. "It will be too late when the soldiers arrive."

Notwithstanding the tumult in the city the Piazza of St. Peter's was silent and deserted. Not the sound of a footfall, not the rattle of a carriage-wheel; only the swish-swish of the fountains, whose waters were playing in the lamplight through the falling snow, and the echoing hammer of the clock of the Basilica.

THE ETERNAL CITY

The porter of the Palazzo Leone was asleep in his lodge, and Rossi passed upstairs.

"I'll bring the man to justice now," he thought. "He imagined we were only tame cats and would submit to anything. He was wrong. We'll show him we know how to punish tyrants. Haven't we always done so, we Romans? He has a sharp tongue for the people, but I have a sharper one here for him."

And he felt for the revolver in his breast-pocket to make certain it was there.

The lackey in knee-breeches and yellow stockings who answered the inside bell was almost speechless at the sight of the white face which confronted him at the door. No, the Baron was not at home. He had not been there since early in the evening. Had he gone to the Prefettura? Possibly. Or the Consulta? Perhaps.

"Which, man, which?" said Rossi, and to say something the lackey stammered "The Consulta," and closed the door.

Rossi set his face towards the Foreign Office. There was a light in the stained-glass windows of the Pope's private chapel—the Holy Father was at his prayers. A canvas-covered barrow containing a man who had been injured by the soldiers was being wheeled into the Hospital of Santo Spirito, and a woman and a child were walking and crying beside it.

The streets were covered with broken tiles which had been thrown on to the heads of the cavalry as they galloped through the principal thoroughfares. Carabineers, with revolvers in hand, were dragging themselves on their stomachs along the roofs, trying to surprise the rioters who were hiding behind chimney-stacks. Some one shouted: "Cut the electric wires," and men were clambering up the tall posts and breaking the electric lamps.

The Consulta, the office of the Minister of Foreign Affairs, stands in the Piazza of the Quirinal, and when Rossi reached it the great square of the King was as silent as the great square of the Pope had been.

Two sentries were in boxes on either side of the royal gate, and one Carabineer was in the doorway. The gardens down the long corridor lay dark in the shadows, but the fountain with sculptured horses, the splashing water, and the front of the building were white under the electric lamps as if from a dazzling moon.

Before turning into the silent courtyard of the Consulta, Rossi paused and listened to the noises that came from the city. Men were singing and women were screaming. The rattle of musketry mingled with the cries of children. And over all were the steady downfall of the snow and the dull rumble of distant thunder.

Rossi held his head between his hands to prevent his senses from leaving him. His rage was ebbing away, and he was beginning to tremble. Nevertheless, he forced himself to go on. As he rang the bell at the Foreign Office, he was partly conscious of a secret desire that the Prime Minister might not be there.

The porter was not sure. The Baron's carriage had just gone. Let him ask on the telephone. . . . No, there had been a messenger from the Minister of the Interior, but the Minister himself had not been there that night.

Rossi took a long breath of relief and went away. He had returned to the bright side of the piazza when the lights seemed to be wiped out as though by an invisible wing, and the whole city was plunged in darkness. At the next moment a squadron of cavalry galloped up to the Quirinal, and the gates of the royal palace and of the Consulta were closed.

Midnight struck.

For two hours the soldiers had been charging the crowds by the light of lanterns and torches. They had arrested hundreds of persons. Chained together, two and two, the insurgents had been taken to the places of detention, amid the cries of their women and children. " Who knows whether we shall see each other again? " said the prisoners, as they passed into the " House of Pain." One old woman went on her knees to the soldiers and begged them to have pity on the people. " They are your brothers, my sons," she cried.

One o'clock struck.

The streets were still dark, but a searchlight from Monte Mario was sweeping over the city like a flash of a supernatural eye. With tottering limbs and his head on his breast, David Rossi was walking down the Via due Macelli towards the column of the Immaculate Conception, when a young girl spoke to him.

" Honourable," she said, " is it true that the little boy is dead? . . . It is? Oh, dear! I met him in the Corso, and brought him up as far as the Variétés, and if I had only taken him all the way. . . . Oh, I shall never forgive myself!"

The city was quiet and all was hushed on every side when Rossi found himself on a flight of steps at the back of Roma's apartment. From these steps a door opened into the studio. One panel of the door was glazed, and a light was shining from within. Going cautiously forward, Rossi looked into the room. Roma was seated on a stool with her hands clasped in her lap and her hair hanging loose. She was very pale. Her face expressed unutterable sadness.

Rossi listened for a moment, but there was not a sound to be heard except that of the different clocks chiming the quarter. Then he tapped lightly on the glass.

"Roma!" he said in a low tone. "Roma!"

She rose up and shrank back. Then coming to the door, and shielding her eyes from the light, she put her face close to the pane. At the next moment she threw the door open.

"Is it you?" she said in a tremulous voice, and taking his hand she drew him hurriedly into the house.

XII

AFTER the Baron was gone, Roma had sat a long time in the dark among the ruins of the broken bust. When twelve o'clock struck she was feeling hot and feverish, and, in spite of the coldness of the night, she rose and opened the window. The snow had ceased to fall, the thunder was gone, and the city was quiet.

At that moment the revolving searchlight on Monte Mario passed over the room. The white flash lit up the broken fragments at her feet, and brought a new train of reflections. The bust she destroyed had been only the plaster cast; the piece-mould remained, and might be a cause of danger.

She closed the window, took a candle, and went down to the studio to put the mould out of the way. She had done so, and was sitting to rest and to think when Rossi's knock came at the door. In a moment all her dreams were gone. She was clasped in his arms and had put up her mouth to be kissed.

"Is it you?"

"Roma!"

It was not at first that she realised what was happening,

but after a moment she recovered from her bewilderment, and extinguished the candle lest Rossi should be seen from outside.

They were in the dark, save at intervals when the revolving light in its circuit of the city swept across the studio, and lit up their faces as by a flash of lightning. He seemed to be dazed. His weary eyes looked as if their light were almost extinct.

"You are safe? You are well?" she asked.

"O God! what sights!" he said. "You have heard what has happened?"

"Yes, yes! But you are not injured?"

"The people were peaceful and meant no evil, but the soldiers were ordered to fire, and our little boy is dead."

"Don't let us speak of it. . . . The police were told to arrest you, but you have escaped thus far, and now . . ."

"Bruno is taken, and hundreds of others are in prison."

"But you are safe? You are well? You are uninjured?"

"Yes," he answered between his teeth, and then he covered his face with his hands. "God knows I did my best to prevent this bloodshed—I would have laid down my life to prevent it."

"God *does* know it."

"Take this."

He drew something from his breast-pocket and put it into her hands.

It was the revolver.

"I cannot trust myself any longer."

"You haven't used it?"

"No."

"Thank God!"

"I should have done so if I could have met the man face to face."

"The Baron?"

"I searched for him everywhere, and couldn't find him. God kept him out of my way to save me from sin and shame."

With a frightened cry she put down the revolver and clasped her hands about his neck. He began to recover his dazed senses and to smooth the hair on her damp forehead.

"My poor Roma! You didn't think we were to part like this?"

Her arms slackened, and she dropped her head on to his shoulder.

"Last night you told me to fly, and I wouldn't do so. There was no man in Rome I was afraid of then. But to-night there is some one I am afraid of. I am afraid of myself."

"You intend to go?"

"Yes! I shall feel like a captain who deserts his sinking ship. Would to God I could have gone down with her! . . . Yet no! She is not lost yet. Everything is in God's hands. Perhaps there is work for me abroad, now that the paths are closed to me at home. Let us wait and see."

They were both silent for a while.

"Then it's all over," she said, gulping down a sob.

"God forbid! This black night in Rome is only the beginning of the end. It will be the dawn of the resurrection everywhere."

"But it is all over between you and me."

"Indeed, no. No, no! I cannot take you with me. That is impossible. I couldn't see you suffer hunger and thirst and the privations of exile, but . . ."

"Our marriage cannot be celebrated now, and that being so . . ."

"The banns are good for half a year, Roma, and before that time I shall be back. Have no fear! The immortality stirring beneath the ruins of this old city will give us victory all over Italy. I will return and we shall be very happy. How happy we shall be!"

"Yes, yes," she brought out at intervals.

"Be brave, my girl, be brave!"

"Yes, yes."

The revolving searchlight flashed through the room at that moment, and she dropped her face again.

"Dearest," she said faintly, "if I should not be here when you come back . . ."

He started and seized her arm.

"Roma, you cannot intend to submit to the will of that man?"

She shook her head as it rested on his shoulder.

"The man is a monster. He may put pressure upon you."

"It is not that."

" He may even make you suffer for my sake."

" Nor that either."

" By-and-by he may require everybody to take an oath of allegiance to the King."

" I have taken mine already—to *my* king."

" Roma, if you wish me to stay I will do so in spite of everything."

" I wish you to go, dearest."

" Then what is it you fear?"

" Nothing—only . . ."

" But you are sad. Why is it?"

" A foreboding. I feel as if we were parting for ever."

He passed his hands through her hair. " It may be so. Only God can tell."

" It was too sweet dreaming. I was too happy for a little while."

" If it must be, it must be. But let us be brave, dear! We, who take up a life like this, must learn renunciation. . . . Crying, Roma?"

" No! Oh, no! But renunciation! That's it—renunciation." She could feel the beating of her heart against his breast. " Love comes to every one, but to some it comes too late, and then it comes in vain." She was striving to keep down her sobs. " They have only to conquer it and renounce it, and to pray God to unite them to their loved ones in another life." She was choking, but she struggled on. " Sometimes I think it must be my lot to be like that. Other women may dream of love and home and children . . ."

" Don't unman me, Roma."

" Dearest, promise me that whatever happens you will think the best of me."

" Roma!"

" Promise me that whoever says anything to the contrary you will always believe I loved you."

" Why should we talk of what can never happen?"

" If we are parting for ever . . . if we are saying a long farewell to all earthly affections, promise me . . ."

" For God's sake, Roma!"

" Promise me!"

" I promise!" he said. " And you?"

" I promise too—I promise that as long as I live, and wherever I am and whatever becomes of me, I will . . . yes, because I cannot help it . . . I will love you to the last."

Saying this in passionate tones, she drew down his head and he met her kiss with his lips.

"It is our marriage, David. Others are married in church and by the hand, and with a ring. We are married in our spirits and our souls."

A long time passed, during which they did not speak. The searchlight flashed in on them again and again with its supernatural eye, and as often as it did so Rossi looked at her with strange looks of pity and of love.

Meantime, she cut a lock from her hair, tied it with a piece of ribbon, and put it in his pocket with his watch. Then she dried her eyes with her handkerchief and pushed it in his breast.

The night went on, and nothing was to be heard but the chiming of clocks outside. At length through the silence there came a muffled rumble from the streets.

"You must go now," she said, and when the next flash came round she looked up at him with a steadfast gaze, as if trying to gather into her eyes her last memories of his face.

"Adieu!"

"Not yet."

"It is still dark, but the streets are patrolled and every gate is closed, and how are you to escape?"

"If the soldiers had wished to take me they could have done so a hundred times."

"But the city is stirring. Be careful for my sake. Adieu!"

"Roma," said Rossi, "if I do not take you with me it is partly because I want your help in Rome. Think of the poor people I leave behind me in poverty and in prison. Think of Elena when she awakes in the morning, alone with her terrible grief. Some one should be here to represent me for a time at all events—to take the messages I must send, the instructions I shall have to give. It will be a dangerous task, Roma, a task that can only be undertaken by some one who loves me, some one who . . ."

"That is enough. Tell me what I can do," she said.

They arranged a channel of correspondence, and then Roma began her farewells afresh.

"Roma," said Rossi again, "since I must go away before our civil marriage can be celebrated, is it not best that our spiritual one should have the blessing of the Church?"

Roma looked at him and trembled.

"When I am gone God knows what may happen. The Baron may be a free man any day, and he may put pressure on you to marry him. In that case it will be strength and courage to you to know that in God's eyes you are married already. It will be happiness and comfort to me, too, when I am far away from you and alone."

"But it is impossible."

"Not so. A declaration before a parish priest is all that is necessary. 'Father, this is my wife.' 'This is my husband.' That is enough. It will have no value in the eye of the law, but it will be a religious marriage for all that."

"There is no time. You cannot wait . . ."

"Hush!" The clocks were striking three. "At three o'clock there is mass at St. Andrea delle Frate. That is your parish church, Roma. The priest and his acolytes are the only witnesses we require."

"If you think . . . that is to say . . . if it will make you happy, and be a strength to me also . . ."

"Run for your cloak and hat, dearest—in ten minutes it will be done."

"But think again." She was breathing audibly. "Who knows what may happen before you return? Will you never repent?"

"Never!"

"But . . . but there is something . . . something I ought to tell you—something painful. It is about the past."

"The past is past. Let us think of the future."

"You do not wish to hear it."

"If it is painful to you—no!"

"Will nothing and nobody divide us?"

"Nothing and nobody in the world."

She gulped down another choking sob and threw both arms about his neck.

"Take me, then. I am your wife before God and man."

XIII

IT was still dark overhead, and the streets with their thin covering of snow were as silent as a catacomb. Through the door of the church, when the leather covering was lifted, there came the yellow light of the candles burning on the altar. The priest in his gold vestments stood with his face to the glistening shrine, and his acolytes knelt beside him. There was only one worshipper, an old woman who was kneeling before a chair in the gloom of a side chapel. The tinkle of the acolytes' bell and the faint murmur of the priest's voice were the only sounds that broke the stillness.

Rossi and Roma stepped up on tiptoe, and as the Father finished his mass and turned to go they made their declaration. The old man was startled and disturbed, but the priest commits no crime who listens to the voice of conscience, and he took their names and gave them his blessing. They parted at the church door.

"You will write when you cross the frontier?"

"Yes."

"Adieu then, until we meet again!"

"If I am long away from you, Roma . . ."

"You cannot be long away. You will be with me every day and always."

She was assuming a lively tone to keep up his courage, but there was a dry glitter in her eyes and a tremor in her voice.

He took her full, round form in his arms for a last embrace. "If the result of this night's work is that I am arrested and brought back and imprisoned . . ."

"I can wait for you," she said.

"If I am banished for life . . ."

"I can follow you."

"If the worst comes to the worst, and one way or another death itself should be the fate that falls to me . . ."

"I can follow you there, too."

"If we meet again we can laugh at all this, Roma."

"Yes, we can laugh at all this," she faltered.

"If not . . . Adieu!"

"Adieu!"

She disengaged her clinging arms with one last caress; there was an instant of unconsciousness, and when she recovered herself he was gone.

At the next moment there came through the darkness the measured tramp, tramp, tramp of the patrol. With a quivering heart Roma stood and listened. There was a slight movement among the soldiers, a scarcely perceptible pause, and then the tramp, tramp, tramp as before. Rossi looked back as he turned the corner, and saw Roma, in her light cloak, gliding across the silent street like a ghost.

Three or four hundred yards inside the gate of St. John Lateran in one of the half-finished tenement houses on the outskirts of Rome, there is a cellar used as a resting-place and eating-house by the carriers from the country who bring wine into the city. This cellar was the only place that seemed to be awake when Rossi walked towards the city walls. Some eight or nine men, in the rude dress of wine-carriers, lay dozing or talking on the floor. They had been kept in Rome overnight by the closing of the gate, and were waiting for it to be opened in the morning.

Without a moment's hesitation David Rossi stepped down and spoke to the men.

"Gentlemen," he said, "you know who I am. I am Rossi. The police have orders to arrest me. Will you help me to get out of Rome?"

"What's that?" shouted a drowsy voice from the smoky shadows of the cellar.

"It's the Honourable Rossi," said a lad who had shambled up. "The oysters are after him, and will we help him to escape?"

"Will we? It's not *will* we; it's *can* we, Honourable," said a thick-set man, who lifted his head from an upturned horse-saddle.

In a moment the men were all on their feet, asking questions and discussing chances. The gate was to be opened at six, and the first train north was to go out at half-past nine. But the difficulty was that everybody in Rome knew Rossi. Even if he got through the gate he could not get on to the train within ten miles of the city without the certainty of recognition.

"I have it!" said the thick-set man with the drowsy voice. "There's young Carlo. He got a scratch in the leg last night from one of the wet nurses of the Government, and he'll have to lie upstairs for a week at least. Why can't he lend his clothes to the Honourable? And why can't the Honourable drive Carlo's cart back to Monte Rotondo, and then go where he likes when he gets there?"

"That will do," said Rossi, and so it was settled.

When the train which left Rome for Florence and Milan at 9.30 in the morning arrived at the country station of

Monte Rotondo, eighteen miles out, a man in top-boots, blue trousers, a white waistband and a red-lined overcoat got into the people's compartment. The train was crowded with foreigners who were flying from the risks of insurrection, and even the third-class carriages were filled with well-dressed strangers. They were talking bitterly of their experiences the night before. Most of them had been compelled to barricade their bedroom doors at the hotels, and some had even passed the night at the railway station.

"It all comes of letting men like this Rossi go at large," said a young Englishman with the voice of a pea-hen. "For my part, I would put all these anarchists on an uninhabited island and leave them to fight it out among themselves."

"Say, Rossi isn't an anarchist," said a man with an American intonation.

"What is he?"

"A dreamer of dreams."

"Bad dreams, then," said the voice of the pea-hen. and there was general laughter.

PART SIX—THE ROMAN OF ROME

I

ROMA awoke next morning with a feeling of joy. The dangers of last night were over and David Rossi had escaped. Where would he be by this time? She looked at her little round watch and reckoned the hours that had passed against the speed of the train.

Natalina came with the tea and the morning newspaper. The maid's tongue went faster than her hands as she rattled on about the terrors of the night and the news of the morning. Meantime Roma glanced eagerly over the columns of the paper for its references to Rossi. He was gone. The authorities were unable to say what had become of him.

With boundless relief Roma turned to the other items of intelligence. The journal was the organ of the Government, and it contained an extract from the Official Gazette and the text of a proclamation by the Prefect. The first announced that the riot was at an end and Rome was quiet; the second notified the public that by royal decree the city was declared to be in a state of siege, and that the King had nominated a Royal Commissioner with full powers.

Besides this news there was a general account of the insurrection. The ringleaders were anarchists, socialists, and professed atheists, determined on the destruction of both throne and altar by any means, however horrible. Their victims had been drawn, without seeing where they were going, into a vortex of disorder, and the soldiers had defended society and the law. Happily the casualties were few. The only fatal incident had been the death of a child, seven years of age, the son of a workman. The people of Rome had to congratulate themselves on the promptness of a Government which had reinstated authority with so small a loss of blood.

Roma remembered what Rossi had said about Elena— "Think of Elena when she awakes in the morning, alone

237

with her terrible grief "—and putting on a plain dark cloth dress she set off for the Piazza Navona.

It was eleven o'clock, and the sun was shining on the melting snow. Rome was like a dead city. The breath of revolution had passed over it. Broken tiles lay on the pavement of the slushy streets, and here and there were the remains of abandoned barricades. The shops, which are the eyes of a city, were nearly all closed and asleep.

At a flower-shop, which was opened to her knock, Roma bought a wreath of white chrysanthemums. A group of men and women stood at the door in the Piazza Navona, and she received their kisses on her hands. The Garibaldian followed her up the stairs, and his old wife, who stood at the top, called her " Little Sister," and then burst into tears.

The boy lay on the couch, just where Roma had first seen him, when David Rossi was lifting him up asleep. He might have been asleep now, so peaceful was his expression under the mysterious seal of death. The blinds were drawn, and the sun came through them with a yellow light. Four candles were burning on chairs at the head and two at the feet. The little body was still dressed in the gay clothes of the festival, and the cocked hat and gilt-headed mace lay beside it. But the chubby hands were clasped over a tiny crucifix, and the hair of the shock head was brushed smooth and flat.

" There he is," said Elena, in a cracked voice, and she went down on her knees between the candles.

Roma, who could not speak, put the wreath of chrysanthemums on the brave little breast, and knelt by the mother's side. At that they all broke down together.

The old Garibaldian wiped his rheumy eyes and began to talk of David Rossi. He was as fond of Joseph as if the boy had been his own son. But what had become of the Honourable? Before daybreak the police had made a domiciliary perquisition in the apartment, carried off his papers and sealed up his rooms.

" Have no fear for him," said Roma, and then she asked about Bruno. All they knew was that Bruno had been arrested and locked up in the prison called Regina Cœli.

" Poor Bruno! He'll be dying to know what is happening here," said Elena.

" I'll see him," said Roma.

It was well she had come early. In the stupefaction of their sorrow the three poor souls were like helpless children

and had done nothing. Roma sent the Garibaldian to the
sanitary office for the doctor who was to verify the death,
to the office of health to register it, and to the municipal
office to arrange for the funeral. It was to be a funeral of
the third category, with a funeral car of two horses and a
coach with liveried coachmen. The grave was to be one of
the little vaults, the Fornelli, set apart for children. The
priest was to be instructed to buy many candles and order
several Frati. The expense would be great, but Roma undertook to bear it, and when she left the house the old people
kissed her hands again and loaded her with blessings.

II

THE Roman prison with the extraordinary name, "The
Queen of Heaven," is a vast yellow building on the Trastevere side of the river. Behind it rises the Janiculum, in front
of it runs the Tiber, and on both sides of it are narrow lanes
cut off by high walls.

On the morning after the insurrection a great many persons had gathered at the entrance of this prison. Old men,
who were lame or sick or nearly blind, stood by a dead wall
which divides the street from the Tiber, and looked on with
dazed and vacant eyes. Younger men nearer the entrance
read the proclamations posted up on the pilasters. One of
these was the proclamation of the Prefect announcing the
state of siege; another was the proclamation of the Royal
Commissioner calling on citizens to consign all the arms in
their possession to the Chief of Police under pain of imprisonment.

In the entrance-hall there was a crowd of women, each
carrying a basket or a bundle in a handkerchief. They were
young and old, dressed variously as if from different prov-
inces, but nearly all poor, untidy, and unkempt.

An iron gate was opened, and an officer, two soldiers, and
a warder came out to take the food which the women had
brought for their relatives imprisoned within. Then there
was a terrible tumult. "Mr. Officer, please!" "Please, Mr.
Officer!" "Be kind to Giuseppe, and the saints bless you!"
"My turn next!" "No, mine!" "Don't push!" "You're
pushing yourself!" "You're knocking the basket out of my
hands!" "Get away!" "You cat! You . . ."

" Silence! Silence! Silence!" cried the officer, shouting the women down, and meantime the men in the street outside curled their lips and tried to laugh.

Into this wild scene, full of the acrid exhalations of human breath, and the nauseating odour of unclean bodies, but moved, nevertheless, by the finger of God Himself, the cab which brought Roma to see Bruno discharged her at the prison door.

The officer on the steps saw her over the heads of the women with their outstretched arms, and judging from her appearance that she came on other business, he called to a Carabineer to attend to her.

" I wish to see the Director," said Roma.

" Certainly, Excellency," said the Carabineer, and with a salute he led the way by a side door to the offices on the floor above.

The Governor of Regina Cœli was a middle-aged man with a kindly face, but under the new order he could do nothing.

" Everything relating to the political prisoners is in the hands of the Royal Commissioner," he said.

" Where can I see him, Cavaliere?"

" He is with the Minister of War to-day, arranging for the military tribunals, but perhaps to-morrow at his office in the Castle of St. Angelo . . ."

" Thanks! Meantime can I send a message into the prison?"

" Yes."

" And may I pay for a separate cell for a prisoner, with food and light, if necessary?"

" Undoubtedly."

Roma undertook the expense of these privileges and then scribbled a note to Bruno.

" DEAR FRIEND,—Don't lose heart! Your dear ones shall be cared for and comforted. He whom you love is safe and your darling is in heaven. Sleep well! These days will pass.
                                                      " R. V."

III

THAT night Roma wrote the first part of a letter to David Rossi:

" David—my David! It is early days to call you by a

dearer name, but the sweet word is on the tip of my pen, and I can hardly help myself from scribbling it. You wished me to tell you what is happening in Rome, and here I am beginning to write already, though when and how and where this letter is to reach you, I must leave it to Fate and to yourself to determine. Fancy! Only eighteen hours since we parted! It seems inconceivable! I feel as if I had lived a lifetime.

"Do you know, I did not go to bed when you left me. I had so many things to think about. And, tired as I was, I slept little, and was up early. The morning dawned beautifully. It was perfectly tragic. So bright and sunny after that night of slaughter. No rattle of cars, no tinkle of trams, no calls of the water-carriers and of the pedlars in the streets. It was for all the world like that awful quiet of the sea the morning after a tempest, with the sun on its placid surface and not a hint of the wrecks beneath.

"I remembered what you said about Elena, and went down to see her. The poor girl has just parted with her dead child. She did it with a brave heart, God pity her! taking comfort in the Blessed Virgin, as the mother in heaven who knows all our sorrows and asks God to heal them. Ah, what a sweet thing it must be to believe that! Do you believe it?"

Here she wanted to say something about her great secret. She tried, but she could not do it.

"I couldn't see Bruno to-day, but I hope to do so to-morrow, and meantime I have ordered food to be supplied to him. If I could only do something to some purpose! But five hundred of your friends are in Regina Cœli, and my poor little efforts are a drop of water in a mighty ocean.

"Rome is a deserted city to-day, and but for the soldiers, who are everywhere, it would look like a dead one! The steps of the Piazza di Spagna are empty, not a model is to be seen, not a flower is to be bought, and the fountain is bubbling in silence. After sunset a certain shiver passes over the world, and after an insurrection something of the same kind seems to pass over a city. The churches and the hospitals are the only places open, and the doctors and their messengers are the only people moving about.

"Just one of the newspapers has been published to-day, and it is full of proclamations. Everybody is to be indoors by nine o'clock and the cafés are to be closed at eight. Arms are to be consigned at the Questura, and meetings of more than four persons are strictly forbidden. Rewards of pardon are offered to all rioters who will inform on the ringleaders of the insurrection, and of money to all citizens who will denounce the conspirators. The military tribunals are to sit to-morrow and domiciliary visitations are already being made. Your own apartments have been searched and sealed and the police have carried off papers.

"Such are the doings of this evil day, and yet—selfish woman that I am—I cannot for my life think it is all evil. Has it not given me you? And if it has taken you away from me as well, I can wait, I can be patient. Where are you now, I wonder? And are you thinking of me while I am thinking of you? Oh, how splendid! Think of it! Though the train may be carrying you away from me every hour and every minute, before long we shall be together. In the first dream of the first sleep I shall join you, and we shall be cheek to cheek and heart to heart. Good-night, my dear one!"

Again she tried to say something about her secret. But no! "Not to-night," she thought, and after switching off the light and kissing her hand in the darkness to the stars that hung over the north, she laughed at her own foolishness and went to bed.

IV

ROMA awoke next day with a sense of pain. Thus far she had beaten the Baron—yes! But David Rossi? Had she sinned against God and against her husband? She must confess. There was no help for it. And there must be no hesitation and no delay.

Natalina came into the bedroom and threw open the shutters. She was bringing a telegram, and Roma almost snatched it out of her hands. It was from Rossi and had been sent off from Chiasso. "Crossed frontier safe and well."

Roma made a cry of joy and leapt out of bed. All day long that telegram was like wings under her heels and made her walk with an elastic step.

While taking her coffee she remembered the responsibilities she had undertaken the day before—for the boy's funeral and Bruno's maintenance—and for the first time in her life she began to consider ways and means. Her ready money was getting low, and it was necessary to do something.

Then Felice came with a sheaf of papers. They were tradesmen's bills and required immediate payment. Some of the men were below and refused to go away without the cash.

There was no help for it. She opened her purse, discharged her debts, swept her debtors out of the house, and sat down to count what remained.

Very little remained. But what matter? The five words of that telegram were five bright stars which could light up a darker sky than had fallen on her yet.

In this high mood she went down to the studio—silent now in the absence of the humorous voice that usually rang in it, and with Bruno's chisels and mallet lying idle, with his sack on a block of half-hewn marble. Uncovering her fountain, she looked at it again. It was good work; she knew it was good; she could be certain it was good. It should justify her yet, and some day the stupid people who were sheering away from her now would come cringing to her feet afresh.

That suggested thoughts of the Mayor. She would write to him and get some money with which to meet the expenses of yesterday as well as the obligations which she might perhaps incur to-day or in the future.

"Dear Senator Palomba," she wrote, "no doubt you have often wondered why your much-valued commission has not been completed before. The fact is that it suffered a slight accident a few days ago, but a week or a fortnight ought to see it finished, and if you wish to make arrangements for its reception you may count on its delivery in that time. Meantime as I am pressed for funds at the moment, I shall be glad if you can instruct your treasurer at the Municipality to let me have something on account. The price mentioned, you remember, was 15,000 francs, and as I have not had anything hitherto, I trust it may not be unreasonable to ask for half now, leaving the remainder until the fountain is in its place."

Having despatched this challenge by Felice, not only to the Mayor, but also to herself, her pride, her poverty, and to the great world generally, she put on her cloak and hat and drove down to the Castle of St. Angelo.

When she returned, an hour afterwards, there was a dry

glitter in her eyes, which increased to a look of fever when she opened the drawing-room door and saw who was waiting there. It was the Mayor himself. The little oily man in patent-leather boots, holding upright his glossy silk hat, was clearly nervous and confused. He complimented her on her appearance, looked out of the window, extolled the view, and finally, with his back to his hostess, began on his business.

"It is about your letter, you know," he said awkwardly. "There seems to be a little misunderstanding on your part. About the fountain, I mean."

"None whatever, Senator. You ordered it. I have executed it. Surely the matter is quite simple."

"Impossible, my dear. I may have encouraged you to an experimental trial. We all do that. Rome is eager to discover genius. But a simple member of a corporate body cannot undertake . . . that is to say, on his own responsibility, you know . . ."

Roma's breath began to come quickly. "Do you mean that you didn't commission my fountain?"

"How could I, my child? Such matters must go through a regular form. The proper committee must sanction and resolve . . ."

"But everybody has known of this, and it has been generally understood from the first."

"Ah, understood! Possibly! Rumour and report perhaps."

"But I could bring witnesses—high witnesses—the very highest if needs be . . ."

The little man smiled benevolently.

"Surely there is no witness of any standing in the State who would go into a witness-box and say that, without a contract, and with only a few encouraging words . . ."

The dry glitter in Roma's eyes shot into a look of anger. "Do you call your letters to me a few encouraging words only?" she said.

"My letters?" the glossy hat was getting ruffled.

"Your letters alluding to this matter, and enumerating the favours you wished me to ask of the Prime Minister."

"My dear," said the Mayor after a moment, "I'm sorry if I have led you to build up hopes, and though I have no authority . . . if it will end matters amicably . . . I think I can promise . . . I might perhaps promise a little money for your loss of time."

THE ROMAN OF ROME

" Do you suppose I want charity?"

" Charity, my dear?"

" What else would it be? If I have no right to everything I will have nothing. I will take none of your money. You can leave me."

The little man shuffled his feet, and bowed himself out of the room, with many apologies and praises which Roma did not hear. For all her brave words her heart was breaking, and she was holding her breath to repress a sob. The great bulwark she had built up for herself lay wrecked at her feet. She had deceived herself into believing that she could be somebody for herself. Going down to the studio, she covered up the fountain. It had lost every quality which she had seen in it before. Art was gone from her. She was nobody. It was very, very cruel.

But that glorious telegram rustled in her breast like a captive song-bird, and before going to bed she wrote to David Rossi again.

" Your message arrived before I was up this morning, and not being entirely back from the world of dreams, I fancied that it was an angel's whisper. This is silly, but I wouldn't change it for the greatest wisdom, if, in order to be the most wise and wonderful among women, I had to love you less.

" Business first and other things afterwards. Most of the newspapers have been published to-day, and some of them are blowing themselves out of breath in abuse of you, and howling louder than the wolves of the Capitol before rain. The military courts began this morning, and they have already polished off fifty victims. Rewards for denunciations have now deepened to threats of imprisonment for non-denunciation. General Morra, Minister of War, has sent in his resignation, and there is bracing weather in the neighbourhood of the Palazzo Braschi. An editor has been arrested, many journals and societies have been suppressed, and twenty thousand of the contadini who came to Rome for the meeting in the Coliseum have been despatched to their own communes. Finally, the Royal Commissioner has written to the Pope, calling on him to assist in the work of pacifying the people, and it is rumoured that the Holy Office is to be petitioned by certain of the Bishops to denounce the 'Republic of Man' as a secret society (like the Freemasons) coming within the ban of the Pontifical constitutions.

" So much for general news, and now for more personal

intelligence. I went down to the Castle of St. Angelo this morning, and was permitted to speak to the Royal Commissioner. Recognised him instantly as a regular old-timer at the heels of the Baron, and tackled him on our ancient terms. The wretch—he squints, and he smoked a cigarette all through the interview—couldn't allow me to see Bruno during the private preparation of the case against him, and when I asked if the instruction would take long he said, ' Probably, as it is complicated by the case of some one else who is not yet in custody.' Then I asked if I might employ separate counsel for the defence, and he shuffled and said it was unnecessary. This decided me, and I walked straight to the office of the great lawyer Napoleon Fuselli, promised him five hundred francs by to-morrow morning, and told him to go ahead without delay.

"But heigh-ho, nonny! Coming home I felt like the witches in ' Macbeth.' ' By the pricking of my thumbs, something wicked this way comes.' It was Senator Tom-Tit, the little fat Mayor of Rome. His great ambition is to wear the green ribbon of St. Maurice and Lazarus, as none know better than myself. Wanting money on my fountain, I had written to the old wretch, but the moment we met I could see what was coming, so I braved it out, bustled about and made a noise. It was a mistake! There had been no commission at all! But if a little money would repay me for a loss of time . . .

"It wasn't so much that I cared about the loss of the fees, badly as I needed them. It was mainly that I had allowed the summer flies who buzzed about me for the Baron's sake to flatter me into the notion that I was an artist, when I was really nobody for myself at all.

"This humour lasted all afternoon, and spoiled my digestion for dinner, which was a pity, for there was some delicious wild asparagus. But then I thought of you and your work, and the future when you will come back with all Rome at your feet, and my vexation disappeared and I was content to be nothing and nobody except somebody whom you loved and who loved you, and that was to be everything and everybody in the world.

"I don't care a rush about the matter now, but what do you think I've done? Sold my carriage and horses! Actually! The little job-master, with his tight trousers, close-cropped head, and chamois-leather waistcoat, has just gone off after cheating me abominably. No matter! What do I want with a grand carriage while you are going about as an exile and an outcast? I want nothing you have not got, and all I have I wish you to have too, including my heart and my soul and everything that is in them . . ."

She stopped. This was the place to reveal her great secret. But she could not find her way to begin. " To-morrow will do," she thought, and so laid down the pen.

V

EARLY next morning Roma received a visit from the lawyer who conducted the business of her landlord. He was a middle-aged man in pepper-and-salt tweeds, and his manner was brusque and aggressive.

" Sorry to say, Excellency, that I've had a letter from Count Mario at Paris saying that he will require this apartment for his own use. He regrets to be compelled to disturb you, but having frequently apprised you of his intention to live here himself . . ."

" When does he want to come? " said Roma.

" At Easter."

" That will do. My aunt is ill, but if she is fit to be moved . . ."

" Thanks! And may I perhaps present . . ."

A paper in the shape of a bill came from the breast-pocket of the pepper-and-salt tweeds. Roma took it, and, without looking at it, replied:

" You will receive your rent in a day or two."

" Thanks again. I trust I may rely on that. And meantime . . ."

" Well? "

" As I am personally responsible to the Count for all moneys due to him, may I ask your Excellency to promise me that nothing shall be removed from this apartment until my arrears of rent have been paid? "

" I promise that you shall receive what is due from me in two days. Is not that enough? "

The pepper-and-salt tweeds bowed meekly before Roma's flashing eyes.

" Good-morning, sir."

" Good-morning, Excellency."

THE ETERNAL CITY

The man was hardly out of the house when a woman was shown in. It was Madame Sella, the fashionable modiste.

"So unlucky, my dear! I'm driven to my wits' end for money. The people I deal with in Paris are perfect demons, and are threatening all sorts of pains and penalties if I don't send them a great sum straight away. Of course if I could get my own money in, it wouldn't matter. But the dear ladies of society are so slow, and naturally I don't like to go to their gentlemen, although really I've waited so long for their debts that if . . ."

"Can you wait one day longer for mine?"

"Donna Roma! And we've always been such friends, too!"

"You'll excuse me this morning, won't you?" said Roma, rising.

"Certainly. I'm busy, too. So good of you to see me. Trust I've not been *de trop*. And if it hadn't been for those stupid bills of mine . . ."

Roma sat down and wrote a letter to one of the *strozzini* (stranglers), who lend money to ladies on the security of their jewels.

"I wish to sell my jewellery," she wrote, "and if you have any desire to buy it, I shall be glad if you can come to see me for this purpose at four o'clock to-morrow."

"Roma!" cried a fretful voice.

She was sitting in the boudoir, and her aunt was calling to her from the adjoining room. The old lady, who had just finished her toilet, and was redolent of perfume and scented soap, was propped up on pillows between the mirror and her Madonna, with her cat purring on the cushion at the foot of her bed.

"Ah, you do come to me sometimes, don't you?" she said, with her embroidered handkerchief at her lips. "What is this I hear about the carriage and horses? Sold them! It is incredible. I will not believe it unless you tell me so yourself."

"It is quite true, Aunt Betsy. I wanted money for various purposes, and among others to pay my debts," said Roma.

"Goodness! It's true! Give me my salts. There they are—on the card-table beside you. . . . So it's true! It's really true! You've done some extraordinary things already, miss, but this . . . Mercy me! Selling her horses! And she isn't ashamed of it! . . . I suppose you'll sell your clothes next, or perhaps your jewels."

" That's just what I want to do, Aunt Betsy."

" Holy Virgin! What are you saying, girl? Have you lost all sense of decency? Sell your jewels! Goodness! Your ancestral jewels! You must have grown utterly heartless as well as indifferent to propriety, or you wouldn't dream of selling the treasures that have come down to you from your own mother's breast, as one might say."

" My mother never set eyes on any of them, auntie, and if some of them belonged to my grandmother, she must have been a good woman because she was the mother of my father, and she would rather see me sell them all than live in debt and disgrace."

" Go on! Go on with your English talk! Or perhaps it's American, is it? You want to kill me, that's what it is! You will, too, and sooner than you expect, and then you'll be sorry and ashamed . . . Go away! Why do you come to worry me? Isn't it enough . . . Natalina! Nat-a-*lina!*"

Late that night Roma resumed her letter to David Rossi:

" DEAREST,—You are always the last person I speak to before I go to bed, and if only my words could sail away over Monte Mario in the darkness while I sleep, they would reach you on the wings of the morning.

" You want to know all that is happening, and here goes again. The tyrannies of military rule increase daily, and some of its enormities are past belief. Military court sat all day yesterday and polished off eighty-five poor victims. Ten of them got ten years, twenty got five years, and about fifty got periods of one month to twelve.

" Lawyer Napoleon F. was here this afternoon to say that he had seen Bruno and begun work in his defence. Strangely enough he finds a difficulty in a quarter from which it might least be expected. Bruno himself is holding off in some unaccountable way which gives Napoleon F. an idea that the poor soul is being got at. Apparently—you will hardly credit it—he is talking doubtfully about you, and asking incredible questions about his wife. Lawyer Napoleon actually inquired if there was ' anything in it,' and the thing struck me as so silly that I laughed out in his face. It was very wrong of me not to be jealous, wasn't it? Being a woman, I suppose I ought to have leapt at the idea, according to all the natural laws of love. I didn't, and my heart is still tranquil. But poor Bruno was more human, and Napoleon has an idea that something is going on inside the prison. He is to go there again to-morrow and to let me know.

"Such doings at home too! I've been two years in debt to my landlord, and at the end of every quarter I've always prayed like a modest woman to be allowed to pass by unnoticed. Celebrity has fallen on me at last, though, and I'm to go at Easter. Madame de Trop, too, has put the screw on, and everybody else is following suit. Yesterday, for example, I had the honour of a call from every one in the world to whom I owed twopence. Remembering how hard it used to be to get a bill out of these people, I find their sudden business ardour humorous. They do not deceive me nevertheless. I see the die is cast, the fact is known. I have fallen from my high estate of general debtor to everybody and become merely an honest woman.

"Do I suffer from these slings of fortune? Not an atom. When I was rich, or seemed to be so, I was often the most miserable woman in the world, and now I'm happy, happy, happy!

"There is only one thing makes me a little unhappy. Shall I tell you what it is? Yes, I *will* tell you because your heart is so true, and like all brave men you are so tender to all women. It is a girl friend of mine—a very close and dear friend, and she is in trouble. A little while ago she was married to a good man, and they love each other dearer than life, and there ought to be nothing between them. But there is, and it is a very serious thing too, although nobody knows about it but herself and me. How shall I tell you? Dearest, you are to think my head is on your breast and you cannot see my face while I tell you my poor friend's secret. Long ago—it seems long—she was the victim of another man. That is really the only word for it, because she did not consent. But all the same she feels that she has sinned and that nothing on earth can wash away the stain. The worst fact is that her husband knows nothing about it. This fills her with measureless regret and undying remorse. She feels that she ought to have told him, and so her heart is full of tears, and she doesn't know what it is her duty to do.

"I thought I would ask you to tell me, dearest. You are kind, but you mustn't spare her. I didn't. She wanted to draw a veil over her frailty, but I wouldn't let her. I think

she would like to confess to her husband, to pour out her
heart to him, and begin again with a clean page, but she is
afraid. Of course she hasn't really been faithless, and I could
swear on my life she loves her husband only. And then her
sorrow is so great, and she is beginning to look worn with
lying awake at nights, though some people still think she is
beautiful. I dare say you will say, serve her right for deceiving a good man. So do I sometimes, but I feel strangely inconsistent about my poor friend, and a woman has a right to
be inconsistent, hasn't she? Tell me what I am to say to her,
and please don't spare her because she is a friend of mine."

She lifted her pen from the paper. "He'll understand,"
she thought. "He'll remember our other letters and read
between the lines. Well, so much the better, and God be
good to me!"

"Good-night! Good-night! Good-night! I feel like a
child—as if the years had gone back with me, or rather as
if they had only just begun. You have awakened my soul
and all the world is different. Nearly everything that seemed
right to me before seems wrong to me now, and *vice versa.*
Life? That wasn't life. It was only existence. I fancy it
must have been some elder sister of mine who went through
everything. Think of it! When you were twenty and I was
only ten! I'm glad there isn't as much difference now. I'm
catching up to you—metaphorically, I mean. If I could
only do so physically! But what nonsense I'm talking! In
spite of my poor friend's trouble I can't help talking nonsense
to-night."

VI

Two days later Natalina, coming into Roma's bedroom,
threw open the shutters and said:

"Letter with a foreign postmark, Excellency—'Sister
Angelica, care of the Porter.' It was delivered at the Convent, and the porter sent it over here."

"Give it to me," said Roma eagerly. "It's quite right.
I know whom it is for, and if any more letters come for the
same person bring them to me immediately."

Almost before the maid had left the room Roma had torn
the letter open. It was dated from a street in Soho.

"MY DEAR WIFE,—As you see, I have reached London,
and now I am thinking of you always, wondering what suffer-

ings are being inflicted upon you for my sake and how you meet and bear them. To think of you there, in the midst of our enemies, is a spur and an inspiration. Only wait! If my absence is cruel to you it is still more hard to me. I will see your lovely eyes again before long, and there will be an end of all our sadness. Meantime continue to love me, and that will work miracles. It will make all the slings and slurs of life seem to be a long way off and of no account. Only those who love can know this law of the human heart, but how true it is and how beautiful!

"We reached London in the early morning, when the grey old city was beginning to stir after its sleepless rest. I had telegraphed the time of my arrival to the committee of our association, and early as it was some hundreds of our people were at Charing Cross to meet me. They must have been surprised to see a man step out of the train in the disguise of driver of a wine-cart on the Campagna, but perhaps that helped them to understand the position better, and they formed into procession and marched to Trafalgar Square as if they had forgotten they were in a foreign country.

"To me it was a strange and moving spectacle. The mist like a shroud over the great city, some stars of leaden hue paling out overhead, the day dawning over the vast square, the wide silence with the far-off hum of awakening life, the English workmen stopping to look at us as they went by to their work, and our company of dark-bearded men, emigrants and exiles, sending their hearts out in sympathy to their brothers in the south. As I spoke from the base of the Gordon statue and turned towards St. Martin's Church, I could fancy I saw your white-haired father on the steps with his little daughter in his arms.

"I will write again in a day or two, telling you what we are doing. Meantime I enclose a Proclamation to the People, which I wish you to get printed and posted up. Take it to old Albert Pelegrino in the Stamperia by the Trevi. Tell him to mention the cost and the money shall follow. Call at the Piazza Navona and see what is happening to Elena. Poor girl! Poor Bruno! And my poor dear little darling!

"Take care of yourself, my dear one. I am always thinking of you. It is a fearful thing to have taken up the burden of one who is branded as an outcast and an outlaw. I cannot help but reproach myself. There was a time when I saw my duty to you in another way, but love came like a hurricane

252

out of the skies and swept all sense of duty away. My wife!
my Roma! You have hazarded everything for me, and some
day I will give up everything for you.   D. R."

VII

"DEAREST,—Your letter to Sister Angelica arrived safely,
and worked more miracles in her cloistered heart than ever
happened to the 'Blessed Bambino.' Before it came I was
always thinking, 'Where is he now? Is he having his breakfast? Or is it dinner, according to the difference of time and
longitude?' All I knew was that you had travelled north,
and though the sun doesn't ordinarily set in that direction,
the sky over Monte Mario used to glow for my special pleasure like the gates of the New Jerusalem.

"Your letters are so precious that I will ask you not to
fill them with useless things. Don't tell me to love you. The
idea! Didn't I say I should think of you always? I do! I
think of you when I go to bed at night, and that is like opening a jewel-case in the moonlight. I think of you when I am
asleep, and that is like an invisible bridge which unites us
in our dreams; and I think of you when I wake in the morning, and that is like a cage of song-birds that sing in my
breast the whole day long.

"But you are dying to hear what is really happening in
Rome, so your own special envoy must send off her budget
as a set-off against those official telegrams. 'Not a day without a line,' so my letter will look like words shaken out of
a literary pepper-box. Let me bring my despatches up to
date.

"Military rule severer than ever, and poverty and misery
on all sides. Families of reserve soldiers starving, and meetings of chief citizens to succour them. Donation from the
King and from the 'Black' Charity Circle of St. Peter.
Even the clergy are sending francs, so none can question their
sincerity. Bureau of Labour besieged by men out of work,
and offices occupied by Carabineers. People eating maize
in polenta and granturco with the certainty of sickness to
follow. Red Cross Society organised as in time of war, and
many sick and wounded hidden in houses.

"And now for more personal matters. The proclamation
is in hand, and paid for, and will be posted first thing in the

morning. From the printer's I went on to the Piazza Navona and found a wilderness of woe. Elena has gone away, leaving an ambiguous letter behind her, saying that she wished her Madonna to be given to me, as she would have no need of it in the place she was going to. This led the old people to believe that for the loss of her son and husband she had become demented and had destroyed herself. I pretended to think differently, and warned them to say nothing of their daughter's disappearance, thinking that Bruno might hear of it, and find food for still further suspicions.

"Lawyer Napoleon F. has seen the poor soul again, and been here this evening to tell me the result. It will seem to you incredible. Bruno will do nothing to help in his own defence. Talks of 'treachery' and the 'King's pardon.' Napoleon F. thinks the Camorra is at work with him, and tells how criminals in the prisons of Italy have a league of crime, with captains, corporals, and cadets. My own reading of the mystery is different. I think the Camorra in this case is the Council, and the only design is to entrap by treachery one of the 'greater delinquents not in custody.' I want to find out where Charles Minghelli is at present. Nobody seems to know.

"As for me, what do you suppose is my last performance? I've sold my jewels! Yesterday I sent for one of the *strozzini*, and the old Shylock came this evening and cheated me unmercifully. No matter! What do I want with jewellery, or a fine house, and servants to follow me about as if I were a Cardinal? If *you* can do without them so can I. But you need not say you are anxious about what is happening to me. I'm as happy as the day is long. I am happy because I love you, and that is everything.

"Only one thing troubles me—the grief of the poor girl I told you of. She follows me about, and is here all the time, so that I feel as if I were possessed by her secret. In fact, I'm afraid I'll blab it out to somebody. I think you would be sorry to see her. She tries to persuade herself that because her soul did not consent she was really not to blame. That is the thing that women are always saying, isn't it? They draw this distinction when it is too late, and use it as a quibble to gloss over their fault. Oh, I gave it her! I told her she should have thought of that in time, and died rather than yield. It was all very fine to talk of a minute of weakness—mere weakness of bodily will, not of virtue, but the world splits no straws of that sort. If a woman has fallen she has fallen, and there is no question of body or soul.

"Oh dear, how she cried! When I caught sight of her red eyes, I felt she ought to get herself forgiven. And after all I'm not so sure that she should tell her husband, seeing that it would so shock and hurt him. She thinks that after one has done wrong the best thing to do next is to say nothing about it. There *is* something in that, isn't there?

"One thing I must say for the poor girl—she has been a different woman since this happened. It has converted her. That's a shocking thing to say, but it's true. I remember that when I was a girl in the convent, and didn't go to mass because I hadn't been baptized and it was agreed with the Baron that I shouldn't be, I used to read in the Lives of the Saints that the darkest moments of ' the drunkenness of sin' were the instants of salvation. Who knows? Perhaps the very fact by which the world usually stamps a woman as bad is in this case the fact of her conversion. As for my friend, she used to be the vainest young thing in Rome, and now she cares nothing for the world and its vanities.

"Two days hence my letter will fall into your hands— why can't I do so too? Love me always. That will lift me up to your own level, and prove that when you fell in love with me love wasn't quite blind. I'm not so old and ugly as I was yesterday, and at all events nobody could love you more. Good-night! I open my window to say my last good-night to the stars over Monte Mario, for that's where England is! How bright they are to-night! How beautiful! ROMA."

VIII

NEXT morning the Countess was very ill, and Roma went to her immediately.

"I must have a doctor," she said. "It's perfectly heartless to keep me without one all this time."

"Aunt Betsy," said Roma, "you know quite well that but for your own express prohibition you would have had a doctor all along."

"For mercy's sake, don't nag, but send for a doctor immediately. Let it be Dr. Fedi. Everybody has Dr. Fedi now."

Fedi was the Pope's physician, and therefore the most costly and fashionable doctor in Rome.

THE ETERNAL CITY

Dr. Fedi came with an assistant who carried a little case of instruments. He examined the Countess, her breast, her side, and the glands under her arms, shot out a solemn underlip, put two fingers inside his collar, twisted his head from side to side, and announced that the patient must have a nurse immediately.

"Do you hear that, Roma? Doctor says that I must have a nurse. Of course I must have a nurse. I'll have one of the English nursing Sisters. Everybody has them now. They're foreigners, and if they talk they can't do much mischief."

The Sister was sent for. She was a mild and gentle creature, in blue and white, but she talked perpetually of her Mother Superior, who had been bedridden for fifteen years, yet smiled sweetly all day long. That exasperated the Countess and fretted her. When the doctor came again the patient was worse.

"Your aunt must have dainties to tempt her appetite and so keep up her strength."

"Do you hear, Roma?"

"You shall have everything you wish for, auntie."

"Well, I wish for strawberries. Everybody eats them who is ill at this season."

The strawberries were bought, but the Countess scarcely touched them, and they were finally consumed in the kitchen.

When the doctor came a third time the patient was much emaciated and her skin had become sallow and earthy.

"It would not be right to conceal from you the gravity of your condition, Countess," he said. "In such a case we always think it best to tell a patient to make her peace with God."

"Oh, don't say that, doctor," whimpered the poor withered creature on the bed.

"But while there's life there's hope, you know; and meantime I'll send you an opiate to relieve the pain."

When the doctor was gone, the Countess sent for Roma.

"That Fedi is a fool," she said. "I don't know what people see in him. I should like to try the Bambino of Ara Cœli. The Cardinal Vicar had it, and why shouldn't I? They say it has worked miracles. It may be dear, but if I die you will always reproach yourself. If you are short of money you can sign a bill at six months, and before that the poor maniac woman will be gone and you'll be the wife of the Baron."

"If you really think the Bambino will . . ."

"It will! I know it will."

"Very well, I will send for it."

Roma sent a letter to the Superior of the Franciscans at the Friary of Ara Cœli asking that the little figure of the infant Christ, which is said to restore the sick, should be sent to her aunt, who was near to death.

At the same time she wrote to an auctioneer in the Via due Macelli, requesting him to call upon her. The man came immediately. He had little beady eyes, which ranged round the dining-room and seemed to see everything except Roma herself.

"I wish to sell up my furniture," said Roma.

"All of it?"

"Except what is in my aunt's room and the room of her nurse, and such things in the kitchen, the servants' apartments, and my own bedroom as are absolutely necessary for present purposes."

"Quite right. When?"

"Within a week if possible."

The Bambino came in a carriage with two horses, and the people in the street went down on their knees as it passed. One of the friars in priest's surplice carried it in a box with the lid open, and two friars in brown habits walked before it with lifted candles. But as the painted image in its scarlet clothes and jewels entered the Countess's bedroom with its grim and ghostly procession, and was borne like a baby mummy to the foot of her bed, it terrified her, and she screamed.

"Take it away!" she shrieked. "Do you want to frighten me out of my life? Take it away!"

The grim and ghostly procession went out. Its visit had lasted thirty seconds and cost a hundred francs.

When the doctor came again the outline of the Countess's writhing form had shrunk to the lines of a skeleton under the ruffled counterpane.

"It's not the Bambino you want—it's the priest," he said, and then the poor mortal who was still afraid of dying began to whimper.

"And, Sister," said the doctor, " as the Countess suffers so much pain, you may increase the opiate from a dessertspoonful to a tablespoonful, and give it twice as frequently."

That evening the Sister went home for a few hours' leave, and Roma took her place by the sick-bed. The patient was more selfish and exacting than ever, but Roma had begun to feel a softening towards the poor tortured being, and was trying her best to do her duty.

It was dusk, and the Countess, who had just taken her opiate in the increased doses, was out of pain, and wished to make her toilet. Roma brought up the night-table and the mirror, the rouge-pot, the rabbit's foot, the puff, the pencil, and the other appurtenances of her aunt's toilet-box. And when the fragile thing, so soon to be swallowed up by the earth in its great earthquake, had been propped by pillows, she began to paint her wrinkled face as if going to dance a minuet with death. First the black rings about the languid eyes were whitened, then the earthen cheeks were rouged, and finally the livid lips and nostrils were pencilled with the rosy hues of health and youth.

Roma had turned on the electric light, but the glare oppressed the patient, and she switched it off again. The night had now closed in, and the only light in the room came from the little red oil-lamp which burned before the shrine.

The drug began to operate, and its first effect was to loosen the old lady's tongue. She began to talk of priests in a tone of contempt and braggadocio.

"I hate priests," she said, "and I can't bear to have them about me. Why so? Because they are always about the dead. Their black cassocks make me think of funerals. The sight of a graveyard makes me faint. Besides, priests and confessions go together, and why should a woman confess if she can avoid it? When people confess they have to give up the thing they confess to, or they can't get absolution. Fedi's a fool. Give it up indeed! I might as well talk of giving up the bed that's under me."

Roma sat on a stool by the bedside, listening intently, yet feeling she had no right to listen. The drug was rapidly intoxicating the Countess, who went on to talk as if some one else had been in the room.

"A priest would be sure to ask questions about that girl. I would have to tell him why the Baron put me here to look after her, and then he would prate about the Sacraments and want me to give up everything."

THE ROMAN OF ROME

The Countess laughed a hard, evil laugh, and Roma felt an icy shudder pass over her.

"'I'm tied,' said the Baron. 'But you must see that she waits for me. Everything depends upon you, and if all comes out well . . .'"

The old woman's tongue was thickening, and her eyes in the dull red light were glazed and stupid.

Roma sat motionless and silent, watching with her own dilated eyes the grinning sinner, as she poured out the story of the plot for her capture and corruption. At that moment she hated her aunt, the unclean, malignant, unpitying thing who had poisoned her heart against her father and tried to break down every spiritual impulse of her soul.

The diabolical horse-laughter came again, and then the devil who had loosened the tongue of the dying woman in the intoxication of the drug made her reveal the worst secret of her tortured conscience.

"Why did I let him torment me? Because he knew something. It was about the child. Didn't you know I had a child? It was born when my husband was away. He was coming home, and I was in terror."

The red light was on the emaciated face. Roma was sitting in the shadow with a roaring in her ears.

"It died, and I went to confession. . . . I thought nobody knew. . . . But the Baron knows everything. . . . After that I did whatever he told me."

The thick voice stopped. Only the ticking of a little clock was audible. The Countess had dozed off. All her vanity of vanities, her intrigues, her life-long frenzies, her sins and sufferings were wrapt in the innocence of sleep.

Roma looked down at the poor, wrinkled, rouged face, now streaked with sweat and with black lines from the pencilled eyebrows, and noiselessly rose to go. She was feeling a sense of guilt in herself that stirred her to the depths of abasement.

The Countess awoke. She was again in pain, and her voice was now different.

"Roma! Is that you?"

"Yes, aunt."

"Why are you sitting in the darkness? I have a horror of darkness. You know that quite well."

Roma turned on the lights.

"Have I been speaking? What have I been saying?"

Roma tried to prevaricate.

"You are telling me a falsehood. You know you are. You gave me that drug to make me tell you my secrets. But I know what I told you and it was all a lie. You needn't think because you've been listening . . . It was a lie, I tell you . . ."

The Sister came back at that moment, and Roma went to her room. She did not write her usual letter to David Rossi that night. Instead of doing so, she knelt by Elena's little Madonna, which she had set up on a table by her bed.

Her own secret was troubling her. She had wanted to take it to some one, some woman, who would listen to her and comfort her. She had no mother, and her tears had begun to fall.

It was then that she thought of the world-mother, and remembered the prayer she had heard a thousand times but never used before.

"Holy Mary, Mother of God, pray for us sinners, now, and at the hour of death—Amen!"

When she rose from her knees she felt like a child who had been crying and was comforted.

IX

FOR some days after this the house was in a tumult. Men in red caps labelled "Casa di Vendita" were tearing up carpets, dragging out pieces of furniture and marking them. The catalogue was made, and bills were posted outside the street door announcing a sale of "Old and New Objects of Art" in the "Appartamento Volonna." Then came the "Grand Esposizione"—it was on Sunday morning—and the following day the auction.

Roma built herself an ambush from prying eyes in one corner of the apartment. She turned her boudoir into a bedroom and sitting-room combined. From there she heard the shuffling of feet as the people assembled in the large dismantled drawing-room without. She was writing at a table when some one knocked at the door. It was the Commendatore Angelelli, in light clothes and silk hat. At that moment the look of servility in his long face prevailed over the look of arrogance.

"Good-morning, Donna Roma. May I perhaps . . ."

THE ROMAN OF ROME

"Come in."

The lanky person settled himself comfortably and began on a confidential communication.

"The Baron, sincerely sorry to hear of your distresses, sends me to say that you have only to make a request and this unseemly scene shall come to an end. In fact, I have authority to act on his behalf—as an unknown friend, you know—and stop these proceedings even at the eleventh hour. Only a word from you—one word—and everything shall be settled satisfactorily."

Roma was silent for a moment, and the Commendatore concluded that his persuasions had prevailed. Somebody else knocked at the door.

"Come in," said the Commendatore largely.

This time it was the auctioneer. "Time to begin the sale, Signorina. Any commands?" He glanced from Roma to Angelelli with looks of understanding.

"I think her Excellency has perhaps something to say," said Angelelli.

"Nothing whatever. Go on," said Roma.

The auctioneer disappeared through the door, and Angelelli put on his hat.

"Then you have no answer for his Excellency?"

"None."

"*Bene*," said the Commendatore, and he went off whistling softly.

The auction began. At a table on a platform where the piano used to stand sat the chief auctioneer with his ivory hammer. Beneath him at a similar table sat an assistant. As the men in red caps brought up the goods the two auctioneers took the bidding together, repeating each other in the manner of actor and prompter at an Italian theatre.

The English Sister came to say that the Countess wished to see her niece immediately. The invalid, now frightfully emaciated and no longer able to sit up, was lying back on her lace-edged pillows. She was plucking with shrivelled and bony fingers at her figured counterpane, and as Roma entered she tried to burst out on her in a torrent of wrath. But the sound that came from her throat was like a voice shouted on a windy headland, and hardly louder than the muffled voices of the auctioneers as they found their way through the walls.

Roma sat down on the stool by the bedside, stroked the

cat with the gold cross suspended from its neck, and listened to the words within the room and without as they fell on her ear alternately.

"Roma, you are treating me shamefully. While I am lying here helpless you are having an auction—actually an auction—at the door of my very room."

"Camera da letto della Signorina! Bed in *noce*, richly ornamented with fruit and flowers." "Shall I say fifty?" "Thank you, fifty." "Fifty." "Fifty-five." "Fifty-five." "No advance on fifty-five?" "Gentlemen, gentlemen! The beautiful bed of a beautiful lady, and only fifty-five offered for it! . . ."

"If you wanted money you had only to ask the Baron, and if you didn't wish to do that, you had only to sign a bill at six months, as I told you before. But no! You wanted to humble and degrade me. That's all it is. You've done it, too, and I'm dying in disgrace. . . ."

"Secretaire in walnut! Think, ladies, of the secrets this writing-desk might whisper if it would! How much shall I say?" "Sixty lire." "Sixty." "Sixty-five." "Sixty-five." "Writing-desk in walnut with the love letters hardly out of it, and only sixty-five lire offered! . . ."

"This is what comes of a girl going her own way. Society is not so very exacting, but it revenges itself on people who defy the respectabilities. And quite right, too! Pity they could not be the only ones to suffer, but they can't. Their friends and relations are the real sufferers; and as for me . . ."

The Countess's voice broke down into a maudlin whimper. Without a word Roma rose up to go. As she did so she met Natalina coming into the room with the usual morning plate of forced strawberries. They had cost four francs the pound.

Some time afterwards, from her writing-table in the boudoir-bedroom, Roma heard a shuffling of feet on the circular iron stairs. The people were going down to the studio. Presently the auctioneer's voice came up as from a vault.

"And now what am I offered for this large and important work of modern art?"

There was a ripple of derisive laughter.

"A fountain worthy, when finished, to rank with the masterpieces of ancient Rome."

More derisive laughter.

"Now is the time for anti-clericals. Gentlemen, don't all speak at once. Every day is not a festa. How much? Nothing at all? Not even a soldo? Too bad. Art is its own reward."

Still more laughter, followed by the shuffling of feet coming up the iron stairs, and a familiar voice on the landing—it was the Princess Bellini's—"Madonna mia! what a fright it is, to be sure!"

Then another voice—it was Madame Sella's—"I thought so the day of the private view, when she behaved so shockingly to the dear Baron."

Then a third voice—it was the voice of Olga the journalist—"I said the Baron would pay her out, and he has. Before the day is over she'll not have a stick left or a roof to cover her."

Roma dropped her head on to the table. Try as she might to keep a brave front, the waves of shame and humiliation were surging over her.

Some one touched her on the shoulder. It was Natalina with a telegram: "Letter received; my apartment is paid for to end of June; why not take possession of it?"

From that moment onward nothing else mattered. The tumultuous noises in the drawing-room died down, and there was no sound but the voices of the auctioneer and his clerk, which rumbled like a drum in the empty chamber.

It was four o'clock. Opening the window, Roma heard the music of a band. At that a spirit of defiance took possession of her, and she put on her hat and cloak. As she passed through the empty drawing-room, the auctioneer, who was counting his notes with the dry rustle of a winnowing machine, looked up with his beady eyes and said:

"It has come out fairly well, Madame—better than we might have expected."

On reaching the piazza she hailed a cab. "The Pincio!" she cried, and settled in her seat. When she returned an hour afterwards she wrote her usual letter to David Rossi.

"High doings to-day! Have had a business on my own account, and done a roaring trade! Disposed of everything in the shop except what I wanted for myself. It isn't every trades-woman who can say that much, and I'm only a beginner to boot!

"Soberly, I've sold up. Being under notice to leave this

apartment, I didn't want all this useless furniture, so I thought I might as well get done with it in good time. Besides, what right had I to soft beds and fine linen while you were an exile, sleeping Heaven knows where? And then my aunt, who is very ill and wants all sorts of luxuries, is rather expensive. So for the past week my drawing-room has been as full of fluting as a frog-pond at sunset, and on Sunday morning people were banging away at my poor piano as if it had been a hurdy-gurdy at an osteria.

"But, oh dear! how stupid the world is! People thought because I was selling what I didn't want I must be done. You would have laughed to hear their commentaries. To tell you the truth, I was so silly that I could have cried, but just at the moment when I felt a wee bit badly, down came your telegram like an angel from Heaven—and what do you think I did? The old Adam, or say the new Eve, took possession of me, and the minute the people were gone I hired a cab—a common garden cab, Roman variety, with a horse on its last legs and a driver in ragged tweeds—and drove off to the Pincio! I wanted to show those fine folk that I *wasn't* done, and I did! They were all there, my dear friends and former flatterers—every one of them who has haunted my house for years, asking for this favour or that, and paying me in the coin of sweetest smiles. It seemed as if fate had gathered them all together for my personal inspection and wouldn't let a creature escape.

"Did they see me? Not a soul of them! I drove through them and between them, and they bowed across and before and behind me, and I might have been as invisible as Asmodeus for all the consciousness they betrayed of my presence. Was I humiliated? Confused? Crushed? Oh, dear no! I was proud. I knew the day would come, the day was near, when they must try to forget all this and to persuade themselves it had never been, when for my own sake, even mine, and for yours, most of all for yours, they would come back humble, so humble and afraid.

"So I gave them every chance. I was bold and I did not spare them. And when the sun began to sink behind St. Peter's and the band stopped, and we turned to go, I know which of us went home happy and unashamed. Oh, David Rossi! If you could have been there!

"I must write again on other matters. Meantime, one item of news. Lawyer Napoleon, who continues to go to

Regina Cœli to see the bewildering Bruno, saw Charles Minghelli there in prison clothes! If the God who settles the question of sex had only remembered to make your wife the procurator-general, think how different the history of the world would have been! The worst of it is he mightn't have remembered to make you a woman; and in any case, things being so nicely settled as they are, I don't think I want to be a man. I waft a kiss to you on the wings of the wind. It's ponente to-day, so it ought to be warm.

" ROMA.

"P.S.—My poor friend is still in trouble. Although not a religious woman, she has taken to saying a 'Hail Mary' every night on going to bed, and if it wasn't for that I'm afraid she would commit suicide, so frightful are the visions that enter her head sometimes. I've told her how wrong it would be to do away with herself, if only for the sake of her husband, who is away. Didn't I tell you he was away at present? It would hurt you dreadfully if *I* were to die before *you* return, wouldn't it? But I'm dying already to hear what you think of her. Write! Write! Write!"

X

WHEN the King of Terrors could no longer be beaten back the Countess sent for the priest. Before he arrived she insisted on making her toilet and receiving him in the dressing-gown which she used to wear when people made ante-camera to her in the days of her gaiety and strength.

During the time of the Countess's confession Roma sat in her own room with a tremor of the heart which she had never felt before. Something personal and very intimate was creeping over her soul. She heard the indistinct murmur of the priest's voice at intervals, followed by a sibilant sound as of whispers and sobs.

The confession lasted fifteen minutes and then the priest came out of the room. "Now that your relative has made her peace with God," he said, "she must receive the Blessed Sacrament, Extreme Unction, and the Apostolic Blessing."

He went away to prepare for these offices, and the English Sister came to see Roma. "The Countess is like another woman already," she said, but Roma did not go into the sick-room.

THE ETERNAL CITY

The priest returned in half-an-hour. He had now two assistants, one carrying the cross and banner, the other a vessel of holy water and the volume of the Roman ritual. The Sister and Felice met them at the door with lighted candles.

"Peace be to this house!" said the priest.

And the assistants said, "And to all dwelling in it."

Then the priest took off an outer cloak, revealing his white surplice and violet stole, and followed the candles into the Countess's room. The little card-table had been covered with a damask napkin and laid out as an altar. All the dainty articles of the dying woman's dressing-table, her scent-flasks, rouge pots and puffs, were huddled together with various medicine bottles on a chest of drawers at the back. It was two o'clock in the afternoon and the sun was shining, so the curtains were drawn and the shutters closed. In the darkened room the candles burned like stars.

The ghostly viaticum being over, the priest and his assistants left the house. But the pale, grinning shadow of death continued to stand by the perfumed couch.

Roma had not been present at the offices, and presently the English Sister came to say that the Countess wished to see her.

"It's perfectly miraculous," said the Sister. "She's like another woman."

"Has she had her opiate lately?" said Roma, and the Sister answered that she had.

Roma found her aunt in a kind of mystical transport. A great light of joy, almost of pride, was shining in her face.

"All my pains are gone," she said. "All my sorrows and trials too. I have laid them all on Christ, and now I am going to mount up with Him to God."

Clearly she had no sense of her guilt towards Roma. She began to take a high tone with her, the tone of a saint towards a sinner.

"You must conquer your worldly passions, Roma. You have been a sinner, but you must not die a bad death. For instance, you are selfish. I am sorry to say it, but you know you are. You must confess and dedicate your life to fighting the sin in your sinful heart, and commend your soul to His mercy who has washed me from all stain."

But the Countess's ethereal transports did not wholly eclipse her worldly vanities when she proceeded to preparations for her funeral.

THE ROMAN OF ROME

"Let there be a Requiem Mass, Roma. Everybody has it. It costs a little, certainly, but we can't think of money in a case like this. And send for the Raveggi Company to do the funeral pomps, and see they don't put me on a tressel. I am a noble and have a right to be laid on the church floor. See they bury me on high ground. The little Pincio is where the best people are buried now, above the tomb of Duke Massimo."

Roma continued to say "Yes," and "Yes," and "Yes," though her very heart felt sore.

Two hours afterwards the Countess was in her death agony. The tortured body had prevailed over the rapturous soul, and she was calling for more and more of the opiate. Everybody was odious to her, and her angular face was snapping all round.

The priest came to say the prayers for the dying. It was near to sunset, but the shutters were still closed, and the room had a grim solemnity. A band was playing on the Pincio, and the strains of an opera mingled with the petitions of the "breathing forth."

Everybody knelt except Roma. She alone was standing, but her heart was on its knees and her whole soul was prostrate.

The priest put a crucifix in the Countess's hand and she kissed it fervently, pronouncing all the time with gasping breath the name, "Gesù, Gesù, Gesù!"

The passing bell of the parish church was tolling in slow strokes, and the priest was praying fast and loud:

"May Christ who called thee receive thee, and let angels lead thee into the bosom of Abraham."

At one moment the crucifix dropped from the dying woman's hands, and her diamond rings, now too large for the shrivelled fingers, fell on to the counterpane. A little later her wig fell off, and for an instant her head was bald. Her forehead was perspiring; her breath was rattling in her chest. At last she became delirious.

"It's a lie!" she cried. "Everything I've said is a lie! I didn't kill it!" Then she rolled aside, and the crucifix fell on to the floor.

The priest, who had been praying faster and faster every moment, rose to his feet and said in an altered tone, "We commend to Thee, O Lord, the soul of Thy handmaiden, Elizabeth, that being dead to the world she may live to

Thee, and those sins which through the frailty of human life she has committed Thou by the indulgence of Thy loving kindness may wipe out, through Christ our Lord, Amen."

The priest's voice died down to an inarticulate murmur and then stopped. A moment afterwards the curtains were drawn back, the shutters parted, and the windows thrown open. A flood of sunset light streamed into the room. The candles burnt yellow and went out. The mystic rites were at an end.

Roma fled back to her own room. Her storm-tossed soul was foundering.

The band was still playing on the Pincio, and the sun was going down behind St. Peter's, when Roma took up her pen to write.

"She is dead! The life she clung to so desperately has left her at last. How she held on to it! And now she has gone to give an account of the deeds done in this body. Yet who am I to talk like this? Only a poor, unhappy fellow-sinner.

"After confession she thought she was forgiven. She imagined she was pure, sinless, soulful. Perhaps she was so, and only the pains of death made her seem to fall away. But what a power in confession! Oh, the joy in her poor face when she had lifted the burden of her sins and secrets off her soul! Forgiveness! What a thing it must be to feel one's self forgiven! . . .

"I cannot write any more to-day, my dear one, but there will be news for you next time, great and serious news."

XI

ROMA fulfilled her promise. The funeral pomps, if the Countess could have seen them, would have satisfied her vain little mind. On going to the parish church the procession covered the entire length of the street. First the banner with skull, cross-bones, and hour-glass, then a confraternity of lay people, then twenty paid mourners in evening dress, then fifty Capuchins at two francs a head with yellow candles at three francs each, then the cross, then the secular clergy two and two, then the parish priest in surplice and black stole with servitors and acolytes, then a stately funeral car with four horses richly harnessed, and finally four coaches with coachmen and footmen in gala livery. The bier was loaded with flowers and streamers, and the cost of the cortège was nearly a thousand francs.

As Roma passed out of the church with head down some one spoke to her. It was the Baron, carrying his hat, on which there was a deep black band. His tall spare figure, high forehead, straight hair, and features hard as iron, made a painful impression.

" Sorry I cannot go on to the Campo Santo," he said, and then he added something about breaks in the chain of life which Roma did not hear.

" I trust it is not true, as I am given to understand, that on leaving your apartment you are going to live in the house of a certain person whom I need not name. That would, I assure you, be a grave error, and I would earnestly counsel you not to commit it."

She made no reply but walked on to the door of the carriage. He helped her to enter it, and then said: " Remember, my attitude is the same as ever. Do not deny me the satisfaction of serving you in your hour of need."

When Roma came to full possession of herself after the Requiem Mass, the cortège was on its way to the cemetery. There was a line of carriages. Most of them were empty as the mourning of which they formed a part. The parish priest sat with his acolyte, who held a crucifix before his eyes so that his thoughts might not wander. He took snuff and said his Matins for to-morrow.

The necropolis of Rome is outside the Porta San Lorenzo, by the church of that name. The bier drew up at the House of Deposit. When the coaches discharged their occupants, Roma saw that except the paid servants of the funeral she was the only mourner. The Countess's friends, like herself, disliked the sight of churchyards.

The House of Deposit, a low-roofed chamber under a chapel, contained tressels for every kind and condition of the dead. One place was labelled " Reserved for distinguished corpses." The coffin of the Countess was put to rest there until the buriers should come to bury it in the morning, the wreaths and flowers and streamers were laid over it, the priest sprinkled it again with holy water, and then the funeral was at an end.

" I will not go back yet," said Roma, and thereupon the

priest and his assistants stepped into the carriages. The drivers lit cigarettes and started off at a brisk trot.

It had been a gorgeous funeral, and the soul of the Countess would have been satisfied. But the grinning King of Terrors had stood by all the time, saying, "Vanity of vanities, all is vanity."

Roma bought a wreath of wild flowers at a stall outside the cemetery gates, and by help of a paper given to her in the office she found the grave of little Joseph. It was in a shelf of vaults like ovens, each with its marble door, and a photograph on the front. They were all photographs of children, sweet smiling faces, a choir of little angels, now singing round the throne in heaven. The sun was shining on them, and the tall cypress trees were singing softly in the light wind overhead. Here and there a mother was trimming an oil-lamp that hung before her baby's face, and listening to the little voice that was not dead but speaking to her soul's soul.

Roma hung her wreath on Joseph's vault and turned away. Going out of the gates she met a great concourse of people. At their head was a Capuchin carrying a black wooden cross with sponge, spear, hammer and nails attached. Two boys in blue and white carried candles by his side. The crowd behind were of the poorest, chiefly women and girls with shawls and handkerchiefs on their heads. It was Friday, and they were going to the Church of San Lorenzo to make the procession of the Stations of the Cross. Scarcely knowing why she did so, Roma followed them.

The people filled the Basilica. Their devotion was deep and touching. As they followed the friar from station to station they sang in monotonous tones the strophes of the *Stabat Mater.*

"Ah, Mother, fountain of love, make me feel the strength of sorrow that I may mourn with thee."

Their prayer seemed hardly needful. They were the starving wives and daughters of men in prison, men in hospital, and reserve soldiers. Poor wrecks on life's shore, thrown up by the tide, they had turned to religion for consolation, and were sending up their cry to God.

When they had finished their course and ended their canticles of grief they gathered about the pulpit and the Capuchin got up to preach. He was a bearded man with a face full of light, almost of frenzy, and a cross and a rosary hung from his girdle. He spoke of their poverty, their lost ones, their privations, of the dark hour they were passing through, and of answers to prayer in political troubles. During this time the silence was breathless; but when he told them that God had sent their sufferings upon them for their sins, that they must confess their sins, in order that their holy mother, the Church, might save them from their sins, there was a deep hum in the air like the reverberation in a great shell.

A line of confessional boxes stood in each of the church aisles, and as the preacher described the sorrows of the man-God, His passion, His agony, His blood, the women and girls, weeping audibly, got up one by one and went over to confess. No sooner had one of them arisen than another took her place, and each as she rose to her feet looked calm and comforted.

The emotion of the moment was swelling over Roma like a flood. If she could unburden her heart like that! If she could cast off all the trouble of her days and nights of pain! One of the confessional boxes had a penitential rod protruding from it, and going past the front of it she had seen the face of a priest. It was a soft, kindly, human face. She had seen it before somewhere—perhaps in the Pope's procession.

At that moment a poor girl with a handkerchief on her head, who had knelt down crying, was getting up with shining eyes. Roma was shaken by violent tremors. An overpowering desire had come upon her to confess. For a moment she held on to a chair, lest she should fall to the floor. Then by a sudden impulse, in a kind of delirium, scarcely knowing what she was doing until it was done, she flung herself in the place the girl had risen from, and with a palpitating heart said in a tremulous voice through the little brass grating:

"Father, I am a great sinner—hear me, hear me!"

The measured breathing inside the confessional was arrested, and the peaceful face of the priest looked out at the hectic cheeks and blazing eyes.

"Wait, my daughter, do not agitate yourself. Say the Confiteor."

She tried to speak, but her words were hardly audible or coherent.

"I confess . . . I confess . . . I cannot, Father."

A pinch of snuff dropped from the old man's fingers.

"Are you not a Christian?"

"I have not been baptized, but I was educated in a convent, and . . ."

"Then I cannot hear your confession. Baptism is the door of the Church, and without it . . ."

"But I am in great trouble. For Our Lady's sake, listen to me. Oh, listen to me, Father, only listen to me."

Although accustomed to the sufferings of the human heart, a measureless pity came over the old priest, and he said in a kind and tender voice:

"Go on, my daughter. I cannot give you absolution, for you are not a child of the Church; but I am an old man, and if I can help your poor soul to bear its burden, God forbid that I should turn you away."

In a torrent of hot words Roma poured out her trouble, hiding nothing, extenuating nothing, and naming and blaming no one. At length the throbbing breath and quivering voice died down, and there was a moment's silence, in which the dull rumble in the church seemed to come from far away. Then the voice behind the grating said in tender tones:

"My daughter, you have committed no sin in this case and have nothing to repent of. That you should be troubled by scruples shows that your soul is pure and that you are living in communion with God. Your bodily health is reduced by nervousness and anxiety, and it is natural that you should imagine that you have sinned where you have not sinned. That is the sweet grace of most women, but how few men! What sin there has been is not yours; therefore go home, and God comfort you."

"But, dear Father . . . it is so good of you, but have you forgotten . . ."

"Your husband? No! Whether you should tell him it is beyond my power to say. In itself I should be against it, for why should you disturb his conscience and endanger the peace of a family? Your scruples about Nature coming to convict you, being without grounds of reason, are temptations of the devil and should be put behind your back. But that your marriage was a religious one only, that the other person (you did right not to name him, my child) may use that circumstance to separate you, and that your confession to your husband, if it came too late, would come prejudiced and worse than in vain, these are facts that make it difficult to advise you for your safety and peace of mind. Let me consult some one wiser than myself. Let me, perhaps, take your secret to a high place, a kindly ear, a saintly heart, a venerable and holy head. Come again, or leave me your name if you will, and if that holy person has anything to say you shall hear of it. Meantime go home in peace and content, my daughter, and may God bring you into His true fold at last."

When Roma got up from the grating of the confessional she felt like one who had passed through a great sickness and was now better. Her whole being was going through a miraculous convalescence. A great weight had been lifted off; she was renewed as with a new soul and her very body felt light as air.

The preacher was still preaching in his tremulous tones, and the women and girls were still crying, as Roma passed out of the church, but now she heard all as in a dream. It was not until she reached the portico, and a blind beggar rattled his can in her face, that the spell was broken, so sudden and mysterious was the transition when she came back from heaven to earth.

XII

By the first post next morning " Sister Angelica " received a letter from David Rossi.

" DEAREST,—Your budget arrived safely and brought me great joy and perhaps a little sadness. Apart from the pain I always suffer when I think of our poor people, there was a little twinge as I read between the lines of your letter. Are you not dissimulating some of your happiness to keep up my spirits and to prevent me from rushing back to you at all hazards? You shall be really happy some day, my dear one. I shall hear your silvery laugh again as I did on that glorious day in the Campagna. Wait, only wait! We are still young and we shall live.

" Pray for me, my heart, that what my hand is doing may not be done amiss. I am working day and night. Meetings, committees, correspondence early and late. A great scheme is afoot, dearest, and you shall hear all about it presently. I am proud that I judged rightly of the moral grandeur of your nature, and that it is possible to tell you everything.

" We have elected a centre of action and mapped out our organisation. Everybody agrees with me on the necessity for united action. Europe seems to be ready for a complete change, but the first great act must be done in Rome. I find encouragement everywhere. The brotherly union of the peoples is going on. A power stronger than brute force is sweeping through the world.

"Poor Bruno! You are no doubt right that pressure is being put upon him to betray me. It is not for myself only that I am troubled. It would be a lasting grief to me if his mind were poisoned. Charles Minghelli being in prison in the disguise of a prisoner means that anything may happen. When the man came to me after his dismissal in London, it was to ask help to assassinate the Baron. I refused it, and he went over to the other side. The secret tribunal in which cases are prepared for public trial is a hellish machine for cruelty and injustice. It has been abolished in nearly every other civilised country, but the courts and jails of our beautiful Italy continue to be the scene of plots in which helpless unfortunates are terrorised by expedients which leave not a trace of crime. A prisoner is no longer a man, but a human agent to incriminate others. His soul is corrupted, and a price is put upon treachery. See Bruno yourself if you can, and save him from himself and the people whose only occupation in life is to secure convictions.

"And now, as to your friend. Comfort her. The poor girl is no more guilty than if a traction engine had run over her or a wild beast had broken on her out of his cage. She must not torture herself any longer. It is not right, it is not good. Our body is not the only part of use that is subject to diseases, and you must save her from a disease of the soul.

"As to whether she should tell her husband, I can have but one opinion. I say, Yes, by all means. In the court of conscience the sin, where it exists, is not wholly or mainly in the act. That has been pardoned in secret as well as in public. God pardoned it in David. Christ pardoned it in the woman of Jerusalem. But the concealment, the lying and duplicity, these cannot be pardoned until they have been confessed.

"Another point, which your pure mind, dearest, has never thought of. There is the other man. Think of the power he holds over your friend. If he still wishes to possess her in spite of herself, he may intimidate her, he may threaten to reveal all to her husband. This would make her miserable, and perhaps in the long run, her will being broken, it might even make her yield. Or the man may really tell her husband in order to insult and outrage both of them. *If he does so, where is she? Is her husband to believe her story then?*

"To meet these dangers let her speak out now. Let her trust her husband's love and tell him everything. If he is a man he will think, 'Only her purity has prompted her to tell me,' and he will love her more than ever. Some momentary spasm he may feel. Every man wishes to believe that the flower he plucks is flawless. But his higher nature will conquer his vanity and he will say, 'She loves me, I love her, she is innocent, and if any blow is to be struck at her it must go through me.'

"My love to you, dearest. Your friend must be a true woman, and it was very sweet of you to be so tender with her. It was noble of you to be severe with her too, and to make her go through purgatorial fires. That is what good women always do with the injured of their own sex. It is a kind of pledge and badge of their purity, and it is a safeguard and shield, whatever the unthinking may say. I love you for your severity to the poor soiled dove, my dear one, just as much as I love you for your tenderness. It shows me how rightly I judged the moral elevation of your soul, your impeccability, your spirit of fire and heart of gold. Until we meet again, my darling,   D. R."

XIII

"MY DEAR DAVID ROSSI,—All day long I've been carrying your letter round like a reliquary, taking a peep at it in cabs, and even, when I dare, in omnibuses and the streets.

"What you say about Bruno has put me in a fever, and I have written to the Director-General for permission to visit the prison. Even Lawyer Napoleon is of opinion that Bruno is being made a victim of that secret inquisition. No Holy Inquisition was ever more unscrupulous. Lawyer N. says the authorities in Italy have inherited the traditions of a bad régime. To do evil to prevent others from doing it is horrible. But in this case it is doing evil to prevent others from doing good. I am satisfied that Bruno is being tempted to betray you. If I could only take his place! *Would their plots have any effect upon me?* I should die first.

"And now about my friend. I can hardly hold my pen when I write of her. What you say is so good, so noble. I might have known what you would think, and yet . . .

" Dearest, how can I go on? Can't you divine what I wish to tell you? Your letter compels me to confess. Come what may, I can hold off no longer. Didn't you guess who my poor friend was? I thought you would remember our former correspondence when you pretended to love somebody else. You haven't thought of it apparently, and that is only another proof—a bitter sweet one this time—of your love and trust. You put me so high that you never imagined that I could be speaking of myself. I was, and my poor friend is my poor self.

" It has made me suffer all along to see what a pedestal of purity you placed me on. The letters you wrote before you told me you loved me, when you were holding off, made me ashamed because I knew I was not worthy. More than once when you spoke of me as so good, I couldn't look into your eyes. I felt an impulse to cry, ' No, no, no,' and to smirch the picture you were painting. Yet how could I do it? What woman who loves a man can break the idol in his heart? She can only struggle to lift herself up to it. That was what I tried to do, and it is not my fault that it is not done.

" I have been much to blame. There were moments when duty should have made me speak. One such moment was before we married. Do you remember that I tried to tell you something? You were kind, and you would not listen. ' The past is past,' you said, and I was only too happy to gloss it over. You didn't know what I wished to say, or you would not have silenced me. *I* knew, and I have suffered ever since. I *had* to speak, and you see how I have spoken. And now I feel as if I had tricked you. I have got you to commit yourself to opinions and to a line of conduct. Forgive me! I will not hold you to anything. Take it all back, and I shall have no right to complain.

" Besides, there are features in my own case which I did not present to you in my friend's. One of them was the fear of being found out. Dearest, I must not shield myself behind the sweet excuse you find for me. I *did* think of the other man. It wasn't that I was afraid that he would intimidate me, and so corrupt my love. Not all the tyrannies of the world could do that now. But if from revenge or a desire to wrest me away from you by making you cast me off he told you his story before I had told you mine! That was a day-long and night-long terror, and now I confess it lest you should think me better than I am.

"Another thing you did not know. Dearest, I would give my life to spare you the explanation, but I must tell you everything. You know who the man is, and it is true before God that he alone was to blame. But my own fault came afterwards. Instead of cutting him off, I continued to be on good terms with him, to take the income he allowed me from my father's estate, and even to think of him as my future husband. And when your speech in the piazza seemed to endanger my prospects I set out to destroy you.

"It is terrible. How can I tell you and not die of shame? Now you know how much I deceived you, and the infamy of my purpose makes me afraid to ask for pardon. To think that I was no better than a Delilah when I met you first! But Heaven stepped in and saved you. How you worked upon me! First, you re-created my father for me, and I saw him as he really was, and not as I had been taught to think of him. Then you gave me my soul, and I saw myself. Darling, do not hate me. Your great heart could not be capable of a cruelty like that if you knew what I suffered.

"Last of all love came, and I wanted to hold on to it. Oh, how I wanted to hold on to it! That was how it came about that I went on and on without telling you. It was a sort of gambling, a kind of delirium. Everything that happened I took as a penance. Come poverty, shame, neglect, what matter? It was only wiping out a sinful past, and bringing me nearer to you. But when at last he who had injured me threatened to injure you *through me*, I was in despair. You could never imagine what mad notions came to me then. I even thought of killing myself, to end and cover up everything. But no, I could not break your heart like that. Besides, the very act would have told you something, and it was terrible to think that when I was dead you might find out all this pitiful story.

"Now you know everything, dearest. I have kept nothing back. As you see, I am not only my poor friend, but some one worse—myself. Can you forgive me? I dare not ask it. But put me out of suspense. Write. Or better still, telegraph. One word—only one. It will be enough.

"I would love to send you my love, but to-night I dare not. I have loved you from the first, and I can never do anything but love you, whatever happens. I think you would forgive me if you could realise that I am in the world only to love you, and that the worst of my offences comes of loving you more than reason or honour itself. Whatever you do, I am yours, and I can only consecrate my life to you.

"It is daybreak, and the cross of St. Peter's is hanging spectral white above the mists of morning. Is it a symbol of hope, I wonder? The dawn is coming up from the south-east. It would travel quicker to the north-west if it loved you as much as I do. I have been writing this letter over and over again all night long. Do you remember the letter you made me burn, the one containing all your secrets? Here is a letter containing mine—but how much meaner and more perilous! Your poor unhappy girl, ROMA."

XIV

NEXT day Roma removed into her new quarters. A few trunks containing her personal belongings, the picture of her father and Elena's Madonna, were all she took with her. A broker glanced at the rest of her goods and gave a price for the lot. Most of the plaster casts in the studio were broken up and carted away. The fountain, being of marble, had to be put in a dark cellar under the lodge of the old Garibaldian. Only one part of it was carried upstairs. This was the mould for the bust of Rossi and the block of stone for the head of Christ.

Except for her dog, Roma went alone to the Piazza Navona, Felice having returned to the Baron and Natalina being dismissed. The old woman was to clean and cook for her and Roma was to shop for herself. It didn't take the neighbours long to sum up the situation. She was Rossi's wife. They began to call her Signora.

Coming to live in Rossi's home was a sweet experience. The room seemed to be full of his presence. The sitting-room with its piano, its phonograph, and its portraits brought back the very tones of his voice. The bedroom was at first a sanctuary, and she could not bring herself to occupy it until she had set upon the little Madonna. Then it became a bower, and to sleep in it brought a tingling sense which she had never felt before.

Living in the midst of Rossi's surroundings, she felt as if she were discovering something new about him every minute. His squirrels on the roof made her think of him as a boy, and his birds, which were nesting, and therefore singing from their little swelling throats the whole day long, made her thrill and think of both of them. His presents from other women were a source of almost feverish interest. Some came from England and America, and were sent by women who had never even seen his face. They made her happy, they made her proud, they made her jealous.

It was Rossi, Rossi, always Rossi! Every night on going to bed in her poor quarters her last thought was a love-prayer in the darkness, very simple and foolish and childlike, that he would love her always, whatever she was, and whatever the world might say or evil men might do.

This mood lasted for a week and then it began to break. At the back of her happiness there lay anxiety about her letter. She counted up the hours since she posted it, and reckoned the time it would take to receive a reply. If Rossi telegraphed she might hear from him in three days. She did not hear.

"He thinks it better to write," she told herself. Of course he would write immediately, and in five days she would receive his reply. On the fifth day she called on the porter at the convent. He had nothing for "Sister Angelica."

"There must be snow on the Alps, and therefore the mails are delayed," she thought, and she went down to Piale's, where they post up telegrams. There *was* snow in Switzerland. It was just as she imagined, and her letter would be delivered in the morning. It was not delivered in the morning.

"How stupid of me! It would be Sunday when my letter reached London." She had not counted on the postal arrangements of the English Sabbath. One day more, only one, and she would hear from Rossi and be happy.

But one day went by, then another and another, and still no letter came. Her big heart began to fail and the rainbow in the sky of her life to pale away. The singing of the birds on the roof pained her now. How could they crack their little throats like that? It was raining and the sky was dark.

Then the Garibaldian and his old wife came upstairs with scared looks and with papers in their hands. They were summoned to give evidence at Bruno's trial. It was to take place in three days.

"Well, I'm deaf, praise the saints! and they can't make much of me," said the old woman.

Roma put on her simple black straw hat with a quill through it and set off for the office of the lawyer, Napoleon Fuselli.

"Just writing to you, dear lady," said the great man, dropping back in his chair. "Sorry to say my labour has been in vain. It is useless to go further. Our man has confessed."

"Confessed?" Roma clutched at the lapel of her coat.

"Confessed, and denounced his accomplices."

"His accomplices?"

"Rossi in particular, whom he has implicated in a serious conspiracy."

"What conspiracy?"

"That is not yet disclosed. We shall hear all about it the day after to-morrow."

"But why? With what object?"

"Pardon! Apparently they have promised the clemency of the court, and hence in one sense our object is achieved. It is hardly necessary to defend the man. The authorities will see to that for us."

"What will be the result?"

"Probably a trial in contumacy. As soon as Parliament rises for Easter Rossi will be summoned to present himself within ten days. But you will be the first to know all about it, you know."

"How so?"

"The summons will be posted upon the door of the house he lived in, and on the door of any other house he is known to have frequented."

"But if he never hears of it, or if he takes no heed?"

"He will be tried all the same, and when he is a condemned man his sentence will be printed in black and posted up in the same places."

"And then?"

"Then Rossi's life in Rome will be at an end. He will be interdicted from all public offices and expelled from Parliament."

"And Bruno?"

"He will be a free man the following morning."

Roma went home dazed and dejected. A letter was waiting for her. It was from the Director of the Roman prisons. Although the regulations stipulated that only relations should visit prisoners, except under special conditions, the Director

had no objection to Bruno Rocco's former employer seeing
him at the ordinary bi-monthly hour for visitors to-morrow,
Sunday afternoon.

At two o'clock next day Roma set off for Regina Cœli.

XV

The visiting-room of Regina Cœli is constructed on the
principle of a rat-trap. It is an oblong room divided into
three compartments longitudinally, the partition walls being
composed of wire and resembling cages. The middle compartment is occupied by the armed warder in charge who
walks up and down; the compartment on the prison side is
divided into many narrow boxes each occupied by a prisoner,
and the compartment on the world side is similarly divided
into sections each occupied by a visitor.

When Roma entered this room she was deafened by a roar
of voices. Thirty prisoners and as many of their friends
were trying to talk at the same time across the compartment
in the middle, in which the warder was walking. Each batch
of friends and prisoners had fifteen minutes for their interview, and everybody was shouting so as to be heard above
the rest.

A feeling of moral and physical nausea took possession of
Roma when she was shown into this place. After some minutes of the hellish tumult she had asked to see the Director.
The message was taken upstairs, and the Director came down
to speak to her.

"Do you expect me to speak to my friend in this place
and under these conditions?" she asked.

"It is the usual place, and these are the usual conditions,"
he answered.

"If you are unable to allow me to speak to him in some
other place under some other conditions, I must go to the
Minister of the Interior."

The Director bowed. "That will be unnecessary," he
said. "There is a room reserved for special circumstances,"
and, calling a warder, he gave the necessary instructions. He
was a good man in the toils of a vicious system.

A few minutes afterwards Roma was alone in a small bare
room with Bruno, except for two warders who stood in the
door. She was shocked at the change in him. His cheeks,

which used to be full and almost florid, were shrunken and pale; a short grizzly beard had grown over his chin, and his eyes, which had been frank and humorous, were fierce and evasive. Six weeks in prison had made a different man of him, and, like a dog which has been changed by sickness and neglect, he knew it and growled.

"What do you want with me?" he said angrily, as Roma looked at him without speaking.

She flushed and begged his pardon, and at that his jaw trembled and he turned his head away.

"I trust you received the note I sent in to you, Bruno?"

"When? What note?"

"On the day after your arrest, saying your dear ones should be cared for and comforted."

"And were they?"

"Yes. Then you didn't receive it?"

"I was under punishment from the first."

"I also paid for a separate cell with food and light. Did you get that?"

"No, I was nearly all the time on bread and water."

His sulkiness was breaking down and he was showing some agitation. She lifted her large dark eyes on him and said in a soft voice:

"Poor Bruno! No wonder they have made you say things."

His jaw trembled more than ever. "No use talking of that," he said.

"Mr. Rossi will be the first to feel for you."

He turned his head and looked at her with a look of pity. "She doesn't know," he thought. "Why should I tell her? After all, she's in the same case as myself. What hurts me will hurt her. She has been good to me. Why should I make her suffer?"

"If they've told you falsehoods, Bruno, in order to play on your jealousy and inspire revenge . . ."

"Where's Rossi?" he said sharply.

"In England."

"And where's Elena?"

"I don't know."

He wagged his poor head with a wag of wisdom, and for a moment his clouded and stupefied brain was proud of itself.

"It was wrong of Elena to go away without saying where she was going to, and Mr. Rossi is in despair about her."

THE ROMAN OF ROME

" You believe that? "

" Indeed I do."

These words staggered him, and he felt mean and small compared to this woman. " If she can believe in them why can't I? " he thought. But after a moment he smiled a pitiful smile and said largely, " You don't know, Donna Roma. But I do, and they don't hoodwink me. A poor fellow here —a convict, he works on the Gazette and hears all the news— he told me everything."

" What's his name? " said Roma.

" Number 333, penal part. He used to occupy the next cell."

" Then you never saw his face? "

" No, but I heard his voice, and I could have sworn I knew it."

" Was it the voice of Charles Minghelli? "

" Charles Ming . . ."

" Time's up," said one of the warders at the door.

" Bruno," said Roma, rising, " I know that Charles Minghelli, who is now an agent of the police, has been in this prison in the disguise of a prisoner. I also know that after he was dismissed from the embassy in London he asked Mr. Rossi to assist him to assassinate the Prime Minister."

" Right about," cried the warder, and with a bewildered expression the prisoner turned to go. Roma followed him through the open courtyard, and until he reached the iron gate he did not lift his head. Then he faced round with eyes full of tears, but full of fire as well, and raising one arm he cried in a resolute voice:

" All right, sister! Leave it to me, damn me! I'll see it through."

The private visiting-room had one disadvantage. Every word that passed was repeated to the Director. Later the same day the Director wrote to the Royal Commissioner:

" Sorry to say the man Rocco has asked for an interview to retract his denunciation. I have refused it, and he has been violent with the chief warder. But inspired by a sentiment of justice I feel it my duty to warn you that I have been misled, that my instructions have been badly interpreted, and that I cannot hold myself responsible for the document I sent you."

The Commissioner sent this letter on to the Minister of the Interior, who immediately called up the Chief of Police.

"Commendatore," said the Baron, "what was the offence for which young Charles Minghelli was dismissed from the embassy in London?"

"He was suspected of forgery, your Excellency."

"The warrant for his arrest was drawn out but never executed?"

"That is so, and we still hold it at the office . . ."

"Commendatore!"

"Your Excellency?"

"Let the papers that were taken at the domiciliary visitation in the apartments of Deputy Rossi and his man Bruno be gone through again—let Minghelli go through them. You follow me?"

"Perfectly, Excellency."

"Let your Delegate see if there is not a letter among them from Rossi to Bruno's wife—you understand?"

"I do."

"If such a letter can be found let it be sent to the Under Prefect to add to his report for to-morrow's trial, and let the Public Prosecutor read it to the prisoner."

"It shall be done, your Excellency."

XVI

At eight o'clock the next morning Roma was going into the courtyard of the Castle of St. Angelo when she met the carriage of the Prime Minister coming out. The coachman was stopped from inside, and the Baron himself alighted.

"You look tired, my child," he said.

"I *am* tired," she answered.

"Hardly more than a month, yet so many things have happened!"

"Oh, that! That's nothing—nothing whatever."

"Why should you pass through these privations? Roma, if I allowed these misfortunes to befall you it was only to let you feel what others could do for you. But I am the same as ever, and you have only to stretch out your hand and I am here to lighten your lot."

"All that is over now. It is no use speaking as you spoke before. You are talking to another woman."

"Strange mystery of a woman's love! That she who set

284

out to destroy her slanderer should become his slave! If he were only worthy of it!"

"He *is* worthy of it."

"If you should hear that he is not worthy—that he has even been untrue to you?"

"I should think it is a falsehood, a contemptible falsehood."

"But if you had proof, substantial proof, the proof of his own pen?"

"Good-morning! I must go."

"My child, what have I always told you? You will give the man up at last and carry out your first intention."

With a deep bow and a scarcely perceptible smile the Baron turned to the open door of his carriage. Roma flushed up angrily and went on, but the poisoned arrow had gone home.

The military tribunal had begun its session. A ticket which Roma presented at the door admitted her to the well of the court where the advocates were sitting. The advocate Fuselli made a place for her by his side. It was a quiet moment and her entrance attracted attention. The judges in their red armchairs at the green-covered horse-shoe table looked up from their portfolios, and there was some whispering beyond the wooden bar where the public were huddled together. One other face had followed her, but at first she dared not look at that. It was the face of the prisoner in his prison clothes sitting between two Carabineers.

The secretary read the indictment. Bruno was charged not only with participation in the riot of the 1st of February, but also with being a promoter of associations designed to change violently the constitution of the state. It was a long document, and the secretary read it slowly and not very distinctly.

When the indictment came to an end the Public Prosecutor rose to expound the accusation, and to mention the clauses of the Code under which the prisoner's crime had to be considered. He was a young captain of cavalry, with restless eyes and a twirled-up moustache. His long cloak hung over his chair, his light gloves lay on the table by his side, and his sword clanked as he made graceful gestures. He was an elegant speaker, much preoccupied about beautiful phrases, and obviously anxious to conciliate the judges.

"Illustrious gentlemen of the tribunal," he began, and

then went on with a compliment to the King, a flourish to the name of the Prime Minister, a word of praise to the army, and finally a scathing satire on the subversive schemes which it was desired to set up in place of existing institutions. The most crushing denunciation of the delirious idea which had led to the unhappy insurrection was the crude explanation of its aims. A universal republic founded on the principles enunciated in the Lord's Prayer! Thrones, armies, navies, frontiers, national barriers, all to be abolished! So simple! So easy! So childlike! But alas, so absurd! So entirely oblivious of the great principles of political economy and international law, and of impulses and instincts profoundly sculptured in the heart of man!

After various little sallies which made his fellow-officers laugh and the judges smile, the showy person wiped his big moustache with a silk handkerchief, and came to Bruno. This unhappy man was not one of the greater delinquents who, by their intelligence, had urged on the ignorant crowd. He was merely a silly and perhaps drunken person, who if taken away from the wine-shop and put into uniform would make a valiant soldier. The creature was one of the human dogs of our curious species. His political faith was inscribed with one word only—Rossi. He would not ask for severe punishment on such a deluded being, but he would request the court to consider the case as a means of obtaining proof against the dark if foolish minds (fit subjects for Lombroso) which are always putting the people into opposition with their King, their constitution, and the great heads of government.

The sword clanked again as the young soldier sat down. Then for the first time Roma looked over at Bruno. His big rugged face was twisted into an expression of contempt, and somehow the " human dog of our curious species," sitting in his prison clothes between the soldiers, made the elegant officer look like a pet pug.

" Bruno Rocco, stand up," said the president. " You are a Roman, aren't you ? "

" Yes, I am—I'm a Roman of Rome," said Bruno.

The witnesses were called. First a Carabineer to prove Bruno's violence. Then another Carabineer, and another, and another, with the same object. After each of the Carabineers had given his evidence the president asked the prisoner if he had any questions to ask the witnesses.

"None whatever. What they say is true. I admit it," he said.

At last he grew impatient and cried out, "I admit it, I tell you. What's the good of going on?"

The next witness was the Chief of Police. Commendatore Angelelli was called to prove that the cause of the revolt was not the dearness of bread but the formation of subversive associations, of which the "Republic of Man" was undoubtedly the strongest and most virulent. The prisoner, however, was not one of the directing set, and the police knew him only as a sort of watch-dog for the Honourable Rossi.

"The man's a fool. Why don't you go on with the trial?" cried Bruno.

"Silence," cried the usher of the court, but the prisoner only laughed out loud.

Roma looked at Bruno again. There was something about the man which she had never seen before, something more than the mere spirit of defiance, something terrible and tremendous.

"Francesca Maria Mariotti," cried the usher, and the old deaf mother of Bruno's wife was brought into court. She wore a coloured handkerchief on her head as usual, and two shawls over her shoulders. Being a relative of the prisoner, she was not sworn.

"Your name and your father's name?" said the president.

"Francesca Maria Mariotti," she answered.

"I said your father's name."

"Seventy-five, your Excellency."

"I asked you for your father's name."

"None at all, your Excellency."

A Carabineer explained that the woman was nearly stone deaf, whereupon the president, who was irritated by the laughter his questions had provoked, ordered the woman to be removed.

"Tommaso Mariotti," said the president, after the preliminary interrogations, "you are porter at the Piazza Navona, and will be able to say if meetings of political associations were held there, if the prisoner took part in them, and who were the organising authorities. Now answer me, were meetings ever held in your house?"

The old man turned his pork-pie hat in his hand, and made no answer.

"Answer me. We cannot sit here all day doing nothing."

"It's the Eternal City, Excellency—we can take our time," said the old man.

"Answer the president instantly," said the usher. "Don't you know he can punish you if you don't?"

At that the Garibaldian's eyes became moist, and he looked at the judges. "Generals," he said, "I am only an old man, not much good to anybody, but I was a soldier myself once. I was one of the 'Thousand,' the 'Brave Thousand' they called us, and I shed my blood for my country. Now I am more than threescore years and ten, and the rest of my days are numbered. Do you want me for the sake of what is left of them to betray my comrades?"

"Next witness," said the president, and at the same moment a thick, half-stifled voice came from the bench of the accused.

"Why the —— don't you go on with the trial?"

"Prisoner," said the president, "if you continue to make these interruptions I shall stop the trial and order you to be flogged."

Bruno answered with a peal of laughter. The president —he was a bald-headed man with the heavy jaw of a bloodhound—looked at him attentively for a moment, and then said to the men below:

"Go on."

The next witness was the Director of Regina Cœli. He deposed that the prisoner had made a statement to him which he had taken down in writing. This statement amounted to a denunciation of the Deputy David Rossi as the real author of the crime of which he with others was charged.

After the denunciation had been read the president asked the prisoner if he had any questions to put to the witness, and thereupon Bruno cried in a loud voice:

"Of course I have. It is exactly what I've been waiting for."

He had risen to his feet, kicked over a chair which stood in front of him, and folded his arms across his breast.

"Ask him," said Bruno, "if he sent for me late at night and promised my pardon if I would denounce David Rossi."

"It was not so," said the Director. "All I did was to

advise him not to observe a useless silence which could only condemn him to further imprisonment if by speaking the truth he could save himself and serve the interests of justice."

" Ask him," said Bruno, " if the denunciation he speaks of was not dictated by himself."

" The prisoner," said the Director, " made the denunciation voluntarily, and I rose from my bed to receive it at his urgent request."

" Ask him if I said one word to denounce David Rossi."

" The prisoner had made statements to a fellow-prisoner, and these were embodied in the document he signed."

The advocate Fuselli interposed. " Then the Court is to understand that the Director who dictated this denunciation knew nothing from the prisoner himself ? "

The Director hesitated, stammered, and finally admitted that it was so. " I was inspired by a sentiment of justice," he said. " I acted from duty."

" This man fed me on bread and water," cried Bruno. " He put me in the punishment cells and tortured me in the strait-waistcoat with pains and sufferings like Jesus Christ's, and when he had reduced my body and destroyed my soul he dictated a denunciation of my dearest friend and my unconscious fingers signed it."

" Don't shout so loud," said the president.

" I'll shout as loud as I like," said Bruno, and everybody turned to look at him. It was useless to protest. Something seemed to say that no power on earth could touch a man in a mood like that.

The next witness was the chief warder. He deposed that he was present at the denunciation, that it was made voluntarily, and that no pressure whatever was put upon the prisoner.

" Ask him," cried Bruno, " if on Sunday afternoon, when I went into his cabinet to withdraw the denunciation, he refused to let me."

" It is not true," said the witness.

" You liar," cried Bruno, " you know it is true; and when I told you that you were making me drag an innocent man to the galleys I struck you, and the mark of my fist is on your forehead still. There it is, as red as a Cardinal, while the rest of your face is as white as a Pope."

The president no longer tried to restrain Bruno. There

was something in the man's face that was beyond reproof. It was the outraged spirit of Justice.

The chief warder went on to say that at various times he had received reports that Rocco was communicating important facts to a fellow-prisoner.

"Where is this fellow-prisoner? Is he at the disposition of the court?" said the president.

"I'm afraid he has since been set at liberty," said the witness, whereupon Bruno laughed uproariously, and pointing to some one in the well, he shouted:

"There he is—there! The dandy in cuffs and collar. His name is Minghelli."

"Call him," said the president, and Minghelli was sworn and examined.

"Until recently you were a prisoner in Regina Cœli, and have just been pardoned for public services?"

"That is true, your Excellency."

"It's a lie," cried Bruno.

Minghelli leaned on the witness's chair, caressed his small moustache, and told his story. He had occupied the next cell to the prisoner, and talked with him in the usual language of prisoners. The prisoner had spoken of a certain great man and then of a certain great act, and that the great man had gone to England to prepare for it. He understood the great man to be the Deputy Rossi, and the great act to be the overthrow of the constitution and the assassination of the King.

"You son of a priest," cried Bruno, "you lie!"

"Bruno Rocco," said the president, "do not agitate yourself. You are under the protection of the law. Be calm and tell us your own story."

XVII

"Your Excellency," said Bruno, "this man is a witness by profession, and he was put into the next cell to torture me and make me denounce my friends. I didn't see his face, and I didn't know who he was until afterwards, and so he tore me to pieces. He said he was a proof-reader on the Official Gazette and heard everything. When my heart was bleeding for the death of my poor little boy—only seven years of age, such a curly-headed little fellow, like a sunbeam in a fog, killed in the riot, your Excellency—he poisoned my mind about my wife, and said she had run away with Rossi. It was a lie, but I was brought down by flogging and bread and water and I believed it, because I was mad and my soul was exhausted and dead. But when I found out who he was I tried to take back my denunciation, and they wouldn't let me. Your Excellency, I tell you the truth. Everybody should tell the truth here. I alone am guilty, and if I have accused anybody else I ask pardon of God. As for this man, he is an assassin and I can prove it. He used to be at the embassy in London, and when he was sacked he came to Mr. Rossi and proposed to assassinate the Prime Minister. Mr. Rossi flung him out of the house, and that was the beginning of everything."

" This is not true," said Minghelli, red as the gills of a turkey.

" Isn't it? Give me the cross, and let me swear the man a liar," cried Bruno.

Roma was breathing hard and rising to her feet, but the advocate Fuselli restrained her and rose himself. In six sentences he summarised the treatment of Bruno in prison, and denounced it as worthy of the cruellest epochs of tyrannical domination, in which men otherwise honourable could become demons in order to save the dynasty and the institutions and to make their own careers.

" Mr. President," he cried, " I call on you in the name of humanity to say that justice in Italy has nothing to do with a barbarous system which aims at obtaining denunciations through jealousy and justice through revenge."

The president was deeply moved. " I have made a solemn promise under the shadow of that venerable image "—he pointed to the effigy above him—" to administer justice in this case, and to the last I will do my duty."

The Public Prosecutor rose again and obtained permission to interrogate the prisoner.

" You say the witness Minghelli told you that your wife had fled with the Honourable Rossi?"

" He did, and it was a lie, like all the rest of it."

" How do you know it was a lie?"

Bruno made no answer, and the young officer took up a letter from his portfolio.

" Do you know the Honourable Rossi's handwriting?"

" Do I know my own ugly fist?"

"Is that the Honourable Rossi's writing?" said the officer, handing the envelope to the usher to be shown to Bruno.

"It is," said Bruno.

"Sure of it?"

"Sure."

"You see it is a letter addressed to your wife?"

"I see. But you needn't go on washing the donkey's head, Mister—I know what you are getting at."

"You must not speak like that to him, Rocco," said the president. "Remember, he is the honourable representative of the law."

"Mustn't I, Excellency? Then tell his honourableness that David Rossi and my wife are like brother and sister, and anybody who makes evil of that isn't stuff to take with a pair of tongs."

Saying this, Bruno flung the letter back on to the table.

"Don't you want to read it?"

"Not I! It's somebody else's correspondence, and I'm not an honourable representative of the law."

"Then permit me to read it to you," said the Public Prosecutor, and taking the letter out of the envelope he began in a loud voice:

"'Dearest Elena . . .'"

"That's nothing," Bruno interrupted. "They're like brother and sister, I tell you."

The Public Prosecutor went on reading:

"'I continue to be overwhelmed with grief for the death of our poor little Joseph.'"

"That's right! That's David Rossi. He loved the boy the same as if he had been his own son. Go on."

"'. . . Our child—your child—my child, Elena.'"

"Nothing wrong there. Don't try to make mischief of that," cried Bruno.

"'But now that the boy is gone, and Bruno is in prison, perhaps for years, the obstacles must be removed which have hitherto prevented you from joining your life to mine and living for me, as I have always lived for you. Come to me then, my dear one, my beloved . . .'"

Here Bruno, who had been stepping forward at every word, snatched the letter out of the Public Prosecutor's hand.

"Stop that! Don't go reading out of the back of your head," he cried.

THE ROMAN OF ROME

No one protested, everybody felt that whatever he did this injured man must be left alone. Roma felt a roaring in her ears, and for some minutes she could scarcely command herself. In a vague way she was conscious of the same struggle in her own heart as was going on in the heart of Bruno. This, then, was what the Baron referred to when he spoke of Rossi being untrue to her, and of the proof of his disloyalty in his own handwriting.

Bruno, who was running his eyes over the letter, read parts of it aloud in a low husky voice:

"'And now that the boy is gone and Bruno is in prison . . . perhaps for years . . . the obstacles must be removed . . .'"

He stopped, looked up, and stared about him. His face had undergone an awful change. Then he returned to the letter, and in jerky sentences he read again:

"'Come to me then . . . my dear one . . . my beloved . . .'"

Until that moment an evil spirit in Roma had been saying to her, in spite of herself: "Can it be possible that while you have been going through all those privations for his sake he has been consoling himself with another woman?" Impossible! The letter was a manifest imposture. She wouldn't believe a word of it.

But Bruno was still in the toils of his temptation. "Look here," he said, lifting a pitiful face. "What with the bread and water and the lashes I don't know that my head isn't light, and I'm fancying I see things . . ."

The paper of the letter was crackling in his hand, and his husky voice was breaking. Save for these sounds and the tramp—tramp—tramp of the soldiers drilling outside, there was a dead silence in the court.

"You are not fancying at all, Rocco," said the Public Prosecutor. "We are all sorry for you, and I am sure the illustrious gentlemen of the tribunal pity you. Your comrade, your master, the man you have followed and trusted, is false to you. He is a traitor to his friend, his country, and his King. The denunciation you made in prison is true in substance and in fact. I advise you to adhere to it, and to cast yourself on the clemency of the court."

"Here—you—shut up your head and let a man think," said Bruno.

Roma tried to rise. She could not. Then she tried to cry

out something, but her tongue clave to the roof of her mouth. Would Bruno break down at the last moment?

Bruno, whose face was convulsed with agony, began to laugh in a delirious way. "So my friend is false to me, is he? Very well, I'll be revenged."

He reeled a little and the letter dropped from his hand, floated a moment in the air, and fell to the ground a pace or two farther on.

"Yes, by God, I'll be revenged," he cried, and he laughed again.

He stopped, lifted one leg, seemed to pull at his boot, and again stood erect.

"I always knew the hour would come when I should find myself in a tight place, and I've always kept something about me to help me to get out of it. Here it is now."

In an instant, before any one could be aware of what he was doing, he had uncorked a small bottle which he held in his hand and swallowed the contents.

"Long live David Rossi!" he cried, and he flung the empty bottle over his head.

Everybody was on his feet in a moment. It was too late. In thirty seconds the poison had begun its work, and Bruno was reeling in the arms of the Carabineers. Somebody called for a doctor. Somebody else called for a priest.

"That's all right," said Bruno. "God is a good old saint. He'll look after a poor devil like me." Then he began to sing:—

> "The tombs are uncovered,
> The dead arise,
> The martyrs are rising
> Before our eyes."

"Long live David Rossi!" he cried again, and at the next moment he was being carried out of court.

In the tumult that ensued everybody was standing in the well of the judges' horse-shoe table. The deaf old woman, with her shawls slipping off her shoulders, was wringing her hands and crying. "God will think of this," she said. The Garibaldian was gazing vacantly out of his rheumy eyes and saying nothing. Roma, who had recovered control of herself, was looking at the letter, which she had picked up from the floor.

"Mr. President," she cried over the heads of the others,

"GOD WILL LOOK AFTER A POOR DEVIL LIKE ME."

"this letter is not in Mr. Rossi's handwriting. It is a forgery. I am ready to prove it."

At that moment one of the Carabineers came back to tell the judges that all was over.

" Gone! " said one after another, more often with a motion of the mouth than with the voice.

The president was deeply agitated. " This court stands adjourned," he said, " but I take the Almighty to witness that I intend to ascertain all responsibility in this case and to bring it home to the guilty ones, whosoever and whatsoever they may be."

XVIII

" MY DEAR DAVID ROSSI,—You will know all about it before this letter reaches you. It is one of those scandals of the law that are telegraphed to every part of the civilised world. Poor Bruno! Yet no, not poor—great, glorious, heroic Bruno! He ended like an old Roman, and killed himself rather than betray his friend. When they played upon his jealousy, and tempted him by a forged letter, he cried, ' Long live David Rossi!' and died. Oh, it was wonderful. The memory of that moment will be with me always like the protecting and strengthening hand of God. I never knew until to-day what human nature is capable of. It is divine.

" But how mean and little I feel when I think of all I went through in the court this morning! I was really undergoing the same tortures as Bruno, the same doubt and the same agony. And even when I saw through the whole miserable machination of lying and duplicity I was actually in terror for Bruno lest he should betray you in the end. Betray you! His voice when he uttered that last cry rings in my ears still. It was a voice of triumph—triumph over deception, over temptation, over jealousy, and over self.

" Don't think, David Rossi, that Bruno died of a broken heart, and don't think he went out of the world believing that you were false. I feel sure he came to that court with the full intention of doing what he did. All through the trial there was something in his bearing which left the impression of a purpose unrevealed. Everybody felt it, and even the judges ceased to protest against his outbursts. The poor prisoner in convict clothes, with dishevelled hair and bare neck, made every one else look paltry and small. Behind him was something mightier than himself. It was Death. Then remember his last cry, and ask yourself what he meant by it. He meant loyalty, love, faith, fidelity. He intended to say, ' You've beaten me, but no matter; I believe in him, and follow him to the last.'

"As you see, I am here in your own quarters, but I keep in touch with ' Sister Angelica,' and still have no answer to my letter. I invent all manner of excuses to account for your silence. You are busy, you are on a journey, you are waiting for the right moment to reply to me at length. If I could only continue to think so, how happy I should be! But I cannot deceive myself any longer.

"It is perhaps natural that you should find it hard to forgive me, but you might at least write and put me out of suspense. I think you would do so if you knew how much I suffer. Your great soul cannot intend to torture me. To-night the burden of things is almost more than I can bear, and I am nearly heartbroken. It is my dark hour, dearest, and if you had to say you could never forgive me, I think I could easier reconcile myself to that. I have been so happy since I began to love you; I shall always love you even if I have to lose you, and I shall never, never be sorry for anything that has occurred.

"Not receiving any new letters from you, I am going back on the old ones, and there is a letter of only two months ago in which you speak of just such a case as mine. May I quote what you say?

"'Yet even if she were not so (*i.e.* worthy of your love and friendship), even if there were, as you say, a fault in her, who am I that I should judge her harshly? . . . I reject the monstrous theory that while a man may redeem the past a woman never can. . . . And if she has sinned as I have sinned, and suffered as I have suffered, I will pray for strength to say, ' Because I love her we are one, and we stand or fall together.'

"It is so beautiful that I am even happy while my pen copies the sweet, sweet words, and I feel as I did when the old priest spoke so tenderly on the day I confessed, telling me I had committed no sin and had nothing to repent of. Have I never told you about that? My confessor was a Capuchin, and perhaps I should have waited for his advice before going farther. He was to consult his General or his Bishop or some one, and to send for me again.

"But all that is over now, and everything depends upon you. In any case, be sure of one thing, whatever happens. Bruno has taught me a great lesson, and there is not anything your enemies can do to me that will touch me now. They have tried me already with humiliation, with poverty, with jealousy, and even with the shadow of shame itself. There is nothing left but death. *And death itself shall find me faithful to the last.* Good-bye! Your poor unforgiven girl,   ROMA."

The morning after writing this letter Roma received a visit from one of the Noble Guard. It was the Count de Raymond.

"I am sent by the Holy Father," he said, "to say that he wishes to see you."

PART SEVEN—THE POPE

I

On the morning appointed for the visit to the Vatican, Roma dressed in the black gown and veil prescribed by etiquette for ladies going to an audience with the Pope.

The young Noble Guard in civilian clothes was waiting for her in the sitting-room. When she came out of the bedroom he was standing with a solemn face before the bust of David Rossi, which she had lately cast afresh and was beginning to point in marble.

"This is wonderful," he said. "Perfectly wonderful! A most astonishing study."

Roma smiled and bowed to him.

"Christ of course, and such reality, such feeling, such love! But shall I tell you what surprises me most of all?"

"What?"

"What surprises me most is the extraordinary resemblance between your Christ and the Pope."

"Really?"

"Indeed yes! Didn't you know it? No? It is almost incredible. Younger certainly, but the same features, the same expression, the same tenderness, the same strength! Even the same vertical lines over the nose which make the shako dither on one's head when something goes wrong and His Holiness is indignant."

Roma's smile was dying off her face like the sun off a field of corn, and she was looking sideways out of the window.

"Has the Pope any relations?" she asked.

"None whatever, not a soul. The only son of an only son. You must have been thinking of the Holy Father himself, and asking yourself what he was like thirty years ago. Come now, confess it!"

Roma laughed. The soldier laughed. "Shall we go?" she said.

A carriage was waiting for them, and they drove by the

THE POPE

Tor di Nona, a narrow lane which skirts the banks of the Tiber, across the bridge of St. Angelo, and up the Borgo.

Roma was nervous and preoccupied. Why had she been sent for? What could the Pope have to say to her?

"Isn't it unusual," she asked, "for the Pope to send for any one—especially a woman, and a non-Catholic?"

"Most unusual. But perhaps Father Pifferi . . ."

"Father Pifferi?"

"He is the Holy Father's confessor."

"Is he a Capuchin?"

"Yes. The General at San Lorenzo."

"Ah, now I understand," said Roma. Light had dawned on her and her spirits began to rise.

"The Pope is very tender and fatherly, isn't he?"

"Fatherly? He is a saint on earth, that's what he is! Impetuous, perhaps, but so sweet and generous and forgiving. Makes you shake in your shoes if you've done anything amiss, but when all is over and he puts his arm on your shoulder and tells you to think no more about it, you're ready to die for him even at the stake."

Roma's spirits were rising every minute, and her nervousness was fading away. Since things had fallen out so, she could take advantage of her opportunities. She would tell the Pope everything, and he would advise with her and counsel her. She would speak about David Rossi, and the Pope would tell her what to do.

The great clock of the Basilica was striking ten with a solemn boom as the carriage rattled over the stones of the Piazza of St. Peter's—wet with the play of the fountains and bright with the rainbows made by the sun.

They alighted at the bronze gate, ascended the grand staircase, crossed a courtyard, passed through many gorgeous chambers, and arrived finally at an apartment hung with tapestries and occupied by a Noble Guard, who wore a brass helmet and held a drawn sword. The next room was the throne room, and beyond it were the Pope's private apartments.

A chaplain of the Pope's household came to say that by request of Father Pifferi the lady was to step into an anteroom; and Roma followed him into a small adjoining chamber, carpeted with cocoanut matting and furnished with a marble-topped table and two wooden chest-seats, bearing the papal arms. The little room opened on to a corridor overlooking a courtyard, a secret way to the Pope's private rooms, and it had a door to the throne room also.

"The Father will be here presently," said the chaplain, "and His Holiness will not be long."

Roma, who was feeling some natural tremors, tried to re-assure herself by asking questions about the Pope. The chaplain's face began to gleam. He was a little man, with round red cheeks and pale grey eyes, and the usual tone of his voice was a hushed and reverent whisper.

"Faint? Yes, ladies do faint sometimes—often, I may say—and they nearly always cry. But the Holy Father is so gentle, so sweet."

The door to the throne room opened and there was a gleam of violet and an indistinct buzz of voices. The chaplain disappeared, and at the next moment a man in the dress of a waiter came from the corridor carrying a silver soup dish.

"You're the lady the Holy Father sent for?"

Roma smiled and assented.

"I'm Cortis—Gaetano Cortis—the Pope's valet, you know—and of course I hear everything."

Roma smiled again and bowed.

"I bring the Holy Father a plate of soup every morning at ten, but I'm afraid it is going to get cold this morning."

"Will he be angry?"

"Angry? He's an angel, and couldn't be angry with any one."

"He must indeed be good; everybody says so."

"He is perfect. That's about the size of it. None of your locking up his bedroom when he goes into the garden and putting the key into the pocket of his cassock, same as in the old Pope's days. I go in whenever I like, and he lets me take whatever I please. At Christmas some rich Americans wanted a skull-cap to save a dying man, and I got it for the asking. Now an old English lady wants a stocking to cure her rheumatism, and I'll get that too. I've saved a little hair from the last cutting, and if you hear of anybody . . . "

The valet's story of his perquisites was interrupted by the opening of the door of the throne room and the entrance of a friar in a brown habit. It was Father Pifferi.

"Don't rise, my daughter," he said, and closing the door

behind the valet, he gathered up the skirts of his habit and sat down on the chest-seat in front of her.

"When you came to me with your confidence, my child, and I found it difficult to advise with you for your peace of mind, I told you I wished to take your case to a wiser head than mine. I took it to the Pope himself. He was touched by your story, and asked to see you for himself."

"But, Father . . ."

"Don't be afraid, my daughter. Pius the Tenth as a Pope may be lofty to sternness, but as a man he is humble and simple and kind. Forget that he is a sovereign and a pontiff, and think of him as a tender and loving friend. Tell him everything. Hold nothing back. And if you must needs reveal the confidences of others, remember that he is the Vicar of Him who keeps all our secrets."

"But, Father . . ."

"Yes."

"He is so high, so holy, so far above the world and its temptations . . ."

"Don't say that, my daughter. The Holy Father is a man like other men. Shall I tell you something of his life? The world knows it only by hearsay and report. You shall hear the truth, and when you have heard it you will go to him as a child goes to its father, and no longer be afraid."

II

"THIRTY-FIVE years ago," said Father Pifferi, "the Holy Father had not even dreamt of being Pope. He was the only child of a Roman banker, living in a palace on the opposite side of the piazza. The old Baron had visions, indeed, of making his son a great churchman by the power of wealth, but these were vain and foolish, and the young man did not share them. His own aims were simple but worldly. He desired to be a soldier, and to compromise with his father's disappointed ambitions he asked for a commission in the Pope's Noble Guard."

The old friar put his hands into the vertical pockets in the breast of his habit, and looked up at the ceiling as he went on speaking.

"All this is no secret, but what follows is less known. The soldier, who had the charm of an engaging personality, led the life of an ordinary young Roman of his day, frequenting cafés, concerts, theatres, and balls. In this character he met a poor woman of the people, and came to love her. She was a good girl, with soft and gentle manners, but a heart of gold and a soul of fire. He was a good man and he meant to marry her. He did marry her. He married her according to the rites of the Church, which are all that religion requires and God calls for."

Roma was leaning forward on her seat and breathing between tightly-closed lips.

" Unhappily, then as now, a godless legislature had separated a religious from a civil marriage, and the one without the other was useless. The old Baron heard of what had happened and tried to defeat it. A cardinal had just been created in Australia, and an officer of the Noble Guard had to be sent with the Ablegate to carry the biglietto and the skull-cap. At the request of the Baron his son was appointed to that mission and despatched in haste."

Roma could scarcely control herself.

" The young husband being gone, the father set himself to deal with the wife. He had not yet relinquished his hopes of seeing his son a churchman, and marriage was a fatal impediment. A rich man may have many instruments, and the Baron was able to use some that were evil. He played upon the conscience of the girl, who was pure and virtuous; told her she was not legally married, and that the laws of her country thought ill of her. Finally, he appealed to her love for her husband, and showed her that she was standing in his way. He was not a bad man, but he loved his son beyond truth and to the perversion of honour, and was ready to sacrifice the woman who stood between them. She allowed herself to be sacrificed. She wiped herself out that she might not be an obstacle to her husband. She drowned herself in the Tiber."

Roma could not control herself any longer, and made a half-stifled exclamation.

" Then the young husband returned. He had been travelling constantly, and no letters from his wife had reached him. But one letter was waiting for him at Rome, and it told him what she had done. It was then all over; there was no help for it, and he was overwhelmed with horror. He could not blame the poor dead girl, for all she had done had been done in love; he could not blame himself, for he had meant no wrong in making the religious marriage, and had hastened home to complete the civil one; and he could not reproach his father, for if the Baron's conduct had led to fearful consequences, it had been prompted by affection for himself. But the hand of God seemed to be over him, and his soul was shaken to its foundations. From that time forward he renounced society and all worldly pleasures. For eight days he went into retreat and prayed fervently. On the ninth day he joined a religious house, the Novitiate of the Capuchins at San Lorenzo. The young soldier, so gay, so handsome, so fond of social admiration, became a friar."

The old Capuchin looked tenderly at Roma, whose wet eyes and burning cheeks seemed to tell of sympathy with his story.

"In those days, my daughter, the nuns of Thecla served the Foundling of Santo Spirito."

Roma began to look frightened and to feel faint.

"It was usual for a member of our house to live in the hospital in order to baptize the children and to confess the sick and the dying. We took it in turns to do so, staying one year, two years, three years, and then going back to the monastery. I was myself at Santo Spirito for this purpose at the time I speak about, and it was not until three or four years afterwards that I became Superior of our House and returned to San Lorenzo. There I found the young Noble Guard, and, wisely or unwisely, I told him a new phase of his own story."

"There was a child?" said Roma, in a strange voice.

The Capuchin bent his head. "That much he knew already by the letter his wife had left for him. She had intended that the child should die when she died, and he supposed that it had been so. But pity for the little one must have overtaken the poor mother at the last moment. She had put the babe in the rota of the hospital, and thus saved the child's life before carrying out her purpose upon her own."

The Capuchin crossed his knees, and one of his bare feet in its sandal showed from under the edge of his habit.

"We had baptized the boy by a name which the mother had written on a paper attached to his wrist, and the identity of that name with the name of the Noble Guard led to my revelation. Nature is a mighty thing, and on hearing what I told him the young brother became restless and unhappy. The instincts of the man began to fight with the feelings of the religious, and at last he left the friary in order to fulfil the duty which he thought he owed to his child."

"He did not find him?"

"He was too late. According to custom, the boy had been put out to nurse on the Campagna, by means of the little dower that, was all his inheritance from the State. His foster parents passed him over to other hands, and thus by the abuse of a good practice the child was already lost."

Roma tried to speak, but she could not utter a word.

"What happened then is a long story. The old Baron was now dead and the young friar had inherited his princely fortune. Dispensations got over canonical difficulties, and in due course he took holy orders. His first work was to establish in Rome an asylum for friendless orphans. He went out into the streets to look for them, and brought them in with his own hands. His fame for charity grew rapidly, and he knew well what he was doing. He was looking for the little fatherless one who owned his own blood and bore his name."

Roma was now sitting with drooping head, and her tears were falling on her hands.

"Five years passed, and at length he came upon a trace of the boy and heard that he had been sent to England. The unhappy father obtained permission and removed to London. There he set up the same work as before and spent in the same way his great wealth. He passed five years more in a fruitless search, looking for his lost one day and night, winter and summer, in cold and heat, among the little foreign boys who play organs and accordions in the streets. Then he gave up hope and returned to Rome. His head was white and his heart was humble, but in spite of himself he rose from dignity to dignity until at length the old Baron's perverted ambitions were fulfilled. For his great and abounding charity, and still greater piety, he was promoted to be Bishop; seven years afterwards he was created Cardinal; and now he is Pope Pius the Tenth, the saint, the saviour of his people, once the storm-tossed, sorrowing, stricken man . . ."

"David Leone?"

The Capuchin bowed. "That was the Holy Father's name. He committed no sin and has nothing to reproach himself with, but nevertheless he has known what it is to fall and to rise again, to suffer and be strong. Tell me, my daughter, is there anything you would be afraid to confide to him?"

"Nothing! Nothing whatever!" said Roma, with tears choking her voice and streaming down her cheeks.

The door to the throne room opened again and a line of Cardinals came out and passed down the secret corridor, talking together as they walked, old men in violet, most of them very feeble and looking very tired. At the next moment the chaplain came in for Roma.

"The Holy Father will be ready to receive you presently," he said in a hushed and reverent whisper, and she rose to follow him.

A moment later Roma was at the door of the grand throne room. A chamberlain took charge of her there, and passed her to a secret chamberlain at the door of an anteroom adjoining. This secret chamberlain handed her on to a Monsignor in a violet cassock, and the Monsignor accompanied her to the door of the room in which the Pope was sitting.

"As you approach," he said in a low tone, "you will make three genuflexions—one at the door, another midway across the floor, the third at the Holy Father's feet. You feel well?"

"Yes," she faltered.

The door was opened, the Monsignor stepped one pace into the room, and then knelt and said—

"Donna Roma Volonna, your Holiness."

Roma was on her knees at the threshold; a soft, full, kindly voice, which she could have believed she had heard before, called on her to approach; she rose and stepped forward, the Monsignor stepped back, and the door behind her was closed.

She was in the Presence.

III

THE Pope, dressed wholly in white, was seated in a simple chair by a little table in a homely room, surrounded by bookcases and some busts of former pontiffs. There were little domesticities of intimate life about him, an empty soup-dish, a cruet-stand, a plate and a spoon. He had a face of great sweetness and spirituality, and as Roma approached he bent his head and smiled a fatherly smile. She knelt and kissed his ring, and continued to kneel by his chair, putting one hand on the arm. He placed his own mittened hand over hers and patted it tenderly, while he looked into her face.

The little nervous perturbation with which Roma had entered the room began to leave her, and in the awful wearer of the threefold crown she saw nothing but a simple, loving human being. A feminine sense crept over her, a sense of nursing, almost of motherhood, and at that first moment she felt as if she wanted to do something for the gentle old man. Then he began to speak. His voice had that tone which comes to the voice of a man who has the sense of sex strong in him, when a woman is with him and his accents soften perceptibly.

"My daughter," he said, "Father Pifferi has spoken about you, and by your permission, as I understand it, he has repeated the story you told him. You have suffered, and you have my sympathy. And though you are not among the number of my children, I sent for you, that, as an old man to a young woman, by God's grace I might strengthen you and support you."

She kissed his ring again and continued to kneel by the arm of his chair.

"Long ago, my child, I knew one who was in something like the same position, and perhaps it is the memory of what befell that poor soul which impels me to speak to you. . . . But she is dead, her story is dead too; let time and nature cover them."

His voice had a slight tremor. She looked up. There was a hush, a momentary thrill. Then he smiled again and patted her hand once more.

"You must not let the world weaken you, my child, or cause you to doubt the validity of your marriage. Whether it is a good marriage, in effect as well as intention (one of you being still unbaptized), it is for the Church, not the world, to decide."

Again Roma kissed the ring of the Pope, and again he patted the hand that lay under his.

"Nevertheless, there is something I wish you to do, my daughter," he said, in the same low tones. "I wish you to tell your husband."

"Holy Father," said Roma, "I have already told him. I had done so before I spoke to Father Pifferi, but only under the disguise of another woman's story."

"And what did your husband say?"

"He said what your Holiness says. He was very charitable and noble; so I took heart and told him everything."

"And what did he say then?"

A cloud crossed her face. "Holy Father, he has not yet said anything."

"Not anything?"

"He is away; he has not replied to my letter."

"Has there been time?"

"More than time, your Holiness, but still I hear nothing."

"And what is your conclusion?"

"That my letter has awakened some pity, but now that he knows *I* am the wife I spoke about and *he* is the husband intended, he cannot forgive me as he said the husband would forgive, and his generous soul is in distress."

"My daughter, could you wish *me* to speak to him?"

The cloud fled from her face. "It is more than I deserve, far more, but if the Holy Father would do that . . ."

"Then I must know the names—you must tell me everything."

"Yes, yes!"

"Who is your father, my child?"

"My father died in banishment. He was a Liberal—he was Prince Prospero Volonna."

"As I thought. Who was the other man?"

"He was a distant kinsman of my father's, and I have lately discovered that he was the principal instrument in my father's deportation. He was my guardian, a Minister and a great man in Italy. It is the Baron Bonelli, your Holiness."

"Just so, just so!" said the Pope, tapping his foot in obvious heat. "But go on, my child. Who is your husband?"

"My husband is a different kind of man altogether."

"Ah!"

"He has done everything for me, Holy Father—everything. Heaven knows what I should have been now without him."

"God bless him! God bless both of you!"

"I came to know him by the strangest accident. He is a

THE ETERNAL CITY

Liberal too, and a Deputy, and thinking of the corruptions of the Government, he pointed to me as the mistress of the Minister. It was not true, but I was degraded, and . . . and I set out to destroy him."

" A terrible vengeance, my child. Only the Minister could have thought of it."

" Then I found that my enemy was one of my father's friends, and a true and noble man. Holy Father, I had begun in hate, but I could not hate him. The darkness faded away from my soul, and something bright and beautiful came in its place. I loved him, and he loved me. With all our hearts we loved each other."

" And then ? "

" Then *he* came back to me. I knew all the secrets I had set out to learn, but I could not give them up, and when I refused he threatened me."

" And what did you do ? "

" I married my husband and withstood every temptation. It wasn't so very hard, for I cared nothing for wealth and luxury now. I only wanted to be good. God Himself should see how good I could be."

The Pope's eyes were moist. He was patting the young woman's trembling hand.

" My blessing rest on you, my daughter, and may the man you have married be worthy of your love and trust."

" Indeed, indeed he is," said Roma.

" He was your father's friend, you tell me ? "

" Yes, your Holiness, and although we met again so recently, I had known him in England when I was a child."

" A Liberal, you say ? "

" Yes, your Holiness."

" The enmity of the Minister was the fruit of political warfare ? "

" Nothing but that at first, though now . . ."

" I see, I see. And the secrets you speak of are only . . ."

" Only the doings of twenty years ago, which are dead and done with."

" Then your husband is older than you are ? "

The young woman broke into a sunny smile, which set the Pope smiling.

" Only ten years older, your Holiness. He is thirty-four."

" Where does he come from, and what was his father ? "

THE POPE

" He was born in Rome, but he does not know who his father was."

" What is he like to look upon? "

" He is like . . . I have never seen any one so like . . . will your Holiness forgive me? "

The colour had mounted to her eyes, her two rows of pearly teeth seemed to be smiling, and the sunny old face of the Pope was smiling too.

" Say what you please, my daughter."

" I have never seen any one so like the Holy Father," she said softly.

Her head was held down and there was a little nervous tremor at her heart. The Pope patted her hand affectionately.

" Have I asked you his name, my child? "

" His name is David Rossi."

The Pope rose suddenly from his seat, and for the first time his face looked dark and troubled.

" David Rossi? " he repeated in a husky voice.

Roma began to tremble. " Yes," she faltered.

" David Rossi, the Revolutionary? "

" Indeed no, your Holiness, he is not that."

" But, my child, my child, he is the founder of a revolutionary society which this very day the Holy Father has condemned."

He walked across the room and she rose to her feet and looked after him.

" One of the men who are conspiring against the peace of the Church—banded together to fight the Church and its head."

" Don't say that, your Holiness. He is religious, deeply religious, and far more an enemy of the Government and the King."

She began to talk wildly, almost aimlessly, trying to defend Rossi at all costs.

" Holy Father," she said, " shall I tell you a secret? There is nobody else in the world to whom I could tell it, but I can tell it to you. My husband is now in England organising a great scheme among the exiles and refugees of Italy. What it is I don't know, but he has told me that it will lead to the conquest of the country and the downfall of the throne. Whether it is to be a conspiracy in the ordinary sense, or a constitutional plan of campaign, he has not said, but everything tells me that it is directed against the politics of Rome, and not against its religion, and is intended to over-throw the King, and not the Pope."

The Pope, who had been standing with his back to Roma, turned round to her with a look of fright. His eyebrows had met over the vertical lines on his forehead, and this further reminder of another face threw Roma into still greater confusion.

" 'When I come back, it will be with such a force behind me as will make the prisons open their doors and the thrones of tyrants tremble.' That's what he said, your Holiness. The movement will come soon, too, I am sure it will, and then your Holiness will see that, instead of being irreligious men, the leaders of the people . . ."

The Pope held up his hand. " Stop! " he cried. " Say no more, my child. God knows what I must do with what you have said already."

Then Roma saw what she had done in the wild gust of her emotion, and in her terror she tried to take it back.

" Holy Father, you must not think from what I say that David Rossi is for revolution and regicide . . ."

" Don't speak, my child. You cannot know what an earthquake you have opened at my feet. Let me think! "

There was silence for a moment, and then Roma gulped down the great lumps in her throat and said: " I am only an ignorant woman, Holy Father, and perhaps I have said too much, and do not understand. But what I have told your Holiness was told me in love and confidence. And the Holy Father is wise and good, and whatever he does will be for the best."

The Pope returned to his chair with a bewildered look, and did not seem to hear. Roma sank to her knees by his side and said in a low, pleading tone:

" My husband's faith in me is so beautiful, your Holiness. Oh, so beautiful. I am the only one in the world to whom he has told all his secrets, and if any of them should ever come back to him . . ."

" Don't be afraid, my daughter. What you said in simple confidence shall be as sacred as if it had been spoken under the seal of the confessional."

" If I could tell your Holiness more about him—who he is and where he comes from—a place so lowly and humble, your Holiness . . ."

" Tell me no more, my child. It is better I should not

know. Pity ought to have no place in what duty tells me to do. But I can love David Rossi for all that. I do love him. I love him as a lost and wayward son, whose hand is raised against his Father, though he knows it not."

There was a bell button on the Pope's chair. He pressed it, and the Participante returned to the room without knocking. The Pope rose and took Roma's hand.

"Go in peace and with my blessing, my child. I bless you! May my fatherly blessing keep you pure in heart, may it strengthen you in all temptations, comfort you in all trials, avert from you every evil omen, and bring you into the fold of Christ's children at the last."

The Participante stepped forward and signed to Roma to withdraw. She rose and left the presence chamber, stepping backward and too much moved to speak. Not until the door had been closed did she realise that she was crossing the throne room, and that the Bussolante was walking beside her.

IV

When the Pope walked in his garden that afternoon as usual, the old Capuchin was with him. From the door of the Vatican they drove in the Pope's landau with two of the Noble Guard riding beside the carriage, and one of the chamberlains walking behind it, through lanes enshrouded in laurel and ilex, until they reached the summer-house on the top of the hill. There the old men stepped down, the Pope in his white cassock, white overcoat and red hat, the Capuchin in his brown habit, skull-cap and sandals. The Pope's cat, a creature of reddish coat, which followed him into the garden as a dog follows his master, leapt out of the carriage after them.

The Pope was more than usually grave and silent. Once or twice the Capuchin said, "And how did you find my young penitent this morning?"

"*Bene, bene!*" the Pope replied.

But at length the Pope, scraping the gravel at his feet with the ferrule of his walking-stick, began to speak on his own initiative.

"Father!"

"Your Holiness?"

"The inscrutable decree of God which made me your Pontiff has not altered our relations to each other as men?"

The Capuchin took snuff and answered, "Your Holiness is always so good as to say so."

"You are my master now just as you were thirty years ago, and there is something I wish to ask of you."

"What is it, your Holiness?"

"You have been a confessor many years, Father?"

"Forty years, your Holiness."

"In that time you have had many difficult cases?"

"Very many."

"Father, has it ever happened that a penitent has revealed to you a conspiracy to commit a crime?"

"More than once it has happened."

"And what have you done?"

"Persuaded him to reveal it to the civil authorities, or else tell it to me outside the confessional."

"Has the penitent ever refused to do so?"

"Never."

"But if . . . if the case were such as made it difficult for the penitent to reveal the conspiracy to the civil authorities, having regard to the penalties the revelation would bring with it . . . if by reason of ties of blood and affection such revelation were humanly impossible, and it would even be cruel to ask for it, what would you do then?"

"Nothing, your Holiness."

"Not even if the crime to be committed were a serious one, and it touched you very nearly?"

The Capuchin shook out his coloured print handkerchief and said, "That could make no difference, your Holiness."

"But suppose you heard in confession that your brother is to be assassinated, what is your duty?"

"My duty to the penitent who reveals his soul to me is to preserve his secret."

"And what is your duty to God?"

The handkerchief dropped from the Capuchin's hand.

The Pope paused, scraped the gravel with the ferrule of his stick, and said:

"Father, I am in the position of the confessor who has guilty knowledge of a conspiracy against the life of his enemy."

The Capuchin pushed his handkerchief into his sleeve and dropped back into his seat. After a moment the Pope told the story of what Roma had said of Rossi's plans abroad.

"A conspiracy," he said, "plainly a conspiracy."

"And what do you understand the conspiracy to be?"

"Who can say? Perhaps a recurrence to the custom of the Middle Ages, when citizens who had been banished by their opponents used to apply themselves in exile to attempt the reconquest of their country by stirring up the factions at home."

"You think that is Rossi's object?"

"I do."

The Capuchin shifted uneasily the skull-cap on his crown and said:

"Holy Father, I trust your Holiness will leave the matter alone."

"Why so?"

"In reading history I do not find that such enterprises have usually been successful. I see, rather, how commonly they have failed. And if it was so in the Middle Ages when the arts of war were primitive, how much less likely are the conspiracies of secret societies, the partial and superficial risings of refugees, to be serious now in the days of standing armies."

"True. But is that a good reason for doing nothing in this instance?"

"But, Holy Father, think. You cannot disclose the secrets this poor lady has revealed to you. Her confession was only a confidence, but your Holiness knows well that there is such a thing as a natural secret which it would be a great fault to reveal. Facts which of their own nature are confidential belong to this order. They are assimilated to the confessional, and as such they should be respected."

"Indeed they should."

"Then it is not possible for your Holiness to reveal what you heard this morning without bringing trouble to the penitent and wronging her in relation to her husband."

"God forbid that I should do so, whatever happens. But is a priest forbidden to speak of a sin heard in confession if he can do so in such a way that the identity of the penitent cannot be discovered?"

"Your Holiness intends to do that?"

"Why not?"

"The Holy Father knows best. For my own part, your Holiness, I think it a danger to tamper with the secrets of a soul, whatever the good end in view or the evil to be prevented."

The Capuchin looked round to where the horses were pawing the path and the Guards stood by the carriage.

"Thirty-five years ago we had a terrible lesson in such dangers, your Holiness."

The Pope dropped his head and continued to scrape the gravel.

"Your Holiness remembers the poor young woman who told her confessor she was about to marry a rich young man. The confessor thought it his duty to tell the young man's father in general terms that such a marriage was to be contracted. What was the result? The marriage took place in secret and ended in grief and death."

The Pope rose uneasily. "We will not speak of that. It was a case of a father's pride and perverted ambition. This is a different case altogether. A man who is a prey to diabolical illusions, an enemy of the Church and of social order, is hatching a plot which can only end in mischief and bloodshed. The Holy Father knows it. Shall he keep this guilty knowledge locked in his own bosom? God forbid!"

"Then you intend to warn the civil authorities?"

"I must. It is my duty. How could I lay my head on my pillow and not do it? But I will do it discreetly. I will commit no one, and this poor lady shall remain unknown."

The venerable old men, each leaning on his stick, walked down a path lined by clipped yews, shaded by cypresses, and almost overgrown with crocus, anemone, and violet. Suddenly from the bushes there came a flutter of wings, followed by the scream of a bird, and in a moment the Pope's cat had leapt on to a marble which stood in the midst of the jungle. It was an ancient sarcophagus, placed there as a fountain, but the spring that had fed it was dry, and in its moss-grown mouth a bird had made its nest. The cat was about to pounce down on the eggs when the Pope laid hold of it.

"Ah, Meesh, Meesh," he said, "what an anarchist you are, to be sure! . . . Monsignor!"

"Yes, your Holiness," said the chamberlain, coming up behind.

"Take this *gatto rosso* back to the carriage, and keep him in *domicilio coatto* until we come."

The Monsignor laughed and carried off the cat, and the Pope put his mittened hand gently on the little speckled eggs.

"Poor things! they're warm. Listen! That's the mother bird screaming in the tree. Hark! She's watching us, and waiting for us to go. How snugly she thought she had kept her secret."

The Capuchin drew a long breath. "Yes, nature has the same cry for fear in all her offspring."

"True," said the Pope.

"It makes me think of that poor girl this morning."

The Pope walked back to the carriage without saying a word. As he returned to the Vatican, the Angelus was ringing from all the church bells of Rome, the city was bathed in crimson light, the sun was sinking behind Monte Mario, and the stone pines on the crest of the hill, standing out against the reddening sky, were like the roofless columns of a ruined temple.

V

NEXT day Francesca came up with a letter. The porter from Trinità de' Monti had brought it and he was waiting below for a present. In a kind of momentary delirium Roma snatched at the envelope and emptied her purse into the old woman's hand.

"Santo Dio!" cried Francesca, "all this for a letter?"

"Never mind, godmother," said Roma. "Give the money to the good man and let him go."

"It's from Mr. Rossi, isn't it? Yes? I thought it was. You've only to say three Ave Marias when you wake in the morning and you get anything you want. I knew the Signora was dying for a letter, so . . ."

"Yes, yes, but the poor man is waiting, and I must get on with my work, and . . ."

"Work? Ah, Signora, in paradise you won't have to waste your time working. A lady like you will have violins and celestial bread and . . ."

"The man will be gone, godmother," said Roma, hustling the deaf old woman out of the room.

But even when Roma was alone she could not at first find courage to open the envelope. There was a certain physical thrill in handling it, in turning it over, and in looking at the stamps and the postmark. The stamps were French and the postmark was of Paris. That fact brought a vague gleam of joy. Rossi had been travelling, and perhaps he had not yet received her letter.

With a trembling kiss and a little choking prayer she

broke the seal at last, and as the letter came rustling out of the envelope she glanced at the closing lines:

"Your Faithful Husband."

She caught her breath and waited a moment, tingling all over. Then she unfolded the paper and read:—

"DEAREST,—A telegram from Rome, published in the Paris newspapers this morning, reports the trial and death of Bruno. To say that I am shocked is to say little. I am shaken to my foundations. My heart is bursting and my hand can with difficulty hold the pen.

"The news first reached me last evening, when I was in a restaurant with a group of journalists. We were at dinner, but I was compelled to rise and return to my lodgings. I must have been almost in delirium the whole night long. More than once I started from my sleep with the certainty that I heard Bruno's voice calling to me. Once I went to the window and looked out into the silent street. And yet I knew all the time that my poor friend lay dead in prison.

"Poor Bruno! I do not hold with suicide under any circumstances. A man's life does not belong to himself. Each of us is a soldier, and no sentinel ought to kill himself at his post. Who knows what the next turn of the battle will be? It is our duty to the General to see the fight out. But when the sentinel dies rather than pass a false watchword, suicide is sacrifice, death is victory, and God takes His martyr under the wings of His mercy.

"The poor fellow died believing I had been false to him! I knew him for eight years, and during that time he was more faithful to me than my shadow. He was the bravest, staunchest friend man ever had. And now he has left me, thinking I have wronged him at the last. Oh, my brother, do you not know the truth at last? In the world to which you are gone, does no heavenly voice tell you? Does not death reveal everything? Can you not look down and see all, tearing away the veil that clouded your vision here below? Is it only vouchsafed to him who remains on earth to know that he was true to the love you bore him? God forbid it! It cannot, cannot be.

"Dearest, I came to Paris unexpectedly ten days ago . . ."

Roma lifted her swimming eyes. "Then he hasn't received it," she thought.

"Called in haste, not only to organise our Italian people for the new crusade, but to compose by a general principle the many groups of Frenchmen who, under different names, have the same aspirations—Marxists, Possibilists, Boulangists, Guesdists, and Central Revolutionists, with their varying propaganda, co-operative, trade-unionist, anti-semite, national, and I know not what—I had almost despaired of any union of interests so pitifully subdivided when the news of Bruno's death came like a trumpet-blast, and the walls of the social Jericho fell before it. Everybody feels that the moment of action has arrived, and what I thought would be an Italian movement is likely to become an international one. A great outrage on the spirit of Justice breaks down all barriers of race and nationality.

"God guide us now. What did our Master say? ' The dagger of the conspirator is never so terrible as when sharpened on the tombstone of a martyr.' With all the heat of my own blood I tremble when I think what may be the effect of these tyrannies. Of course the ruling classes at home will wash their hands of this affair. When a Minister wants to play Macbeth he has no lack of grooms to dabble with Duncan's blood. But the people will make no nice distinctions. I wouldn't give two straws for the life of the King when this crime has touched the conscience of the people. He didn't do it? No, he does nothing, but he stands for all. Anarchists did not invent regicide. It has been used in all ages by people who think the spirit of Justice violated. And the names of some who practised it are written on marble monuments in letters of gold."

Roma began to tremble. Had the Pope been right after all? Was it really revolution and regicide which Rossi contemplated?

"Dearest, don't think that because I am so moved by all this that other and dearer things are not with me always. Never a day or an hour passes but my heart speaks to you as if you could answer. I have been anxious at not hearing from you for ten days, although I left my Paris address in London for your letters to be sent on. Sometimes I think my enemies may be tormenting you, and then I blame myself for not bringing you with me, in spite of every disadvantage. Sometimes I think you may be ill, and then I have an impulse to take the first train and fly back to Rome. I know I cannot be with you always, but this absence is cruel. Happily it will soon be over, and we shall see an end of all sadness. Don't suffer for me. Don't let my cares distress you. Whatever happens, nothing can divide us, because love has united our hearts for ever.

"That's why I'm sure of you, Roma, sure of your love and sure of your loyalty. Otherwise how could I stay an hour longer after this awful event, tortured by the fear of a double martyrdom—the martyrdom of myself and of the one who is dearest to me in the world?

"The spring is coming to take me home to you, darling. Don't you smell the violets? Adieu!

"Your Faithful Husband."

Roma slept little that night. Joy, relief, disappointment, but, above all, fear for Rossi, apprehension about his plans, and overpowering dread of the consequences kept her awake for hours. Early next day a man in a blue uniform brought a letter from the Braschi Palace. It ran:—

"Dear Roma,—I must ask you to come across to my office this morning, and as soon as convenient. You will not hesitate to do so when I tell you that by this friendly message I am saving you the humiliation of a summons from the police. Yours, as always, affectionately, Bonelli."

VI

The Minister of the Interior sat in his cabinet before a table covered with blue-books and the square sheets of his "projects of law," and the Commendatore Angelelli, with his usual extravagant politeness, was standing and bowing by his side.

"And what is this about proclamations issued by Rossi?" said the Baron, fixing his eye-glasses and looking up.

"We have traced the printer who published them," said Angelelli. "After he was arrested he gave the name of the person who paid him and provided the copy."

The Baron bowed without speaking.

"It was a certain lady, Excellency," said Angelelli in his thin voice, "so we thought it well to wait for your instructions."

"You did right, Commendatore. Leave that part of the matter to me. And Rossi himself—he is still in England?"

"In France, your Excellency, but we have letters from both London and Paris detailing all his movements."

THE POPE

" Good."

" The Chief Commissioner writes that during his stay in London Rossi lodged in Soho, and received visits from nearly all the representatives of revolutionary parties. Apparently he united many conflicting forces, and not only the Democratic Federations and the Socialist and Labour Leagues, but also the Radical organisations and various religious guilds and unions gathered about him."

The Baron made a gesture of impatience. " It's a case of birds of a feather. London has always been the central home of anarchy under various big surnames. What does the Commissioner understand to be Rossi's plan? "

" Rossi's plan, the Commissioner thinks, is to send back the Italian exiles, and to disperse them, with money and literature gathered abroad, among the excited millions at home."

" Wonderful! " said the Baron.

Angelelli laughed his thin laugh, like a hen cackling over its nest. Then he said:

" But the Prefect of Paris has formed a more serious opinion, your Excellency."

" What is it? "

" That Rossi is conspiring to assassinate the King."

The Baron blinked the glasses from his nose and sat upright.

" Apparently he was having less success in Paris, where the moral plea has been overdone, when reports of the Rocco incident . . ."

" A most unlucky affair, Commendatore."

" Meeting at cafés in order to avoid the control of the police . . . In short, although he has no exact information, the Prefect warns us to keep double guard over the person of his Majesty."

The Baron rose and perambulated the hearthrug. " A pretty century, truly, for fools who pass for wise men, and for weaklings who threaten when the distance is great enough! . . . Commendatore, have you mentioned this matter to anybody else? "

" To nobody whatever, Excellency."

" Then think no more about it. It's nothing. The public mind must not be alarmed. Tighten the cord about our man in Paris. Adieu! "

The Baron's next visitor was the Prefect of the Province, who looked more solemn and soldierly than ever.

"Senator," said the Baron, "I sent for you to say that the Council has determined to put an end to the state of siege."

The Prefect bowed again severely.

"The insurrection has been suppressed, the city is quiet, and the severities of military rule begin to oppress the people."

The Prefect bowed again and assented.

"The Council has also resolved, dear Senator, that the country shall celebrate the anniversary of the King's accession with general rejoicings."

"Excellent idea, sir," said the Prefect. "To wipe out the depression of the late unhappy times by a public festival is excellent policy. But the time is short."

"Very short. The anniversary falls on Easter Monday. That is to say, a week from to-day. You will therefore take the matter in hand immediately and push it on without further delay. The details we will discuss later, and arrange all programmes of presentations and processions. Meantime I have written a proclamation announcing the event. Here it is. You can take it with you."

"Good!"

"The King will also sign a decree of amnesty to all the authors and accomplices of the late acts and attempts at rebellion who were not the organising and directing minds. That is also written. Here it is. But his Majesty has not yet signed it."

The Prefect took a second paper from the Baron's hand, glanced his eyes over it, and read certain passages. "'Seeing that on a day of public rejoicing we could not restrain an emotion of grief . . . turning a pitying eye upon the inexperienced youths drawn into a vortex of political disorder . . . we therefore decree and command the following acts of sovereign clemency . . .' May I expect to receive this in the course of the day, your Excellency?"

"Yes. And now for your own part of the enterprise, dear Senator. You will order all mayors of towns to assemble in Rome to complete the preparations. You will arrange a procession to the Quirinal, when the people will call the King on to the balcony and sing the National Hymn. You will order banners to be made bearing suitable watchwords, such as 'Long live the King,' 'May he govern as well as reign,' 'Long live the Crown,' the 'Flag,' and (perhaps) the 'Army.' You will oppose these generating ideas to 'Atheism' and

'Anarchy.' The essential point is that the people must be caused by festivals, songs, bands of music, and processions to think of the throne as their bulwark and the King as their saviour, and to take advantage of every opportunity to attest their gratitude to both. You follow me?"

" Perfectly."

" Then lose no time, Senator. . . . One moment."

The Prefect had risen and reached the door.

" If you can double the King's guard and change the company every day until the festival is over . . ."

" Easily, your Excellency. But wait; the Vatican Chief of Police has asked for help on Holy Thursday."

" Give it him. Let the timid old man of the Sacred College have no excuse for saying we take more care of the King than of the Pope."

The Minister of Justice was the next of the Baron's visitors. He was a short man with a smiling and rubicund face, and he wore yellow kid gloves.

" All goes well and wisdom is justified of her children," said the Baron, rising again and promenading the hearthrug. " The national sentiment, dear colleague, is a sword, and either we must use it on behalf of the Government and the King, or stand by and see it used by the hostile factions."

" Men like Rossi are not slow to use it, sir," said the little Minister.

" Tut! It's not Rossi I'm thinking of now. It's the Church, the clergy, rich in money and in the faith of the populace. That's why I wanted to do something as a set-off against those mourning demonstrations which the Pope has appointed."

" Yes, the old gentleman of the Vatican knows the instincts and cravings of our people, doesn't he, sir? He knows they like a show, and the seasoning of their pleasures with a little religion."

" It's the rustiest old weapon in the Pope's arsenal, dear colleague, but it may serve unless we do something. If the people can be persuaded that the Pope is their one friend in adversity, there couldn't be a better feather in the Papal cap. Happily our people love to sing and to dance as well as to weep and to pray. So we needn't throw up the sponge yet."

Both laughed, and the little Minister said, " Besides, it is so easy to change religious processions into political ones.

And then the Vatican is always intriguing with the powers of rebellion and preaching obedience to the Pope alone."

The creaking of the Baron's patent-leather boots stopped, and he drew up before his colleague.

"Watch that sharply," he said, "and if you see any sign on the part of the Vatican of intriguing with men like Rossi, any complicity with conspiracy, or any knowledge of plots pointing to revolution and regicide, let the Council hear of it immediately!"

The Baron's face had suddenly whitened with passion, and his little colleague looked at him in alarm. A secretary entered the room and handed the Baron a card. The Baron fixed his eye-glasses and read: "MONSIGNOR MARIO, Cameriere Segreto Partecipante di Sua Santità Pio X. Vaticano."

"St. Anthony! Talk of the angels . . ." muttered the little Minister.

"Will you perhaps . . ."

"Certainly," said the Minister, and he left the room.

"Show the Monsignor in," said the Baron.

VII

THE Monsignor was young, tall, slight, almost fragile, and had thin black hair and large spiritual eyes. As he entered in the long black overcoat, which covered his cassock, he bowed and looked slowly round the room. His subdued expression was that of a sheep going through a gate where the dogs may be, and his manner suggested that he would fly at the first alarm.

The Baron looked over his eye-glasses and measured his man in a moment. "Pray sit," he said, and at the next moment the young Monsignor and the Baron were seated at opposite sides of the table.

"I am sent to you by a venerable and illustrious personage . . ."

"Let us say the Pope," said the Baron.

The young Monsignor bowed and continued, "to offer on his behalf a word of counsel and of warning."

"It is an unusual and distinguished honour," said the Baron.

"I am instructed to inform you that the Holy Father has reason to believe a further and more serious insurrection is preparing, and to warn you to take the necessary steps to secure public order and to prevent bloodshed."

The Baron did not move a muscle. "If the Holy Father has special knowledge of a plot that is impending . . ."

"Not special, only general, but sufficient to enable him to tell you to hold yourself in readiness."

"How long has the Holy Father been aware of this?"

"Not long. In fact, only since yesterday morning," said the Monsignor, and fearing he had said too much he added, "I only mention this to show you that the Holy Father has lost no time."

"But if the Holy Father knows that a conspiracy is afoot, he can no doubt help us to further information."

The Monsignor shook his head.

"You mean that he will not do so?"

"No."

"Am I, then, to understand that the information with which his Holiness honours me came to him secretly?"

"Yes, sir, secretly, and it is, therefore, not open to further explanation."

"So it reached him by the medium of the confessional?"

The Monsignor rose from his seat. "Your Excellency cannot be in earnest."

"You mean that it did not reach him by the medium of the confessional?"

"Certainly not."

"Then he is able to tell me everything, if he will?"

The Monsignor became agitated. "The Holy Father's information came through a channel that is assimilated to the confessional, and is almost as sacred and inviolate."

"But obedience to the Pope obliterates from all other responsibility. His Holiness has only to say 'Speak,' and his faithful child must obey."

The Monsignor became confused. "His informant is not even a Catholic, and he has, therefore, no right to command her."

"So it is a woman," said the Baron, and the young ecclesiastic dropped his head.

"It is a woman and a non-Catholic, and she visited the Holy Father at the Vatican yesterday morning; is that so?"

"I do not assert it, sir, and I do not deny it."

The Baron did not speak for a moment, but he looked

22

steadily over his eye-glasses at the flushed young face before him. Then he said in a quiet tone:

"Monsignor, the relations of the Pope and the Government are delicate, and if anything occurred to carry the disagreement further it might result in a serious fratricidal struggle."

The Monsignor was trying to regain his self-possession, and he remained silent.

"But whatever those relations, it cannot be the wish of the Holy Father to cover with his mantle the upsetters of order who are cutting at the roots of the Church as well as the State."

"Therefore I am here now, sir, thus early and thus openly," said the Monsignor.

"Monsignor," said the Baron, "if anything should occur to—for example—the person of the King, it cannot be the wish of his Holiness that anybody—myself, for instance—should be in a position to say to Parliament and to the Governments of Europe, 'The Pope knew everything beforehand, and therefore, not having revealed the particulars of the plot, the venerable Father of the Vatican is an accomplice of murderers.'"

The young ecclesiastic lost himself utterly. "The Pope," he said, "knows nothing more than I have told you."

"Yes, Monsignor, the Pope knows one thing more. He knows who was his informant and authority. It is necessary that the Government should know that also, in order that it may judge for itself of the nature of the conspiracy and the source from which it may be expected."

The Monsignor was quivering like a limed bird. "I have delivered my message, and have only to add that in sending me here his Holiness desired to prevent crime, not to help you to apprehend criminals."

The Baron's eye-glasses dropped from his nose, and he spoke sharply and incisively. "The Government must at least know who the lady was who visited his Holiness at the Vatican yesterday morning, and led him to believe that a serious insurrection was impending."

"That your Excellency never will, or can, or shall know."

The Monsignor was bowing himself out of the room when the Baron's secretary opened the door and announced another visitor.

"Donna Roma, your Excellency."

The Monsignor betrayed fresh agitation, and tried to go.

"Bring her in," said the Baron. "One moment, Monsignor."

"I have said all I am authorised to say, sir, and I feel warned that I must say no more."

"Don't say that, Monsignor. . . . Ah, Donna Roma!"

Roma, who had entered the room, replied with reserve and dignity.

"Allow me, Donna Roma, to present Monsignor Mario of the Vatican," said the Baron.

"It is unnecessary," said Roma. "I met the Monsignor yesterday morning."

The young ecclesiastic was overwhelmed with confusion.

"My respectful reverence to his Holiness," said the Baron, smiling, "and pray tell him that the Government will do its duty to the country and to the civilised world, and count on the support of the Pope."

Monsignor Mario left the room without a word.

VIII

THE Baron pushed out an easy-chair for Roma and twisted his own to face it.

"How are you, my child?"

"One lives," said Roma, with a sigh.

"What is the matter, my dear? You are ill and unhappy."

She eluded the question and said, "You sent for me—what do you wish to say?"

He told her the printer of certain seditious proclamations had been arrested, and in the judicial inquiry preparatory to his trial he had mentioned the name of the person who had employed and paid him.

"You cannot but be aware, my dear, that you have rendered yourself liable to prosecution, and that nothing—nothing whatever—could have saved you from public exposure but the good offices of a powerful friend."

Roma drew her lips tightly together and made no answer.

"But what a situation for a Minister! To find himself ruled by his feelings for a friend, and thus weakened in the eyes of his servants, who ought to have no possible hold on him."

Roma's gloomy face began to be compressed with scorn.

"You have perhaps not realised the full measure of the indignity that might have befallen you. For instance—a cruel necessity—the police would have been making a domiciliary visitation in your apartment at this moment."

Roma made a faint, involuntary cry, and half rose from her seat.

"Your letters and most secret papers would by this time be exposed to the eyes of the police. . . . No, no, my child; calm yourself, be seated; thanks to my intervention, this will not occur."

Roma looked at him, and found him more repulsive to her at that moment than he had ever been before. Even his daintiness repelled her—the modified perfume about his clothes, his waxed moustache, his rounded finger-nails, and all the other refinements of the man who loves himself and sets out to please the senses of women.

"You will allow, my dear, that I have had sufficient to humiliate me without this further experience. A ward who persistently disregards the laws of propriety and exposes herself to criticism in the most ordinary acts of life was surely a sufficient trial. But that was not enough. Almost as soon as you have passed out of my legal control you join with those who are talking and conspiring against me."

Roma continued to sit with a gloomy and defiant face.

"How am I to defend myself against the humiliations you put upon me in your own mind? You give me no chance to defend myself. I cannot know what others have told you. I know no more than you repeat to me, and that is nothing at all."

Roma was biting her compressed lips and breathing audibly.

"How am I to defend myself against the humiliations I suffer in the minds of the public? There is only one way, and that is to allow it to be believed that, in spite of all appearances, you are still playing a part, that you are going to all lengths to punish the enemy who traduced you and publicly degraded you."

Roma tried to laugh, but the laugh was broken in her throat by a rising sob.

"I have only to whisper that, dear friend, and society, at

all events, will credit it. Already it knows the very minute details of your life, and it will believe that when you threw away every shred of propriety and went to live in that man's apartment, it was only in order to play the old part—shall I say the Scriptural part?—of possessing yourself of *the inmost secrets of his soul.*"

The clear, sharp whisper in which the Baron spoke his last words cut Roma like a knife. She threw up her head with scorn.

"Let it believe what it likes," she said. "If society cares to think that I have allowed my life to be turned upside down for the sake of hatred, let it do so."

The Baron's secretary interrupted by opening the door.

"Nazzareno, Excellency," said the secretary.

"Ah! Let him come in," said the Baron. "You remember Nazzareno, Roma? My steward at Albano?"

An elderly man with a bronzed face and shaggy eyebrows, bringing an odour of the fields and the farmyard, was ushered into the room.

"Come in, Nazzareno! You've not forgotten Donna Roma? You planted a rosebush on her first Roman birthday, you remember. It's a great tree by this time, perhaps."

"It is, Excellency," said the steward, bowing and smiling, "and nearly as full of bloom as the Signorina herself."

"Well, what news from Albano?"

The steward told a long story of operations on the estates—planting birch in the top fields, and eucalyptus in the low meadow, fencing, draining, and sowing.

"And . . . and the Baroness?" said the Baron, turning over some papers.

"Ah! her Excellency is worse," said the old man. "The nurse and the doctor thought you had better be told exactly, and that is the object of my errand."

"Yes?" The papers rustled in the Baron's fingers as he shuffled and sorted them.

The steward told another long story. Her Excellency was weaker, or she would be quite ungovernable. And so changed! When he was called in yesterday she was so much altered that he would not have known her. It was a question of days, and all the servants were saying prayers to Mary Magdalene.

"Have some dinner downstairs before you return, Nazzareno," said the Baron. "And when you see the doctor this evening, say I'll come out some time this week if I can. Good-morning!"

The repulsion the Baron had inspired in Roma deepened to loathing when he began to speak affectionately the moment the door had closed on the steward.

"Look at this, dearest. It's from his Majesty."

She did not look at the letter he put before her, so he told her what it contained. It offered him the Collar of the Annunziata, the highest order in Italy, making him a cousin to the King.

She could not contain herself any longer. "I want to tell you something," she said, "so that you may know once for all that it is useless to waste further thought on me."

He looked at her with an indulgent smile.

"I am married to Mr. Rossi," she said.

"But that is impossible. There was no time."

"We were married religiously, in the parish church, on the morning he left Rome."

The indulgent smile gave way to a sarcastic one.

"Then why did he leave you behind? If he thought *that* was a good marriage, why didn't he take you with him? But perhaps he had his own reason, and the denunciation of the poor man in prison was not so far amiss."

"That was an official lie, a cowardly lie," said Roma, and her eyes burned with anger.

"Was it? Perhaps it was. But I have just heard something else about Mr. Rossi that is undoubtedly true. I have heard from the Prefect of Paris that he is organising a conspiracy for the assassination of the King."

A look of fear which she could not restrain crossed Roma's face.

"More than that, and stranger than that, I have just heard also that the Pope has some knowledge of the plot."

Roma felt terror seizing her, and she said in a constrained voice, "Why? What has the Pope told you?"

"Only that an insurrection is impending. It seems that his informant is a woman. . . . Who can she be, I wonder?"

The Baron was fixing his eyes on her and she tried to elude his gaze.

"Whoever she is she must know more," he said in a severe voice, "and whatever it is she must reveal it."

Roma got up, looking very pale, and feeling very feeble.

When she reached the door the Baron was smiling and holding out his hand.

"Will you not shake hands with me?" he said.

"What is the use?" she answered. "When people shake hands it means that they wish each other well. You do not wish me well. You are trying to force me to betray my husband. . . . *But I'll die first*," she said, and then turned and fled.

When Roma was gone the Baron wrote a letter to the Pope:

"Your Holiness,—Providential accident, as your chamberlain would tell you, has enabled his Majesty's Government to judge for itself of that source of your Holiness's information which your Holiness very properly refused to reveal. At the same time official channels have disclosed to his Majesty's Government the nature of the conspiracy of which your Holiness so patriotically forewarned them. This conspiracy appears to be no less serious than an attempt to assassinate the King, but as detailed knowledge of so vile a plot is necessary in order to save the life of our august sovereign, his Majesty's Government asks you to grant the Prime Minister the honour of an audience with your Holiness in the cause of order and public security. Hoping to hear of your Holiness's convenience, and trusting that your Holiness will not disappoint the hopes of those who are dreaming even yet of a reconciliation of Church and State, I am, with all reverence, your Holiness's faithful son and servant, Bonelli."

IX

Roma went home full of uncertainty, and wrote in a nervous and straggling hand a hasty letter to Rossi.

"My dearest," she said, "your letter reached me safely last evening, and though I cannot answer it properly at the present moment, I must send a brief reply by mid-day's mail, because there are two or three things it is imperative I should say immediately.

"The first is that I wrote you a very important letter to London twelve days ago, and it is clear that you have not yet received it. The contents were of the greatest seriousness and also of the greatest secrecy, and I should die if any other eye than yours were to read them; therefore do not lose a moment until you ask for the letter to be sent after you to Paris. Write to London by the first post, and when the letter has come to your hand, do telegraph to me saying so. 'Received,' that will be sufficient, but if you can add one other little word expressing your feeling on reading what I wrote—'Forgiven,' for instance—my feeling will not be happiness, it will be delirium.

"The next thing I have to say, dearest, is about your letters. You know they are more precious to me than my heart's blood, and there is not a word or a line of them I would sacrifice for a queen's crown. But they are so full of perilous opinions and of hints of programmes for dangerous enterprises, that for your sake I am afraid. It is so good of you to tell me what you are thinking and doing, and I am so proud to be the woman who has the confidence as well as the love of the most-talked-of man in Europe, that it cuts at my heart to ask you to tell me no more about your political plans. Nevertheless, I must. Think what would happen if the police took it into their heads to make a domiciliary visitation in this house. And then think of what a fearful weapon it puts into the hands of your enemies, if, hearing that I know so much, they put pressure upon me that I cannot withstand! Of course, that is impossible. I would die first. But still . . .

"My last point, dearest . . ."

Her pen stopped. How was she to put what she wished to say next? David Rossi was in danger—a double danger —danger from within as well as danger from without. His last letter showed plainly that he was engaged in an enterprise which his adversaries would call a plot. Roma remembered her father, doomed to a life-long exile and a lonely death, and asked herself if it was not always the case that the reformer partly reformed his age, and was partly corrupted by it.

If she could only draw David Rossi away from associations that were always reeking of revolution, if she could bring him back to Rome before he was too far involved in plots and with plotters! But how could she do it? To tell him the plain truth that he was going headlong to *domicilio coatto* was useless. She must resort to artifice. A light shot through her brain, her eyes gleamed, and she began again:

"My last point, dearest, is that I am growing jealous. Yes, indeed, jealous! I know you love me, but knowing it doesn't help me to forget that you are always meeting women who must admire and love you. I tremble to think you may be happy with them. I want you to be happy, yet I feel as if it would be treason for you to be happy without me. What an illogical thing love is! But where Love reigns jealousy is always the Prime Minister, and in order to banish my jealousy you must come back immediately . . ."

Her pen stopped again. The artifice was too trivial, too palpable, and he would certainly see through it. She tore up the sheet and began afresh.

"My last point, dearest, is that I fear you are forgetting me in your work. While thinking of the revolution you are making in Europe, you forget the revolution you have already made in this poor little heart. Of course I love your glory more than I love myself, yet I am afraid it is taking you away from me, and will end by leading you up, up, up, out of a woman's reach. Why didn't I give you my portrait to put in your watch-case when you went away? Don't let this folly disgust you, dearest. A woman is a foolish thing, isn't she? But if you don't want me to make a torment of everything you will hasten back in time to . . ."

She threw down the pen and began to cry. Hadn't she promised him that, come what would, her love for him should never stand in his way? In the midst of her tears a little stab at her heart made her think of something else, and she took up the pen again.

"My last point, dearest, is that I am ill, and very, very anxious to see you soon. My health has been failing ever since you left Rome. Perhaps the anxieties I have gone through have been partly the cause of this, but I am sure that your absence is chiefly responsible, and that no doctor and no medicine would be so good for me as one rush into your arms. Therefore come and give me back all my health and happiness. Come, I beg of you. Leave it to others to do your work abroad. Come at once *before things have gone too far;* come, come, come!"

She hesitated, wanting to say, "Not that I am *very* ill . . ." And then, "You mustn't come if there is any risk to yourself . . ." And again, "I would never forgive myself if . . ." But she crushed down her qualms, sealed her letter, and sent the Garibaldian to post it.

Then she gathered up the entire body of David Rossi's letters, and putting some light firewood into the stove she sat on the ground to burn them. It was necessary to remove all evidence that could be used against him in the event of a domiciliary visitation. One by one as the letters were passed into the fire she read parts of them, and some of the passages seemed to stand out afresh in the flames. "Your friend must be a true woman, and it was very sweet of you to be so tender with her." . . . "There is always a little twinge when I read between the lines of your letters. Are you not dissimulating? . . . to keep up my spirits?" . . . "You shall smile and recover all your girlish spirits. . . . I shall hear your silvery laugh again as I did on that glorious day in the Campagna." . . . "It shows how rightly I judged the moral elevation of your soul, your impeccability, your spirit of fire and your heart of gold."

While the letters were burning she felt herself to be under the influence of a kind of delirium. It was almost as though she were committing murder.

X

The Pope had begun the day with the long task of administering the sacrament to the lay members of his household, yet at eight o'clock he was back in his library in the midst of his morning receptions surrounded by a bevy of camerieri, monsignori, and messengers. First came a Cardinal Prefect of Propaganda to report the doings of his congregation; then an ambassador from Spain to tell of the suppression of religious orders; and finally the majordomo to recite the official programme for the public ceremonies which the Pope had ordered for Holy Thursday.

It was now ten o'clock, and Cortis, the valet, brought the usual plate of soup. Then came a large man with bold features and dark complexion, wearing a purple robe edged with red and a red biretta. It was the Cardinal Secretary of State.

"What news this morning, your Eminence?" said the Pope.

"The Government," said the Cardinal Secretary, "has just published a proclamation announcing a jubilee in honour of the King's accession. It is to begin on Monday next, and there are to be great feasts and rejoicings."

"A jubilee at a time like this! What a wild mockery of the people's woes! How many poor women and children must go hungry before this royal orgy has been paid for! God be with us! Such injustice and tyranny in the Satanic guise of clemency and indulgence is almost enough to explain the homicidal theories of the demagogues and to justify men like Rossi. . . . Any further news of him?"

"Yes. He is at present in Paris, in close intercourse with the leaders of every abominable sect."

"You have seen this man Rossi, your Eminence?"

"Once. I saw him on the morning of the jubilee of your Holiness, when he attempted to present a petition."

"What is he like to look upon—the typical demagogue; no?"

"No. I am bound to say no, your Holiness. And his conversation, though it is full of the jargon of modern Liberalism, has none of the obscenities of Voltaire."

"Some one said . . . who was it, I wonder? . . . some one said he resembled the Holy Father."

"Now that you mention it, your Holiness, there is perhaps a remote resemblance."

"Ah! who knows what service for God and humanity even such a man might have done if in early life his lines had been cast in better places."

"They say he was an orphan from his infancy, your Holiness."

"Then he never knew a father's care and guidance! Unhappy son! Unhappy father!"

"Monsignor Mario," said the low voice of a chamberlain, and at the next moment the Pope's messenger to the Prime Minister was kneeling in the middle of the floor.

In nervous tones and broken sentences the Monsignor told his story. The Pope listened intently, the vertical lines on his forehead deepening and darkening every moment, until at length he burst out impatiently:

"But, my son, you do not say that you said all this in addition to your message?"

"I was drawn into doing so in defence of your Holiness."

"You told the Minister that my information came through the channel of a simple confidence?"

"He insinuated that the Holy Father was perhaps breaking the seal of the confessional . . ."

"That my informant was a non-Catholic and a woman?"

"He implied that your Holiness had only to command her to reveal the conspiracy to the civil authorities, and therefore . . ."

"And you said she was here on Saturday morning?"

"He hinted that the Holy Father was an accomplice of criminals if he had known this without revealing it before, and that was why . . ."

"And she came in at that moment, you say?"

"At that very moment, your Holiness, and said she had met me on Saturday morning."

"Man, man, what have you done?" cried the Pope, rising from his seat and pacing the room.

The chamberlain continued to kneel in utter humility, until the Pope, recovering his composure, put both hands on his shoulders and raised him to his feet.

"Forgive me, my son. I was more to blame than you were. It was wrong to trust any one with a verbal message in the cabinet of a fox. The Holy Father should have no intercourse with such persons. But this is God's hand. Let us leave everything to the Holy Spirit."

At that moment the Papal Majordomo returned with a letter. It was the Baron's letter to the Pope. After the Pope had read it he stepped into a little adjoining room which contained nothing but a lounge and an easy-chair. There he lay on the lounge and turned his face to the wall.

XI

At four o'clock in the afternoon the Pope and Father Pifferi were again walking in the garden. The groves of Judas trees were shedding their crimson blossoms and the path had a covering of bloom; the atmosphere was full of the odour of honey-suckle and violet, and through the sunlit air the swallows were darting with shrill cries and the glitter of wings.

"And what does your Holiness intend to do?" asked the Capuchin.

"Providence will direct us," said the Pope with a sigh.

THE POPE

"But your Holiness will refuse the request of the Government?"

"How can I do so without exposing myself to misunderstanding? Suppose the King is assassinated, what then? The Government will tell the world that the Pope knew all and did nothing."

"Let them. It will not be an incident without parallel in the history of the Church. And the world will only honour your Holiness the more for standing firm on your sanctity of the human soul."

"Yes, if the confessional were in question. The world knows that the seal of the confessional is sacred, and must be observed at all costs. But this is not a case of the confessional."

"Didn't your Holiness say you would observe it as such?"

"And I shall. But what about the public? Accident has told the Government that this is not a case of the confessional, and the Government will tell the world. What follows? If I refuse to do anything the enemies of the Church will give it out that the Holy Father is an accomplice of a regicide, ready and willing to intrigue with the agents of rebellion to regain the temporal power."

"Then you will receive the Prime Minister?"

"No! Or if so, only in the company of his superior."

"The King?"

"Yes."

The Capuchin removed his skull-cap with an uneasy hand, and walked some paces without speaking.

"Will he come, your Holiness?"

"If he thinks I hold the secret on which his life depends, assuredly he will come."

"But you are sovereign as well as Pope—is it possible for you to receive him?"

"I will receive him as the King of Sardinia, the King of Italy, if you will, but not as the King of Rome."

The Capuchin took his coloured handkerchief from his sleeve and rolled it in his palms, which were hot and perspiring.

"But, Holy Father," he said, "what will be the good? Say that all difficulties of etiquette can be removed, and you can meet as man to man, as David Leone and Albert Charles —why will the King come? Only to ask you to put pressure upon your informant to give more information."

THE ETERNAL CITY

The Pope drew himself up on the gravel path and smote his breast with indignation. "Never! It would be an insult to the Church," he said. "It is one thing to expect the Holy Father to do his duty as a Christian even to his enemy, it is another thing to ask him to invade the sanctity of a private confidence."

The Capuchin did not reply, and the two old men walked on in silence. As the light softened the swallows increased their clamour, and song-birds began to call from neighbouring trees. Suddenly a startled cry burst from the foliage, and, turning quickly, the Pope lifted up the cat which, as usual, was picking its way at his heels.

"Ah, Meesh, Meesh! I've got you safely this time. . . . It was the poor mother-bird again, I suppose. Where is her nest, I wonder?"

They found it in the old sarcophagus, which was now almost lost in leaves. The eggs had been hatched, and the fledglings, with eyes not yet opened, stretched their featherless necks and opened their beaks when the Pope put down his hand to touch them.

"Monsignor," said the Pope over his shoulder, "remind me to-morrow to ask the gardener for some worms."

The cat, from his prison under the Pope's arm, was watching the squirming nest with hungry eyes.

"Naughty Meesh! Naughty!" said the Pope, shaking one finger in the cat's face. "But Meesh is only following the ways of his kind, and perhaps I was wrong to let him see the quarry."

The Pope and the Capuchin walked back to the Vatican for joy of the sweet spring evening with its scent of flowers and song of birds.

"You are sad to-day, Father Pifferi," said the Pope.

"I'm still thinking of that poor lady," said the Capuchin.

At the first hour of night the Pope attended the recitation of the rosary in his private chapel, and then returning to his private study, a room furnished with a table and two chairs, he took a light supper, served by Cortis in the evening dress of a civilian. His only other company was the cat, which sat on a chair on the opposite side of the table. After supper he wrote a letter. It ran:

"SIRE,—Your Minister informs us that through official channels he has received warning of a plot against your life,

336

and believing that we can give information that will help him to defeat so vile a conspiracy, he asks us for a special audience. It is not within our power to promise more assistance than we have already given; but this is to say that if your Majesty yourself should wish to see us, we shall be pleased to receive you, with or without your Minister, if you will come in private and otherwise unattended, at the hour of 21½ on Holy Thursday, to the door of the Canons' House of St. Peter's, where the bearer of this message will be waiting to conduct you to the Sacristy.

"Nil timendum nisi a Deo.   PIUS P.P.X."

XII

THE ceremonies in St. Peter's on Maundy Thursday exceeded in pomp and magnificence anything that could be remembered in Rome.

It was a great triumph for the Church. In the face of the anti-religious Governments of Europe she had proved that the mightiest sentiment of the people was the sentiment of religion.

The Papal Court was proud of itself. Some of its members made no effort to conceal their delight at the blow they had struck at the ruling classes. But there was one man in Rome who felt no joy in his triumph. It was the Pope.

At nine o'clock at night he visited the "urn" called the "Sepulchre." Borne amid the light of torches on his *sedia* with his *flabelli* waving on either hand, under a white canopy upheld by prelates, he passed through the glittering rooms of his own palace, along the dark corridors of the Vatican and down the marble stairs, accompanied by his guards in helmets and preceded by the papal cross covered with a violet veil, into the great Basilica, lit only by large candles in iron stands, and looking plain and barn-like and full of shadows in the gloom and the smoky air. But after he had visited the Sepulchre, gorgeously illuminated, while the cantors sang the *Verbum Caro*, after he had knelt in silence and had risen, and the torches of his procession had been put out, and he had returned to his chair to be borne into the Sacristy, and the poor people, lifted to a height of emotion not often reached by the human soul, had broken again into a last delirious shout of affection, he dropped his head and wept.

At that moment the Sacristy was empty save for the custodian in black cassock and biretta, who was warming his hands over a large bronze scaldino; but in the Archpriest's room adjoining, with its gilt arm-chair and stools of red plush, Father Pifferi in his ordinary brown habit was waiting for the Pope. The bearers put down the chair, knelt and kissed the Pope's feet in spite of his protest, backed themselves out with deep obeisance, and left the two old men together.

" Have they arrived? " asked the Pope.

" Not yet, your Holiness," said the Capuchin.

" Father, have you any faith in presentiments? "

" Sometimes, your Holiness. When they continue and are persistent . . ."

" I have had a presentiment which has been with me all my life—all my life as Pope, at all events. The blessed God who abases and lifts up has thought fit to raise my lowliness to the most sublime dignity that exists on earth, but I have always lived in the fear that some day I should be torn down from it, and the Church would suffer."

" God forbid, your Holiness! "

" That was why I refused every place and every honour. You know how I refused them, Father! "

" Yes, but God knew better, your Holiness, and He preserved you to be a blessing and a comfort to His people."

" His holy will be done! But the shadow which has been over me will not be lifted. Cause prayers to be said for me. Pray for me yourself, Father."

" Your Holiness is in low spirits. And to-day of all days! Ah, how happy is the Church which has seen the hand of God place in the chair of St. Peter a soul capable of comprehending the necessities of His children and a heart desirous of satisfying them! "

" I hardly know what is to come of this interview, Father, but I must leave myself in the hands of the Holy Spirit."

" There is no help for it now, your Holiness."

" Perhaps I should not have gone so far but for this wave of anarchy which is sweeping over the world. . . . You believe the man Rossi is secretly an anarchist? "

" I am afraid he is, your Holiness, and one of the worst enemies of the Church and the Holy Father."

" They say he was an orphan from his infancy, and never knew father, or mother, or home."

" Pitiful, very pitiful! "

"I have heard that his public life is not without a certain perverted nobility, and that his private life is pure and good."

"His relation to the lady would seem to say so, your Holiness."

"But the Holy Father may be sorry for a wayward son, and yet be forced to condemn him for all that. He must cut himself off from all such men, lest his adversaries should say that, while preaching peace and the moral law, he is secretly encouraging the devilish agents of atheism, anarchy, and rebellion."

"Perhaps so, your Holiness."

"Father, do you think the care of temporal things is ever a danger and temptation?"

"Sometimes I think it is, your Holiness, and that the Holy Father would be better without lands or fleshly armies."

"How late they are!" said the Pope; but at the same moment the door opened, and a Noble Guard knelt on the threshold.

"Well?"

"The personages you expect have come, your Holiness."

"Bring them in," said the Pope.

XIII

THE young King, who wore the uniform of a cavalry officer, with sword and long blue cloak, knelt to the Pope and kissed his ring, while the Prime Minister, who was in ordinary civilian costume, bowed deeply, but remained standing.

"Pray sit," said the Pope, seating himself in the gilded arm-chair, with the Capuchin on his left.

The King sat on one of the wooden stools in front of the Pope, but the Baron continued to stand by his side. Between the Pope and the King was a wooden table on which two large candles were burning. The young King was pale, and the expression of his twitching face was one of pain.

"It was good of your Holiness to see us," he said, "and perhaps the gravity of our errand may excuse the informality of our visit."

The Pope, who was leaning forward on the arms of his chair, only bent his head.

"His Excellency," said the King, indicating the Baron,

"tells me he has gained proof of an organised conspiracy against my life, and he says that your Holiness holds the secret of the conspirators."

The Pope, without responding, looked steadily into the face of the young King, who became nervous and embarrassed.

"Not that I'm afraid," he said, "personally afraid. But naturally I must think of others—my family—my people— even of Italy—and if your Holiness . . . if your . . . your Holiness . . ."

The Baron, who had been standing with one arm across his breast, and the other supporting his chin, intervened at this moment.

"Your Majesty," he said, "with your Majesty's permission, and that of his Holiness," he bowed to both sovereigns, "it may be convenient if I state shortly the object of our visit."

The young King drew a breath of relief, and the Pope, who was still silent, bent his head again.

"Some days ago your Holiness was good enough to warn his Majesty's Government that from private sources of information you had reason to fear that an assault against the public peace was to be attempted."

The Pope once more assented.

"Since then the Government has received corroboration of the gracious message of your Holiness, coupled with very definite predictions of the nature of the revolt intended. In short, we have been told by our correspondents abroad that a conspiracy of European proportions, involving the subversive elements of England, France, and Germany, is to be directed against Rome as a centre of revolution, and that an attempt is to be made to assail constituted society by striking at our King."

"Well, sir?"

"Your Holiness may have heard that it is the intention of the Government and the nation to honour the anniversary of his Majesty's accession by a festival. The anniversary falls on Monday next, and we have reason to fear that Monday is the day intended for the outbreak of this vile conspiracy."

"Well?"

"Your Holiness may have differences with his Majesty, but you cannot desire that the cry of suffering should mingle with the strains of the royal march."

"If your Government knows all this, it has its remedy—let it alter the King's plans."

"The advice with which your Holiness honours us is scarcely practicable. For the Government to alter the King's plans would be to alarm the populace, demoralise the services, and to add to the unhappy excitement which it is the object of the festival allay."

"But why do you come to me?"

"Because, your Holiness, our information, although conclusive, is too indefinite for effective action, and we believe your Holiness can supply the means by which we may preserve public order, and"—with an apologetic gesture—"save the life of the King."

The Pope was moving uneasily in his chair. "I will ask you to be good enough to speak more plainly," he said.

The Baron's heavy moustache rose at one corner to a fleeting smile. "Your Holiness," he said, "is already aware that accident disclosed to us the source of your information. It was a lady. This knowledge enabled us to judge who was the subject of her communication. It was the lady's lover. Official channels give us proof that he is engaged abroad in plots against public order, and thus . . ."

"If you know all this, sir, what do you want with me?"

"Your Holiness may not be aware that the person in question is a Deputy, and that a Deputy cannot be arrested without the fulfilment of various conditions prescribed by law. One of those conditions is that some one should be in a position to denounce him."

The Pope half rose from his chair. "You ask me to denounce him?"

The Baron bowed very low. "The Government does not presume so far," he said. "It only hopes that your Holiness will require your informant to do so."

"Then you want me to outrage a confidence?"

"It was not a confession, your Holiness, and even if it had been, as your Holiness knows better than we do, it would not be without precedent to reveal the facts which are necessary to be known in order to prevent crime."

The Capuchin's sandals were scraping on the floor, but the Pope raised his left hand, and the friar fell back.

"You are aware," said the Pope, "that the lady you speak of as my informant is married to the Deputy?"

"We are aware that she thinks she is."

"Thinks?" said the indignant voice of the Capuchin, but the Pope's left hand was raised again.

"In short, sir, you ask me to require the wife to sacrifice her husband."

"If your Holiness calls it so,—to perform an act that will preserve the public peace . . ."

"I *do* call it so."

The Baron bowed, the young King was restless, and there was a moment's silence. Then the Pope said:

"Putting aside the extreme unlikelihood that the lady knows more than she has said, and we have already communicated, what possible inducement do you expect us to offer her that she should sacrifice her husband?"

"Her husband's life," said the Baron.

"His life?"

"Your Holiness may not know that the Governments of Europe, having ascertained the existence of a widespread plot against civil society, have joined in measures of repression. One of these is the extension to all countries of what is called the Belgian clause in treaties, whereby persons guilty of regicide or of plots directed against the lives of sovereigns are made liable to extradition."

"Well?"

"The Deputy Rossi is now in Berlin. If he were denounced with the conditions required by law as conspiring against the life of the King, we might have him arrested tonight and brought back as a common murderer."

"Well?"

"Your Holiness may not have heard that since the late unhappy riots the Parliament, in spite of the protests of his Majesty, has re-established capital punishment for all forms of high treason."

"Therefore," said the Pope, "if the wife were to denounce her husband for participation in this conspiracy he would be sentenced to death."

"For this conspiracy—yes," said the Baron. "But the present is not the only conspiracy the man Rossi has engaged in. Eighteen years ago he was condemned in contumacy for conspiracy against the life of the late King. He has not yet suffered for his crime, because of the difficulty of bringing it home. In that case, as in this, there is only one person known to the authorities who can fulfil the conditions required by law. That person is the informant of your Holiness."

THE POPE

"Well?"

"If your Holiness can prevail upon the lady to identify her lover as the man condemned for the former conspiracy, you will be helping her to save her husband's life from the penalty due for the present one."

"How so?"

"His Majesty is willing to promise your Holiness that, whatever the result of a new trial in assize to follow the old one in contumacy, he will grant a complete pardon."

"And then?"

"Then the Deputy Rossi will be banished, the threatened conspiracy will be crushed, the public peace will be preserved, and the King's life will be saved."

The Pope leaned forward on the arms of his chair, but he did not speak, and there was silence for some moments.

"Thus your Holiness must see," said the Baron suavely, "that, in asking you to obtain the denunciation of the man Rossi, the Government is only looking to your Holiness to fulfil the mission of mercy to which your venerated position has destined you."

"And if I refused to exercise this mission of mercy?"

The Baron bowed gravely. "Your Holiness will not refuse," he said.

"But if I do—what then?"

"Then . . . your Holiness . . . I was about to say something."

"I am listening."

"The man we speak of is the bitterest enemy of the Church. Whatever his hypocrisies, he is at once an atheist and a freemason, sworn to allow no private interests or feelings, no bonds of patriotism or blood, to turn him aside from his purpose, which is to overthrow Society and the Church."

"Well?"

"He is also a bitter personal enemy of the Holy Father, and knows no object so dear as that of tearing him from his place and shaking the throne of St. Peter."

"Well, sir?"

"The police and the army of the Government are the only forces by which the Holy Father can be protected, and without them the bad elements which lurk in every community would break out, the Holy Father would be driven from Rome, and his priests assaulted in the streets."

343

" But what will happen if I refuse to outrage the sanctity of an immortal soul in spite of all this danger ? "

" Your Holiness asks me what will happen if you refuse to obtain the denunciation of a man whom your Holiness knows to be conspiring against public order ? "

" I do."

" What will happen will be . . . your Holiness, I am speaking . . ."

" Go on."

" That, if the crime is committed and the King is killed, I, the Minister of his Majesty, will be in a position to say— and to call upon this friar to witness—that the Pope knew of it beforehand, and under the most noble sentiments about the sanctity of an immortal soul gave a supreme encourage-ment of regicide."

" And then, sir ? "

" The world draws no nice distinctions, your Holiness, and the Vatican is now at war with nearly all the powers and peoples of Europe. In the presence of a monstrous crime against the most innocent and the most highly placed, the world would say that what the Pope did not prevent the Pope desired, what the Pope desired the Pope designed, and that the Vicar of the Prince of Peace attempted to rebuild his temporal power by means of the plots of conspirators and the daggers of assassins."

The sandals of the Capuchin were scraping the floor again, and once more the Pope put up his hand.

" You come to me, sir, when you have exhausted all other means of obtaining your end ? "

" Naturally the Government wishes if possible to spare your Holiness an unusual and painful ordeal."

" The lady has resisted all other influences ? "

" She has resisted all influences which can be brought to bear upon her by the proper authorities."

" I have heard of it, sir. I have heard what your ' authori-ties ' have done to humble a helpless woman. She had been the victim of a heartless man, and by knowledge of that fact your ' authorities ' have tempted and tried her. They tried her with poverty, with humiliation, with jealousy and the shadow of shame. But the blessed God upheld her in the love which had awakened her soul, and she withstood them to the last."

The Baron, for the first time, looked confused.

THE POPE

"I have also heard that in order to achieve the same end one of your gaols has been the scene of a scandal which has outraged every divine and human law."

"Your Holiness must not accept for truth all that is printed in the halfpenny papers."

"Is it true that in the cell where a helpless unfortunate was paying the penalty of his crime your 'authorities' introduced a police agent in disguise to draw him into a denunciation of his accomplice?"

"These are matters of state, your Holiness. I do not assert them and I do not deny."

"In the name of humanity I ask you are such 'authorities' punished, or do they sit in the cabinets of your Ministers of the Interior?"

"No doubt the officials went too far, your Holiness; but shall we, for the sake of a miserable malefactor who told one story to-day and another to-morrow, drag our public service through courts of law? Pity for such persons is morbid sentimentality, your Holiness, unworthy of a strong and enlightened Government."

"Then God destroy all such Governments, sir, and the bad and unchristian system which supports them! Allow that the man *was* a miserable malefactor, it was not he alone that was offended, but in his poor, degraded person the spirit of Justice. What did your 'authorities' do? They tortured the man by his love for his wife, by the memory of his murdered child, by all that was true and noble and divine in him. They crucified the Christ in that helpless man, and you stand here in the presence of the Vicar of Christ to excuse and defend them."

The Pope had risen in his chair and lifted one hand over his head with a majestic gesture. Involuntarily the young King, who had been ashen pale for some moments, dropped to his knees, but the Baron only folded his arms and stiffened his legs.

"Have you ever thought, sir, of the end of the unjust Minister? Think of his dying hour, tortured with the memory of young lives dissolved, mothers dead, widows desolate, and orphans in tears. Think of the day after his death, when he who has passed through the world like the scourge of God lies at its feet, and no one so mean but he may spurn the dishonoured carcass. You are aiming high, your Excellency, but beware, beware!"

345

The Pope sat, and the King rose to his feet.

"Your Majesty," said the Pope, "the day will come when we must both present ourselves before God to render to Him an account of our deeds, and I, being far more advanced in years, will assuredly be the first. But I would not dare to meet the eye of my Judge if I did not this day warn you of the dangers in which you stand. Only God knows by what inscrutable decree of Providence one man is made a Pope or a King, while another man, his equal or superior, is made a beggar or a slave. But God who made Popes and Kings meant them to be the fathers, not the seducers of their subjects. A sovereign may be a man of good intentions, but if he is weak, and allows himself to fall into the hands of despotic Ministers, he is a worse affliction than the cruellest tyrant. Think well, your Majesty! A throne may be a quagmire, and a man may be buried in it, and buried alive."

The young King began to falter some incoherent words, but without listening the Pope rose to end the audience.

"You promise me," said the Pope, "that if—I say if—in order to avoid bloodshed and to prevent a crime, I obtain from this lady the identification of her husband as the person condemned for the former conspiracy, you will spare and pardon him whatever happens?"

"Holy Father, I give you my solemn word for it."

"Then leave me! Let me think! . . . Wait! If she consents, where must she go to?"

"To the Procura by the Ponte Ripetta, and, as time presses, at ten o'clock on Saturday morning," said the Baron.

"Leave me! Leave me!"

The King knelt again and kissed the Pope's hand, but the Baron only bowed as he passed out behind his sovereign.

The opening of the doors let in a wave of sound that was like the roll of a great wind in a cave. Tenebræ had been going on for some time in the Basilica, and the people were singing the Miserere.

"Did you hear him, Father?" said the Pope. "Isn't it almost enough to justify a man like Rossi that he has to meet a despot like that?"

"We'll talk of it to-morrow," said the Capuchin.

The friar touched a bell, and the *palfrenieri* returned with the chair.

THE POPE

XIV

NEXT day, being Good Friday, was passed by the Pope in religious retreat, which was interrupted by indispensable business only. After Mass of the Presanctified he sat in his study with his confessor, while his chaplain in black passed through on tiptoe from the private chapel, and his chamberlains, tired out by the ceremonies of yesterday, dozed on their stools in the outer hall.

The day was bright but the room was darkened, and the hearts of the two old men were heavy. Over the face of the Pope there was a cloud of trouble, and the countenance of the Capuchin was solemn to the point of sternness. The friar sat in the old-fashioned easy-chair with his bare feet showing from under the edge of his brown habit; the Pope lay on the lounge with both hands in the vertical pockets of his white woollen cassock.

" Your Holiness is not well this morning? "

" Not very well, Father Pifferi."

" Your Holiness was disturbed by the interview in the Sacristy. But you should think no more about it. In any case, what the Minister proposed was impossible, therefore you must dismiss it from your mind. To ask a wife to reveal the secrets of her husband would be tyranny worse than the rack. Besides, it would be uncanonical, and your Holiness could never consider it."

" How so? "

" Didn't your Holiness promise that whatever the nature of this poor lady's confidence you would hold it as sacred as the confessional? "

" Well? "

" What is the confessional, your Holiness? It is a tribunal in which the priest is judge and the penitent a prisoner who pleads guilty. Is the priest to call witnesses to prove other crimes? He has no right and no power to do so."

" But where the penitent wittingly or unwittingly is in the position of an accomplice, what then, Father Pifferi? "

" Even then it is expressly forbidden to demand the names of others upon the plea of preventing evil. How can you hold this lady's confidence as sacred and yet ask her to denounce her husband? "

The Pope rose with a face full of pain, walked to the bookcase, and took down a book. "Listen, Father," he said, and he began to read:—

"*If the penitent was obliged under pain of mortal sin to reveal his accomplices to repair a common injury, I have maintained against other theologians that even then the confessor cannot oblige him to do so.*"

"There!" cried the Capuchin. "What did I say? Gaume is wise, and the other theologians, who are they?"

"*Only,*" continued the Pope, turning a page and holding up one finger, "*he can and must oblige him to make known his accomplices to other persons who can arrest the scandal.*"

The Capuchin took a long breath. "Is that what the Holy Father intends to do in this instance?"

"He *can* and *must.*"

The Capuchin dropped his head, and there was a long pause, in which the Pope walked nervously about the room.

"Poor child!" said the Capuchin. "But perhaps her heart has been too much set on human love."

The Pope sighed.

"Yet who are we, whose hearts are closed to earthly affection, to prescribe a limit to human love?"

"Who indeed?" said the Pope.

"Do you recall her resemblance to any one, your Holiness?"

The Pope stopped in his walk and looked towards the curtained window.

"The same soft voice and radiant smile, the same attitude of idolatry towards the husband she is devoted to, the same . . ."

"The Sisters of the Sacred Heart will take her when all is over," said the Pope.

"And the man, too, whatever his errors, has a certain grandeur of soul, that lifts him far above these chief gaolers and detectives who call themselves statesmen and diplomatists, these scavengers of civilisation."

"He must go back to America and begin life again," said the Pope.

Two hours later Father Pifferi went off to fetch Roma, and the Pope sat down to his mid-day meal. The room was very quiet, and in the absence of the church bells the city seemed to sit in silence. Cortis stood behind the Pope's chair, and the cat sat on a stool at the opposite side of the table.

The chamberlains, lay and ecclesiastical, waited in the

antecamera, and the Swiss and Noble Guards, the Palatine Guards, and the *palfrenieri* dotted the decorated halls that led to the royal stairs.

But the saintly old man, who had a palace yet no home, servants yet no family, an army yet no empire, who was the father of all men, yet knew no longer the ordinary joys and sorrows of human life, sat alone in his little plain apartment and ate his simple dish of spinach and beans.

XV

Good Friday's Ministerial paper announced in its official column that late the night before the King, attended by the Minister of the Interior, had paid a surprise visit to the Mint, which was in the Via Fondamenta, a lane approached by way of the silent passage which leads to the lodging of the Canons of St. Peter's. Roma was puzzling over the inexplicable announcement, when old John, one of Rossi's pensioners, knocked at her door. His face and his lips were white, and when Roma offered him money he put it aside impatiently.

"You mustn't think a gold hammer can break the gate of heaven, Eccellenza," the old man said.

Then he told his story. The King had seen the Pope in secret the night before, and there was something going on about the Honourable Rossi. John knew it because his grandson had left Rome that morning for Chiasso, and another member of the secret police had started for Modane. If Donna Roma knew where the Honourable was to be found, she had better tell him not to return to Italy.

"Better be a wood-bird than a cage-bird, you know," the old man whispered.

Roma thanked him for his news, and then warned him of the risk he ran, being dependent on his grandson and his grandson's wife.

"That's nothing," he said, "nothing at all *now*."

Last night he had dreamed a dream. He thought he was a strong man again, with his children about him, and beholden to no one. How happy he had been! But when he awoke, and found it was not true, and that he was old and feeble, he felt that he could bear it no longer.

"I'm in the way and taking the food of the children, so

it can't last long, Eccellenza," he said in a tremulous voice, smiling with his toothless mouth, and nodding slightly as he went away.

In the uneasy depths of Roma's soul only one thing was now certain. Her husband was in danger, and he must not attempt to cross the frontier. Yet how was he to be prevented? The difficulty was enormous. If only Rossi had replied to her letter by telegram, as she had asked him to do, she might have found some means of communication. At length an idea occurred to her, and she sat down to write a letter.

" Dearest," she wrote, while her eyes shone with a kind of delirium and tears trickled down her cheeks, " I am very ill, and as you cannot come to me I must go to you. Don't think me too weak and womanish, after all my solemn promises to be so strong and brave. But I can only live by love, dearest, and your absence is more than I can bear. You will think I ought to be content with your letters, and certainly they have been very sweet and dear to me; but they are so few, and they come at such long intervals, and now they seem to have stopped altogether. Perhaps at the bottom of my selfish heart, too, I think your letters might be a wee bit more lover-like, but then men don't write real love letters, and nearly every woman would confess, if she told the truth, and she is a little disappointed in that regard.

" I know my husband has other things to think about, great things, high and noble aims and objects, but I am only a woman in spite of my loud pretences, and I must be loved, or I shall die. Not that I am afraid of dying, because I know that if I die I shall be with you in a moment, and this cruel separation will be at an end. But I want to live, and I'm certain I shall begin to feel better after I have passed a few moments at your side. So I shall pack up immediately and start away on the wings of the morning.

" Don't be alarmed if you find me looking pale and thin and old and ugly. How could I be anything else when the particular world I live in has been sunless all these weeks? I know your work is very pressing, especially now when so many things are happening; but you will put it aside for a little while, won't you, and take me up into the Alps somewhere, and nurse me back to health and happiness? Fancy! We shall be boy and girl again, as in the days when you used to catch butterflies for me, and then look sad when, like a naughty child, I scrunched them!

"*Au revoir*, dearest. I shall fall into your hands nearly as soon as this letter. I tremble to think you may be angry with me for following you and interrupting your work. If you show it in your face I shall certainly expire. But you will be good to your poor pilgrim of love and comfort and strengthen her. All the time you have been away she has never forgotten you for a moment—no, not one waking moment. An ordinary woman who loved an ordinary man would not tell him this, but you are not ordinary, and if I am I don't care a pin to pretend.

"Expect me, then, by the fastest train leaving Rome tomorrow morning, and don't budge from Paris until I arrive.

"ROMA."

The strain of this letter, with its conscious subterfuge and its unconscious truth, put Roma into a state of fever; and when she had finished it and sent it to the post, her head was light, and she was aware for the first time that she was really ill.

The deaf old woman, who helped her to pack, talked without ceasing of Rossi and Bruno and Elena and little Joseph, and finally of the King and his intended jubilee.

"I don't take no notice of Governments, Signora. It's the same as it used to be in the old days. One Pope died, and his soul went into the next. First an ugly Pope, then a handsome one, but the soul was the same in all. Wet soup or dry—that's all I trouble about now; and I don't care who gets the taxes so long as I can pay. . . . What do you say, Tommaso?"

The Garibaldian had come upstairs smiling and winking, and holding out a letter. "From Trinità de' Monti," he whispered. Flushing crimson and trembling visibly, Roma took the letter out of the old man's hands with as much apprehension as if he had tried to deal her a blow, and went off to her room.

"What do I say, Francesca? I say it's a good thing to be a Christian in these days, and that's why I always carry a sharp knife and a rosary."

THE ETERNAL CITY

XVI

The letter bore the Berlin postmark.

"My dear Wife,—I left Paris rather unexpectedly three days ago and arrived here on Tuesday. The reason of this sudden flight was the announcement in the Paris papers of the festivities intended in Rome in honour of the King's accession. Such a shameless outrage on the people's sufferings in the hour of their greatest need seemed to call for immediate and effectual protest, and it was thought wise to push on the work of organisation with every possible despatch . . ."

"There is a train north at 9.30," thought Roma. "I must leave to-night, not in the morning."

"Oh, Roma, Roma, my dear Roma, I understand your father now, and can sympathise with him at last. He held that even regicide might become a necessary weapon in the warfare of humanity, and though I knew that some of the greatest spirits had recourse to it, I always thought this belief the defect of your father's quality as a prophet and the limit of his vision. But now I see that the only difference between us was that his heart was bigger than mine, and that in those cruel crises where the people are helpless and can do nothing by constitutional means, revolution, not evolution, may *seem* to be their only hope . . ."

Roma felt hysterical. There could no longer be any doubt of Rossi's intention.

"I don't tell you anything definite about our plans, dearest, partly because of the danger of this letter going astray, and partly because I don't think it right to saddle my wife with the responsibility of knowing a programme that is weighted with issues of such immense importance to so many. I know there is not a drop of blood in her veins that isn't ready to flow for me, but that is no reason for exposing her to the danger of even the prick of her little finger.

"Briefly our cry is 'Unite! Unite! Unite!' As soon as our scheme is complete, and associates all over Europe receive the word to commence concerted movement, the tyrants at the heads of the States will find the old edifices riddled and honeycombed, and ready to fall."

Roma imagined she could see everything as it was intended to be—the signal, the rising, the regicide. "There is a train at 2.30; I must catch that one," she thought.

"Dearest, don't attempt to reply to this letter, for I may leave Berlin at any moment, but whether for Geneva or Zurich I don't yet know. I can give you no address for letter or telegram, and perhaps it is best that at the critical moment I should cut myself off from all connection with Rome. Before many days I shall be with you; my absence will be over, and, God willing, I shall never leave your side again . . ."

Roma was growing dizzy. Rossi was rushing on his death, and there was no help for him. It was like the awful hand of the Almighty driving him blindly on.

"Adieu, my darling. Keep well. A friend writes that letters from Rome are following me from London. They must be yours, but before they overtake me I shall be holding you in my arms. How I long for it! I am more than ever full of love for you, and if I have filled my letter with business I have other things to say to you the very moment that we meet. Don't expect me until you see me in your room. Be brave! Now is the moment for all your courage. Remember you promised to be my soldier as well as my wife—'ready and waiting when her captain calls.'   D."

Roma was standing with Rossi's letter in her hand—her face and lips white, and her head full of a roaring noise—when a knock came to the bedroom door. Before answering she thrust the letter into the stove and set a match to it.

"Donna Roma! Are you there, Signora?"

"Wait . . . come in."

The old woman's head, in its coloured handkerchief, appeared through the half-opened door.

"A Frate in the sitting-room to see you, Signora."

It was Father Pifferi. The old man's gentle face looked troubled. Roma gave him a rapid, penetrating, and fearful glance.

"The Holy Father wishes to see you again," he said.

Roma thought for a moment; then she said, "Very well, let us go," and she went back to her room to make ready. The last of the letter was burning in the stove.

XVII

ROMA returned to the Vatican with the Capuchin. There were the same gorgeous staircases and halls, the same soldiers, chamberlains, Bussolanti and Monsignori, the same atmosphere of the palace of an emperor. But in the little plain apartment which they entered, not as before by way of the throne room, but by a secret corridor with cocoanut matting and narrow frosted windows, the Pope stood waiting, like a simple priest, in a white woollen cassock.

He smiled as Roma approached, a sad smile, and his weary eyes, when she looked timidly into his face, were full of the measureless pity that is in the eyes of the surgeon who is about to vivisect a dumb creature because it is necessary for the welfare of the human race.

She knelt and kissed his ring. He raised her and put her to sit on the lounge, sitting in the arm-chair himself, and continuing to hold her hand. The Capuchin stood by the window, holding the curtain aside as if looking out on the piazza.

"You believe the Holy Father would not send for you to injure you?" he said.

"I am sure he would not, your Holiness," she answered.

"And though I disapprove of your husband's doings, you know I would not willingly do him any harm?"

"The Holy Father would not do harm to any one; and my husband is so good, and his aims are so noble, that nobody who really knew him could ever try to injure him."

He looked into her face; it shone with a frightened joy, and pity grew upon him.

"Your devotion to your husband is very sweet and beautiful, my daughter, and it grieves the Holy Father's heart to trouble it. But it seems to be his duty to do so, and he must do his duty."

Again she looked up timidly, and again the sense came to him of dumb eyes full of entreaty.

"My daughter, your husband's motives may not be bad. They may even be good and noble. It is often so with men of his sympathies. They see the disparity of wealth and poverty, and their hearts are torn with anger and with pity. But, my child, they do not know that true and lasting reforms, such as affect the whole human family, can only be accomplished by God and by the authority of His Holy Church and Pontificate, and that it must be the bell of St. Peter's which announces them to the world."

As the Pope was speaking the colour ran up Roma's face like a flag of distress. She looked helplessly round at the Capuchin. The dumb eyes seemed to ask when the blow would fall.

" As a consequence, what is he doing, my daughter? Ignoring the Church, which like a true mother is ever anxious to bear the burden of human weakness and suffering; he is setting up a new gospel, such as would reduce mankind to a worse barbarism than that from which Christ freed us. Is this conduct worthy of your devotion, my child? "

Roma fixed her timid eyes on the Pope's face and answered:

" I have nothing to do with my husband's opinions, your Holiness. I have only to be true to the friendship he gives me and the love I bear him."

" My child," said the Pope, " ask yourself what your husband is doing at this moment. Not content with sowing the seeds of discord in Parliament and by the press, he is wandering through Europe, gathering up the adventurers who work in darkness in every country, and hatching a conspiracy which would lead to a state of anarchy throughout the world."

Roma withdrew her hand from the hand of the Pope and made an exclamation of dissent.

" Ah, I know what you would say, my daughter. He did not set out to produce anarchy. Such men never do. They begin with evolution and end with revolution. They begin with peace and end with violence. And the only sequel to your husband's aims must be the destruction of civil society, of Government, and of the Church."

Roma's fingers were clasped convulsively in her lap. She lifted her timid but passionate face and said:

" I know nothing about that, your Holiness. I only know that whatever he is doing his heart laid it upon him as a duty, and his heart is pure and noble."

" My daughter, your husband may be the greatest of patriots in spirit and intention, but nevertheless he is one of the criminal and visionary teachers of this unhappy time who are deluding the ignorant crowd with promises that can never be realised. Anarchy, chaos, the uprooting of religion and morality, of justice, human dignity, and the purity of domestic life—these are the only possible fruits of the seed he is sowing."

The timid eyes began to flash. "I did not come here to hear this, your Holiness." The Pope put his hand tenderly on her hands.

"Remember, my child, what you said yourself on your former visit."

Roma dropped her head.

"The authorities know all about it."

"Holy Father!"

"It was necessary."

"Then . . . then somebody must have told them."

"I told them. The Holy Father revealed no more than was necessary to relieve his conscience and to prevent crime. It was your own tongue that told the rest, my daughter."

He recalled what had passed in the cabinet of the Prime Minister, and Roma felt as if something choked her. "No matter!" she said, with the same frightened but passionate face. "David Rossi is prepared for anything, and he will be prepared for this."

"The authorities already knew more than I could tell them," said the Pope. "They knew where your husband was and what he was doing. They know where he is now, and they are preparing to arrest him."

Roma's nerves grew more and more excited, the timid look gave place to a look of defiance.

"They tell me that he is in Berlin at this moment. Is it true?"

Roma did not reply.

"They say their advices from official sources leave no doubt that he is engaged in conspiracy."

Still Roma did not reply.

"They say confidently that the conspiracy points to rebellion, and is intended to include regicide. Is it so?"

Roma bit her lip and remained silent.

"Can't you trust me, my child? Don't you know the Holy Father? Only give me some hope that these statements are untrue, and the Holy Father is ready to withstand all evil influences against you, and face the world in your defence."

Roma felt as if something would snap within her brain. "I cannot say . . . I do not know," she faltered.

"But have you any uncertainty, my daughter? If you have the least reason to believe that these statements are slanders of malicious imaginations, tell me so, and I will give your husband the benefit of the doubt."

Roma rose to her feet, but she held on to the edge of the table that stood by her side, rigid, quivering, frail and silent. The Pope looked up at her with weary eyes, and continued in a caressing tone:

"If unhappily you have no doubt that your husband is engaged in dangerous enterprises, can you not dissuade him from them?"

"No," said Roma, struggling with her tears, "that is impossible. Whether he is right or wrong, it is not for me to sit in judgment upon him. Besides, long ago, before we were married, I promised that I would never stand between him and his work, and I never can—never."

"But if he loves you, my child, would he not wish for your sake to avoid the danger?"

"I can't ask him. I told him to go on without thinking of me, and I would take care of myself whatever happened."

Her eyes were now shining with her tears. The Pope patted the hand on the table.

"Can you not at least go to him and warn him, and thus leave him to judge for himself, my daughter?"

"Yes . . . no, that is impossible also."

"Why so, my child?"

"Because I don't know where he is, and I shouldn't know where to find him. In his last letter he said it was better I should not know."

"Then he has cut himself off from you entirely?"

"Entirely. I am to see him next in Rome."

"And meantime, that he may not run the risk of being traced by his enemies, he has stopped all channels of communication with his friends?"

"Yes."

The Pope's face whitened visibly, and an inward voice said to him, "This is God's hand. Death is waiting for the man in Rome, and he is walking blindly on to it."

The weary eyes looked with compassion on Roma's quivering face. "There's no help for it," thought the Pope.

"Suppose, my child . . . suppose it were within your power to hinder evil consequences, would you do it?"

"I am a woman, Holy Father. What can a woman do to hinder anything?"

"In the history of nations it has sometimes happened that a woman has been able to save life and protect society by raising a little hand like this."

The Pope lifted Roma's quivering fingers from the table.

"If there is anything I can do, your Holiness, without breaking my promise or betraying my husband . . ."

"It is a terrible ordeal, my child. For a wife, God knows how terrible."

"No matter! If it will save my husband . . . Tell me, your Holiness."

He told her the proposal of the Prime Minister and the promise of the King. His voice vibrated. He was like a man who was wounding himself at every word. She looked at him until he had finished, without ability to speak.

"You ask me to *denounce* my husband?"

"It is the only way to save him, my daughter."

She looked round the room with helpless eyes, full of a dumb appeal for mercy or the chance of escape.

"Holy Father," she said in a choking voice, "that is what his enemies have been asking me to do all this time, and because I have refused they have persecuted me with poverty and shame. And now that I come to you for refuge and shelter, thinking your fatherly arms will protect me, you . . . even you . . ."

She broke off as by a sudden thought, and said: "But it is impossible. He is my husband, therefore I cannot witness against him."

"My heart bleeds for you, my child, and I am ashamed to gainsay you. But an oath is not necessary to a denunciation, and if it were so the law of this unchristian country would not recognise you as Rossi's wife."

"But he will know who has denounced him. I am the only one in the world to whom he has told his secrets, and he will hate me and part from me."

"You will have saved his life, my daughter."

"What is it to me to have saved his life if he is lost to me for ever?"

"Is it you that say that, my child—you that have sacrificed so much already? Doesn't the highest love remember first the welfare of the loved one and think of itself the last?"

"Yes, yes; I didn't know what I was saying. But he will curse me for destroying his cause."

"His cause will be destroyed in any case. It is doomed already. And when his visionary schemes are in the dust, and all is lost and vain, and your tears are powerless to bring back the past . . ."

"But he will be banished, and I shall never see him again."

"It will be the less of two evils, my child," said the Pope. And in the solemn, vibrating voice that rang in Roma's ears like the voice of Rossi, he added, "'Whosoever sheds man's blood by man shall his blood be shed.'"

Again Roma held on to the table, feeling at every moment as if she might fall with a crash.

"That's what would come to your husband if he were arrested and condemned for a conspiracy to kill the King. And even if the humane spirit of the age snatched him from death—what then? A cell in a prison on a volcanic rock in the sea, a stone sepulchre for the living dead, buried like a toad in a hole left by the running lava of life, guarded, watched, tortured in body and soul—a figure of tremendous tragedy, the hapless man once worshipped by the people spreading impotent hands to the outer world, until madness comes to his relief and suicide helps him to escape into eternity and leave only his wasted body on the earth."

Roma could bear the nervous tension no longer. "I'll do it," she said.

"My brave child!" said the Capuchin, turning from the window, with a face broken up by emotion.

"It is one thing to repeat a secret if it is to harm any one, and quite another thing if it is to do good, isn't it?" said Roma.

"Indeed it is," said the Capuchin.

"He will never forgive me—I know that quite well. He will never imagine I would have died rather than do it. But I shall know I have done it for the best."

"Indeed you will."

Roma's eyes were shining with fresh tears, and she was struggling to keep back her sobs. "When we parted on the night he went away he said perhaps we were parting for ever. I promised to be faithful to death itself, but I was thinking of my own death, not his, and I didn't imagine that to save his life I must betray his . . ."

But at that moment she broke down utterly, and the Pope, who had returned to his seat, rose again to comfort her.

"Calm yourself, my daughter," he said. "What you are going to .do is an act of heroic self-sacrifice. Be brave and Heaven will reward you."

She grew calmer after a while, and then Father Pifferi made arrangements for the visit to the Procura. He would call for her at ten in the morning.

"Wait!" said Roma. A new light had come into her face—the light of a new idea.

"What is it, my daughter?" said the Pope.

"Holy Father, there is something I had forgotten. But I must tell you before it is too late. It may alter your view of everything. When you hear it you may say, 'You must not speak a word. You shall not speak. It is impossible.'"

"Tell me, my child."

Roma hesitated and looked from the Capuchin to the Pope. "How can I tell you," she said. "It is so difficult. I hadn't meant to tell any one."

"Go on, my daughter."

"My husband's name . . ."

"Well?"

"Rossi is not really his name, your Holiness. It is the name he took on returning to Italy, because the one he had borne abroad had been involved in trouble."

"Just so," said the Pope.

"Holy Father, David Rossi was a friendless orphan."

"I have heard so," said the Pope.

"He never knew his father—not even by name. His mother was a poor unhappy woman who had been cruelly deceived by everybody. She drowned herself in the Tiber."

"Poor soul," said the Pope.

"He was nursed in the Foundling, your Holiness, and brought up in a straw hut in the Campagna, and then sold as a boy into England."

The Pope moved uneasily in his seat.

"My father found him on the streets of London on a winter's night, your Holiness, carrying a squirrel and an accordion. He wore a ragged suit of velveteens which used to be laughed at by the London boys, and that was all that sheltered his little body from the cold. 'Some poor man's child,' my father thought. But who can say if it was so, your Holiness?"

The Pope was silent. A sudden change had come over his face. Roma's eyes were held down, her voice was agitated, she was scarcely able to speak.

"My father was angry with the boy's father, I remember, and if at that time he had known where to find him I think he would have denounced him to the public or even the police."

The Pope's head sank on his breast; the Capuchin looked steadfastly at Roma.

"But who knows if he was really to blame, your Holiness? He may have been a good man after all—one of those who have to suffer all their lives for the sins of others. Perhaps . . . perhaps that very night he was walking the streets of London, looking in vain among its waifs and outcasts for the little lost boy who owned his own blood and bore his name."

The Pope's face was white and quivering. His elbows rested on the arms of his chair and his wrinkled hands were tightly clasped.

Roma stopped. There was a prolonged silence. The atmosphere of the room seemed to be whirling round with frightful rapidity to one terrific focus.

"Holy Father," said Roma at length, in a low tone, "if David Rossi were *your own son*, would you still ask me to denounce him?"

The Pope lifted a face full of suffering and said in his deep, vibrating voice, "Yes, yes! More than ever for that—a thousand times more than ever."

"Then *I will do it*," said Roma.

The Pope rose up in great emotion, laid both hands on her shoulder, and said, "Go in peace, my daughter, and may God grant you at least a little repose."

XVIII

AFTER recitation of the Rosary, the Pope, who had kept his religious retreat throughout the day, announced, to the astonishment of his chamberlains, his desire to walk in the garden at night. With Father Pifferi carrying a long Etruscan lamp he walked down the dark corridors with their surprised *palfrenieri*, and across the open courtyards with their startled sentinels, to where the arches of the Vatican opened upon the soft spring sky.

The night was warm and quiet, and the moon, which had just risen and was near the full, shone with steady brilliance.

The venerable old men walked without speaking, and only the beating of their sticks on the gravel seemed to break the empty air. At length the Pope stopped and said:

"How strange it all was, Father Pifferi!"

"Very strange, your Holiness," said the Capuchin.

"Rossi is not his name, it seems."

"'Not *really* his name' was what she said."

"His mother was deceived by every one, and she drowned herself in the Tiber."

"That was so, your Holiness."

"He was nursed in the Foundling, brought up in the Campagna, and then sold as a boy into England."

"It is really extraordinary," said Father Pifferi.

"Most extraordinary," repeated the Pope.

They looked steadily at each other for a moment, and then walked on in silence. Little sparks of blue light pulsed and throbbed and floated before their faces, and the moon itself, like a greater firefly, came and went in the interstices of the thin-leaved trees. The Pope, who shuffled in his walking, stopped again.

"Your Holiness?"

"Who can he be, I wonder?"

The Capuchin drew a deep breath. "We shall know everything to-morrow morning."

"Yes," said the Pope, "we shall know everything to-morrow morning."

Some dark phantom of the past was hovering about them, and they were afraid to challenge it.

At that moment the silence of the listening air was broken by a long clear call, which rang out through the night without any warning, and then stopped as suddenly.

"The nightingale," said the Pope.

A mighty flood of melody floated down from some unseen place, in varying strains of divine music broken by many pauses, and running through every phase of jubilation, sorrow, and pain. It ended in a low wail of unutterable sadness, a pleading, yearning cry of anguish, which seemed to call on God Himself to hear. When it was over, and all was hushed around, the world seemed to have become void.

The Pope's feet shuffled on the gravel. "I shall never forget it," he said.

"It was wonderful," said the Capuchin.

"I was thinking of that poor lady," said the Pope. "Her pleading voice will ring in my ears as long as I live."

"Poor child!" said the Capuchin.

"After all, we could not have acted otherwise. Don't you think so, Father Pifferi? Considering everything, we could not possibly have acted otherwise."

"Perhaps we could not, your Holiness."

They turned the bend of an avenue, where the path under their feet rustled with the thick blossom shed from the over-hanging Judas trees.

"Surely this is where the little mother bird used to be," said the Pope.

"So it is," said the friar.

"Strange, she has not sprung out as usual. Ah, Meesh is not here, and perhaps that's the reason." And feeling for the old sarcophagus, the Pope put his hand gently down into it. A moment afterwards he said in another tone: "Father, the young birds are gone."

"Flown, no doubt," said the friar.

"No. See," said the Pope, and he brought up a little nest filled with a ruin of fluff and feathers.

"Meesh has been here indeed," said the friar.

The venerable old men walked on in silence until they re-entered the vaulted courtyards of the Vatican. Then the Pope turned to the Capuchin and said in a breaking voice, "You'll go with the poor lady to the Procura in the morning, Father Pifferi. If the magistrates ask questions which they should not ask, you will protect her, and even forbid her to reply, and if she breaks down at the last moment you will support and comfort her. After that . . . we must leave all to the Holy Spirit. God's hand is in this thing . . . it is in everything. He will bring out all things well—well for us, well for the Church, well for the poor lady, and even for her husband, whoever he may be."

"Whoever he may be," repeated the Capuchin.

XIX

EARLY in the morning of Holy Saturday, Roma was summoned as a witness before the Penal Tribunal of Rome. The citation, which was signed by a magistrate, required that she should present herself at the Procura at ten o'clock the same day, "to depose about facts on which she would then be interrogated," and she was warned that if she did not appear, "she would incur the punishment sanctioned by Article 176 of the Code of Penal Procedure."

Roma found Father Pifferi waiting for her at the door of the Procura. The old Capuchin looked anxious. He glanced at her pale face and quivering lips and inquired if she had slept. She answered that she was well, and they turned to go upstairs.

On the landing of the first floor Commendatore Angelelli, who was wearing a flower in his buttonhole, approached them with smiles and quick bows to lead them to the office of the magistrate.

"Only a form," said the Questore. "It will be nothing— nothing at all."

Commendatore Angelelli led the way into a silent room furnished in red, with carpet, couch, armchairs, table, a stove, and two large portraits of the King and Queen.

"Sit down, please. Make yourselves comfortable," said the Chief of Police, and he passed into an adjoining room.

A moment afterwards he returned with two other men. One of them was an elderly gentleman, who wore with his frockcoat a close-fitting velvet cap decorated with two bands of gold lace. This was the Procurator General, and the other, a younger man, carrying a portfolio, was his private secretary. A marshal of Carabineers came to the door for a moment.

"Don't be afraid, my child. No harm shall come to you," whispered Father Pifferi. But the good Capuchin himself was trembling visibly.

The Procurator General was gentle and polite, but he dismissed the Chief of Police, and would have dismissed the Capuchin also, but for vehement protests.

"Very well, I see no objection; sit down again," he said.

It was a strange three-cornered interview. Father Pifferi, quaking with fear, thought he was there to protect Roma. The Procurator General, smiling and serene, thought she had come to complete a secret scheme of personal revenge. And Roma herself, sitting erect in her chair, in her black Eton coat and straw hat, and with her wonderful eyes turning slowly from face to face, thought only of Rossi, and was silent and calm.

THE POPE

The secretary opened his portfolio on the table and prepared to write. The Procurator General sat in front of Roma and leaned slightly forward.

"You are Donna Roma Volonna, daughter of the late Prince Prospero Volonna?"

"I am."

"You were born in England and lived there as a child?"

"Yes."

"Although you were young when you lost your father, you have a perfect recollection both of him and of his associates?"

"Of some of his associates."

"One of them was a young man who lived in his house as a kind of adopted son?"

"Yes."

"You are aware that your father was unhappily involved in political troubles?"

"I am."

"You know that he was arrested on a serious charge?"

"I do."

"You also know that, when condemned to death by a military tribunal for conspiring against the person of the late sovereign, his sentence was commuted by the King, but that one of his associates, condemned at the same time, and for the same crime, escaped all punishment because he was not then at the disposition of the law?"

"Yes."

"That was the young man who lived with him as his adopted son?"

"It was."

There was a moment's pause during which nothing could be heard but the quick breathing of the Capuchin and the scratching of the secretary's pen.

"During the past few months you have made the acquaintance in Rome of the Deputy David Rossi?"

"I have."

The Capuchin moved in his seat. "Acquaintance! The lady is married to the Deputy."

The Procurator General's eyes rose perceptibly. "Married!"

"That is to say religiously married, which is all the Church thinks necessary."

"Ah, I see," said the Procurator General, suppressing a

smile. "Still I must ask the lady to make her statement in her natal name."

"Go on, sir," said the Capuchin.

"Your intimacy with the Honourable Rossi has no doubt led him to speak freely on many subjects?"

"It has."

"He has perhaps told you that Rossi was not his father's name."

"Yes."

"That it was his mother's name, and though strictly his legal name also, he has borne it only since his return to Rome?"

"That is so."

It was the Capuchin's turn to look surprised. His sandalled feet shuffled on the carpet, and he prepared to take snuff.

"The Honourable Rossi has been some weeks abroad, and during his absence you have no doubt received letters from him?"

"I have."

"Can you tell me if in any of these letters he has said anything of a certain revolutionary propaganda?"

The Capuchin, with his finger and thumb half raised, stopped and said, "I forbid the question, sir."

"Father General!"

"I mean that I counsel the lady not to answer it."

The Procurator General suppressed another smile, directed this time at Roma, and said, "*Bene!*"

"Be calm, my daughter," whispered the Capuchin.

"At least," said the Procurator General, "you can now be certain that you had seen the Honourable Rossi before you met him in Rome?"

"I can."

"In fact you recognise in the illustrious Deputy the young man condemned in contumacy eighteen years ago?"

"I do."

"Perhaps in his letters or conversations he has even admitted the identity?"

"He has."

"Only one more question, Donna Roma," said the Procurator General, with another smile. "Your father's name in England was Doctor Roselli, and the name of his young confederate——"

"Courage, my child," whispered the Capuchin, taking Roma's ice-cold hand in his own trembling one.

"The name of his young confederate was——"

"David Leone," said Roma, lifting her eyes to the face of Father Pifferi.

"So David Leone and David Rossi are one and the same person?"

"Yes," said Roma, and the Capuchin dropped back in his seat as if he had been dealt a blow.

"Thank you. I need trouble you no more. My secretary will now prepare the *précis.*"

Commendatore Angelelli returned with the Carabineer, and there was some talking in low tones. "Report for the Committee of the Chamber, sir?" "That is unnecessary at this moment, the House having risen for Easter." "Warrant for the arrest, then?" "Certainly. Here is the form. Fill it up, and I will sign."

While the secretary wrote his *précis* at one side of the table, the Chief of Police prepared his *mandato* at the other side, repeating the words to the Carabineer who stood behind his chair. "We . . . considering the conclusions of the Public Minister . . . according to Article 187 of the Code . . . order the arrest of David Leone, commonly called David Rossi . . . imputed guilty of attempted regicide in the year . . . and tried and condemned in contumacy for the crime contemplated in Article. . . . And to such effects we require the Corps of the Royal Carabineers to conduct him before us to be interrogated on the facts above stated, and call on all officials and agents of the public force to lend a strong hand for the execution of the present warrant. Age, 34 years. Height, 1.79 metres. Forehead, lofty. Eyes, large and dark. Nose, Roman. Hair, black with short curls. Beard and moustache, clean shaven. *Corporatura,* distinguished."

When the secretary had finished his *précis* he read it aloud to Roma and his superior.

"Good! Give the lady the pen. You will sign this paper, Donna Roma—and that will do."

Roma and Father Pifferi had both risen. "Courage," the Capuchin tried to say, but his quivering lips emitted no sound. Roma stood a moment with the pen in her fingers, and her great eyes looked slowly round the room. Then she stooped and wrote her name rapidly.

At the same moment the Procurator General signed the warrant, whereupon the Chief of Police handed it to the Carabineer, saying, " Lose no time—Chiasso," and the soldier went out hurriedly.

Roma held the pen a moment longer, and then it dropped out of her fingers.

" Come," said the Capuchin, and they left the room.

There was a crowd on the embankment by the corner of the Ripetta bridge. The body of a beggar had been brought out of the river, and it was lying there for the formal inspection of the officials who report on cases of sudden death. Roma stopped to look at the dead man. It was Old John. He had committed suicide.

XX

It was said at the Vatican that the Pope had not slept all night. The attendant whose duty it was to lie awake while the Holy Father expected to sleep said he heard him praying in the dark hours, and at one moment he heard him singing a hymn.

To the Pope it had been a night of searching self-examination. Pictures of his life had passed before him in swift review, pulsing and throbbing out of the darkness like the light of a firefly, now come, now gone.

First the Conclave, the three scrutators, and himself as one of them. The first scrutiny, the second scrutiny, the third scrutiny and his own name going up, up, up, as he proclaimed the votes in a loud voice so that all in the chapel might hear. One vote more to his own name, another, still another; his fear, his fainting; the gentle tones of an old Cardinal, saying, " Take your time, brother; rest, repose a while." Then the election, the awful sense of being God's choice, the almost unearthly joy of the supreme moment when he became the Vicar of Christ on earth.

Then the stepping forth from the dim conclave into the full light of day to be proclaimed the representative of the Almighty, the living voice of God, the infallible one. The sunless chapel, the white and crimson vestments, the fisherman's ring, the vast crowd in the blazing light of the piazza, the sudden silence, and the clear cry of the Cardinal Deacon ringing out under the blue sky, " I announce to you joyful tidings—the Most Eminent and Reverend Cardinal Leone,

having taken the name of Pius X., is elected Pope." Then
the call of silver trumpets, the roar of ten thousand human
throats, the surging mass of living men below the balcony,
and the joy-bells ringing out the glad news from every
church tower in Rome, that a new King and Pontiff had
been given by God to His World.

Somewhere in the dark hours the Pope dozed off, and
then Sleep, the maker of visions, dispelled his dream. Another picture—a picture which had pursued him at intervals
both in sleeping and waking hours, ever since the great day
when he stepped out on to the balcony and was saluted as a
god—came to him again that night. He called it his presentiment. The scene was always the same. A darkened
room, a chapel, an altar, himself on his knees, with the
sense of Someone bending over him, and an awful voice saying into his ears:—"You, the Vicar of Jesus Christ; you,
the rock on which the Saviour built His Church; you, the
living voice of God; you, the infallible one; you, who fill
the most exalted dignity on earth—*remember you are but
clay!*"

The Pope awoke with a start, and to break the oppression
of painful thoughts he turned on the light, propped himself
up in bed, and taking a book from the night table, he began
to read. It was the Catholic legend of a father doomed to
destroy his son, or suffer the son to destroy the father. They
had been separated early in the son's life, and now that they
met again they met as foes, and the son drew his sword upon
his father without knowing who he was!

One by one the incidents of the history linked themselves with the incidents of the day before, and the lonely
old man of the Vatican—childless, kinless, homeless for all
his state, and cut off from every human tie—began to think
of things that were still farther back than the conclave and
the proclamation—things of the dead past which nature had
seemed to bury with so kind a hand, covering the grave with
grass and flowers.

A sweet young face, timid and trustful; a sudden shock
such as makes the world crumble beneath a man's feet; a
vague sense of guilt and shame, unreasonable, unmerited, un-
justifiable, yet not to be put away; a blank period of humiliation; the opening of eyes in a new world; the humblest place
in a religious house, the kitchen of the Noviciate. Then a
great yearning, a great restlessness; coming out of the con-

vent; dispensations; holy orders; works of charity; travels in foreign lands and searchings day and night in the streets of a cruel city for some one who had been lost and was never found.

The Pope put down the book and turned out the light. It was then that he sang and prayed.

When Cortis came with the Pope's breakfast in the frayed edge of the morning, the chamberlain outside the bedroom door whispered to the valet, " The Holy Father has been with the angels all night long."

There was a Papal " Chapel " in St. Peter's that morning, with a procession of white vestments in honour of the Mass of the Resurrection, but the Pope did not attend. He sat alone in his simple chamber, with curtains drawn across the marble columns to obscure the bed, fingering the crucifix which hung from his neck, and waiting for the ringing of the Easter bells.

The little door to the private corridor opened quietly, and Father Pifferi entered the room.

" Well? " said the Pope.

" It is all over," said the Capuchin.

" Did the poor child . . . did she bear up bravely? "

" Very bravely, your Holiness."

" No weakness, no hysteria? She did not faint or break down at the end? "

" On the contrary, she was composed—perfectly composed and quiet."

" Thank God! "

" It was most extraordinary. A woman denouncing her husband, and yet so calm, so terribly calm."

" God helped her to bear her burden. God help all of us in our hour of need! "

The Pope lifted the crucifix to his lips, and added, " And the man? "

" Rossi? "

" Yes."

" After she had signed the denunciation a warrant for his arrest was made out and given to the Carabineers."

" It mentioned everything? "

" Everything."

" Who he is and all about him? "

" Yes, your Holiness."

The Pope fingered his crucifix again, and said, " Who is he, Father Pifferi? "

THE POPE

The Capuchin did not reply.

"Father Pifferi, I ask you who he is?"

Still the Capuchin did not reply, and the Pope smiled a pitiful smile, touched the friar's arm with a caressing gesture, and said, "Don't be afraid for the Holy Father, carissimo. If that poor child, who would have died rather than sacrifice her husband, could be so calm and strong . . ."

"Holy Father," said the Capuchin, "when you asked the lady to denounce David Rossi you thought of him only as an enemy of the Church and of its head, trying to pull down both and destroy civil society—isn't that so?"

The Pope bent his head.

"Holy Father, if . . . if you had known that he was something more than that . . . something nearer . . . if, for example, you had been told that . . . that he was the relative of a priest, would you have asked for his denunciation just the same?"

The old Capuchin had stammered, but the Pope answered in a firm voice, "That would have made no difference, my son. The blessed Scriptures do not conceal the sin of Judas, and shall we conceal the offences of those who come within the circle of our own families?"

"Holy Father," said the Capuchin, "if you had been told that he was related to a prelate of your domestic household . . ."

He stopped, and the Pope answered in a voice that trembled slightly, "Still it would have made no difference. The enemies of the Almighty are watching day and night, and shall His holy Church be imperilled and abased by the weakness of His servant?"

"Holy Father, if . . . if you had been told that . . . that he was the kinsman of a Cardinal?"

The Pope was struggling to control himself. "Even then it would have made no difference. I am old and weak, but God would have supported me, and though I had been called upon to cut off my right hand, or give my body to be burned, still . . ."

His voice quivered and died in his throat, and there was a moment's pause.

"Holy Father," said the Capuchin, turning his eyes away, "if you had been told that he was the nearest of kin to the Pope himself . . ."

The Pope dropped the crucifix which was trembling in his

hand, and half rose from his chair. "Then . . . even then . . . it would have . . . but the will of God be done," he said, and he could not utter another word.

At that moment the Easter bells began to ring. The deep-toned bells of St. Peter's came first with its joyful peal, and then the bells of the other churches of the city took up the rapturous melody. In the Basilica the veil before the altar had been rent with a loud crash, and the Gloria in Excelsis was being sung.

At the same moment a prelate vested in a white tunic entered the Pope's room, and kneeling in the middle of the floor, he said, "Holy Father, I announce to you a great joy. Hallelujah! The Lord is risen again."

The Pope tried to rise from his seat, but could not do so. "Help me, Monsignor," he said faintly, and the prelate raised him to his feet. Then leaning on the prelate's arm, he walked to the door of his private chapel. On reaching it he looked back at Father Pifferi, who was going silently out of the room.

"Addio, carissimo," he said, in a pitiful voice, but the Capuchin could not reply.

Some moments afterwards the Pope was quite alone. The arched windows of the little chapel were covered with heavy red curtains, but the clanging of the brass tongues in the cupola, the deep throb of the organ, and the rolling waves of the voices of the people singing the grand Hallelujah, found their way into the darkened chamber. But above all other sounds in the ears of the Pope as he lay prostrate on the altar steps was the sound of a voice which said, "You, the Vicar of Jesus Christ; you, the rock on which the Saviour built His Church; you, the living voice of God; you, the infallible one; you, who fill the most exalted dignity on earth—*remember you are but clay.*"

XXI

"Acqua Acetosa!" "Roba Vecchia!" "Rannocchie!"
The street cries were ringing through the Navona, the piazza was alive with people, and strangers were saluting each other as they passed on the pavement when Roma returned home. At the lodge the Garibaldian wished her a good Easter, and at the door of the apartment the curate of the parish,

THE POPE

who in cotta and biretta was making his Easter call to sprinkle the rooms with holy water, gave her a smile and his blessing, while old Francesca, inside the house, laying the Easter sideboard of cakes, sausages, and eggs, put both hands behind her back, like a child playing a game, and cried—

"Now, what does the Signora think I've got for her?"

It was a letter, and as the old woman produced it she was glowing with happiness at the joy she was bringing to Roma.

"The porter from Trinità de' Monti brought it," she said, "and he told me to tell you there's a lay sister called Sister Angelica at the convent now, and he is afraid that other letters may go astray . . . Aren't you glad you've got a letter, Signora? I thought Signora would die of delight, and I gave the man six soldi."

Roma was turning the envelope over and over in her hands, thinking what a call to joy a letter of Rossi's used to be, and wondering if she ought to open this one.

"Well, that was the way with me too when Tommaso was at the wars. But this is Easter, Signora, and the Blessed Virgin wouldn't bring you bad news to-day. Listen! That's the Gloria. I can always hear the church bells on Holy Saturday. The first time after I was deaf Joseph was a baby, and I took the wrappings off his little feet while the bells were ringing, and he walked straight away! Ah, my poor darling! . . . But I'm making the Signora cry."

The letter was dated from Zürich. It ran:—

"MY DEAR ROMA,—Your letters and I seem to be running a race which shall return to you first. I was compelled to leave Berlin before my long-delayed correspondence could arrive from London, and now it seems probable that I must leave Zürich before it can follow me from Berlin. As a consequence I have not heard from you for weeks—not since your letter about your friend, you remember—and I am in agonies of impatience to know what has happened to you in the interval.

"I came to Switzerland the day before yesterday, pushed on by the urgency of affairs at home. Here we hold the last meeting of our international committee before I go back to Italy. This will be to-morrow (Friday) night, and according to present plans I set out for Rome on Saturday morning.

"How different my return will be from my flight a few weeks ago! Then I was plunged in despair, now I am

373

buoyed up with hope; then my soul was furrowed by doubts, now it is braced up with certainties; then my idea was a dream, now it is a practical reality.

" O Roma, my Roma, it is a good thing to live. After all, the world is no Gethsemane, and when a man has a beautiful life like yours belonging to him he may be forgiven if he forgets the voices which assail him with fears. They have come to me sometimes, dearest, in this long and cruel silence, and I have asked myself hideous questions. What is happening to my dear one in the midst of my enemies? What sufferings are being inflicted upon her for my sake? She is brave, and will bear anything, but did I do right to leave her behind? Bruno died rather than betray me, and she will do more—infinitely more in her eyes—she will see *me* die, rather than imperil a cause which is a thousand times more dear to me than my life.

" Addio, carissima! Set me as a seal upon thine heart, as a seal upon thine arm, for love is strong as death. If there were any possibility of our love increasing it *would* increase after going through dangers like these. Keep well, dearest. Preserve that sweet life which is so precious to me that I cannot live without it. Do you remember, it was the 2nd of February when we parted in the darkness at the church door, and now it is Easter, and the day after to-morrow we shall hear the Easter bells! Spring is here, and in the unchangeable changeableness of nature I see the resurrection of humanity and listen to the Gloria of God.

" You cannot answer this letter, dear, because I shall already be on the way to Rome before it reaches you, but you can send me a telegram to Chiasso. Do so. I shall look out for the telegraph boy the moment the train stops at the station. Say you are well and happy and waiting for me, and it will be like a smile from your lovely lips and eyes on the frontier of my native land.

" My train is due to arrive on Sunday morning at seven o'clock. Meet me at the railway station, and let your face be the first I see when the train draws up in Rome. Then . . . let me hear your voice, and let my heart become a King.
" D. R."

Roma had grown paler and paler as she read this letter. The man's love and trust were crushing her. Tears filled her eyes and flooded her face. But her soul, which had been stunned and had fallen, recovered itself and arose.

PART EIGHT—THE KING

I

EARLY on the morning of Holy Saturday a little crowd of Italians stood on the open space in front of the platform at the Bahnhof of Zürich. Most of them wore the blue smocks and peaked caps of porters and street-sweepers, but in the centre of the group was a tall man in a frockcoat and a soft felt hat.

It was Rossi. He was noticeably changed since his flight from Rome. His bronzed face was paler, his cheeks thinner, his dark eyes looked larger, his figure stooped perceptibly, and he had the air of a man who was struggling to conceal a consuming nervousness.

The bell rang for the starting of a train and Rossi shook hands with everybody.

" Going straight through, Honourable? "

" No, I shall sleep at Milan to-night and go on to Rome in the morning."

" *Addio, Onorevole!* "

" *Addio!* "

The moment the train started, Rossi gave himself up to thoughts of Roma. Where was she now? He closed his eyes and tried to picture her. She was reading his letter. He recalled particular passages, and saw the smile with which she read them. Peace be with her! The light pressure of her soft fingers was on his hands already, and through the *tran-tran* of the train he could hear her softest tones.

Nature as well as humanity seemed to smile on Rossi that day. He thought the lakes had never looked so lovely. It was early when they ran along the shores of Lucerne, and the white mists, wrapping themselves up on the mountains, were gliding away like ghosts. One after another the great peaks looked over each other's shoulders, covered with pines as with vast armies crossing the Alps, thick at the bottom and with thinner files of daring spirits at the top. The sun danced on the waters of the lake like fairies on a floor of glass, and when the train stopped at Fluelen the sound of waterfalls mingled with the singing of birds and the ringing of the church bells. It was the Gloria. All the earth was singing its Gloria. "Glory to God in the highest."

Rossi's happiness became almost boyish as the train approached Italy. When the great tunnel was passed through, the signs of a new race came thick and fast. Shrines of the Madonna, instead of shrines of the Christ; long lines of field-workers, each with his hoe, instead of little groups with the plough; grey oxen with great horns and slow step, instead of brisk horses with tinkling bells.

Signs of doubtful augury for the most part, but Rossi was in no mood to think of that. He let down the carriage window that he might drink in the air of his own country. In spite of his opinions he could not help doing that. The mystic call that comes to a man's heart from the soil that gave him birth was coming to him also. He heard the voice of the vine-dresser in the vineyard singing of love—always of love. He saw the oranges and lemons, and the roses white and red. He caught a glimpse of the first of the little cities high up on the crags, with its walls and tower, and Campo Santo outside. His lips parted, his breast swelled. It was home! Home!

The day waned, the sky darkened, and the passengers in the train, who had been talking incessantly, began to doze. Rossi returned to his seat, and thought more seriously about Roma. All his soul went out to the young wife who had shared his sufferings. In his mind's eye he was reading between the lines of her letters, and beginning to reproach himself in earnest. Why had he imposed his life's secret upon her, seeing the risk she ran, and the burden of her responsibility?

The battle with his soul was short. If he had not trusted Roma, he would never have loved her. If he had not stripped his heart naked before her, he would never have known that she loved him. And if she had suffered in his absence he would make it all up to her on his return. He thought of their joyous day on the Campagna, and then of the unalloyed hours before them. What would she be doing now? She would be sending off the telegram he was to receive at Chiasso. God bless her! God bless everybody!

The thought of Roma's telegram filled the whole of the

THE KING

last hour before he reached the frontier. He imagined the words it would contain: "Well and waiting. Welcome home." But was she well? It was weeks since he had heard from her, and so many things might have happened. If he had managed his personal affairs with more thought for himself, he might have received her letters.

Heavy clouds began to shut out the landscape. The temperature had fallen suddenly, and the wind must have risen, for the trees, as they flashed past, were being beaten about. Rossi stood in the corridor again, feeling feverish and impatient.

At length the train slackened speed, the noise of the wheels and the engine abated, and there came a clap of thunder. After a moment there was a far-off sound of church bells which were being rung to avert the lightning, and then came a donwpour of rain. It was raining in torrents when the train drew up at Chiasso, but the carriages were hardly under cover of the platform when Rossi was ready to step out.

"All baggage ready!" "Hand baggage out!" "Chiasso!" "The Customs!"

The station hands and porters were shouting by the stopping train, and Rossi's dark eyes with their long lashes were looking through the line of men for some one who carried a yellow letter.

"Facchino!"

"Signore?"

"Seen the telegraph boy about?"

"No, Signore."

Rossi leapt down to the platform, and at the same moment three Carabineers, who had been working their heads from right to left to peer into the carriages as they passed, stepped up to him and offered a folded white paper.

He took it without speaking, and for a moment he stood looking at the soldiers as if he had been stunned. Then he opened the paper and read: "*Mandato di Cattura* . . . We . . . order the arrest of David Leone, commonly called David Rossi . . ."

A cold sweat burst in great beads from his forehead. Again he looked into the faces of the soldiers. And then he laughed. It was a fearful laugh—the laugh of a smitten soul.

The scene had been observed by passengers trooping to

the Customs, and a group of English and American tourists
were making apposite comments on the event.

"It's Rossi." "Rossi?" "The anarchist." "Travelled
in our train?" "Sure." "My!"

The marshal of Carabineers, a man with shrunken cheeks
and the eyes of a hawk, dressed in his little brief authority,
strode with a lofty look through the spectators to telegraph
the arrest to Rome.

II

When the train started again, Rossi was a prisoner sitting between two of the Carabineers with the marshal of
Carabineers on the seat in front of him. His heart felt
cold and his chin buried itself in his breast. He was asking
himself how many persons knew of his identity with David
Leone, and could connect him with the trial of eighteen
years ago. *There was but one.*

Rossi leapt to his feet with a muttered oath on his lips.
The thing that had flashed through his mind was impossible,
and he was himself the traitor to think of it. But even when
the imagined agony had passed away, a hard lump lay at
his heart and he felt sick and ashamed.

The marshal of Carabineers, who had mistaken Rossi's
gesture, closed the carriage window and stood with his back to
it until the train arrived at Milan. A police official was waiting for them there with the latest instructions from Rome.
In order to avoid the possibility of a public disturbance in
the capital on the day of the King's Jubilee, the prisoner
was to be detained in Milan until further notice.

"Seems you're to sleep here to-night, Honourable," said
the soldier. Remembering that it had been his intention to
do so when he left Zürich, Rossi laughed bitterly.

It was now dark. A prison van stood at the end of a
line of hotel omnibuses, and Rossi was marched to it between
the measured steps of the Carabineers. News of his arrest
had already been published in Milan, and crowds of spectators were gathered in the open space outside the station. He
tried to hold up his head when the people peered at him,
telling himself that the arrest of an innocent man was not his
but the law's disgrace; yet a sense of sickness surprised him
again and he dropped his head as he buried himself in
the van.

THE KING

On the dark drive to the prison in the Via Filangeri the Carabineers grumbled and swore at the hard fate which kept them out of Rome at a time of public rejoicing. There was to be a dinner on Monday night at the barracks on the Prati, and on Tuesday morning the King was to present medals.

Rossi shut his eyes and said nothing. But half-an-hour later, when he had been put in the "paying" cell, and the marshal of Carabineers was leaving him, he could not forbear to speak.

"Officer," he said, fumbling his copy of the warrant, "would you mind telling me where you received this paper?"

"At the Procura, of course," said the soldier.

"Some one had denounced me there—can you tell me who it was?"

"That's no business of mine, Honourable. Still, as you wish to know . . ."

"Well?"

"A lady was there when the warrant was made out, and if I had to guess who she was . . ."

Rossi saw the name coming in the man's face, and he flung out at him in a roar of wrath.

During the long hours of the night he tried to account for his arrest to the exclusion of Roma. He thought of every woman whom he had known intimately in England and America, and finally of Elena and old Francesca. It was useless. There was only one woman in the world who knew the secrets of his early life. He had revealed some of them himself, and the rest she knew of her own knowledge.

No matter! There was no traitor so treacherous as circumstance. He would not believe the lie that fate was thrusting down his throat. Roma was faithful, she would die rather than betray him, and he was a contemptible hound to allow himself to think of her in that connection. He recalled her letters, her sacrifices, her brave and cheerful renunciation, and the hard lump that had settled at his heart rose up to his throat.

Morning broke at last. As the grey dawn entered the cell the Easter bells were ringing. Rossi remembered in what other conditions he had expected to hear them, and again his heart grew bitter. A good-natured warder came with his breakfast of bread and water, and a smuggled copy of a morning journal called the *Perseveranza*. It contained an account of his arrest, and a leading article on his career as a thing closed and ruined. The public would learn with astonishment that a man who had attained to great prominence in Parliament and lived several years in the fierce light of the world's eye, had all the time masqueraded in a false character, being really a criminal convicted long ago for conspiring against the person of the late King.

The sun shone, the sparrows chirped, the church bells rang the whole day long. Towards evening the warder came with another newspaper, the *Corriere della Sera*. It explained that the sensational arrest of the illustrious Deputy, which had fallen on the country like a thunderbolt, was not intended as punishment for an offence long past and forgotten, but as a means of preventing a political crime that was on the eve of being committed. The Deputy had been abroad since the unhappy riots of the First of February, and advices from foreign police left no doubt whatever that he had contemplated a preposterous raid of the combined revolutionary clubs of Europe against Italy, timed with almost fiendish imagination to break out on the festival of the King's Jubilee.

Rossi slept as little on Sunday night as on the night before. The horrible doubts which he had driven away were sucking at his heart like a vampire. He tried to invent excuses for Roma. She was intimidated; she was a woman and she could not help herself. Useless, and worse than useless! "I thought the daughter of Joseph Roselli would have died first," he told himself.

The good-natured warder brought him another newspaper in the morning, the *Secolo*, an organ of his own party. Its tone was the bitterest of all. "We have reason to believe that the unfortunate event, which cannot but have the effect of setting back the people's cause, is due to the betrayal of one of their leaders by a certain fashionable woman who is near to the person of the President of the Council. It is the old story over again, the story of man's weakness and woman's deception, with every familiar circumstance of humiliation, folly, and shame."

There could be no doubt of it. It was Roma who had betrayed him. Whatever her reasons or excuse, the result was the same. She had given up the deepest secrets of his soul, and his life's work was in the dust.

The marshal of Carabineers came to say that they were to go on to Rome, and at nine o'clock they were again in the train. People in holiday dress were promenading the platform and the station was hung with flags. A gentleman in a white waistcoat was about to step into the compartment with the Carabineers and their prisoner, when, recognising his travelling companions, he bowed and stepped back. It was the Sergeant of the Chamber, returning after the Easter vacation from his villa on one of the lakes. Rossi sent a ringing laugh after the man, and that brought him back.

"I'm sorry for you, Honourable, very sorry," he said. "You've deceived us all, but now you are seen in your true colours, and apparently throwing off all disguise."

The Sergeant was so far right that Rossi was another man. Whatever had been tender and sweet in him was now hard and bitter. The train started for Rome, and the soldiers drew the straws out of their Tuscan cigars and smoked. Rossi coiled himself up in his corner and shut his eyes. Sometimes a sneer curled his lips, sometimes he laughed aloud.

They were travelling by the coast route, and when the train ran into Genoa a military band at the foot of the monument to Mazzini was playing the royal hymn. But the festivities of the King's Jubilee were eclipsed in public interest by the arrest of Rossi and the collapse of the conspiracy which it was understood to imply. The marshal of the Carabineers bought the local papers, and one of them was full of details of "The Great Plot." An exact account was given from a semi-military standpoint of the plan of the supposed raid. It included the capture of the arsenal at Genoa and the assassination of the King at Rome.

The train ran through countless tunnels like the air through a flute, now rumbling in the darkness, now whistling in the light. Rossi closed his eyes and shut out the torment of passing scenes, and straightway he was seeing Roma. He could only see her as he had always seen her, with her golden complexion, her large violet eyes and long curved lashes, her mouth which had its own gift of smiling, and her glow of health and happiness. Whatever she had done he knew that he must always love her. This worked on him like madness, and once again he leapt to his feet and made for the corridor, whereupon the Carabineers, who had been sleeping, got up and shut the door.

Night fell, and the moon rose, large and blood-red as a setting sun. When the train shot on to the Roman Campagna, like a boat gliding into open sea, the great and solemn desolation seemed more than ever withdrawn from the sights and sounds of the living world. Rossi remembered the joy of joys with which he had expected to cross the familiar country. Then he looked across at the soldiers who were snoring in their seats.

When the train stopped at Civita Vecchia, the Carabineers opened the door to the corridor that their prisoner might stretch his legs. Some evening papers from Rome were handed into the carriage. Rossi put out his hand to pay for them, and to his surprise it was seized with an eager grasp. The newsman, who was also carrying a tray of coffee, was a huge creature, with a white apron and a paper cap.

" Caffé, sir? Caffé? " he called, and then in an undertone, " Don't you know me, old fellow? Caffé, sir? Thank you."

It was one of Rossi's colleagues in the House of Deputies.

" Milk, sir? With pleasure, sir. Venti centesimi, sir. . . . 'All right, old chap. Keep your eyes open at the station at Rome. . . . Change, sir? Certainly sir. . . . Coupé, waiting on the left side. Look alive. Addio! . . . Caffé! Caffé! "

The lusty voice died away down the platform, and the train started again. Rossi felt giddy. He staggered back to his seat and tried to read his evening papers.

The *Sunrise*, the paper founded by Rossi himself, seemed to be full of the Prime Minister. He had that day put the crown on a career of the highest distinction; the King had conferred the Collar of the Annunziata upon him; and in view of the continued rumblings of unrest it was even probable that he would be made Dictator.

The *Avanti* seemed to Rossi to be full of himself. When the country recovered from the delirium of that day's ridiculous doings, it would know how to judge of the infamous methods of a Minister who had condescended to use the devices of a Delilah for the defeat and confusion of a political adversary.

Rossi felt as if he were suffocating. He put a hand into a side-pocket, for his copy of the warrant crinkled there under his twitching fingers. If he could only meet with Roma for a moment and thrust the damning document in her face!

When the train ran along the side of the Tiber, they could see a great framework of fireworks which had been erected on the Pincio. It represented a gigantic crown and was all ablaze. At length the train slowed down and entered the terminus at Rome. Rossi remembered how he had expected to enter it, and he choked with wounded pride.

There were the thumpings and clankings and the blinding flashes of white light, and then the train stopped. The station was full of people. Rossi noticed Malatesta among them, the man whose life he had spared in the duel he had been compelled to fight.

"Now, then, please!" said the marshal of Carabineers, and Rossi stepped down to the platform. A soldier marched on either side of him; the marshal walked in front. The people parted to let the four men pass, and then closed up and came after them. Not a word was spoken.

With pale lips and a fixed gaze which seemed to look at nobody, Rossi walked to the end of the platform, and there the crush was greatest.

"Room!" cried the marshal of Carabineers, making for the gate at which a porter was taking tickets. A black van stood outside.

Suddenly the marshal was struck on the shoulder by a hand out of the crowd. He turned to defend himself, and was struck on the other side. Then he tried to draw a weapon, but before he could do so he was thrown to the ground. One of the two other Carabineers stooped to lift him up, and the third laid hold of Rossi. At the next instant Rossi felt the soldier's hand fall from his arm as by a sword cut, and somebody was crying in his ear:

"Now's your time, sir. Leave this to me and fly."

It was Malatesta. Before Rossi fully knew what he was doing, he crossed the lines to the opposite platform, passed through the barrier by means of his Deputy's medal permitting him to travel on the railways, and stepped into a coupé that stood waiting with an open door.

"Where to, signore?"

"Piazza Navona—*presto*."

As the carriage rattled across the end of the Piazza Margherita a company of Carabineers was going at quick march towards the station.

III

At ten o'clock on Saturday night the screamers in the Piazza Navona were crying the arrest of Rossi. The telegrams from the frontier gave an ugly account of his capture.

He was in disguise, and he made an effort to deny himself, but thanks to the astuteness of the Carabineer charged with the warrant the device was defeated, and he was now lodged in the prison at Milan, where it was probable that he would remain some days.

Roma's feelings took a new turn. Her crushing self-reproach at the degradation of David Rossi, fallen, lost, and in prison, gave way to an intense bitterness against the Baron, successful, radiant, and triumphant. She turned a bright light upon the incidents of the past months and saw that the Baron was responsible for everything. He had intimidated her. His intimidation had worked upon her conscience and driven her to the confessional. The confessional had taken her to the Pope, and the Pope in love and loyalty and fatal good faith had led her to denounce her husband. It was a chain of damning circumstances, helped out by the demon of chance, but the first link had been forged by the Baron, and he was to blame for all.

On Monday morning bands of music began to promenade the streets. Before breakfast the rejoicings of the day had begun. Towards midday drunken fellows in the piazza were embracing and crying, " Long live the King," and then " Long live the Baron Bonelli."

Roma's disgust deepened to contempt. Why were the people rejoicing? There was nothing to rejoice at. Why were they shouting and singing? It was all got-up enthusiasm, all false, all a lie. By a sort of clairvoyance, Roma could see the Baron in the midst of the scenes he had prearranged. He was sitting in the carriage with the King and Queen, smiling his icy smile, while the people bellowed by their side. And meantime David Rossi was lying in prison in Milan, in a downfall worse than death, crushed, beaten, and broken-hearted.

Old Francesca brought a morning paper. It was the *Sunrise,* and it contained nothing that did not concern the Baron. His wife had died on Saturday—there were three lines for that incident. The King had made him a Knight of the Order of Annunziata—there was half a column on the new cousin to the royal family. A state dinner and ball were to be held at the Quirinal that night, when it might be expected that the President of the Council would be nominated Dictator.

In another column of the *Sunrise* she found an interview

with the Baron. The journal called for exemplary punishment on the criminals who conspired against the sovereign and endangered the public peace; the Baron, in guarded words, replied that the natural tendency of the King would be to pardon such persons, where their crimes were of old date, and their present conspiracies were averted, but it lay with the public to say whether it was just to the throne that such lenity ought to be encouraged.

When Roma read this a red light seemed to flash before her eyes, and in a moment she understood what she had to do. The Baron intended to make the King break his promise to save the life of David Rossi, casting the blame upon the country, to whose wish he had been forced to yield. There was no earthly tribunal, no judge or jury, for a man who could do a thing like that. He was putting himself beyond all human law. Therefore one course only was left—to send him to the bar of God!

When this idea came to Roma she did not think of it as a crime. In the moral elevation of her soul it seemed like an act of retributive justice. Her heart throbbed violently, but it was only from the stress of her thoughts and the intensity of her desire to execute them.

One thing troubled her, the purely material difficulties in the way. She revolved many plans in her mind. At first she thought of writing to the Baron asking him to see her, and hinting at submission to his will; but she abandoned the device as a kind of duplicity that was unworthy of her high and noble mission. At last she decided to go to the Piazza Leone late that night and wait for the Baron's return from the Quirinal. Felice would admit her. She would sit in the Council Room, under the shaded lamp, until she heard the carriage wheels in the piazza. Then as the Baron opened the door she would rise out of the red light—and do it.

In the drawer of a bureau she had found a revolver which Rossi had left with her on the night he went away. His name had been inscribed on it by the persons who sent it as a present, but Roma gave no thought to that. Rossi was in prison, therefore beyond suspicion, and she was entirely indifferent to detection. When she had done what she intended to do she would give herself up. She would avow everything, seek no means of justification, and ask for no mercy even in the presence of death. Her only defence would be that the Baron, who was guilty, had to be sent to the supreme tribunal. It would then be for the court to take the responsibility of fixing the moral weight of her motive in the scales of human justice.

With these sublime feelings she began to examine the revolver. She remembered that when Rossi had given it to her she had recoiled from the touch of the deadly weapon, and it had fallen out of her fingers. No such fear came to her now, as she turned it over in her delicate hands and tried to understand its mechanism. There were six chambers, and to know if they were loaded she pulled the trigger. The vibration and the deafening noise shook but did not frighten her.

The deaf old woman had heard the shot, and she came upstairs panting and with a pallid face.

"Mercy, Signora! What's happened? The Blessed Virgin save us! A revolver!"

Roma tried to speak with unconcern. It was Mr. Rossi's revolver. She had found it in the bureau. It must be loaded —it had gone off.

The words were vague, but the tone quieted the old woman. "Thank the saints it's nothing worse. But why are you so pale, Signora? What is the matter with you?"

Roma averted her eyes. "Wouldn't you be pale too if a thing like this had gone off in your hands?"

By this time the Garibaldian had hobbled up behind his wife, and when all was explained the old people announced that they were going out to see the illuminations on the Pincio.

"They begin at eleven o'clock and go on to twelve or one, Signora. Everybody in the house has gone already, or the shot would have made a fine sensation."

"Good-night, Tommaso! Good-night, Francesca!"

"Good-night, Signora. We'll have to leave the street door open for the lodgers coming back, but you'll close your own door and be as safe as sardines."

The Garibaldian raised his pork-pie hat and left the door ajar. It was half-past ten and the piazza was very quiet. Roma sat down to write a letter.

"Dearest," she wrote, "I have read in the newspapers what took place on the frontier and I am overwhelmed with grief. What can I say of my own share in it except that I did it for the best? From my soul and before God, I tell you that if I betrayed you it was only to save your life. And though my heart is breaking and I shall never know another happy hour until God gives me release, if I had to go through it all again I should have to do as I have done. . . .

"Perhaps your great heart will be able to forgive me some day, but I shall never forgive myself or the man who compelled me to do what I have done. Before this letter reaches you in Milan a great act will be done in Rome. But you must know nothing more about it until it is done.

"Good-bye, dearest. Try to forgive me as soon as you can. I shall know it if you do . . . where I am going to—eventually . . . and it will be so sweet and beautiful. Your loving, erring, broken-hearted   ROMA."

A noisy group of revellers were passing through the piazza singing a drinking song. When they were gone a church clock struck eleven. Roma put on a hat and a veil. Her impatience was now intense. Being ready to go out she took a last look round the rooms. They brought a throng of memories—of hopes and visions as well as realities and facts. The piano, the phonograph, the bust, the bed. It was all over. She knew she would never come back.

Her heart was throbbing violently, and she was opening the bureau a second time when her ear caught the sound of a step on the stairs. She knew the step. It was the Baron's.

She stopped, with an indescribable sense of terror, and gazed at the door. It stood partly open as the Garibaldian had left it.

Through the door the Baron was about to enter. He was coming up, up, up—to his death. Some supernatural power was sending him.

She grew dizzy and quaked in every limb. Still the step outside came on. At length it reached the top, and there was a knock at the door. At first she could not answer, and the knock was repeated.

Then the free use of her faculties came back to her. There was more of the Almighty in all this than of her own design. It *was* to be. God intended her to kill this guilty man.

"Come in!" she cried.

IV

WHEN the Baron awoke on Saturday he remembered Roma with a good deal of self-reproach, and everything that happened during the following days made him think of her with tenderness. During the morning an aide-de-camp brought him the casket containing the Collar of the Annunziata, and spoke a formal speech. He fingered the jewelled band and golden pendant as he made the answer prescribed by etiquette, but he was thinking of Roma and the joy she might have felt in hailing him cousin of the King.

Towards noon he received the telegram which announced the death of his maniac wife, and he set off instantly for his castle in the Alban Hills. He remained long enough to see the body removed to the church, and then returned to Rome. Nazzareno carried to the station the little hand-bag full of despatches with which he had occupied the hour spent in the train. They passed by the tree which had been planted on the first of Roma's Roman birthdays. It was covered with white roses. The Baron plucked one of them, and wore it in his button-hole on the return journey.

Before midnight he was back in the Piazza Leone, where the Commendatore Angelelli was waiting with news of the arrest of Rossi. He gave orders to have the editor of the *Sunrise* sent to him so that he might make a tentative suggestion. But in spite of himself his satisfaction at Rossi's complete collapse and possible extermination was disturbed by pity for Roma.

Sunday was given up to the interview with the journalist, the last preparations for the Jubilee, and various secular duties. Monday's ceremonials began with the Mass. The Piazza of the Pantheon was lined with a splendid array of soldiers in glistening breastplates and helmets, a tall bodyguard through which the little King passed to his place amid the playing of the national hymn. In the old Pantheon itself, roofed with an awning of white silk which bore the royal arms, flares were burning up to the topmost cornice of the round walls. A temporary altar decorated in white and gold was ablaze with candles, and the choir, conducted by a fashionable composer of opera, were in a golden cage. The King and Queen and royal princes sat in chairs under a velvet canopy, and there were tribunes for cabinet ministers, senators, deputies, and foreign ambassadors. Religion was necessary to all state functions, and the Mass was a magnificent political demonstration carried out on lines arranged by the Baron himself. He had forgotten God, but he had remembered the King, and he had thought of Roma also. She wept at all religious ceremonies, and would have shed tears if she had been present at this one.

From the Pantheon they passed to the Capitol, amid the playing of bands of music which showered through the streets their hail of sound. The magnificent hall was crowded by a brilliant company in silk dresses and decorations. An address was read by the Mayor, reciting the early misfortunes of Italy, and closing with allusions to the prosperity of the nation under the reigning dynasty. In his reply the King extolled the army as the hope of peace and unity, and ended with a eulogy of the President of the Council, whose powerful policy had dispelled the vaporous dreams of unpractical politicians who were threatening the stability of the throne and the welfare of its loyal subjects.

The Baron answered briefly that he had done no more than his duty to his King, who was almost a republican monarch, and to his country, which was the freest in the world. As for the visionaries and their visions, a few refugees in Zürich, cheered on by the rabble abroad, might dream of constructing a universal republic out of the various nations and races, with Rome as their capital, but these were the delirious dreams of weak minds.

" Dangerous ! " said the Baron, with a smile. " To think of the eternal dreamer being dangerous ! "

The King laughed, the senators cheered, the ladies waved their handkerchiefs, and again the Baron remembered Roma.

The procession to the Quirinal was a prolonged triumph. Every house was hung with flags, every window with red and yellow damask. The clubs in the Corso were crowded with princes, nobles, diplomats, and distinguished foreigners. Civil guards by hundreds in their purple plumes lined the streets, and the pavements were packed with loyal people. It was a glorious pageant, such as Roma loved.

The mayors of the province, followed by citizens under their appointed leaders and flags, came up to the Quirinal as the Baron had appointed, and called the King on to the balcony. The King accepted the call and made a sign of thanks.

Returning to the house the King ordered that papers should be prepared immediately creating the Baron Bonelli by royal decree Dictator of Italy for a period of six months from that date. " If Roma were here now," thought the Baron.

Then night came, and the state dinner at the royal palace was a moving scene of enchantment. One princess came after another, apparently clothed in diamonds. The Baron wore the Collar of the Annunziata, and the foreign ambassadors, who as representatives of their sovereigns were entitled to precedence, gave place to him, and he sat on the right of the Queen.

After dinner he led the Queen to an embroidered throne under a velvet baldachino in a gorgeous chamber which had been the chapel of the Popes. Then the ball began. What torrents of light! What a dazzling blaze of diamonds! What lovely faces and pure white skins! What soft bosoms and full round forms! What gleams of life and love in a hundred pairs of beautiful eyes! But there was a lovelier face and form in the mind of the Baron than any his eyes could see, and excusing himself to the King on the ground of Rossi's expected arrival, he left the palace.

Fireflies in the dark garden of the Quirinal were emitting drops of light as the Baron passed through the echoing courts, and the big square in front, bright with electric light, was silent save for the footfall of the sentries at the gate.

The Baron walked in the direction of the Piazza Navona. His self-reproach was becoming poignant. He remembered the threats he had made, and told himself he had never intended to carry them out. They were only meant to impress the imagination of the person played upon, as might happen in any ordinary affair of public life.

The Baron's memory went back to the last state ball before this one, and he felt some pangs of shame. But the disaster of that night had not been due to the cold calculation to which he had attributed it. The cause was simpler and more human—love of a beautiful woman who was slipping away from him, the girding sense of being bound body and soul to a wife that was no wife, and the mad intoxication of a moment.

No matter! Roma should not lose by what had happened. He would make it up to her. Considering her unconventional conduct, it was no little thing he intended to do, but he would do it, and she would see that others were capable of sacrifice.

The people were on the Pincio and the streets were quiet. When the Baron reached the Piazza Navona there was hardly anybody about, and he had difficulty in finding the house. No one saw him enter, and he met with nobody on the stairs. So much the better. He was half ashamed.

After he had knocked twice a voice which he did not recognise told him to come in. When he pushed the door open Roma, in hat and veil, stood before him, with her back to a bureau. He thought she looked frightened and ill.

V

" My dear Roma," said the Baron, " I bring you good news. Everything has turned out well. Nothing could have been managed better, and I come to congratulate you."

He was visibly excited, and spoke rapidly and even loudly.

" The man was arrested on the frontier—you must have heard of that. He was coming by the night train on Saturday, and to prevent a possible disturbance they kept him in Milan until this morning."

Roma continued to stand with her back to the bureau.

" The news was in all the journals yesterday, my dear, and it had a splendid effect on the opening of the Jubilee. When the King went to Mass this morning the plot had received its death-blow, and our anxiety was at an end. To-night the man will arrive in Rome, and within an hour from now he will be safely locked up in prison."

Every nerve in Roma's body was palpitating, but she did not attempt to speak.

" It is all your doing, my child—yours, not mine. Your clever brain has brought it all to pass. ' Leave the man to me,' you said. I left him to you, and you have accomplished everything."

Roma drew her lips together and tried to control herself.

" But what things you have gone through in order to achieve your purpose! Slights, slurs, insults! No wonder the man was taken in by it. Society itself was taken in. And I—yes, I myself—was almost deceived."

" Shall it be now?" thought Roma. The Baron was on the hearth-rug directly facing her.

" But you knew what you were doing, my dear. It was all a part of your scheme. You drew the man on. In due time he delivered himself up to you. He surrendered every secret of his soul. And when your great hour came you were ready. You met it as you had always intended. 'At the top of his hopes he shall fall,' you said."

Roma's heart was beating as if it would burst its bounds.

"He *has* fallen. Thanks to you, this enemy of civil society, this slanderer of women, is down. Then the Pope too! And the confession to the Reverend Father! Who but a woman could have thought of a thing like that?—making your denunciation so defensible, so pardonable, so plausible, so inevitable! What skill! What patience! What diplomacy! And what will and nerve too! Who shall say now that women are incapable of great things?"

The Baron had thrown open his overcoat, revealing the broad expanse of his shirt-front, crossed by the glittering collar of the Annunziata, and was promenading the hearthrug without a thought of his peril.

"The journals of half Europe will have accounts of the failure of the 'Great Plot.' There was another plot, my dear, which did not fail. Europe will hear of that also, and by to-morrow morning the world will know what a woman may do to punish the man who traduces and degrades her!"

"Why don't I do it?" thought Roma. She was fingering the revolver on the bureau behind her, and breathing fast and audibly.

"You shall have everything back, my dear. Carriages, jewellery, apartments, exactly as you parted with them. I have kept all under my own control, and in a single day you can be reinstated."

Roma's palpitating heart was hurting her.

"But won't you sit down, my child? I have something to tell you. It is important news. The Baroness is dead. Yes, she died on Saturday, poor soul. Should I play the hypocrite and weep? Why should I? For fifteen years a cruel law, which I dare not attempt to repeal by divorce in a Catholic country, has tied me to a living corpse. Shall I pretend to mourn because my burden has fallen away? . . . Roma, sit down, my dear; don't continue to stand there. . . . Roma, I am free, and we can now carry out our marriage, as we always hoped and intended."

"Now!" thought Roma, moving a little forward.

"Ah, don't be afraid of anything. I am not afraid, and you needn't be afraid either. Certainly rumour has coupled our names already. But what matter about that? No one shall insult you, whatever has occurred. Wherever I go you shall go too. If they cannot do without me they shall not do without you, and in spite of everything you shall be received everywhere."

" Is that all you had to say? " said Roma.

" Not all. There is something else, and I couldn't wait for the newspapers to tell you. The King has appointed me Dictator for six months. That means that you will be more courted than the Queen. What a revenge! The women who have been turning their backs upon you will bend their backs before you. You will break down every barrier. You will ... "

" Wait," said Roma.

The Baron had been approaching her, and she lifted her hand.

" You expect me to acquiesce in this lie? "

" What lie, my child? "

" That I denounced David Rossi in order to destroy him. It is true that I did denounce him—unhappy woman that I am—but you know perfectly why I did it. I did it because I was forced to do it. *You* forced me."

At the sound of her own voice, her eyes had begun to fill.

" And now you ask me to pretend that it was all done from an evil motive, and you offer me the rewards of guilt. Do you think I'm a murderer that you can offer me the price of blood? Have you any shame? You come here to ask me to marry you, knowing that I am married already—here of all places, in the house of my husband."

Her eyes were blinded with tears, but her voice thickened with anger.

" My child," said the Baron, " if I have asked you to acquiesce in the idea that what you did was from a certain motive it was only to spare you pain. I thought it would be easier for you to do so now, things being as they are. It was only going back to your original purpose, forgetting all that has intervened."

His voice softened, and he said in a low tone: " If *I* am so much to blame for what has been done, perhaps it was because you were first of all at fault! At the beginning my one offence consisted in agreeing to your proposal. It was the *statesman* who committed that error, and the *man* has suffered for it ever since. You know nothing of jealousy, my child—how can you?—but its pains are as the pains of hell."

He tried to approach her once more.

" Come, dear, try to be yourself again. Forget this moment of fascination, and rise afresh to your old strength and wisdom. I am willing to forget . . . whatever has happened —I don't ask what. I am ready to wipe it all away, just as if it had never been."

In spite of his soft words and gentle tones, Roma was gazing at him with an aversion she had never felt before for any human being.

"Have no qualms about your marriage, my child. I assure you it is no marriage at all. In the eye of the civil law it is frankly invalid, and the Church could annul it at any moment, being no sacrament, because you are unbaptized and therefore not in her sense a Christian."

He took another step towards her and said:

"But if you have lost one husband another is waiting for you—a more devoted and more faithful husband—one who can give you everything in the place of one who can give you nothing. . . . And then that man has gone out of your life for good. Whatever happens now, it is impossible that you and he can ever come together again. But I am here still. . . . Don't answer hastily, Roma. Isn't it something that I am ready to face the opprobrium that will surely come of marrying the most criticised woman in Rome?"

Roma felt herself to be suffocating with indignation and shame.

"You see I am suing to you, Roma—I who have never sued to any human being. Even when I was a child I would not sue to my own mother. Since then I have done something in life—I have justified myself, I have given my country a place among the nations, I stand for it in the eye of the world—and yet——"

"And yet I despise you," said Roma.

There was a moment of silence, and then, recovering himself, the Baron tried to laugh.

"As you will. I must needs accept the only possible interpretation of your words. I thought my devotion in spite of every provocation might burn away your bitterness. But if . . ." (he was getting excited) "if you have no respect for the past, you may have some regard for the future."

She looked at him with a new fear.

"Naturally, I have no desire to humiliate myself further by suing to a woman who despises me. It will be sufficient to punish the man who is responsible for my loss of esteem in the eyes of one who has so many reasons to respect me."

" You mean that you will persuade the King to break his promise? "

" The King need not be persuaded after he has appointed his Dictator."

" So the King's promise to pardon Mr. Rossi will be set aside by his successor? "

" If I leave this room without a better answer . . . yes."

Roma drew from behind the revolver she had held in her hand.

" Then you will never leave this room," she said.

The Baron stood perfectly still, and there was a moment of deadly silence.

Then came the rattle of carriage wheels on the stones of the piazza, followed immediately by a hurried footstep on the stairs.

Roma heard it. She was trembling all over.

A moment afterwards there was a knock at the door. Then another knock, and another. It was imperative, irregular knocking.

Roma, who had forgotten all about the Baron, was rooted to the spot on which she stood. The Baron, who had understood everything, was also transfixed.

Then came a thick, vibrating voice, " Roma! "

Roma made a faint cry, and dropped the revolver out of her graspless hand. The Baron picked it up instantly. He was the first to recover himself.

" Hush! " he said in a whisper. " Let him come in. I will go into this room. I mean no harm to any one; but if he should follow me—if you should reveal my presence— remember what I said before about a challenge. And if I challenge him his shrift will have to be swift and sure."

The Baron stepped into the bedroom. Then the voice came again, " Roma! Roma! "

Roma staggered to the door and opened it.

VI

FLYING from the railway station in the coupé, down the Via Nazionale and the Corso Vittorio Emanuele, Rossi had seen by the electric light the remains of the day's festoons, triumphal arches, banners, embroideries, emblems, and flowers. These things had passed before his eyes like a flash, yet they had deepened the bitterness of his desire to meet with Roma that he might thrust the evidence of her treachery into her face.

But when he came to his own house and Roma opened the door to him, and he saw her, looking so ill, her cheeks so pale, her beautiful eyes so large and timid, and her whole face expressing such acute suffering, his anger began to ebb away, and he wanted to take her into his arms in spite of all.

Roma knew she was opening the door to Rossi, whatever the strange chance which had brought him there, and when she saw him she made a faint cry and a helpless little run toward him, and then stopped and looked frightened. The momentary sensation of joy and relief had instantly died away. She looked at his world-worn face, so disfigured by pain and humiliation, and the arms she had outstretched to meet him she raised above her head as if to ward off a blow.

He saw under the veil she wore the terror which had seized her at sight of him, and by that alone he knew the depths of the abyss between them. But this only increased the measureless pity he felt for her. And he could not look at her without feeling that whatever she had done he loved her, and must continue to love her to the last.

Tears rose to his throat and choked him. He opened his mouth to speak, but at first he could not utter a word. At length he fumbled at his breast, tore at his shirt front, so that his loose neckerchief became untied, and finally drew from an inner pocket a crumpled paper.

"Look!" he said with a kind of gasp.

She saw at a glance what the paper was, and dared not look at it a second time. It was the warrant. She dropped into a chair with bowed head and humble attitude, as if trying to sink out of sight.

"Tell me you know nothing about it, Roma."

She covered her face with both hands and was silent.

"Tell me."

She had expected that he would flame out at her, but his voice was breaking. She lifted her head and tried to look at him. His eyes were fixed on her with an expression she had never seen before. She wanted to speak, and could not do so. Her lip trembled, and she hung her head and covered her face again, unable to say a word.

By this time he knew full well that she was guilty, but

he tried to persuade himself that she was innocent, to make excuses for her, and to find her a way out.

"The newspapers say that the warrant was made at your instruction, Roma—that you were the informer who denounced me. It cannot be true. Tell me it is not true."

She did not speak.

"Look at the name on it—David Leone. There was only one person in the world who knew me by that name— only one."

She began to cry beneath her hands.

"I told you everything myself, Roma. It was in this very room, you remember, the night you came here first. You asked me if I wasn't afraid to tell you, and I answered no. You couldn't deceive the son of your own father. It wasn't natural. I was right, wasn't I?"

She felt him take hold of her hand and draw it down from her face.

"Look at the ring on your hand, dear. And look at this one on mine. You are my wife, Roma. Does a man's wife betray him?"

His voice cracked at every word.

"When we parted you promised that as long as you lived, wherever you might be, and whatever the world might do with us, you would be faithful to me to the last. You have kept your promise, haven't you? It isn't true that you have denounced me to the police."

He paused, but she did not reply, and he dropped her hand, and it fell like a lifeless thing to her side.

"I know it isn't true, dear, but I want to hear it from your own lips. One word—only one. Why shouldn't you speak? Say you know nothing of this warrant. Say that somebody else knew David Leone. It may be so—I cannot remember. Say . . . say anything. Don't you see I will believe you whatever you say, Roma?"

Roma could control herself no longer.

"I know quite well it is impossible for you to forgive me, David."

"Forgive!"

"But if I could explain . . ."

"Explain? What can there be to explain? Did you denounce me to the magistrate?"

"If you could only know what happened . . ."

"Did you denounce me to the magistrate?"

She looked with frightened eyes at the bedroom door, and then dropped to her knees.

"Have pity upon me."

"Did you denounce me to the magistrate?"

"Yes."

His pale face became ashen.

"Then it's true," he said in a voice that hardly passed his throat. "What my friends have been saying all along is true. They warned me against you from the first, but I wouldn't believe them. I was a fool, and *this* is my reward."

So saying he crushed the warrant in his hand and flung it at her feet.

Roma could bear no more. Making a great call on her resolution, she rose, turned towards the bedroom door, and, speaking in a loud voice in order that he who was within might hear, she said:

"David, I don't want to excuse myself or to blame anybody else, whoever it may be, and however wickedly he may have acted. But, from my soul and before God, I tell you that if I denounced you I did it for the best."

"The best!"

He laughed bitterly, but she forced herself to go on.

"When you went away you warned me that your enemies could be merciless. They *have* been merciless. First, they tempted me with the fear of poverty. I had been accustomed to wealth, comfort, luxury. Look round you, David—they are gone. Did I ever regret them? Never! I was rich enough in your love, and I would not have sacrificed that for a queen's crown."

She looked up at his tortured face and saw that it was full of scorn, but still she struggled on.

"Then they tempted me with jealousy. The forged letter which killed Bruno was intended to poison me. Did I believe it? No! I knew you loved me, and if you didn't, if you had deceived me, that made no difference. *I* loved *you*, and even if I lost you I should always love you, whatever happened."

Again she looked up into his face with her glistening eyes. It was not anger she saw there now, but an expression of bewilderment and of pain.

"Last of all, they tempted me with love itself. The treacherous tyrants deceived and intimidated the Pope— the good and saintly Pope—and through him they told me that your arrest was certain, your life in danger, and nothing could save you from your present peril but that I should denounce you for your past offences. The phantom of conspiracy rose up before me, and I remembered my father, doomed to life-long exile and a lonely death. It was my dark hour, dearest, and when they promised me—faithfully promised me—that your life should be spared . . ."

A faint sound came from the bedroom. Roma heard it, but Rossi, in the tumult of his emotion, heard nothing.

"I know what you will say, dear—that you would have given your life a hundred times rather than save it at the loss of all you hold so dear. But I am no heroine, David. I am only a woman who loves you, and I could not see you die."

He felt his soul swell with love and forgiveness, and he wanted to sob like a child, but Roma went on, and without trying to keep back her tears.

"That's all, dear. Now you know everything. It is not your fault that the love you have brought home to me is dead. I hoped that before you came home I might die too. I think my soul must be dead already. I do not hope for pardon, but if your great heart *could* pardon me . . ."

"Roma," said Rossi at last, while tears filled his eyes and choked his voice, "when I escaped from the police I came here to avenge myself; but if you say it was your love that led you to denounce me . . ."

"I do say so."

"Your love, and nothing but your love . . ."

"Nothing! Nothing!"

"Though I am betrayed and fallen, and may be banished or condemned to death, yet . . ."

Her heart swelled and throbbed. She held out her arms to him.

"David!" she cried, and at the next moment she was clasped to his breast.

Again there was a faint sound from the adjoining room.

"The woman lies," said a voice behind them.

The Baron stood in the bedroom door.

VII

The Baron's impulse on going into the bedroom had been merely to escape from one who must be a runaway prisoner, and therefore little better than a madman, whose worst madness would be provoked by his own presence; but when he realised that Rossi was self-possessed, and even magnanimous in his hour of peril, the Baron felt ashamed of his hiding-place, and felt compelled to come out. In spite of his pride he had been forced to overhear the conversation, and he was humiliated by the generosity of the betrayed man, but what humbled him most was the clear note of the woman's love.

Knight of the Annunziata! Cousin of the King! President of the Council! Dictator! These things had meant something to him an hour ago. What were they now?

The agony of the Baron's jealousy was intolerable. For the first time in his life his ideas, usually so clear and exact, became confused. Roma was lost to him. He was going mad.

He looked at the revolver which he had snatched up when Roma let it fall, examined it, made sure it was loaded, cocked it, put it in the right-hand pocket of his overcoat, and then opened the door.

The two in the other room did not at first see him. He spoke, and their arms slackened and they stood apart.

After a moment of silence Rossi spoke. "Roma," he said, "what is this gentleman doing here?"

The Baron laughed. "Wouldn't it be more reasonable to ask what you are doing here, sir?" he asked.

Then trying to put into logical sequence the confused ideas which were besieging his tormented brain, he said, "I understand that this apartment belongs now to the lady; the lady belongs to me, and when she denounced you to the police it was merely in fulfilment of a plan we concocted together on the day you insulted both of us in your speech in the piazza."

Rossi made a step forward with a threatening gesture, but Roma intervened. The Baron gripped firmly the revolver in his pocket, and said:

"Take care, sir. If a man threatens me he must be prepared for the consequences. The lady knows what those consequences may be."

Rossi, breathing heavily, was trying to retain the mastery of himself.

"If you tell me that the lady . . ."

"I tell you that according to the law of nature and of reason the lady is my wife."

"It's a lie."

"Ask her."

" And so I will."

Roma saw the look of triumph with which Rossi turned to her. The terrible moment she had lived in fear of had come to pass. The letters she had written to Rossi had not yet reached him, and her enemy was telling his story before she had told hers.

What was she to do? She would have said anything at that moment and believed herself justified before God. But even lying itself would be of no avail. She remembered the Baron's threat and trembled. If she told the truth her confession, coming at that moment, would be worse than vain. If she told a lie, Rossi would insult the Baron, the Baron would challenge Rossi, and they would fight with all the consequences the Baron had foretold.

" Roma," said Rossi, " forgive me for putting the question, but a falsehood like this, affecting the character of a good woman, ought to be stopped in the slanderer's throat. Don't be afraid, dear. You know I will believe you before anybody in the world. What the man says is a lie, isn't it? "

Roma stood for a moment looking in a helpless way from Rossi to the Baron, and from the Baron back to Rossi. She made an effort to speak, but at first she could not do so. At length she said:

" Can't you trust me, David? "

" Trust you? Answer me on this one point and I will trust you on all the rest. Say the man speaks falsely, and I will stake my life on your word."

Roma did not reply, and the Baron tried to laugh.

" If the lady can deny what I say, let her do so. If she cannot, you must come to your own conclusions."

" Deny it, Roma! Deny it, and I will fling the man's insult in his face."

" David, if I could tell you everything . . ."

" Everything! It's only one thing I want to know, Roma."

" If you had received my letters addressed to England . . ."

" Letters? What matter about letters now. Don't you understand, dear? This gentleman says that before you married me you . . . had already belonged to him. That's what he means, and it's false, isn't it? "

" My mouth is closed. If I could say anything one way or other . . ."

" Yes or no—that is all that is necessary."

Roma looked up at him with a pleading expression, but seeing nothing in his face except the magistrate who was interrogating her, she turned her back and hung her head, and cried like a helpless child.

Rossi laid hold of her arm, twisted her about, and looked into her eyes.

"Crying, Roma? You don't mean to tell me that I am to believe what the man says? Deny it! For God's sake deny it!"

"I . . . I cannot . . . I cannot speak," she stammered, and then there was a dead silence.

When Rossi spoke again his face was dark as a thundercloud, and his voice hoarse as a raven's.

"If that is so, there is nothing more to say."

She looked up at him with a pathetic remonstrance, but he met her eyes with the gaze of a relentless judge who had tried and condemned her.

"I was not to blame, David—I swear before God I was not."

"Yet you allowed me to go on believing that falsehood. The woman who could do a thing like that could do anything. She could pretend to be poor, pretend to be tempted, pretend . . ."

"David, what are you saying?"

Rossi broke into a peal of mad laughter.

"Saying? That you have deceived me from the beginning, when you undertook to betray me to your master and paramour."

"David!"

She tried to protest, but he bore her down with a laugh of scorn, and then wheeled round on the Baron, who had been standing in silence behind them.

"That's why you are here to-night, I suppose. You didn't expect to be disturbed, did you? You didn't expect to see me. You thought I was stowed away in a cell, and you could meet in safety . . . Oh, my brain! my brain! I shall go mad!"

"It isn't true," cried Roma. And turning to the Baron with flame in her eyes she said, "Tell him it isn't true. You know it isn't true."

"True?" Again the Baron tried to laugh. "Of course it's true. Every word the man has uttered is true. Don't ask me to lie to him as you have done from first to last."

THE KING

At that Rossi's mad laughter stopped suddenly, and he stepped up to the Baron with fury in his face.

"You scoundrel!" he said. "You've succeeded, you've separated us, but I understand you perfectly. You have used this unhappy lady's shame to compel her to carry out your infamous designs, and now that she is done with, she must lose the man who played with her as well as the man she has played with."

Roma saw that the Baron was feeling for something in the side pocket of his overcoat, and she called to Rossi to warn him.

"One doesn't quarrel with an escaped criminal," said the Baron. "It is sufficient to call the police . . . Police!" he cried, lifting his voice and taking a step forward.

Rossi stood between the Baron and the door.

"Don't stir," he said. "Don't utter a word, I warn you. I'm a hunted dog to-night, and a hunted dog is dangerous."

"Let me pass," said the Baron.

"Not yet, sir," said Rossi. "You have something to do before you go. You have to go down on your knees and beg the pardon of your victim . . ."

Roma saw the Baron draw the revolver. She saw Rossi spring upon him, and seize him by the collar of the Annunziata which hung over his shirt front. She saw the men go struggling through the door of the sitting-room into the dining-room. She covered her ears with her hands to shut out the sounds from the outer chamber, but she heard Rossi's hoarse voice that was like the growl of a wild beast. Then came the deafening report of a pistol-shot, then the vibration of a heavy fall, and then dead silence.

Roma was still standing with her hands over her ears, shaking with terror and scarcely able to breathe, when footsteps resounded on the floor behind her. Giddy and dazed, with one agonising thought she turned, saw Rossi, and uttered a cry of relief. But he was coming down on her with great staring eyes, and the look of a desperate maniac. For one moment he stood over her in his ungovernable rage, and scalding and blistering words poured out of him in a torrent.

"He's dead. D'you hear me? He's dead. But it's as much your work as mine, and you will never think of yourself henceforward without remorse and horror. I curse you by the love you've wronged and the heart you've broken. I curse you by the hopes you wasted and the truth you've outraged. I curse you by the memory of your father, the memory of a saint and martyr."

Before his last words were spoken Roma had ceased to hear. With a feeble moan, interrupted by a faint cry, she had slowly retreated before him, and then fallen face downwards. Everything about her, Rossi, herself, the room, the lamp on the table and the shadows cast by it, had mingled and blended, and gone out in a complete obscurity.

VIII

When Roma regained consciousness, there was not a sound in the apartment. Even the piazza outside was quiet. Somebody was playing a mandoline a long way off, and the thin notes were trembling through the still night. A dog was barking in the distance. Save for these sounds everything was still.

Roma lay for some minutes in a state of semi-consciousness. Her head was swimming with vague memories, and she was unable at first to disentangle the thread of them. At length she remembered all that had happened, and she wept bitterly.

But when the first tenderness was over the one feeling which seized and held her was hatred of the Baron. Rossi had told her the man was dead, and she felt no pity. The Baron deserved his death, and if Rossi had killed him it was no crime.

She was still lying where she had fallen when a noise as of some one moving came from the adjoining room. Then a voice called to her:

"Roma!"

It was the Baron's voice, broken and feeble. A great terror took hold of her. Then came a sense of shame, and finally a feeling of relief. The Baron was not dead. Thank God! O thank God!

She got up and went into the dining-room. The Baron was on his knees struggling to climb to the couch. His shirt front was partly dragged out of his breast, and the Order of the Annunziata was torn away. There was a streak of blood over his left eyebrow, and no other sign of injury. But his eyes themselves were glassy, and his face was pale as death.

"I'm dying, Roma."

"I'll run for a doctor," she said.

"No. Don't do that. I don't want to be found here. Besides, it's useless. In five minutes a clot of blood will have covered the lacerated brain, and I shall lose consciousness again. Stupid, isn't it?"

"Let me call for a priest," said Roma.

"Don't do that either. You can do me more good yourself, Roma. Give me a drink."

Roma was fighting with an almost unconquerable repugnance, but she brought the Baron a drink of water, and with shaking hands held the glass to his trembling lips.

"How do you feel?" she asked.

"Worse," he answered.

He looked into her eyes with evident contrition, and said, "I wonder if it would be fair to ask you to forgive me? Would it?"

She did not answer, and he stretched himself and sighed. His breathing became laboured and stertorous, his skin hot, and his eyes dilated.

"How do you feel now?" asked Roma.

"I'm going," he replied, and he smiled again.

The human soul was gleaming out of the wretched man at the last, and he was looking at her now with pleading eyes which plainly could not see.

"Are you there, Roma?"

"Yes."

"Promise that you will not leave me."

"I will not leave you now," she answered in a low voice.

After a moment he roused himself with an effort and said, "And this is the end! How absurd! They'll find me here in any case, and what a chatter there'll be! The Chamber—the journals—all the scribblers and speechifiers. What will Europe say? Another Boulanger, perhaps! But I'm sorry for Italy. Nobody can say I did not love my country. Where her interest lay I let nothing interfere. And just when everything seemed to triumph . . ."

He attempted to laugh. Roma shuddered.

"It was the star of the Annunziata that did it. The man threw it with such force. To think that it's been the aim of my life to win that Order and now it kills me! Ridiculous, isn't it?"

Again he attempted to laugh.

"There's a side of justice in that, though, and I'm not going to whine. The Pope tried to paint an awful end, but his nightmare didn't frighten me. We must all bow our heads to the law of compensation—the Pope as well as everybody else. But to die stupidly like this . . ."

He was speaking with difficulty, and dragging at his shirt front. Roma opened it at the neck, and something dropped on to the floor. It was a lock of glossy black hair tied with a red ribbon such as lawyers used to bind documents together. Dull as his sight was, he saw it.

"Yours, Roma! You were ill with fever when you first came to Rome, you remember. The doctors cut off your beautiful hair. This was some of it. I've worn it ever since. Silly, wasn't it?"

Tears began to shine in Roma's eyes. The cynical man who laughed at sentiment had carried the tenderest badge of it in his breast.

"I used to wear some of my mother's in the same place when I was younger. She was a good woman, too. When she put me to bed she used to repeat something: 'Hold Thou my hands,' I think. . . . May I hold your hands, Roma?"

Roma turned away her head, but she held out her hand, and the dying man kissed it.

"What a beautiful hand it is! I think I should know it among all the hands in the world. How stupid! People have been afraid of me all my life, Roma; even my mother was afraid of me when I was a child; but to die without once having known what it was to have some one to love you. . . . I believe I'm beginning to rave."

The mournful irony of the words was belied by the tremulous voice.

"My little comedy is played out, I suppose, and when the curtain is down it is time to go home. Death is a solemn sort of homegoing, Roma, and if those we've injured cannot forgive us before we go . . ."

But the battle of hate in Roma's heart was over. She had remembered Rossi and that had swept away all her bitterness. As the Baron stood to her, so she stood to her husband. They were two unforgiven ones, both guilty and ashamed.

"Indeed, indeed I do forgive you, as I hope to be forgiven," she said, whereupon he laughed again, but with a different note altogether.

Then he asked her to lift up his head. She placed a cushion under it, but still he called on her to lift his head higher.

" Can you lift me in your arms, Roma? . . . Higher still. So! . . . Can you hold me there?"

" How do you feel now?" she asked.

" It won't be long," he answered. His respirations came in whiffs.

Roma began to repeat as much as she could remember of the prayers for the dying which she had heard at the death-bed of her aunt. The dying man smiled an indulgent smile into the young woman's beautiful and mournful face and allowed her to go on. As she prayed faster and faster, saying the same words over and over again, she felt his breathing grow more faint and irregular. At length it seemed to stop, and thinking it was gone altogether, she made the sign of the cross and said:

" We commend to Thee, O Lord, the soul of Thy servant Gabriel, that being dead to the world he may live to Thee, and those sins which through the frailty of human life he has committed, Thou by the indulgence of Thy most merciful loving-kindness may wipe out, through Christ our Lord. Amen."

Then the glazed eyes opened wide and lighted up with a pitiful smile.

" I'm dying in your arms, Roma."

Then a long breath, and then:

" Adieu!"

He had tried to subdue all men to his will, and there was one man he had subdued above all others—himself. There is a greater man than the great man—the man who is too great to be great.

IX

THERE had been no light in the dining-room except the reflection from the lamp in the sitting-room, and now it fell with awful shadows on the whitening face turned upward on the couch. The pains of death had given a distorted expression, and the eyes remained open. Roma wished to close them, but dared not try, and the image of inanimate objects standing in the light was mirrored in their dull and glassy surface. The dog in the distance was still barking, and a company of tipsy revellers were passing through the piazza singing a drinking song with a laugh in it. When they were gone the clocks outside began to strike. It was one o'clock, and the hour seemed to dance over the city in single steps.

Roma's terror became unbearable. Feeling herself to be a murderer, she acted on a murderer's impulse and prepared to fly. When she recalled the emotions with which she had determined to kill the Baron and then deliver herself up to justice, they seemed so remote that they might have existed only in a dream or belonged to another existence.

Trembling from head to foot, and scarcely able to support herself, she fixed her hat and veil afresh, put on her coat, and, taking one last fearful look at the wide-open eyes on the couch, she went backwards to the door. She dared not turn round from a creeping fear that something might touch her on the shoulder.

The door was open. No doubt Rossi had left it so, and she had not noticed the circumstance until now. She had got as far as the first landing when a poignant memory came to her —the memory of how she had first descended those stairs with Rossi, going side by side, and almost touching. The feeling that she had been fatal to the man since then nearly choked and blinded her, but it urged her on. If she remained until some one came, and the crime was discovered, what was she to say that would not incriminate her husband?

Suddenly she became aware of sounds from below—the measured footsteps of soldiers. She knew who they were. They were the Carabineers, and they were coming for Rossi, who had escaped and was being pursued.

Roma turned instantly, and with a noiseless step fled back to the door of the apartment, opened it with her latch-key, closed it silently, and bolted it on the inside. This was done before she knew what she was doing, and when she regained full possession of her faculties she was in the sitting-room, and the Carabineers were ringing at the electric bell.

They rang repeatedly. Roma stood in the middle of the floor, listening and holding her breath.

"Deuce take it!" said a voice outside. "Why doesn't the woman open the door if she doesn't want to get herself into trouble? She's at home, at all events."

"So is he, if I know anything," said a second voice. "He drove here anyway—not a doubt about that."

"Let's see the porter—he'll have another key."

"The old fool is out at the illuminations. But listen . . ." (the door rattled as if some one was shaking it). "This door is fastened on the inside."

There was a chuckling laugh, and then, "All right, boys! Down with it!"

A moment afterwards the door was broken open and four Carabineers were in the dining-room. Roma awaited their irruption without a word. She continued to stand in the middle of the sittting-room looking straight before her.

"Holy saints, what's this?" cried the voice she had heard first, and she knew that the Carabineers were bending over the body on the couch.

"His Excellency!"

"Lord save us!"

Roma's head was dizzy, and something more was said which she did not follow. At the next moment the Carabineers had entered the sitting-room; she was standing face to face with them, and they were questioning her.

"The Honourable Rossi is here, isn't he?"

"No," she answered in a timid voice.

"But he has been here, hasn't he?"

"No," she answered more boldly.

"Do you mean to say that the Honourable Rossi has not been here to-night?"

"I do," she said, with exaggerated emphasis.

The marshal of the Carabineers, who had been speaking, looked attentively at her for a moment, and then he called on his men to search the rooms.

"What's this?" said the marshal, taking up a sealed letter from the bureau and reading the superscription: 'L'on, Davide Rossi, Carceri Giudiziarie, di Milano.'"

"That's a letter I wrote to my husband and haven't yet posted," said Roma.

"But what's this?" cried a voice from the dining-room. "Presented to the Honourable David Rossi by the Italian colony in Zürich."

Roma sank into a seat. It was the revolver. She had forgotten it.

"That's all right," said the marshal, with the same chuckle as before.

Dizzy and almost blind in her terror, Roma struggled to her feet. "The revolver belongs to me," she said. "Mr.

Rossi left it in my keeping when he went away two months ago, and since that time he has never touched it."

" Then who fired the shot that killed his Excellency, Signora ? "

" *I* did," said Roma.

Instinctively the man removed his hat.

Within half-an-hour Roma had repeated her statement at the Regina Cœli, and the Carabineers, to prevent a public scandal, had smuggled the body of the Baron, under the cover of night, to his office in the Palazzo Braschi, on the opposite side of the piazza.

X

ONE thought was supreme in David Rossi's mind when he left the Piazza Navona—that the world in which he had lived was shaken to its foundations and his life was at an end. The unhappy man wandered about the streets without asking himself where he was going or what was to become of him.

Many feelings tore his heart, but the worst of them was anger. He had taken the life of the Baron. The man deserved his death, and he felt no pity for his victim and no remorse for his crime. But that he should have killed the Minister, he who had twice stood between him and death, he who had resisted the doctrine of violence and all his life preached the gospel of peace, this was a degradation too shameful and abject.

The woman had been the beginning and end of everything. " How I hate her! " he thought. He was telling himself for the hundredth time that he had never hated anybody so much before, when he became aware that he had returned to the neighbourhood of the Piazza Navona. Without knowing what he was doing, he had been walking round and round it.

He began to picture Roma as he had seen her that night. The beautiful, mournful, pleading face, which he had not really seen while his eyes looked on it, now rose before the eye of his mind. This caused a wave of tenderness to pass over him against his will, and his heart, so full of hatred, began to melt with love.

All the cruel words he had spoken at parting returned to his memory, and he told himself that he had been too hasty. Instead of bearing her down he should have listened to her explanation. Before the Baron entered the room she had been at the point of swearing that her love, and nothing but her love, had caused her to betray him.

He told himself she had lied, but the thought was hell, and to escape from it he made for the bank of the river again. This time he crossed the bridge of St. Angelo, and passed up the Borgo to the piazza of St. Peter's. But the piazza itself awakened a crowd of memories. It was there in a balcony that he had first seen Roma, not plainly, but vaguely in a summer cloud of lace and sunshades.

Then it occurred to him that it must have been on this spot that Roma was inspired with the plot which had ended with his betrayal. At that thought all the bitterness of his soul returned. He told himself she deserved every word he had said to her, and blamed himself for the humiliation he had gone through in his attempt to make excuses for what she had done. To the curse he had hurled at her at the last moment he added words of fiercer anger, and though they were spoken only in his brain, or to the dark night and the rolling river, they intensified his fury.

" Oh, how I hate her! " he thought.

The piazza was quiet. There was a light in the Pope's windows, and a Swiss Guard was patrolling behind the open wicket of the bronze gate to the Vatican. A porter in gorgeous livery was yawning by the door of the Prime Minister's palace. The man was waiting for his master. He would *have* to wait.

The clock of St. Peter's struck one, and the silent place began to be peopled with many shadows. The scene of the Pope's jubilee returned to Rossi's mind. He saw and heard everything over again. The crowd, the gorgeous procession, the Pope, and last of all his own speech. A sardonic smile crossed his face in the darkness as he thought of what he had said.

" Is it possible that I can ever have believed those fables? "

He was tramping down the Trastevere, picturing his trial for the murder of the Baron, with Roma in the witness-box and himself in the dock. The cold horror of it all was insupportable, and he told himself that there was only one place in which he could escape from despair.

The unhappy man had begun to think of taking his own life. He had always condemned suicide. He had even con-

27   411

demned it in Bruno. But it was the death grip of a man utterly borne down, and there was nothing else to hold on to.

The day began to break, and he turned back towards the piazza of St. Peter's, thinking of what he intended to do and where he would do it. By the end of the Hospital of Santo Spirito there was a little blind alley bounded by a low wall. Below was the quick turn of the Tiber, and no swimmer was strong enough to live long in the turbulent waters at that point. He would do it there.

The streets were silent, and in the grey dawn, that mystic hour of parturition when the day is being born and things are seen in places where they do not exist, when ships sail in the sky and mountains rise around lowland cities, David Rossi became aware in a moment that a woman was walking on the pavement in front of him. He could almost have believed that it was Roma, the figure was so tall and full and upright. But the woman's dress was poorer, and she was carrying a bundle in her arms. When he looked again he saw that her bundle was a child, and that she was weeping over it.

" Taking her little one to the hospital," he thought.

But on turning into the little Borgo he saw that the woman went up to the little Rota, knelt before it, kissed the child again and again, put it in the cradle, pulled the bell, and then, crying bitterly, hastened away.

Rossi remembered his own mother, and a great tide of simple human tenderness swept over him. What he had seen the woman do was what his mother had done thirty-five years before. He saw it all as by a mystic flash of light, which looked back into the past.

Suddenly it occurred to him that the Rota had been long since closed, and therefore it was physically impossible that anybody could have put a child into the cradle. Then he remembered that he had not heard the bell, or the woman's footsteps, or the sound of her voice when she wept.

He stopped and looked back. The woman was returning in the direction of the piazza of St. Peter's. By an impulse which he could not resist he followed her, overtook her, and looked into her face.

Again he thought he was looking at Roma. There was the same nobility in the beautiful features, the same sweetness in the tremulous mouth, the same grandeur in the great dark eyes. But he knew perfectly who it was. It was his mother.

THE KING

It did not seem strange that his mother should be there. From her home in heaven she had come down to watch over her son on earth. She had always been watching over him. And now that he too was betrayed and lost, now that he too was broken-hearted and alone . . .

He was utterly unmanned. "Mother! Mother! I am coming to you! Every door is closed against me, and I have nowhere to go to for refuge. I am coming! . . . I am coming!"

Then the spirit paused, and pointing to the bronze gate of the Vatican, said, with infinite tenderness:

"Go there!"

PART NINE—THE PEOPLE

I

THE Pope awoke next morning in the dreary hour of cock-crow, and rang for his valet while he was still in bed. When the valet came he was greatly agitated.

"What's amiss, Gaetanino?" said the Pope.

"A madman, your Holiness," said the valet. "They wanted me to awaken your Holiness, and I wouldn't do it. A madman is down at the bronze gate, and insists on seeing you."

At this moment the Maestro di Camera came into the room. He also was greatly agitated.

"What is this about some poor madman at the bronze gate?" asked the Pope.

"I have come to tell your Holiness," said the master of the household. "The man declares he is pursued, and demands sanctuary."

"Who is he?"

"He says he will give his name to the Holy Father only; but his face . . ."

"The man's mad," said the valet.

"Be quiet, Gaetanino."

"His face," continued the Maestro di Camera, "is known to the Swiss Guard, and when they sent up word . . ."

The Pope sat up and said, "Is it perhaps . . ."

"It is, your Holiness."

"Where is he now?"

"He has forced his way in as far as the Sala Clementina, and nothing but physical force . . ."

Sounds of voices raised in dispute could be heard in a distant room. The Pope listened and said:

"Let the man come up immediately."

"Here, your Holiness?"

"Here."

The Maestro di Camera had hardly gone from the Pope's

414

bedroom when the Secretary of State entered it with hasty steps.

"Your Holiness," he said, "you will not allow yourself to receive this person? It is sufficiently clear that he must have escaped from the police during the night, probably by the help of confederates, and to shelter him will be to come into collision with the civil authorities."

"The young man demands sanctuary, your Eminence, and whatever the consequences we have no right to refuse it."

"But sanctuary is obsolete, your Holiness."

"Nothing can be obsolete that is of divine institution, your Eminence."

"But, your Holiness, it can only exist by virtue of concession from the State, and the present relation of the Church to the State of Italy . . ."

"Your Eminence, I will ask you to let the young man come in."

"Your Holiness, I beg, I pray, reflect . . ."

"Let the young man come in, your Em . . ."

The Pope had not finished when the words were struck out of his mouth by an apparition which appeared at his bedroom door. It was that of a young man, whose eyes were wild, whose nostrils were quivering, and whose clothes hung about him in rags as if they had been torn in a recent struggle. He had a look of despair and suffering, yet it was the same to the Pope at that moment as if he were looking at his own features in a glass.

The young man was surrounded by Swiss Guards, and the Maestro di Camera pushed in ahead of him. Coming face to face with the Pope propped up in his bed, the loud tones on which he was protesting died in his throat, and he stood in silence on the threshold of the room.

The Pope was the first to speak.

"What is it you wish to say to me, my son?"

The young man seemed to recover his self-possession, but without a genuflexion or even a bow of the head, and with a slightly defiant manner, he said, "My name is David Leone. They call me Rossi, because that was my mother's name, and they said I had no right to my father's. I am a Roman, and I have been two months abroad. For ten years I have worked for the people, and now I am denounced and betrayed to the police. Three days ago I was arrested on returning to Italy, and to-night by the help of friends I have escaped from the Carabineers. But every gate is closed against me, and I cannot get out of Rome. This is the Vatican, and the Vatican is sanctuary. Will you take me in?"

The Pope looked at the Swiss Guard, and said in a tremulous voice, " Gentlemen, you will take this young man to your own quarters, and see that no Carabineer lays hand on him without my knowledge and consent."

" Your Holiness! " protested the Cardinal Secretary, but the Pope raised his hand and silenced him.

Rossi's defiant manner left him. " Wait," he said. " Before you decide to take me in you must know more about me, and what I am charged with. I am the Deputy Rossi who is said to have instigated the late riots. The warrant for my arrest accuses me of treason and an attempt on the person of the late King. It is false, but you must look at it for yourself. Here it is."

So saying he plunged into his pocket for the paper, and then said, " It is gone! I remember now—I flung it at the feet of my betrayer."

" Gentlemen," said the Pope, still addressing the Swiss Guard, " if the civil authorities attempt to arrest this young man, you may tell them they can only do so by giving a written promise of safety for life and limb."

Rossi's wild eyes began to melt. " You are very good," he said, " and I will not deceive you. Although I am innocent of the crime they charge me with, I have broken the law of God and of my country, and if you have any fear of the consequences you must turn me out while there is still time."

" Gentlemen," said the Pope, " instead of taking this young man to your quarters, let him be lodged in the empty apartment below my own, which was formerly occupied by the Secretary of State."

Rossi broke down utterly and fell to his knees. The Pope raised two fingers and blessed him.

" Go to your room and rest, my son, and God grant you a little repose."

" Father! "

By an impulse he could not resist, Rossi had risen from his knees, taken two or three steps forward, knelt again by the side of the bed, and put his lips to the Pope's hand.

With wet eyes that gleamed under his grey brows the

THE PEOPLE

Pope followed the young man out until, surrounded by the Swiss Guard, he had passed from the room. Then he rose and turned into his private chapel for his early Mass.

II

LESS than half-an-hour afterwards a rumour swept through the Vatican like the gust of whistling wind that goes before a storm. The Pope met it as he was coming from Mass.

" What is it, Gaetanino ? " he asked.

" Something about an assassination, your Holiness," said the valet, and the Pope stood as if thunderstruck, for he thought of Rossi and the King.

After a while the vague report became more definite. It was not the King but the Prime Minister who had been assassinated.

The Pope's private room began to fill with pallid faces. The Cardinal Secretary was there, the Maestro di Camera, and at length the little Majordomo. By this time a special message had reached the Vatican from one of its watchers outside, and they were able to discuss the circumstances. The Prime Minister had been found dead in his official palace in the Piazza Navona. He had dined at the Quirinal and remained there for the opening of the State Ball, therefore he could not have reached the Palazzo Braschi before eleven or twelve o'clock. Two shots had been heard about midnight, and the body had been discovered in the early morning.

The Pope listened and said nothing.

The Cardinal Secretary told another story. The Deputy Rossi, who had been brought to Rome by the train from Genoa, which arrived punctually at 11.45, had been rescued by a gang of ruffians at the station. The rescue had been prearranged, and the man had jumped into a coupé and driven off at a gallop. The coupé had gone down the Via Nazionale, and a few minutes before twelve o'clock it had been seen to turn into the Piazza Navona. It was by the accident that the Carabineers had followed in pursuit of the escaped prisoner that the murder had been discovered.

Still the Pope said nothing. But his head was held down, and his soul was full of trouble.

The group of prelates looked into each other's faces with suspicion and terror. A storm was gathering round the Vatican, and who could say what would happen if the Pope persisted in the course he had just taken? At length the Cardinal Secretary approached his Holiness, and said, with a deep genuflexion:

"Holy Father, I fear the tenderness of your fatherly heart has betrayed you into sheltering a criminal. It is not merely that the man Rossi is a revolutionary accused of an attempt to overthrow the Government of his country. There cannot be a question that he is a murderer also, and if you keep him here you will violate the law of every civilised State and expose yourself to the condemnation of the world."

The Pope did not reply. Other words in another voice were drumming in his ears with a new and terrible meaning: "I have broken the law of God and of my country, and if you have any fear of the consequences you must turn me out while there is still time."

"Your Holiness will also remember," said the Cardinal Secretary, "that by the regulation of the civil authorities which guarantees to the Holy Father the rights of sovereignty, it is expressly stated that he holds no powers which are contrary to the laws of the State and of public order. Therefore to conceal and protect a criminal would be of itself to commit a crime, and God alone can say what the consequence might be to the Vatican and to the Church."

"Oh, silence! silence!" cried the Pope, lifting a face full of suffering. "Leave me! leave me!"

The Cardinal Secretary and his colleagues bowed to the Pope and backed out of the room. A moment afterwards the young Monsignor entered. He was bringing a newspaper in his hand, for as Cameriere Participante he was one of the Pope's readers.

"Holy Father," he said in his nervous voice, "I bring you bad news."

"What is it, my son?" said the Pope, with a pitiful expression.

"The assassin of the Prime Minister turns out to be some one . . ."

"Well?"

"Some one known to your Holiness."

THE PEOPLE

"Don't be afraid for the Holy Father. . . . Tell me, Monsignor."

"It is a lady, your Holiness."

"A lady?"

"She has been arrested and has confessed."

"Confessed?"

"It is Donna Roma Volonna, your Holiness. She shot the Prime Minister with a revolver, and her motive was revenge."

The Pope lifted his head, and looked at the young Monsignor with an expression which no language can describe. Relief, joy, shame, and remorse were mingled in one flash on his broken and bankrupt face. He was silent for a moment, and then he said:

"Say nothing of this to the young man in the room below. If he is in sanctuary let him also be in peace. Whatever he is to hear of the world without must come through me alone. Give that as my order to everybody. And may God who has had mercy on His servant be good to us all!"

III

In penance for the joy he had felt on learning that Roma, not Rossi, had assassinated the Minister, the Pope became her advocate in his own mind, and watched for an opportunity to save her. Every day for a week Monsignor Mario read the newspapers to the Pope that he might be fully abreast of what occurred.

The first morning the journals merely reported the crime. The headless one with the fearful hands had stalked over the city in the middle of night in the shape of incarnate murder, and the citizens of Rome would awake to hear the news with consternation, horror, and shame.

The evening journals contained obituary articles and appreciations of the dead man's character. He was the Richelieu of Italy, the chivalrous and devoted servant of his country, and one of the noblest figures of the age.

"Extras" were published giving descriptions of the city under the first effects of the terrible news. Rome was literally draped in mourning. It was a forest of flags at halfmast. All public buildings, embassies, cafés, and places of public amusement were closed.

The Pope was puzzled, and calling a member of his Noble Guard (it was the Count de Raymond) he sent him out into the city to see.

When the Count de Raymond returned he told another story. The people, while deploring the crime, were not surprised at it. Baron Bonelli had refused to understand the wants of the nation. He had treated the people as slaves and shed their blood in the streets. Where such opinions were not openly expressed there was a gloomy silence. Groups could be seen under the great lamps in the Corso reading the evening papers. Sometimes a man would mount a chair in front of the Café Aragno and read aloud from the latest "extra." The crowd would listen, stand a moment, and then disperse.

Next day the journals were full of the assassin. Many things were incomprehensible in her character, unless you approached it with the right key. Young and with a fatal beauty, fantastic, audacious, a great coquette, always giving out a perfume of seduction and feminine ruin, she was one of those women who live in the atmosphere of infamous intrigue, and her last victim had been her first friend.

Once more the Pope was puzzled, and he sent out his Noble Guard again. The Count de Raymond returned to say that in corners of the cafés people spoke of the Baron as a dead dog, and said that if Donna Roma had killed him she did a good act, and God would reward her.

Parliament opened after its Easter vacation, and the Count de Raymond was sent in plain clothes to its first sitting. The galleries and lobbies were filled, and there was suppressed but intense excitement. Rumour said the Government had resigned, and that the King, who was in despair, had been unable to form another ministry. A leader of the Right was heard to say that Donna Roma had done more for the people in a day than the Opposition could have accomplished in a hundred years. "If these agitators on the Left have any qualities of statesmen, now's their time to show it," he said. But what would Parliament say about the dead man? The President entered and took his chair. After the minutes had been read there was a moment's silence. Not a word was uttered, not a voice was raised. "Let us pass on to the next business," said the President.

The assizes happened to be in session, and the opening of

the trial was reported on the following day. When the prisoner was asked whether she pleaded guilty or not guilty, she answered guilty. The court, however, requested her to reconsider her plea, assigned her an advocate, and went through all the formalities of an ordinary case. A principal object of the prosecution had been to discover accomplices, but the prisoner continued to protest that she had none. She neither denied nor extenuated the crime, and she acknowledged it to have been premeditated. When asked to state her motive, she said it was hatred of the methods adopted by the dead man to wipe out political opponents, and a determination to send to the bar of the Almighty one who had placed himself above human law.

The Pope sent his Noble Guard to the next day's hearing of the trial, and when the Count de Raymond came back his eyes were red and swollen. The beautiful and melancholy face of the young prisoner sitting behind iron bars that were like the cage of a wild beast had made a pitiful impression. Her calmness, her total self-abandonment, the sublime feelings that even in the presence of a charge of murder expressed themselves in her sweet voice, had moved everybody to tears. Then the prosecution had been so debasing in its questions about her visits to the Vatican and in its efforts to implicate David Rossi by means of a letter addressed to the prison at Milan.

"But I did it," the young prisoner had said again and again with steadfast fervour, only deepening to alarm when evidence concerning the revolver seemed to endanger the absent man.

There had been some conflicting medical evidence as to whether the death could have been due to a pistol-shot, and certain astounding disclosures of police corruption and prison tyranny. A judge of the Military Tribunal had given startling proof of the Prime Minister's complicity in an infamous case, ending with the suicide of the prisoner's man-servant in open court, and an old Garibaldian among the people, packed away beyond the barrier, had cried out:

"He was just a black-dyed villain, and God Almighty save us from such another."

This laying bare of the machinery of statecraft had made a great sensation, and even the judge on the bench, being a just man, had lowered his eyes before the accused at the bar. As the prisoner was taken back to prison past the Castle of

St. Angelo and the Military College, the crowds had cheered her again and again, and sitting in an open car with a Carabineer by her side, she had looked frightened at finding herself a heroine where she had expected to be a malefactor.

"Poor child!" said the Pope. "But who knows the hidden designs of Providence, whether manifest in the path of His justice or His mercy?"

Next day, when the Noble Guard returned to the Vatican, he could scarcely speak to tell his story. The trial had ended and the prisoner was condemned. Reluctantly the judge had sentenced her to life-long imprisonment. She had preserved the same lofty demeanour to the last, thanked her advocate, and even the judge and jury, and said they had taken the only true view of her act. Her great violet eyes were extraordinarily dilated and dark, and her face was transparent as alabaster.

"You have done right to condemn me," she said, "but God, who sees all, will weigh my conduct in the scale of His holy justice." The entire court was in tears.

When the time came to remove the lady the crowd ran out to see the last of her. There was a van and a company of Carabineers, but the emotion of the people mastered them and they tried to rescue the prisoner. This was near the Castle of St. Angelo, and the gates being open, the military rushed her into the fortress for safety. She was there now.

The Pope sent his Noble Guard to the Castle of St. Angelo to inquire after the prisoner, and the young soldier brought back a pitiful tale. Donna Roma was ill and could not be removed at present. Her nervous system was completely exhausted and nobody could say what might not occur. Nevertheless, she was very brave, very sweet and very cheerful, and everybody was in love with her. The Castle was occupied by a brigade of Military Engineers, and the Major in command was a good Catholic and a faithful son of the Holy Father. He had lodged his prisoner in the bright apartments that used to be the Pope's, although the prison for persons committed by the Penal Tribunals was a dark cell in the middle of the Maschio. She had expressed a desire to be received into the Church, and had asked the Major to send for Father Pifferi.

"Go back and tell the Major that I will go instead," said the Pope.

"Holy Father!"

THE PEOPLE

"Ask him if the secret passage between the Vatican and the Castle of St. Angelo can still be opened up."

Count de Raymond returned to say that the Major would open it. In the present political crisis no one could tell what a day would bring forth, and in any case he would take the consequences.

The Noble Guard held four unopened letters in his hand. They were addressed to the Honourable Rossi in a woman's writing, and had been re-addressed to the Chamber of Deputies from London, Paris, and Berlin.

"An official from the post-office gave me these letters, and asked me if I could deliver them," said the young soldier.

"My son, my son, didn't you see that it was a trap?" said the Pope. "But no matter! Give them to me. We must leave all to the Holy Spirit."

IV

"The dress of a simple priest to-day, Gaetanino," said the Pope, when his valet came to his bedroom on the following morning.

After Mass and the usual visit of the Cardinal Secretary, the Pope called for the young Count de Raymond.

"We'll go down to our guest first," he said, putting into the side-pocket of his cassock the letters which the Noble Guard had given him.

They found Rossi sitting in a large, sparsely furnished room, by an almost untouched breakfast. He lifted his head when he heard steps, and rose as the Pope entered. His pale face was a picture of despair. "Something has died in him," thought the Pope, and an aching sadness, which had been gnawing at his heart for days, returned.

"They make you comfortable in this old place, my son?"

"Yes, your Holiness."

"And you have everything you wish for?"

"More than I deserve, your Holiness."

"You have suffered, my son. But, in the providence of God, who knows what may happen yet? Don't lose heart. Take an old man's word for it—life is worth living. The Holy Father has found it so in spite of many sorrows."

A kind of pitying smile passed over the young man's

miserable face. "Mine is a sorrow your Holiness can know nothing about—I have lost my wife," he said.

There was a moment of silence. Then the Pope said in a voice that shook slightly, "You don't mean that your wife is dead, but only . . ."

"Only," said Rossi, with a curl of the lip, "that it was she who betrayed me."

"It's hard, my son, very hard. But who knows what influences . . ."

"Curse them! Curse the influences, whatever they were, which caused a wife to betray her husband."

The Pope, who was sitting with both hands on the knob of his stick, quivered perceptibly. "My son," he said, "you have much to justify you, and it is not for me to gainsay you altogether. But God rules His world in righteousness, and if this had not happened, who knows but what worse might have befallen you?"

"Nothing worse *could* have befallen me, your Holiness."

There was another moment of silence, and then the Pope said, "Yes, I understand what it is to build one's faith on a human foundation. The foundation fails, and then the heart sinks, the soul totters. But bad as this . . . this betrayal is, you do very wrong if you refuse to see that it saved you from the consequences—the awful consequences before God and man—of your intended conduct."

"What conduct, your Holiness?"

"The terrible conduct which formed the basis of your plans on returning to Rome."

"You mean . . . what the newspapers talked about?"

The Pope bent his head.

"A conspiracy to kill the King?"

Again the Pope bent his head.

"You believed that, your Holiness?"

"Unhappily I was compelled to do so."

"And she . . . do you suppose she believed it?"

"She believed you were engaged in conspiracies. There was nothing else she could believe in the light of what you had said and written."

After a moment Rossi began to laugh. "And yet you say the world is ruled in righteousness!" he said.

The Pope's face was whitening. "Do you tell me it was a mistake?" he asked.

"Indeed I do. The only conspiracies I was engaged in

were conspiracies to found associations of freedom which had been forbidden by the tyrannical new decree. But what matter? If an error like that can lead to results like these, what's the good of trying?" And he laughed again.

The Pope, who was deeply moved, looked up into the young man's tortured face, without knowing that his own tears were streaming. Old memories were astir within him, and he was carried back into the past of his own life. He was remembering the days when he too had reeled beneath the blow of a terrible fate, and all his hopes and beliefs had been mown down as by a scythe. But God had been good. His gracious hand had healed the wound and made all things well.

Taking the letters from the pocket of his cassock, the Pope laid them on the table.

"These are for you, my son," he said, and then he turned away.

Going down the narrow roofed-in passage to the Castle of St. Angelo, with shafts of morning sunshine slanting through its lancet windows, and the voices of children at play coming up from the street below, the Pope told himself that he must be severe with Roma. The only thing irremediable in all that had happened was the assassination, and though that, in God's hands, had been turned to the good of the people, yet it raised a barrier between two unhappy souls that might never in this life be passed.

"Poor child! Poor flower broken by the storms of fate! But I must reprove her. Before I give her the Blessed Sacrament she must confess and show a full contrition."

V

ROMA was lying on a bed-chair in the frescoed room which had once been the Pope's salon. She was wearing a white dress, and it made her unruffled brow look like alabaster. Her large eyes, which were closed, had blue rings on the lids, and her mouth, once so rosy and so gay with laughter and light words, was colourless as marble.

A lay Sister, in a black and white habit, moved softly about the room. It was Bruno's widow, Elena. She was the Sister Angelica who had entered the convent of the Sacred Heart. It was there she had buried her own trouble until, hearing of Roma's, she had begged to be allowed to nurse her.

A door opened and an officer, in a mixed light and dark blue uniform, entered. It was the doctor of the regiment.

"Sleeping, Sister?"

"Yes, sir."

"Poor soul! Let her sleep as long as she can."

But at that moment Roma opened her eyes, and held out her white hand. "Is it you, doctor?" she said with a smile.

"And how is my patient this morning? Better, I think."

"Much better. In fact, I feel no pain at all to-day."

"She never does. She never feels anything if you believe her," said Elena.

"Tired, Sister?"

"Why should I be tired, I wonder?"

"Sitting up all night with me. Your big burden is very troublesome, doctor."

"Tut! You mustn't talk like that."

"If all jailors were as good to their prisoners as mine are to me!"

"And if all prisoners were as good to their jailors. . . . But I forbid that subject. I absolutely forbid it. . . . Ah, here comes your breakfast."

A soldier in uniform trousers and a linen jacket and cap had come in with a tray on which there was a smoking basin.

"You are from Sicily, aren't you, cook?"

"Yes, from Sicily, Signora."

Roma leaned back to Elena and said in an undertone, "That's where *he* has gone to, isn't it?"

"Some people say so, but nobody knows where he is."

"No news yet?"

"None whatever."

"Sicily must be a lovely place, cook?"

"It is, Signora. It's the loveliest place in the world."

"Last night I had such a beautiful dream, doctor. Somebody who had been away came back, and all the church bells rang for him. I thought it was noon, I remember, for the big gun of the Castle had just been fired. But when I awoke it was quite dark, yet there was really something going on, for I could hear people singing in the city and bands of music playing."

"Ah, that . . . I'm afraid that was only . . . only the sequel to the Prime Minister's funeral. Rome is not sorry that Baron Bonelli is dead, and last night a procession of men

426

and women marched along the streets with songs and hymns, as on a night of carnival. . . . But I must be going. Sister, see she takes her medicine as usual, and lies quiet and does not excite herself. Good-morning!"

When the cook also had gone Roma raised herself on her elbow. "Did you hear what the doctor said, Elena? The death of the Baron has altered everything. It was really no crime to kill that man, and by rights nobody should suffer for it."

"Donna Roma!"

"Ah! no, I didn't mean that. Yet why shouldn't I? And why shouldn't you? Didn't he kill Bruno and our poor dear little Joseph? . . ."

Elena was crying. "I'm not thinking of myself," she said.

"I'm not thinking of myself, either," said Roma, "and I'm not going to give in at the eleventh hour. But David Rossi will come back. I am sure he will, and then . . ."

"And then . . . *you*, Donna Roma?"

"I?"

Roma fell back on her bed-chair. "No, *I* shall not be here, that's true. It's a pity, but after all it makes no difference. And if David Rossi has to come back . . . over . . . over my dead body, as you might say . . . who is to know . . . or care . . . except perhaps . . . some day . . . when he . . ."

Roma struggled on, but Elena broke down utterly.

The door opened again, and a sentry on guard outside announced the English Ambassador.

"Ah! Sir Evelyn, is it you?"

The English gentleman held down his head. "Forgive me if I intrude upon your trouble, Donna Roma."

"Sit! Give his Excellency a chair, Sister. . . . Times have changed since I knew you first, Sir Evelyn. I was a thoughtless, happy woman in those days. But they are gone, and I do not regret them."

"You are very brave, Donna Roma. Too brave. Only for that your trial must have gone differently."

"It's all for the best, your Excellency. But was there anything you wished to say to me?"

"Yes. The report of your condemnation has been received with deep emotion in my country, and as the evidence given in court showed that you were born in England, I feel that I am justified in intervening on your behalf."

"But I don't want you to intervene, dear friend."

"Donna Roma, it is still possible to appeal to the Court of Cassation."

"I have no desire to appeal—there is nothing to appeal against."

"There might be much if you could be brought to see that—that . . . In fact so many pleas are possible, and all of them good ones. For instance . . ."

The Englishman dropped both eyes and voice.

"Well?"

"Donna Roma, you were tried and condemned on a charge of going to the Prime Minister's cabinet with the intention of killing him, and of killing him there. But if it could be proved that *he* came to *your* house, and that, to shield *another person not now in the hands of justice*, you . . ."

"What are you saying, your Excellency?"

"Look!"

The Englishman had drawn from his breast-pocket a crumpled sheet of white paper.

"Last night I visited your deserted apartment in the Piazza Navona, and there, amid other signs that were clear and convincing—the marks of two pistol-shots—I found—this."

"What is it? Give it to me," cried Roma. She almost snatched it out of his hand. It was the warrant which Rossi had rolled up and flung away.

"How did that warrant come there, Donna Roma? Who brought it? What other person was with you in those rooms that night? What does he say to this evidence of his presence on the scene of the crime?"

Roma did not speak immediately. She continued to look at the Englishman with her large mournful eyes until his own eyes fell, and there was no sound but the crinkling of the warrant in her hand. Then she said, very softly:

"Excellency, you must please let me keep this paper. As you see, it is nothing in itself, and without my testimony you can make nothing of it. I shall never appeal against my sentence, and therefore it can be no good to me or to anybody. But it may prove to be a danger to somebody else —somebody whose name should be above reproach."

She stretched out a sweet white hand and touched his own.

"Haven't I done enough wrong to him already, and isn't this paper a proof of it? Must I go farther still, and bring him to the galleys? You cannot wish it. Don't you see that the police would have to deny everything? And I—if you forced me to speak, I should deny everything also."

A gentle, brave dauntlessness rang in her voice, and the Englishman could with difficulty keep back his tears.

"Excellency, Sir Evelyn, friend . . . tell me I may keep the paper."

The Englishman rose and turned his head away. "It is yours, Donna Roma—you must do as you please with it."

She kissed the paper and put it in her breast.

"Good-bye, dear friend."

He tried to answer, "Good-bye! God bless you!" But the words would not come.

"The Major!" said the voice of the sentry. The Commandant of the Castle came into the room.

"Ah! Major!" cried Roma.

"The doctor tells me you are better this morning."

"Much better."

"It is my duty—my unhappy duty—to bring you a painful message. The authorities, thinking your presence in Rome a cause of excitement to the populace, have decided to send you to Viterbo."

"When is it to be, Major?"

"To-morrow about mid-day."

"I shall be quite ready. But have you sent for Father Pifferi?"

"I came to speak about that also. Sister, return to your room for the present."

Elena went out.

"Donna Roma, a great personage has asked to see you in the place of the Father General. He will come in through that doorway. It leads by a passage long sealed up to the apartment of the Pope in the Vatican, and he who comes and goes by it must be unknown and unseen by any one except yourself."

"Major!"

But the Major was going hurriedly out of the room. A moment afterwards the Pope entered in his black cassock as a priest.

VI

"RISE, my child! God knows if the Holy Father ought to give you his blessing. Far be it from me to add bitterness to your remorse in finding yourself in this place and guilty of this sin, but . . . Are we alone?"

"Quite alone, your Holiness."

"Sit down. The Holy Father will sit beside you."

He was trying to be severe with her, but it was very difficult. His hand strayed down to hers, and at every hard word there was a tender pressure.

"The Baron is dead. He was a cruel, heartless tyrant, without mercy or humanity. His death has altered everything, and the load that lay on Italy has been lifted away. But none the less you did wrong, very, very wrong, and by the mad act of a moment. . . . My child! My poor child! God help you! God help this little lost one!"

He patted the hand that lay in his as if he had been quieting a crying child.

"My child, I cannot save you from the consequences of your sin. You must go where I cannot follow you. But since the Holy Father induced you to make that cruel denunciation—but let us be calm—let us be calm!"

Roma was perfectly calm, but the Pope could barely control himself.

"I see now that we made a mistake. The conspiracies of David Rossi were not criminal, and his aims were not unrighteous. I have been instructed on this subject, and now I see everything in a different light. Yes, a great mistake, although a natural and excusable one, and if that was the cause and origin of this terrible event, the Holy Father who led you so far . . ."

"Your Holiness!"

"Nay, you must not expect too much. It is little I can do. But now that governments are falling and parliaments are being dissolved, David Rossi must come back . . ."

Roma made a cry of joy, and the Pope raised a warning finger.

"Ah, you must never think of that, my child—you must never think of it. It is a pity, a great pity, but, alas! it cannot be otherwise now. If your husband is to come back, his name must be kept clean and unblemished, and you can never rejoin him whatever happens."

Dizzy with a sense of the Pope's awful error, Roma turned away her face.

"But if you tell me that what you did was due to the compulsion that was put upon you to denounce David Rossi, he must come forward, whatever the consequences, to defend you and plead for you. He must say to the world and to your judges: 'It is true that this poor lady has committed a crime—an awful crime, such as shuts the guilty one out of the fold of the human family—but she was provoked to it by a falsehood. The dead man deceived her. He was her betrayer, her assassin, for he tried to slay her soul. Therefore you will have mercy upon her as you hope for mercy, you will forgive her as you hope for forgiveness, and in the peace and penance of some holy convent she will wipe out the past of her unhappy life as Mary wiped out her sins in the tears with which she washed her Master's feet.'"

He had risen in the exaltation of his emotion, and raised one hand over his head, but Roma, in the toils of the terrible error, had dropped to her knees at his feet.

"Oh, I cannot die with a lie on my lips. Holy Father, let me make my confession."

A vague foreshadowing of the coming revelation seemed to light on the Pope, and he sat down again without a word. Mechanically he prepared to receive the penitent into the Church, questioning her, instructing her, calling on her to repeat the profession of faith, and finally baptizing her conditionally.

"Baptism wipes out all your sins, my daughter," he said, "but if for your soul's comfort you wish to make a full confession before I give you the Blessed Sacrament . . ."

"I do. I have wished it ever since the end of my trial, and that was why I asked for Father Pifferi."

"Then take care—accuse nobody else, my daughter."

Roma put her hands together, repeated the Confiteor, and then said:

"Father, I am a great, great sinner, and when I charged myself in court with having killed the Minister, I told a falsehood to shield another."

"My child!" The Pope had risen to his feet.

There was a moment of painful silence, and then the

Pope sat down again with rigid limbs, saying in a husky voice:

"Go on, my daughter."

Roma went on with her confession. She told of the mad impulse that came to her to kill the Baron after he had forced her to denounce her husband. She told of her preparations for killing him, and of the incidents of the night of the crime when she was making ready to set out on her awful errand.

"But he came to me in my own rooms at that very moment, your Holiness, and then . . ."

"In . . . your own rooms?"

"Yes, indeed, and that was really the cause of everything."

"How so?"

"Somebody else came afterwards."

"Somebody else?"

"A friend."

"A . . . friend?"

She hesitated for a moment, and then put her hand into her breast and drew out the warrant.

"This one," she said, in a voice that was scarcely audible.

The Pope took the paper, and it rustled as he opened it. There was no other sound in the prison cell except the rasping noise of his rapid breathing.

"David Leone! You don't mean to say—to imply . . ."

The Pope's eyes wandered vaguely around, but they came back to the face at his feet, and he said:

"No, no! You cannot mean that, my child. Tell me I have misunderstood you and come to a wrong conclusion."

Roma did not reply. Her head sunk lower and lower, and seeing this, the Pope rose again, and standing over her he cried:

"Tell me! Tell me, I command you! You wish me to believe that it was he, not you, who committed the crime! Out on you! out on you!"

But having said this in a hoarse and angry voice, he passed his arm over his eyes as if to brush away the clouds that had gathered there, and muttered in a broken and feeble way, "O God, Thou knowest my foolishness. I am poor and needy. Make haste unto me, O God! Hide not Thy face from Thy servant, for I am in trouble."

THE PEOPLE

Roma was crying at the Pope's feet, and after a moment he became aware of it, and stooped to lift her up.

"My child! My poor, poor child! You must bear with me. I am an old man now. Only a weak old man. My brain is confused. Things run together in it. But I understand. I think I understand."

She rose and kissed his trembling hand. He was still holding the warrant.

"Where did this paper come from?"

"The English Ambassador brought it this morning. He had found it in our rooms in the Piazza Navona."

"The place where the crime was committed?"

"Yes."

The Pope straightened himself up, and said in a firm voice:

"My daughter, you must permit me to keep this warrant."

"No, no!"

"Yes, yes! If I said before that your husband should come out and defend you, I say now that he shall come out and accuse himself."

"Your Holiness!"

"He shall go to the courts and say: 'This lady is innocent. She sacrificed herself to save my life. I do not ask for mercy. I ask for justice. Liberate her and arrest me.'"

Roma had knelt again, and was fingering the skirt of the Pope's cassock.

"But, Holy Father," she said, "there is something I have not told you. He who killed the Minister did so in self-defence . . ."

"In self-defence!"

"His act was an accident, and if it had not happened the Minister would have killed him, whereas I . . ."

"In self-defence, you say?"

"I am really guilty of the crime, because I intended to commit it."

"But if it was done in self-defence it was no crime, and you must not and shall not suffer."

Roma dropped the Pope's cassock and took hold of his hand.

"Holy Father," she said, "how can I wish to live when he who loved me loves me no longer? I know quite well it is better that I should go, and that when he comes it

433

should be all over. I dreamt of it last night, your Holiness.
I thought my husband had come back and all the church
bells were ringing. Only a dream, and perhaps you do not
believe in such foolishness. But it was very sweet to think
that if I could not live for my love I could die for him,
and so wipe out everything."

The Pope's white head was bent very low.

"And then I cannot suffer very much, your Holiness.
I am ill, really ill, and my trouble will not last very long.
And if God is using what has happened to bring out all
things well, perhaps He intends that I shall give myself
in the place of some one who is better and more necessary."

The Pope could bear no more. His lip quivered and his
voice shook, but his eyes were shining.

"It is not for me to gainsay you, my daughter. I came
here to see Mary Magdalene, and find the soul of the saints
themselves. The world's judgment on a woman who has
sinned is merciless and cruel, but if David Rossi is worthy
of his mother and his name, he will come back to you on
his knees."

"Bless me, your Holiness."

"I bless you, my daughter. May He in whose hands are
the issues of life and death cover your transgressions with
the vast wings of His gracious pardon and bring you joy
and peace."

The Pope went out with a brightening face, and Roma
staggered back to her couch.

VII

DAVID ROSSI sat all day in his room in the Vatican reading the letters the Pope had left with him. They were the
letters which Roma had addressed to him in London, Paris,
and Berlin.

He read them again and again, and save for the tick
of the clock there was no sound in the large gaunt room
but his stifled moans. The most violently opposed feelings
possessed him, and he hardly knew whether he was glad or
sorry that thus late, and after a cruel fate had fallen, these
messages of peace had reached him.

A spirit seemed to emanate from the thin transparent
sheets of paper, and it penetrated his whole being. As he

read the words, now gay, now sad, now glowing with joy, now wailing with sorrow, a world of fond and tender emotions swelled up and blotted out all darker passions.

He could see Roma herself, and his heart throbbed as of old under the influence of her sweet indescribable presence. Those dear features, those marvellous eyes, that voice, that smile—they swam up and tortured him with love and with remorse.

How bravely she had withstood his enemies! To think of that young, ardent, brilliant, happy life sacrificed to his sufferings! And then her poor, pathetic secret—how sweet and honest she had been about it! Only a pure and courageous woman could have done as she did; while he, in his blundering passion and mad wrath, had behaved like a foul-minded tyrant and a coward. What loud protestations of heroic love he had made when he imagined the matter affected another man! And when he had learned that it concerned himself, how his vaunted constancy had failed him, and he had cursed the poor soul whose confidence he had invited!

But above all the pangs of love and remorse, Rossi was conscious of an overpowering despair. It took the form of revolt against God, who had allowed such a blind and cruel sequence of events to wreck the lives of two of His innocent children. When he took refuge in the Vatican he must have been clinging to some waif and stray of hope. It was gone now, and there was no use struggling. The nothingness of man against the pitilessness of fate made all the world a blank.

Rossi had rung the bell to ask for an audience with his Holiness when the door opened and the Pope himself entered.

"Holy Father, I wished to speak to you."

"What about, my son?"

"Myself. Now I see that I did wrong to ask for your protection. You thought I was innocent, and there was something I did not tell you. When I said I was guilty before God and man, you did not understand what I meant. Holy Father, I meant that I had committed murder."

The Pope did not answer, and Rossi went on, his voice ringing with the baleful sentiments which possessed him.

"To tell you the truth, Holy Father, I hardly thought of it myself. What I had done was partly in self-defence, and I did not consider it a crime. And then, he whose life

I had taken was an evil man, with the devil's dues in him, and I felt no more remorse after killing him than if I had trodden on a poisonous adder. But now I see things differently. In coming here I exposed you to danger at the hands of the State. I ask your pardon, and I beg you to let me go."

" Where will you go to?"

" Anywhere—nowhere—I don't know yet."

The Pope looked at the young face, cut deep with lines of despair, and his heart yearned over it.

" Sit down, my son. Let us think. Though you did not tell me of the assassination, I soon knew all about it. . . . Partly in self-defence, you say?"

" That is so, but I do not urge it as an excuse. And if I did, who else knows anything about it?"

" Is there nobody who knows?"

" One, perhaps. But it is my wife, and she could have no interest in saving me now, even if I wished to be saved. . . . I have read her letters."

" If I were to tell you it is not so, my son—that your wife is still ready to sacrifice herself for your safety . . ."

" But that is impossible, your Holiness. There are so many things you do not know."

" If I were to tell you that I have just seen her, and, not-withstanding your want of faith in her, she still has faith in you . . ."

The deep lines of despair began to pass from Rossi's face, and he made a cry of joy.

" If I were to say that she loves you, and would give her life for you . . ."

" Is it possible? Do you tell me that? In spite of every-thing? And she—where is she? Let me go to her. Holy Father, if you only knew! I'll go and beg her pardon. I cursed her! Yes, it is true that in my blind, mad passion I . . . But let me go back to her on my knees. The rest of my life spent at her feet will not be enough to wipe out my fault."

" Stay, my son. You shall see her presently."

" Can it be possible that I shall see her? I thought I should never see her again; but I counted without God. Ah! God is good after all. And you, Holy Father, you are good too. I will beg her forgiveness, and she will forgive me. Then we'll fly away somewhere—we'll escape to Africa, India, anywhere. We'll snatch a few years of happiness, and what more has anybody a right to expect in this miserable world?"

Exalted in the light of his imaginary future, he seemed to forget everything else—his crime, his work, his people.

"Is she at home still?"

"She is only a few paces from this place, my son."

"Only a few paces! Oh, let me not lose a moment more. Where is she?"

"In the Castle of St. Angelo," said the Pope.

A dark cloud crossed Rossi's beaming face and his mouth opened as if to emit a startling cry.

"In . . . in prison?"

The Pope bowed.

"What for?"

"The assassination of the Minister."

"Roma? . . . But what a fool I was not to think of it as a thing that might happen! I left her with the dead man. Who was to believe her when she denied that she had killed him?"

"She did not deny it. She avowed it."

"Avowed it? She said that she had . . ."

The Pope bowed again.

"Then . . . then it was . . . was it to shield me?"

"Yes."

Rossi's eyes grew moist. He was like another man.

"But the court . . . surely no court will believe her."

"She has been tried and sentenced, my son."

"Sentenced? Do you say sentenced? For a crime she did not commit? And to shield me? Holy Father, would you believe that the last words I spoke to that woman . . . but she is an angel. The authorities must be mad, though. Did nobody think of me? Didn't it occur to any one that I had been there that night?"

"There was only one piece of evidence connecting you with the scene of the crime, my son. It was this."

The Pope drew from his breast the warrant he had taken from Roma.

"*She* had it?"

"Yes."

Rossi's emotions whirled within him in a kind of hurricane. The despair which had clamoured so loud looked mean and contemptible in the presence of the mighty passion which had put it to shame. But after a while his swimming eyes began to shine, and he said:

"Holy Father, this paper belongs to me and you must permit me to keep it."

"What do you intend to do, my son?"

"There is only one thing to do now."

"What is that?"

"*To save her.*"

There was no need to ask how. The Pope understood, and his breast throbbed and swelled. But now that he had accomplished what he came for, now that he had awakened the sleeping soul and given it hope and faith and courage to face justice, and even death if need be, the Pope became suddenly conscious of a feeling in his own heart which he struggled in vain to suppress.

"Far be it from me to excuse a crime, my son, but the merciful God who employs our poor passions to His own great purposes has used your acts to great ends. The world is trembling on the verge of unknown events and nobody knows what a day may bring forth. Let us wait a while."

Rossi shook his head.

"It is true that a crime will be the same to-morrow as to-day, but the dead man was a tyrant, a ferocious tyrant, and if he forced you in self-defence . . ."

Again Rossi shook his head, but still the Pope struggled on.

"You have your own life to think about, my son, and who knows but in God's good service . . ."

"Let me go."

"You intend to give yourself up?"

"Yes."

The Pope could say no more. He rose to his feet. His saintly face was full of a dumb yearning love and pride, which his tongue might never tell. He thought of his years of dark searching, ending at length in this meeting and farewell, and an impulse came to him to clasp the young man to his swelling and throbbing breast. But after a moment, with something of his old courageous calm of voice, he said:

"I am not surprised at your decision, my son. It is worthy of your blood and name. And now that we are parting for the last time, I could wish to tell you something."

David Rossi did not speak.

"I knew your mother, my son."

" My mother ? "

The Pope bowed and smiled.

" She was a great soul, too, and she suffered terribly. Such are the ways of God."

Still Rossi did not speak. He was looking steadfastly into the Pope's quivering face and making an effort to control himself.

The Pope's voice shook and his lip trembled.

" Naturally, you think ill of your father, knowing how much your mother suffered. Isn't that so ? "

Rossi put one hand to his forehead as if to steady his reeling brain, and said, " Who am I to think ill of any one ? "

The Pope smiled again, a timid smile.

" David . . ."

Rossi caught his breath.

" If, in the providence of God, you were to meet your father somewhere, and he held out his hand to you, would you . . . wherever you met and whatever he might be . . . would you *shake hands with him?* "

" Yes," said Rossi; " if I were a King on his throne, and he were the lowest convict at the galleys."

The Pope fetched a long breath, took a step forward, and silently held out his hand. At the next moment the young man and the old Pope were hand to hand and eye to eye.

They tried to speak and could not.

" Farewell! " said the Pope in a choking voice, and turning away he tottered out of the room.

VIII

THE doctor of the Engineers, not entirely satisfied with his diagnosis of Roma's illness, prescribed a remedy of unfailing virtue—hope. It was a happy treatment. The past of her life seemed to have disappeared from her consciousness and she lived entirely in the future. It was always shining in her eyes like a beautiful sunrise.

The sunrise Roma saw was beyond the veil of this life, but the good souls about her knew nothing of that. They brought every piece of worldly intelligence that was likely to be good news to her. By this time they imagined they knew where her heart lay, and such happiness was in her white

THE ETERNAL CITY

face when as soldiers of the King they whispered treason that they thought themselves rewarded.

They told her of an attempted attack on the Vatican, with all its results and consequences—army disorganised, the Borgo Barracks shut up, soldiers wearing cockades and marching arm in arm, the Government helpless and the Quirinal in despair.

"I'm sorry for the young King," she said, "but still . . ."

It was the higher power working with blind instruments. Rossi would come back. His hopes, so nearly laid waste, would at length be realised. And if, as she had told Elena, he had to return over her own dead body, so to speak, there would be justice even in that. It would be pitiful, but it would be glorious also. There were mysteries in life and death, and this was one of them.

She was as gentle and humble as ever, but every hour she grew more restless. This conveyed to her guards the idea that she was expecting something. Notwithstanding her plea of guilty, they thought perhaps she was looking for her liberty out of the prevailing turmoil.

"I will be very good and do everything you wish, doctor. But don't forget to ask the Prefect to let me stay in Rome over to-morrow. And, Sister, do please remember to waken me early in the morning, because I'm certain that something is going to happen. I've dreamt of it three times, you know."

"A pity!" thought the doctor. "Governments may fall and even dynasties may disappear, but judicial authorities remain the same as ever, and the judgment of the court must be carried out."

Nevertheless he would speak to the Prefect. He would say that in the prisoner's present condition the journey to Viterbo might have serious consequences. As he was setting out on this errand early the following morning, he met Elena in the anteroom, and heard that Roma was paying the most minute attention to the making of her toilet.

"Strange! You would think she was expecting some one," said Elena.

"She is, too," said the doctor. "And he is a visitor who will not keep her long."

The soldier who brought Roma her breakfast that morning brought something else that she found infinitely more appetising. Rossi had returned to Rome! One of the men below had seen him in the street last night. He was going

440

in the direction of the Piazza Navona, and nobody was attempting to arrest him.

Roma's eyes flashed like stars, and she sent down a message to the Major, asking to be allowed to see the soldier who had seen Rossi.

He was a big ungainly fellow, but in Roma's eyes who shall say how beautiful? She asked him a hundred questions. His dense head was utterly bewildered.

The doctor came back with a smiling face. The Prefect had agreed to postpone indefinitely the transfer of their prisoner to the penitentiary. The good man thought she would be very grateful.

" Ah, indefinitely? I only wished to remain over to-day! After that I shall be quite ready."

But the doctor brought another piece of news which threw her into the wildest excitement. Both Senate and Chamber of Deputies had been convoked late last night for an early hour this morning. Rumour said they were to receive an urgent message from the King. There was the greatest commotion in the neighbourhood of the Houses of Parliament, and the public tribunes were densely crowded. The doctor himself had obtained a card for the Chamber, but he was unable to get beyond the corridors. Nevertheless, the doors being open owing to the heat and crush, he had heard something. Vaguely, for five minutes, he had heard one of their great speakers.

" Was it . . . was it, perhaps . . ."

" It was."

Again the big eyes flashed like stars.

" You heard him speak? "

" I heard his voice at all events."

" It's a wonderful voice, isn't it? And you really heard him? Can it be possible? "

Elena, the sad figure in the background of these bright pathetic scenes, thought Roma was hoping for a reconciliation with Rossi. She hinted as much, and then the fierce joy in the white face faded away.

" Ah, no! I'm not thinking of that, Elena."

Her love was too large for personal thoughts. It had risen higher than any selfish expectations.

They helped her on to the loggia. The day was warm, and the fresh air would do her good. She looked out over the city with a loving gaze, first towards the Piazza Navona, then towards the tower of Monte Citorio, and last of all towards Trinità de' Monti and the House of the Four Winds. But she was seeing things as they would be when she was gone, not to Viterbo, but on a longer journey.

" Elena ? "

" Well ? "

" Do you think he will ever learn the truth ? "

" About the denunciation ? "

" Yes."

" I should think he is certain to do so."

" Why I did it, and what tempted me, and . . . and everything ? "

" Yes, indeed, everything."

" Do you think he will think kindly of me then, and forgive me and be merciful ? "

" I am sure he will."

A mysterious glow came into the pallid face.

" Even if he never learns the truth here, he will learn it hereafter, won't he? Don't you believe in that, Elena—that the dead know all ? "

" If I didn't, how could I bear to think of Bruno ? "

" True. How selfish I am! I hadn't thought of that. We are in the same case in some things, Elena."

The future was shining in the brilliant eyes with the radiance of an unseen sunrise.

" Dear Elena ? "

" Ye-s."

" Do you think it will seem long to wait until he comes ? "

" Don't talk like that, Donna Roma."

" Why not?   It's only a little sooner or later, you know. Will it ? "

Elena had turned aside, and Roma answered herself.

" *I* don't. I think it will pass like a dream—like going to bed at night and awaking in the morning. And then both together—there."

She took a long deep breath of unutterable joy.

" Oh," she said, " that I may sleep until he comes—knowing all, forgiving everything, loving me the same as before, and every cruel thought dead and gone and forgotten."

She asked for pen and paper and wrote a letter to Rossi:

" DEAREST,—I hear the good news, just as I am on the point of leaving Rome, that you have returned to it, and I write to ask you not to try to alter what has happened. Believe me, it is better so. The world wants you, dear, and it doesn't want me any longer. Therefore return to life, be brave and strong and great, and think of me no more until we meet again.

"You will know by what I have done that what you thought was quite unfounded. Whatever people say of me, you must always believe that I loved you from the first, and that I have never loved anybody but you.

"You were angry with me when we parted, but more than ever I love you now. Don't think our love has been wasted. ''Tis better to have loved and lost than never to have loved at all.' How beautiful!   ROMA."

Having written her letter, and put her lips to the enclosure, she addressed the envelope in a bold hand and with a brave flourish: 'All' Illustrissimo Signor Davide Rossi, Camera dei Deputati."

"You'll post this immediately I am gone, Sister," she said.

Elena pretended to put the letter away for that purpose, but she really smuggled it down to the Major, who despatched it forthwith to the Chamber of Deputies.

"And now I'll go to sleep," said Roma.

She slept until mid-day with the sun's reflection from the white plaster of the groined ceiling of the loggia on her still whiter face. Then the twelve o'clock gun shook the walls of the Castle, and she awoke while the church bells were ringing.

"I thought it was my dream coming true, Sister," she said.

The doctor came up at that moment in a high state of excitement.

"Great news, Donna Roma. The King . . ."

"I know!"

"Failing to form a Government to follow that of the Baron, appealed to Parliament to nominate a successor . . ."

"So Parliament . . ."

"Parliament has nominated the Honourable Rossi, the King has called for him, the warrant for his arrest has been cancelled, and all persons imprisoned for the recent insurrection have been set at liberty."

Roma's trembling and exultant eyelids told a touching story.

"Is there anything to see?"

"Only the flag on the Capitol."

"Let me look at it."

He helped her to rise. "Look! There it is on the clock tower."

"I see it. . . . That will do. You can put me down now, doctor."

An ineffable joy shone in her face.

"It *was* my dream after all, Elena."

After a moment she said, "Doctor, tell the Prefect I am quite ready to go to Viterbo. In fact I wish to go. I should like to go immediately."

"I'll tell him," said the doctor, and he went out to hide his emotion.

The Major came to the open arch of the loggia. He stood there for a moment, and there was somebody behind him. Then the Major disappeared, but the other remained. It was David Rossi. He was standing like a man transfixed, looking in speechless dismay at Roma's pallid face with the light of heaven on it.

Roma did not see Rossi, and Elena, who did, was too frightened to speak. Lying back in her bed-chair with a great happiness in her eyes, she said:

"Sister, if he should come here when I am gone . . . no, I don't mean that . . . but if you should see him and he should ask about me, you will say that I went away quite cheerfully. Tell him I was always thinking about him. No, don't say that either. But he must never think I regretted what I did, or that I died broken-hearted. Say farewell for me, Elena. *Addio Carissima!* That's his word, you know. *Addio Carissimo!*"

Rossi, blinded with his tears, took a step into the loggia, and in a low voice, very soft and tremulous, as if trying not to startle her, he cried:

"Roma!"

She raised herself, turned, saw him, and rose to her feet. Without a word he opened his arms to her, and with a little frightened cry she fell into them and was folded to his breast.

By courtesy of Liebler & Co.; from photographs by Byron.

WITH A FRIGHTENED CRY, SHE WAS FOLDED TO HIS BREAST.

THE PEOPLE

IX

It was ten days later. Rossi had surrendered to Parliament, but Parliament had declined to order his arrest. Then he had called for the liberation of Roma, but Roma had neither been liberated nor removed. "It will not be necessary," was the report of the doctor at the Castle to the officers of the Prefetura. The great liberator and remover was on his way.

At Rossi's request Dr. Fedi had been called in, and he had diagnosed the case exactly. Roma was suffering from an internal disease, which was probably hereditary, but certainly incurable. Strain and anxiety had developed it earlier in life than usual, but in any case it must have come.

At first Rossi rebelled with all his soul and strength. To go through this long and fierce fight with life, and to come out victorious, and then, when all seemed to promise peace and a kind of tempered happiness, to be met by Death—the unconquerable, the inevitable—it was terrible, it was awful!

He called in specialists; talked of a change of air; even brought himself, when he was far enough away from Roma, to the length of suggesting an operation. The doctors shook their heads. At last he bowed his own head. His bride-wife must leave him. He must live on without her.

Meantime Roma was cheerful, and at moments even gay. Her gaiety was heart-breaking. Blinding bouts of headache were her besetting trouble, but only by the moist red eyes did any one know anything about that. When people asked her how she felt, she told them whatever she thought they wished to hear. It brought a look of relief to their faces, and that made her very happy.

With Rossi, during these ten days, she had carried on the fiction that she was getting better. This was to break the news to him, and he on his part, to break the news to her, had pretended to believe the story. They made Elena help the little artifice, and even engaged the doctors in their mutual deception.

"And how is my darling to-day?"

"Splendid! There's really nothing to do with me. It's true I have suffered. That's why I look so pale. But I'm better now. Elena will tell you how well I slept last night. Didn't I sleep well, Elena? Elena. . . . Poor Elena is going a little deaf and doesn't always speak when she is spoken to.

But I'm all right, David. In fact, I'll feel no pain at all before long, and then I shall be well."

" Yes, dear, you'll feel no pain at all before long, and then you'll be well."

It was pitiful. All their words seemed to be laden with double meanings. They could find none that were not.

But the time had come when Roma resolved she must speak plainly. Rossi had lifted her into the loggia. He did so every day, carrying her, not on his arm as a woman carries a child, but against his breast, as a man carries his wife when he loves her. She always put her arms around his neck, pretending it was necessary for her safety, and when he had laid her gently in the bed-chair she pulled down his head and kissed him. The two little journeys were the delight of the day to Roma, but to Rossi they were a deepening trouble.

It was the sweetest day of the sweet Roman spring, and Roma wore a light tea-gown with a coil of white silk about her head such as is seen in the portraits of Beatrice Cenci. The golden complexion was quite gone, there was a hard line along the cheek, a deep shadow under the chin, the nostrils were pinched and the mouth was drawn. But the large eyes, though heavy with pain, were full of joy. They did not weep any more, for all their tears were shed, and the light of another world was reflected in their depths.

Rossi sat by her side, and she took one of his hands and held it on her lap between both her own. Sometimes she looked at him and then she smiled. She, who had lost him for a little while, had got him back at last. It was only just in time. A little break, and they would continue this —there. Ah, she was very happy!

Rossi's free hand was supporting his head, and he was trying to look another way. Do what he would to conquer it, the spirit of rebellion was rising in his heart again. " O God, is this just? Is this right? "

They were alone on the loggia. Above was the cloudless blue sky, below was the city, hardly seen or heard.

" David," she began, in a faint voice.

" Dearest? "

" I have been so happy in having you with me again that there is something I have forgotten to tell you."

" What is it, dear? "

" Promise me you will not be shocked or startled."

"What is it, dearest?" he repeated, although he knew too well.

"It is nothing. . . . Yes, hold my hands tight. So! . . . Really it's nothing. And yet it is everything. It is . . . it is death."

"Roma!"

Her eyelids trembled, but she tried to laugh.

"Yes, dear. True! Not immediately. Oh, no! not immediately. But signed and sealed, you know, and not to be put aside that anybody may be happy much longer."

She was laughing almost gaily. But all the same she was watching him closely, and now that her word was spoken she suddenly became conscious of a secret desire which she had not suspected. She wanted him to contradict her, to tell her she was quite wrong, to convince and defeat her.

"Poor little me! Pity, isn't it? It would have been so sweet to go on a little longer—especially after this reconciliation. And when one has kept one's heart under bolt and bar so long . . ."

Her sad gaiety was breaking down. "But it's better so, isn't it?"

He did not reply.

"Ah, yes, it's better so when you come to think of it."

"It's terrible!" said Rossi.

"Don't say that. It's a thing of every day. Here, there, everywhere. God wouldn't allow it to go on if it were terrible."

"It's bitterly cruel for all that."

"Not so cruel as life. Not nearly. For instance, if I lived you would have to put me away, and that would be harder to bear than death—far harder."

"My darling! What are you saying?"

"It's true, dear. You know it's true. God can forgive a woman even if she's a sinner, but the world can't if she's only a victim of sin. It's part of the cruelty of things, but there's no use repining."

"Roma," said Rossi, "I take God to witness that if that were all that stood between us nothing and nobody should separate you and me. I should tell the world that you had every virtue and every heroism, and without you I could do nothing."

Her eyes filled with a fresh joy.

"You set me too high still, dear. Yet you know that I

was far too small and weak for your great work. That was why I failed you at the end. It wasn't my fault that I betrayed you . . ."

"Don't speak of my betrayal. I thank God for it, and see now that it was the best that could have happened."

She closed her eyes. "Is it your own voice, dearest? Really yours? Hush! I shall wake and the dream will pass."

A little jet from his heart of flame burst out in spite of his warning brain, and he was carried away for the moment.

"My poor darling, you must get well for my sake. You must think of nothing but getting well. Then we'll go away somewhere—to Switzerland, as you said in your letter. Or perhaps to England, where you were born, and where your father lived his years of exile. Dear old England! Motherland of liberty! I'll show you all the places."

She was dizzy with the beautiful vision.

"Oh, if I could only go on like this for ever! But I mustn't listen to you, dearest. It's no use, you know. Now, is it?"

The spirit which had exalted him for a moment took flight, and his heart rose into his throat.

"Now, is it?" she repeated.

He did not answer, and she dropped back with a sigh. Ah, it was cruel fencing. Every word was a sword, and it was cutting a hundred ways.

At that moment a band of music passed down the street. Roma, who loved bands of music, asked Rossi to lift her up that she might look at it. A little drummer boy was marching at the head of a procession, gaily rolling his rataplan.

"He reminds me of little Joseph," she said, and she laughed heartily. Strange mystery of life that robs death of all its terrors!

He put his arm about her to support her as they stood by the parapet, and this brought a new tremor of affection, as well as a little of the old physical thrill and a world of fond and tender memories. She looked into his eyes, he looked into hers; they both looked across to Trinità de' Monti, and in the eye-asking between them she said plainly, "Do you remember—over there?"

Roma was assisted back to the bed-chair, and then, conversation being impossible, Rossi began to read. Every day he had read something. Roma had made the selections.

THE PEOPLE

They were always about the great lovers—Francesca and Paolo, Dante and Beatrice, even Alfred de Musset and poor John Keats, with the skull cap which burnt his brain. To-day it was Roma's favourite poem:

> "Teach me, only teach, Love!
> As I ought
> I will speak thy speech, Love,
> Think thy thought . . ."

His right hand held the book. His left was between Roma's hands, lying blue-veined in her lap. She was looking out on the sunlit city as if taking a last farewell of it. He stopped to stroke her glossy black hair and she reached up to his lips and kissed them. Then she closed her eyes to listen. His voice rose and swelled with the ocean of his love, and he felt as if he were pouring his life into her frail body.

> "Meet, if thou require it,
> Both demands,
> Laying flesh and spirit
> In thy hands."

Her blanched lips moved. She took a deep breath and made a faint cry. He rose softly, and bent over her with a trembling heart. Her breathing seemed to have ceased. Had sleep overtaken her? Or had the tender flame expired?

"Roma!"

She opened her eyes and smiled.

"Not yet, dear—soon," she said.

THE END

The illustrations in this book are from scenes of the play as produced by Messrs. LIEBLER & COMPANY, and photographed by Mr. BYRON.

GROSSET & DUNLAP'S
DRAMATIZED NOVELS
A Few that are Making Theatrical History

THE NOVELS OF
GEORGE BARR McCUTCHEON

GRAUSTARK.

A story of love behind a throne, telling how a young American met a lovely girl and followed her to a new and strange country. A thrilling, dashing narrative.

BEVERLY OF GRAUSTARK.

Beverly is a bewitching American girl who has gone to that stirring little principality—Graustark—to visit her friend the princess, and there has a romantic affair of her own.

BREWSTER'S MILLIONS.

A young man is required to spend *one* million dollars in one year in order to inherit *seven*. How he does it forms the basis of a lively story.

CASTLE CRANEYCROW.

The story revolves round the abduction of a young American woman, her imprisonment in an old castle and the adventures created through her rescue.

COWARDICE COURT.

An amusing social feud in the Adirondacks in which an English girl is tempted into being a traitor by a romantic young American, forms the plot.

THE DAUGHTER OF ANDERSON CROW.

The story centers about the adopted daughter of the town marshal in a western village. Her parentage is shrouded in mystery, and the story concerns the secret that deviously works to the surface.

THE MAN FROM BRODNEY'S.

The hero meets a princess in a far-away island among fanatically hostile Musselmen. Romantic love making amid amusing situations and exciting adventures.

NEDRA.

A young couple elope from Chicago to go to London traveling as brother and sister. They are shipwrecked and a strange mix-up occurs on account of it.

THE SHERRODS.

The scene is the Middle West and centers around a man who leads a double life. A most enthralling novel.

TRUXTON KING.

A handsome good natured young fellow ranges on the earth looking for romantic adventures and is finally enmeshed in most complicated intrigues in Graustark.

GROSSET & DUNLAP, 526 WEST 26th ST., NEW YORK

LOUIS TRACY'S
CAPTIVATING AND EXHILARATING ROMANCES

THE STOWAWAY GIRL. Illustrated by Nesbitt Benson.

The story of a shipwreck, a lovely girl who shipped stowaway fashion, a rascally captain, a fascinating young officer and thrilling adventure enroute to South America.

THE CAPTAIN OF THE KANSAS.

A story of love and the salt sea—of a helpless ship whirled into the hands of cannibal Fuegians—of desperate fighting and a tender romance. A story of extraordinary freshness.

THE MESSAGE. Illustrated by Joseph Cummings Chase.

A bit of parchment many, many years old, telling of a priceless ruby secreted in ruins far in the interior of Africa is the "message" found in the figurehead of an old vessel. A mystery develops which the reader will follow with breathless interest.

THE PILLAR OF LIGHT.

The pillar thus designated was a lighthouse, and the author tells with exciting detail the terrible dilemma of its cut-off inhabitants and introduces the charming comedy of a man eloping with his own wife.

THE RED YEAR: A Story of the Indian Mutiny.

The never-to-be-forgotten events of 1857 form the background of this story. The hero who begins as lieutenant and ends as Major Malcolm, has as stirring a military career as the most jaded novel reader could wish. A powerful book.

THE WHEEL O'FORTUNE. With illustrations by James Montgomery Flagg.

The story deals with the finding of a papyrus containing the particulars of the hiding of some of the treasures of the Queen of Sheba. The glamour of mystery added to the romance of the lovers, gives the novel an interest that makes it impossible to leave until the end is reached.

THE WINGS OF THE MORNING.

A sort of Robinson Crusoe *redivivus*, with modern settings and a very pretty love story added. The hero and heroine are the only survivors of a wreck, and have adventures on their desert island such as never could have happened except in a story.

GROSSET & DUNLAP, 526 WEST 26th ST., NEW YORK